NOT QUITE THE FULL CHAPATI

D0888845

NOT QUITE THE FULL CHAPATI

KATH HIRANI

YouCaxton Publications
24 High Street, Bishop's Castle, Shropshire. SY3 8JX
www.youcaxton.co.uk

Produced in Great Britain by YouCaxton
Copyright © Kath Hirani 2014

The Author asserts the moral right to
be identified as the author of this work.

Witch Logo taken from the back of David's coach

ISBN 978-1-909644-15-1
Printed and bound in Great Britain.

All rights reserved. No part of this publication may be reproduced, stored in a
retrieval system, or transmitted in any form or by any means, electronic, mechanical,
photocopying, recording or otherwise, without the prior permission of the publisher.

This book is sold subject to the condition that it shall not, by way of trade or
otherwise, be lent, resold, hired out or otherwise circulated without the publisher's
prior consent in any form of binding or cover other than that in which it is
published and without a similar condition including this condition being imposed
on the subsequent purchaser.

Janice Saheed AKA Jean Nasir

Front cover Rhia Hirani and Laura Shirreffs

So that they never forget, this book is dedicated to
Natasha, Rhia and Dominic Hirani, my three gorgeous children.
Did I ever tell you how much I love you?

Kath Hirani

ACKNOWLEDGEMENTS

A special thank you goes to my parents, Betty and the late Derek Bolton, for providing my sisters and me with such an abundant upbringing and for not being prejudiced in any way. Thank you also to my husband Karim and his family for accepting me in the face of adversity.

I would like to express my appreciation to the many people who did not yawn when I first outlined Not Quite the Full Chapati but instead encouraged me to keep going.

My book is based on a true story but is not a memoir. I am grateful to all those who lie behind the main characters, especially to my sisters, Shirley, Pauline and Carol, who provided support through difficult family times and to Susan Gornall, née Nasir (Jo), who has made my life so interesting and gave permission to include her family.

Lesser characters may be fictional and any semblance of any one of these to anyone in real life coincidental.

Bob Fowke and the team at YouCaxton, you deserve a medal for receiving and patiently responding to a multitude of emails, for editing a book written by a northerner and producing work of quality.

Marion Falle, I am so glad that I met you. Thank you for being so particular and precise when it came to proofreading and for working so quickly.

Finally, my thanks go to my friend Jo Bowers who never gave up hope of seeing this story in print.

PROLOGUE

1964

Helen slipped her feet into the shiny new shoes and fastened the silver buckles. She carefully folded over her crisp white socks and patted them so they lay neatly around her ankles. She looked at her reflection in the mirror and frowned, smoothed the pleats in her skirt and stood tall - or as tall as was possible for a four-year-old. She felt almost grown up because today was her first day at infant school. However, there were butterflies in her stomach that wouldn't go away completely and she felt a little bit sick at the same time.

'Helen!' called Elizabeth from downstairs. 'It's time to go.'

Helen grabbed the brown leather satchel from the end of her bed and ran down the stairs to where Elizabeth held out her arms.

'Just look at you, I can't believe you're off to school already. Give Mummy a big hug.'

Helen grinned and flung her arms around her mother's neck.

'Ready to go? Say bye to your sisters.'

Helen kissed Shelly on the cheek. Shelly was her eldest sister, but her sister Paula wasn't much older than her and when Helen went to give her a kiss, Paula grimaced. Elizabeth laughed.

'Don't be mean, wish her good luck.'

Paula placed her cheek in the vicinity of Helen's lips, scrunching up her face in disgust.

Afterwards she wiped away the wetness with the sleeve of her jumper.

'You two are horrible to each other,' said Elizabeth. 'Don't forget your baby sister, Helen'

Helen kissed the soft, downy cheek of the two-week-old baby in the pram. 'Bye bye, baby Karen,' she whispered, 'and bye, Daddy.'

David was right there. He picked her up and held her close. 'Bye bye, enjoy your day and tell me all about it when you get home.'

She put her arms around his neck and hugged him, inhaling the familiar smell of soap and aftershave.

David had a small travel business consisting of two coaches and a minibus. He had a wicked sense of humour and on the back of each coach was painted the striking emblem of a black witch on a broomstick. David said that for their return journey it helped passengers remember which coach they had travelled on. There was no family car to speak of, apart from his pride and joy, a pristine 1948 black Austin Sheerline, and so Elizabeth used the minibus to ferry her children around. Helen felt the butterflies returning in full force as she climbed its steps. She sat behind the driver's seat so that Elizabeth wouldn't see how nervous she was. They drove along the mile of bumpy road to the old granite school and Helen listened as Elizabeth told her about Shelly's first day at school.

'She skipped straight into class without looking back and I cried all the way home,' she recalled. 'You'll be fine, don't worry.'

Helen smiled with difficulty and stepped from the minibus. Holding tightly onto her mother's hand, she walked along the pavement and through the gates into the playground.

'Helen, stop staring.' Elizabeth tugged Helen's hand, almost pulling her over. But Helen was staring at another little girl and she continued to stare.

'I'm so sorry,' said Elizabeth to the girl's mother. She crouched down to face Helen. 'It's rude to stare. Stop it.'

The woman smiled: 'It's OK, don't worry.'

Helen tried to concentrate on her mother's words but couldn't help glancing to her left.

'Are you listening to me?' Elizabeth whispered. 'Stop!'

Helen had never seen anyone with dark skin before, and had never seen anyone so pretty either so, despite Elizabeth's efforts to distract her, she just couldn't take her eyes off the girl.

'Say hello,' said Elizabeth.

Helen looked from the other girl to Elizabeth and back again. The girl smiled and, barely raising her hand, gave a tiny finger wave. Helen found the courage to smile back and, in that moment, a friendship was born that would last a lifetime.

§

As for little girl's mother, Janice Saheed was a rare breed and she was used to people staring at her daughter. Her husband had come from Pakistan to live in England in 1957. They met soon after he arrived when he began working in the same factory as her in Wigan. The first time she saw him was in the staff canteen where, for obvious reasons, she couldn't help but take notice. It wasn't love at first sight, more intrigue than anything. She had never seen an Asian man close up before, or woman for that matter, and like many others found it hard to resist a furtive glance. On one occasion Mahmood saw her peering at him and winked. Janice quickly turned away, her heart thudded and her cheeks burned as she hurried back to work. Mahmood chuckled; he enjoyed all the attention.

Mahmood was one of the first Asians to settle in England and his new-found freedom gave him a sense of exhilaration. When he first stepped onto English soil and breathed in the cool air, it wasn't muggy and sweltering like in Pakistan. Everything was orderly; there was none of the chaos of the streets back home. It was invigorating and tranquil at the same time, and he found himself eager to explore and try new things - especially the pubs and clubs. But first he must find a job so that he could send money back home to his family, who were poor with no prospects of bettering themselves. He planned to return to Pakistan when he had earned enough to enable him to find a wife and raise a family. In the meantime though, Mahmood couldn't help noticing the pretty young English girls with their pale, smooth skin. And the clothes they wore - dresses that clung to their slim bodies, bare arms and legs on show, and high heels that made them wiggle as they walked.

It was a Friday night and Janice had just finished work. The clank of the clocking-off machine as it marked her card was the best sound in the world. She pulled her coat around her and headed for the bus stop where she stood shivering.

'Janice!'

She almost leapt in the air.

'I'm sorry, I didn't mean to frighten you.'

'Mahmood!'

He smiled, revealing the most perfect white teeth she had ever seen. 'I just wondered if you would like to come with me for a drink before you go home.'

He had taken her by surprise and she couldn't think what to say.

'Er...well I suppose...'

'Just one drink? Yes or no?'

Janice looked around. She was excited, but scared. Shaking her auburn hair off her face, she took a deep breath.

'OK, that would be nice.'

They made their home in that same town - where minds were closed and folk made their opinions known. Janice had opted for a life that drew constant attention and racist comments when she walked down the street with her husband and four children. It was 1964; she was pregnant with her fifth child and too busy to worry what people said. She scrubbed and cleaned like all the rest of the women, but unlike them she could make a curry and knew how to put on a sari. Thankfully, and despite the prejudice and hostility of many, Janice developed a circle of close friends. These young women relied on one another and all accepted Janice and her husband as they were.

§

That evening after school, Helen ran to greet her father when he came home from work, launching herself at him with full force. David was over six feet tall and a big strong man and in one spiralling motion he scooped up his daughter and swung her round. One minute she was up the air, the next she almost touched the ground. She clung to his sweater and laughed till she felt there was no more air left in her lungs.

'Stop, I can't breathe!'

David set her down on the kitchen work surface and kissed her forehead. 'And what have you been doing today?' he asked.

Helen told him about her school and about her new friend, Joanna. He heard that Joanna had beautiful brown skin and that her father was from a country far away called Pakistan, where it is very hot and everyone has brown skin and black hair and brown eyes.

David glanced at Elizabeth to see if this was true; she smiled and nodded. David raised his eyebrows and pursed his lips. He was surprised and he wanted to hear more.

'Joanna has an older brother and two younger brothers, and her mummy is having another baby,' said Helen.

'What's her mummy's name?'

'Janice.'

'But that's an English name.'

'Her mummy's English.'

David's eyes widened and he looked at Elizabeth who was trying not to laugh at his look of surprise.

'Your face was a picture,' she said later, when they were alone. 'Helen has fallen in love with this Asian girl, and I have to say she's adorable.'

'I can't wait to meet her.'

§

His prayers finished, Mahmood quietly folded his mat and tucked it under his arm. He opened the sitting room door to find Joanna waiting to speak to him and he bent and cupped her chin in his outstretched hand.

'Have you been there long? What can I do for you?'

'I have a new friend she's invited me to her house. Please can I go?'

Mahmood's smile faded.

'My little Jojo, you know I don't like you going places on your own.'

'But Daddy you'll like her, I know you will. Her name's Helen.'

'I'll have to speak to your mother about this.'

Mahmood was very protective when it came to his children, especially Joanna, his only daughter. He still felt very new to the English way of life, and wasn't sure how safe they would be, away from his house and his watchful eye. The thought of Joanna out alone perturbed him.

'What if I go too, so I can make sure she's all right?' asked Janice.

'No, I think it's better if her friend comes here.'

'Mahmood, you can't keep her locked up forever. She needs to be independent. I'll take her and bring her back.'

'Janice, we don't know these people. Let Helen come here.'

§

David applied the brakes and the coach glided majestically to a halt outside Janice and Mahmood's house. The side door slid open and out stepped a tiny figure, followed by David's enormous frame. There was no need to knock, the glossy black door of the house swung open and there stood Janice.

'I'm David, I was asked to drop Helen to play with Joanna.'

'Come in.'

Joanna came bounding along the hallway. Janice gestured towards the sitting room, offering tea and biscuits and calling to her husband who approached warily.

'I'm sorry,' said David, 'I don't have time. I have a run to do.'

Mahmood looked puzzled.

'I run a coach business,' said David, 'I have to pick up a group of people and take them to Scarborough'.

'Your daughter is safe with us,' said Mahmood.

'My wife will pick her up at six o'clock, if that's all right with you. This is our telephone number. If you have any problems, please don't hesitate to call.'

When the girls were in the sitting room and out of earshot, Mahmood turned to Janice. 'He seems like a nice man.'

She put her arms around him and pressed her swollen belly into his. 'You have to learn to trust people,' she said. 'Come through to the kitchen and let them play. I'll make us a cup of tea.'

In the dining room that doubled as a playroom, Helen undressed and dressed Joanna's doll several times and placed it in the pram. She wheeled it around the room and then out into the hallway where she stopped abruptly. She could hear a strange noise that scared her. It was a low, muffled mumbling sound. Realising it was coming from the sitting room she turned her head, straining to hear. The door was slightly ajar. It was a man's voice she could hear. Helen gingerly took a step closer, followed by another until she could see through the slit where the hinges were. Her eyes narrowed. She saw Mahmood kneeling on a small mat. He was wearing a tiny white circular cap and was bowing over and over as though kissing the floor. All the time he was muttering something incomprehensible. On the wall behind him was a black and white photograph of some other people with dark skin. The women had beautifully decorated material wrapped round them and the men were wearing fancy pyjamas. Helen went closer trying to get a better view.

'He's saying his prayers.'

Helen sucked in her breath and jerked her head around.

'Dad's always saying his prayers,' Joanna whispered, 'come on, let's play house.'

'Who are those people in the photograph?'

'My grandma and grandad, and my aunties and uncles.'

'What are they wearing?'

'The ladies are wearing saris and the men are wearing salwar kameez.'

'And what's that?' Helen pointed to a small wooden stick that had smoke curling out of the end.

'It makes the room smell nice,' replied Joanna.

'It's on fire!'

'No, it's not; it's just a bit of smoke.'

At that moment, Janice appeared at the door. 'It's OK,' she said. 'It's safe as long as it doesn't touch anything. Joanna's daddy always uses them when he says his prayers.'

At five-thirty Janice called the girls to eat. They were joined by Joanna's three brothers around a large wooden table, and Helen ate her first curry; lamb with potatoes. Janice had also made some thin round doughy pancakes called chapatis.

Helen's tongue tingled.

'Is it hot?' asked one the brothers.

'I like it,' said Helen, gulping a glass of water.

Everyone smiled. Helen and Joanna giggled. A knock at the door brought an end to the visit and Helen left, promising that next time Joanna could go to her house.

§

David threw the cloth over his left shoulder and wiped his forehead on his sleeve.

'Bett, I'm exhausted,' he said, yawning.

'I'm not surprised; you wear yourself out polishing and cleaning all the time. The coaches don't have to be so clean you know. People don't care so long as they look half decent - and they certainly don't care how much rubbish they leave behind.'

'But I care.'

'You're going to kill yourself working.'

'You know what we need? We need a day out. There's nothing in the diary for next Saturday, so why don't we organise something.'

'That would be lovely; shall I ring round and see who's free?'

'You do that. Ask if they'd like to go to Greenfield and walk up to the reservoir.'

David had a severe haircut, but he was a gentle soul and full of fun, always clean-shaven, his clothes clean and pressed, shoes highly polished. He was a perfectionist. In his tool-shed, which the girls called his clinic because it was always so neat and tidy, he made wooden stakes to drive into the ground so that the girls could play rounders in the garden, and wooden stilts for them to strut around on pretending to be circus entertainers or giants. David's whole life revolved around family and work.

The house they had recently moved to was dilapidated. It was out in the countryside, surrounded by fields and with only one neighbour. The two dwellings stood side-by-side approached by a gravel track. The neighbour's house - De Trafford Cottage - was in good repair, but their house - De Trafford House - had fungus growing on the ceilings and many of the windows were without glass. It had always been David's dream to find somewhere idyllic where he could bring up his family safely. There wasn't much money for renovations and he intended to do most of the work himself.

Elizabeth and David worked hard. Elizabeth was a midwife, but she often drove the coaches too. She was one of only a handful of women in England with a Public Service Vehicle licence at that time. Other male drivers were surprised to see a tiny woman, not much more than five feet tall, her shiny brown curls bouncing as she grappled with the massive steering wheel. Elizabeth didn't mind; their plan was to work hard while the children were young and then relax and reap the benefits in years to come.

In what little free time they had, they would gather family and friends together in one of the coaches and drive off into the countryside for a day's hiking. This was David's idea of heaven - to be up on Saddleworth Moor, in the fresh air, miles away from anywhere, surrounded by beautiful views and the people he loved most. Elizabeth picked up the phone and began dialling. She phoned all seven of her sisters and brothers, plus one or two of their friends and invited them and their children for a day out on the moors.

'Would Joanna like to come?' Elizabeth asked Helen.

Helen jumped up and down. 'Can she? Oh please, please, please! Can I ring her?'

After much persuasion, Mahmood agreed to let Joanna go on the trip with Helen and her family and from then on the two girls became inseparable. Janice gave birth to a second daughter, whom Joanna adored, but because her brothers tormented them so much, Joanna and Helen spent more and more time at Helen's house, where she was fondly referred to as their fifth daughter.

Elizabeth and David had very little money; the kitchen was the only habitable downstairs room in the house. Upstairs, Shelly, Paula, Helen and Karen all slept in one huge bedroom, Elizabeth and David in another. But the girls were happy playing out in the fields all day chasing each other and jumping in and out of the unglazed windows. As David planed the wood to make new window frames, the girls tied string across the room and hung the curly shavings up as decorations and sometimes, after he had mowed the huge lawns, the girls made cars out of the grass cuttings, using a crust of bread on a twig as the steering wheel. Eventually, Mahmood didn't mind Joanna being with Helen; he knew she would be having fun without being in danger or getting up to any real mischief.

§

In 1968, following Mahmood's first trip home to Pakistan since his arrival in England, everything changed for Joanna. Mahmood became homesick and longed to be involved with his culture again; he wanted to show his children their heritage and introduce them to the family they had never met. He didn't want them to grow up ignorant of their Pakistani background and he promised himself that he would re-educate them in the Muslim way, teach them his language and show them a 'better way of life'.

Mahmood loved Janice dearly; Helen was used to seeing them snuggled up on the sofa together. But, as the years went by, he came to believe that he had made a mistake in marrying an English woman. He no longer smoked or drank alcohol, he prayed several times a day and eventually he vowed that one day he would set up a local mosque and contact other Muslims to join him. He became convinced that he could put things right by choosing husbands and wives from Pakistan for his children so that his grandchildren could be brought up within his own race and culture.

Fortunately, or unfortunately, Mahmood didn't realise the difficulties of his plan. His children spoke only English. He tried to teach them Urdu and to introduce them to Eastern traditions but this confused them and made them resent him. He would recite the Koran to them but they laughed at him and refused to conform. He found himself isolated and, turning to Islam for solace, prayed that his children would realise that this was the only religion for them to follow.

On the other hand Helen listened and was fascinated when Mahmood spoke to his children in his language hoping that they would learn and understand. She gazed at the family photos, visualising the vibrant colours of the saris and wondering how on earth you put one on. Joanna, or Jo as she became known as she grew older, was a very special friend and Helen felt privileged to share in such a different way of life. Little did she realise the lasting effect their friendship would have on her.

1 THE MYSTERY MAN

1984

'Look, there's Rahim!' exclaimed Jo. 'Hoot your horn!'

A small black poodle, its lead trailing behind it, vanished in front of the car where Jo was a passenger. Helen who was driving, slammed her foot down on the brake pedal bringing the car to an abrupt halt. A brief silence was followed by a loud bang.

'Oh my God!' squealed Jo. 'You OK?'

Helen got slowly out of the car to see that a large white van had driven straight into the back of her beautiful white MGB Roadster, her prized possession and a huge extravagance on her meagre nurse's salary. The once-shiny rear end looked like a crumpled handkerchief.

A middle-aged man leapt from the van. He was wearing a grey undersized T-shirt that allowed an oversized belly to spill out from under it. He remonstrated wildly, the veins in his neck bulging and beads of sweat clinging to his receding hairline. A thought entered Helen's mind: 'This is him! The white van man!' She had seen and heard about him on television so many times and now here he was, face-to-face. She remembered what a television presenter had said: 'The white van man thinks he owns the road, and cares for no-one but himself.'

'What the hell you think you're doing? What did you stop like that for you stupid bitch?'

Tears stabbed Helen's eyes. 'If you hadn't been driving right up my backside, you'd have been able to stop in time.' She spotted a telephone box across the road. 'Look at my car; I'm calling the police!'

'Listen, love, if you'd been driving properly there's no way I'd have run into the back of you. It's me oughtta call the police.'

At that moment, a police car pulled up and out stepped a young WPC. A shop assistant had seen the whole thing and had already called them. She took down the relevant details and a statement from all concerned and quietly dispersed the small crowd that had gathered. When Helen was finally free to pull away, she felt exhausted and her neck ached from the jolt.

'You should go to the hospital to be checked over,' said Jo.

'No way! I can't afford to be signed off work and anyway I wouldn't be seen dead in one those awful surgical collars.'

'OK, OK just a suggestion.'

Helen drove slowly.

'You all right, Jo?'

Jo shifted uncomfortably in her seat. 'I'm fine, I'm really sorry about what happened.'

'Wasn't your fault, it was an accident.' Helen looked across and smiled. She took up the conversation where they had left off. 'Who was he anyway?'

'One of the new doctors in oral surgery. I met him on the ward the other day when he came to see a patient. He seemed nice.' Jo had a pained expression. 'I'm so sorry about your car, Helen. Let me take you for lunch, my treat.'

Later, sitting by the door in the new coffee shop round the corner from where they worked, still dazed by the accident, Helen was only half aware of Jo's chatter, when an Asian man walked in. He smiled as their eyes met and went to sit at a nearby table.

'... he seemed quite nice and apparently he'll be here for some time,' said Jo.

'Who?'

'Rahim, the doctor I was telling you about. Well, actually he's a dentist working in the oral surgery department.'

§

Helen and Jo began their nurse training at Victoria Hospital Blackpool otherwise known as The Vic in 1979 and qualified in the summer of 1983. Jo went to work on a busy surgical ward; she loved the acute nature of the work and the fast turnover of patients. Helen preferred medicine to surgery and began work on a female medical ward. The patients there tended to stay longer and Helen came to know some real characters.

Both girls enjoyed the hospital atmosphere especially during the months of February and August when the doctors changed over and a new batch started. There was a general buzz of excitement in those months and by the end of the first week it was established who was handsome, who had a good sense of humour and who was grumpy when called out in the middle of the night.

'Are you coming out tonight?' Jo asked Helen. It was August after all.

'I don't think so.'

'You should, it'll do you good. We're starting in the hospital social club and going into town later. Come for a drink and see how you feel.'

'I'll think about it.'

Helen had just split up with Robert, who everyone, including herself, had presumed she would marry. He was good-looking and had a steady job with great prospects, so what more could she have asked for? She didn't know, she just felt something was missing and that the relationship wouldn't last. Breaking the news to him had been so hard and now, six months down the line, she still missed him terribly.

From the corner of her eye, Helen had the Asian man in her line of vision; he was looking in their direction. She shot him a quick glance, trying not to be too obvious. He was homing in on their conversation and not in the least bit worried at being spotted. He smiled and took another sip of coffee. Helen tried to concentrate on what Jo was saying, it was more likely to be Jo he was interested in anyway. She always attracted the men with her dark skin and brown eyes. On top of which, she was petite and slim with a more than ample bosom. Helen could not compete, she was much rounder and had pale skin, green eyes and mousy hair.

'What do you think?' said Jo.

'Pardon?'

'What's the matter with you? You're miles away.'

'Sorry, I was thinking of something else.' Helen pushed all thoughts of Robert to the back of her mind and dismissed the attentions of the Asian man to concentrate fully on what Jo was saying.

'I asked if you fancied a spot of flat-hunting tomorrow,' said Jo, 'that's if you feel up to it.'

'OK.'

The lease on their flat was up at the end of the month. The landlord wanted to sell the property so they had to find somewhere else soon. The thought of moving turned Helen's stomach; she had accumulated so many belongings in her three years at The Vic.

Jo was looking at the ads in the local paper spread out beside her coffee. 'This is yesterday's, there's not many to see and they will have gone by now. Why don't we put an advert on the hospital notice board and one in the local shop? You never know.'

The Asian man got up from his seat. As he passed their table, he slowed his pace and smiled again. Helen decided to be bold. She looked him straight in the eye and smiled back.

'Bye!'

Jo turned to see who Helen was talking to.

'That was him! I didn't see him come in!' said Jo.

'Who?'

'Rahim, the dentist I was trying to point out to you earlier.' Jo laughed. 'We could have asked him to join us.'

Steam spiralled towards the ceiling, leaving the smell of lavender oil. Helen allowed her mind to wander and revelled in the warmth of the water. Jo was right; she should make an effort to get out more. She'd become too serious lately and it wasn't like her. She would go out with them that evening. But when she rose to step out of the bath, a searing pain shot down her spine. It was very brief, but she stood for a few seconds too scared to move for fear it would return. Gradually she manoeuvred into an upright position. 'Maybe I stood up too quickly and pulled a muscle.' She decided not to get dressed until later and instead to lie on the bed to read and relax for a while longer.

The sound of the telephone woke her some time later. For a few moments she couldn't fathom where she was or what the time was. It was dark outside. Should she be getting ready for work or was someone ringing to say that something terrible had happened? She jumped up from the bed to get to the phone, but once again was paralysed by an intense pain. The phone continued to ring; she managed to hobble to the hallway and picked up the receiver.

'Hello?'

'Hi, it's me,' said Jo. After they left the restaurant she had gone into town to do some window-shopping. 'I'm still in town. You all right? I was wondering if you were still coming out with us.'

'Yes, but I won't stay late.'

'You should see the dress I bought, I'm going to wear it later. I'll get a newspaper on my way home and we can see if there are any flats worth looking at, OK? And can you stick a pizza in the oven? We can eat when I get back, I'm starving!'

The pain had gone, but the dull ache in the back of Helen's neck was still there and, despite painkillers and a nap, she felt exhausted when Jo returned.

Jo stopped abruptly half in and half out the door.

'You look awful, what's the matter?'

'I'm all right, don't fuss. I'm just a little tired that's all.'

'So you're not coming out?'

'I'll come but I won't be going round town with you after.' All Helen wanted was to crawl right back into bed.

'Good,' said Jo, 'want to see my new dress?'

The dress was beautiful, and looked even better when Jo put it on. It was close-fitting and the dark golden velvet harmonised with her complexion and dark eyes.

'It's lovely, Jo. You look fantastic. What am I going to wear? I'll look like an old frump next to you.'

Normally, Helen might have worried about what to wear, but tonight, despite her words, she didn't care. A paper bag over her head would do. That way she needn't make any effort to speak to anyone.

'I'll find something for you. Is the pizza ready yet? I can't wait any longer.' Jo disappeared into the bedroom and changed into her dressing gown. She emerged with an armful of outfits from her wardrobe.

'Why don't we eat first and do that later, if you're so hungry?' said Helen.

'OK.'

They ate their pizza and searched through the paper for suitable flats. They decided that a penthouse with a balcony looking out to sea would be nice, but there wasn't one in the rental pages this week. They laughed at the prospect, Helen's spirits lifted a little and she actually felt it might be a good idea to go out after all. Eventually they picked out a couple of possible flats and decided to see them the following day. Their first choice had two bedrooms and a large lounge with windows overlooking the park. It was just a short walk from the hospital and sounded ideal. The second was similar but a little further away and, in estate-agents' terms, was in need of slight redecoration.

'But the rent is low and we could always paint it ourselves, couldn't we?' said Jo.

They rang both numbers only to find that both flats had already been taken.

'Unbelievable!' said Jo. 'What are we going to do?'

'Leave it for now and get ready. We'll find something eventually.'

Jo raised her cup: 'To Helen, forever the optimist!'

Helen plumped for the inevitable little black dress, a simple affair that disguised rather than accentuated her womanliness. Tonight, she just wanted to feel comfortable, and having just washed her hair, she decided that it was best to blow-dry it and leave it down. For once it was in good condition and the mid-brown strands looked healthy and shiny. She brushed on some make-up and shouted to Jo to see if she was ready.

Jo emerged from the bedroom looking radiant, dancing like a Latin American.

'How do I look?' she asked.

'You look gorgeous!'

It was seven-thirty when they arrived at the hospital social club. By seven forty-five Helen was unconscious in casualty. Jo had ordered drinks at the bar and was waiting to pay for them when Helen decided to check her appearance in the ladies. She reapplied dark red lipstick and brushed her hair but, as she was leaving, she remembered tossing the tresses from her shoulder and suddenly feeling queasy and dizzy. She reached for the door handle to steady herself, and then - nothing.

The trolley rumbled into Accident and Emergency with an anxious Jo running alongside. A young doctor ran to meet them and escorted them to the resuscitation bay.

'What's your name? Can you hear me?' he shouted, to ascertain the level of the consciousness. 'Has she been drinking? Has she taken anything?' he asked Jo.

'Do you mean drugs?'

'I have to ask this, I need to know and quickly. I haven't got time to argue, just tell me everything.'

Jo's cheeks flared with embarrassment. 'I'm sorry. No, we haven't had anything to drink at all and she certainly hasn't taken any drugs.'

Helen began to stir. The white ceiling and the bright lights loomed down. They blurred and focussed alternately as she tried to open her eyes. The noise around her was deafening, people were calling out and the sound of buzzers screamed in her ears. She tried to sit up but was promptly eased back down.

'You're OK, Helen, try to keep still; you've had a nasty bump to your head,' said Jo.

Aware of the feel of a collar around her neck, Helen began to pull on it to relieve the pressure; it felt tight and strangling. A hand reached out preventing her.

'Don't try and take it off until you've been examined, it could be dangerous.'

As Helen opened her eyes she recognised the face of the man she had seen earlier in the restaurant. She closed her eyes again and screwed up her face. The pain in her head was unbelievable. She put her hand up to where it hurt most. The dressing covering the wound was soaked and the lump beneath was almost the size of a golf ball. Still in a daze, Helen looked to see her fingers covered in blood.

'What happened?'

'You must have fainted,' said Jo, 'and fallen against the sink. Lesley, the nurse from main theatre, found you on the floor when she went to the loo. At least the ambulance didn't have far too come.'

The doctor made a thorough examination and ordered X-rays to be taken.

'Nurse, please could you do half-hourly neurological obs and let me know of any changes.'

Turning to Helen, he continued: 'Your friend told me about the car accident earlier today. Maybe there is a connection between that and what happened to you this evening.'

'I've been having terrible shooting pains down my spine. It's probably from the whiplash,' Helen confessed.

'May well be. I think it would be a good idea to keep the collar on for a while and, because of the concussion, we'll also have to keep you in overnight for observation.'

'I'll go back to the flat and bring your things over,' said Jo. 'Is there anything in particular that you want?'

'Just some toiletries and pyjamas and some clothes for tomorrow, please. I'll be out first thing, hopefully.'

Jo was leaving when a thought occurred and Helen called her back. 'Was that Rahim?'

'Yes, he was in the bar when Lesley came running out of the loo to get help. He rescued the damsel in distress.' Jo laughed at her own fairytale. 'He's gone now though. He had to get back to his girlfriend.'

Next morning, the duty doctor handed over a sick note for one week and asked Helen to make an appointment to be seen in the outpatient department a week later. Lying in bed, Helen remembered the flats they had hoped to see. If they didn't find something soon, they'd be homeless.

'Maybe we could move back to the nurses' home for a while,' she thought, knowing full-well that the old dragon of a warden would soon put a stop to that. Jo and Helen had hardly been her favourites when they lived there before, not after one of Jo's boyfriends had set off the fire extinguisher in the corridor.

The following day, Jo and Helen drafted an advert: 'Two hard-working nurses looking for des res, two bedrooms, near to hospital if possible. Any condition, as considered experts in field of DIY.' They placed one ad in the local shop and the other on the hospital notice board. Helen saw the same young doctor that morning and was allowed home on strict instructions that she kept the surgical collar on and rested until her appointment the following week.

Within two days the girls had a response from the advert on the hospital notice board and were invited to view a ground-floor flat five minutes' walk away. It belonged to a retired hospital consultant and was in need of some decoration.

'Why the hell did we put that?' laughed Jo. 'I couldn't even paint a picture when we were at school.'

'Do you remember that painting competition we entered at the library? I did both our masterpieces and you bloody well won first prize!' said Helen.

'And then someone told the librarian, and she made us stay for two hours to tidy up the books.'

'I wanted to throttle you.'

§

'Come on, Helen, we only have ten minutes. It won't look good if we're late. He'll think that we'll be late with the rent as well.'

Helen was trying to pull her polo-neck jumper over her head to hide the ugly surgical collar.

'I can't go like this; I look like Frankenstein's mother.'

'No you don't, she was much better looking.'

'Ha ha, very funny, I'm taking the damn thing off.'

'Oh no you're not! Anyway, how about if the landlord feels sorry for you and reduces the rent?'

Helen threw the collar at Jo.

'You wear it then.'

'OK, I will.' Jo snatched the collar and put it around her neck. She walked round the bedroom, stooped over and pretended to limp. 'He'll let us have it for free when he sees me.'

Helen had forgotten about her neck, but was quickly reminded by a sharp twinge at the top of her spine.

'Oh - don't make me laugh, it hurts.'

Jo unfastened the collar and handed it back: 'You need it more than I do. Get it on now! Just a small reduction in the rent is better than nothing.'

The taxi arrived and they reached the flat on time. It was perfect. It had two good-sized bedrooms and the lounge was bright and airy, with an L-shaped dining section off to the far end which led into a compact, but perfectly adequate, kitchen. The whole place needed a thorough clean and the landlord hadn't been joking when he said it could do with some redecoration. The paintwork was badly chipped and the walls scraped and dirty. But it was only five minutes' walk from the hospital and they negotiated a lower rent by offering to paint it themselves.

A week later, Helen was given the all-clear from the hospital. The girls had lots of ideas taken from the house-and-garden magazines that littered the floor of their flat; but the landlord insisted on magnolia and said he would provide the paint. They acquired the keys and began scrubbing and cleaning. It was a purpose-built two-storey building containing four flats in total. The main hall and stairway split the building into two.

On the third day they were up early and off to their new home, armed with paintbrushes, rollers and magnolia paint. They worked until lunchtime when Jo had to start her late shift. It was a sunny autumn day with just a light breeze and once she was alone, Helen opened all the windows and doors to let the paint fumes escape. Lionel Ritchie sang 'All night long' on the radio, and she joined in as she sailed away with the paintbrush. It was two-thirty when she realised that she hadn't eaten. She nipped out to a nearby shop for provisions. Staggering back half an hour later she put four bags of shopping down whilst she unlocked the door, placed her keys and two of the carrier bags on the table and then returned to collect the rest of the bags. A voice called out from upstairs.

'Excuse me!'

At that moment, the breeze seized its opportunity and caught the door, swinging it shut, leaving Helen, daubed from head to foot in cream paint, standing on the outside, her keys on the inside.

'Shit, shit, shit,' she hissed.

3 NEW HOME, NEW BEGINNINGS

There was the sound of footsteps coming closer.

'Oh my God, you're locked out. That was my fault.'

The voice belonged to someone with a familiar face, but Helen couldn't be sure where she had seen the girl before.

'It's OK, don't worry,' said Helen. 'My friend has a set of keys. The only thing is, she works at the hospital and I can't go and get them looking like this.'

'Which ward does she work on? I can collect them for you.' A look of recognition spread across the girl's face. 'I know you. You passed out in the ladies' loo at the social club last week. I was there when it happened. I'm Lesley, I work in theatres.'

'I'd hoped to forget that incident, I felt like a complete idiot.'

'Come with me in my car and I'll run into the hospital and get the keys. I was just trying to introduce myself and to ask if you needed anything and look where it got us.'

Helen was only too glad to accept.

'How long have you lived upstairs?' she asked as they headed for the car.

'I don't live here. It's my boyfriend's place. He's at work, but it's my day off. I decided to spend the day here as I'm studying and it's much quieter than in the nurses' home.'

They reached the hospital.

'You stay here and I'll run in.'

Five minutes later, Lesley was back with Jo's keys.

At nine-thirty, having finished her shift, Jo bounced in.

'Isn't that a coincidence?'

'What's a coincidence?' replied Helen.

'Having them in the flat above.'

'You mean Lesley and her boyfriend?'

'You do realise who her boyfriend is, don't you?'

'I haven't a clue.'

'It's Rahim Ismail. Apparently they met on the day he arrived.'

'She seems really nice,' said Helen, thinking back to the tall slim girl with the sleek blonde bob. 'But enough of them, take a look around.'

It was twelve hours since they had taken possession of the flat and Helen had slogged all day. She had painted what remained of the hallway and had almost completed the lounge.

'You've done wonders,' said Jo. She went to give Helen a hug but retreated at the sight of her magnolia-speckled clothing.

'Tell you what; do you want a cup of tea and something to eat? I'll put the kettle on.'

'Mmm, I haven't eaten since three'ish. There's some frozen stuff in the freezer that I bought earlier.'

'On second thoughts, let's order a takeaway to be delivered to the other flat and a taxi to take us back, we should all arrive about the same time. You can have a nice hot bath while I set out the food and open a bottle of wine.'

'Sounds fantastic.'

They sealed the paint cans, left the brushes and rollers to soak in water, and were heading for the door when the taxi drew up.

On the day they moved into their new home, the man from the garage phoned to say that Helen's car was ready. It had been restored it to its former glory, and thanks to the wonderful WPC, Helen hadn't had to pay a penny. The white van man's insurance company had paid the lot immediately. Helen and Jo flopped back onto the sofa of their new home and admired their handiwork.

'Do you remember when we were sixteen,' said Jo, 'how we used to talk about getting married and buying a huge run-down farm in the Lake

District? We were going to split it into two; you one side with your husband and kids and me in the other side with mine.'

'We were going to look after each other's children so we could both carry on working.'

'And we were going to have chickens clucking round the door and horses in the field.'

'You wouldn't get me anywhere near a smelly horse,' said Jo, wrinkling up her nose. 'I only agreed to that to keep you happy.' Jo gazed up at the ceiling. 'Do you think it will ever happen?'

'If you don't have dreams, there's nothing to look forward to.'

'Let's get going on the first part then!'

'Which is what?'

'Let's find ourselves a couple of hunks. We'll go and explore the local pub and do some talent spotting.'

'There's more to life than having a husband and children you know,' said Helen.

'I know, but I think that I'd be happy to settle down. I don't see myself on the career ladder, do you?'

'Actually yes - I want my life to be interesting and a bit different - but I'm not sure how.'

Half an hour later, drinks in hand, the girls stood chatting in the bar of the Horse and Hound. The pub had low ceilings and dark heavy beams and was dimly lit with a big open fire that burned brightly in a cosy sort of way.

Jo said hello to a young man standing alone a few feet away.

'One of my patient's relatives,' she explained. 'His grandma is really ill. I won't be a minute.'

Shortly after, she beckoned to Helen to join them. 'This is Tom Jackson. Tom, this is Helen, my flatmate.'

As the conversation flowed between Jo and Tom, Helen eventually interrupted: 'I've got a headache, she said. 'I think I'll be off, see you back at the flat.'

'Sorry, Helen.'

'Don't worry, wouldn't want to spoil your fun!' Helen grinned. 'I'll see you later. Bye Tom, nice to meet you.'

Later that evening, Helen listened while Jo recounted the episode. 'He's so lovely and caring. How many blokes would be that concerned about their granny? He's very witty and he has a nice little bum!'

'Now where have I heard this before?' said Helen. 'Stop right now, you always fall head-over-heels then end up getting hurt.'

'I was joking! But Tom does seem different, and he's asked me out tomorrow night.'

§

Three weeks after moving into their flat, Helen was at work on the late shift. It was around five o'clock in the afternoon when Ethel, one of her patients, became quite breathless. She sat her upright, supported her with pillows and switched on the oxygen, placing the mask gently over her face. Ethel's skin was a death-like grey and she felt cold and clammy beneath Helen's fingers.

Helen called to the other staff nurse: 'Can you get Dr Shah for me, please? Tell him it's not a dire emergency, but could he come as soon as possible.'

Ethel was frightened, and in her panic, even as she struggled for breath, she tried to pull the oxygen mask off. Helen sat on the bed and held her hand, her voice calm and soothing.

'No Ethel, leave it on. Just breathe in, the oxygen will help you.'

A moment later, Ethel's eyes bulged and stared directly ahead. An initial choking sound faded till she fell silent. There was no sound from her chest and the pale pink of her lips turned blue. Helen shouted Ethel's name several times, with no response. She quickly searched for a pulse before shouting up the ward for someone to put out a crash call. Helen pulled the pillows out from underneath Ethel and the large woman fell unceremoniously flat onto the bed. Helen closed her fist and slammed it down as hard as she could into Ethel's chest, where, in her mind's eye, she could see the woman's heart lying dormant. Helen ripped off the bed-head with an almost super-human strength, and pulled Ethel's chin forward from behind to clear her airway.

A well-rehearsed scenario, and everything happened as if by magic. The crash trolley appeared with its store of drugs and equipment, a screen was shunted into position and work began. Helen inserted an airway in one slick manoeuvre and transferred an enormous breath of air from her own lungs into Ethel's. Footsteps hammered down the corridor and within a few seconds a horde of doctors in white coats took over. Helen passed on as much information as she could and moved aside to let them carry on, staying on hand to assist, drawing up drugs, sending out for equipment and sticking labels on blood samples.

Miraculously, Ethel returned to earth from whatever strange place she had visited. Once her heart rate became regular and her chest rattled in rhythm again, the crash team disappeared. Only Dr Shah remained to stabilise the patient. It was a time-consuming process; testing blood gasses, giving drugs, recording observations and phoning Ethel's relatives. Dr Shah - Aziz as he was known to his friends - took his time tending to every detail meticulously.

It was six in the evening. Helen was in the ward kitchen, brewing a well-earned pot of tea for everyone, when there was a knock on the door.

'Hi, how are you?'

Helen recognised Rahim. 'Oh - I'm fine thanks.' She was flustered. 'Well, much better than the last time I saw you. Actually, I feel a bit embarrassed because I never had the chance to introduce myself or thank you properly. I'm Helen,' she said, holding out her hand.

'That's OK, I'm Rahim.' He shook her hand warmly. 'Glad to see you looking so well. Is Dr Shah around?'

'Aziz? Yes he's on the ward. We just had a cardiac arrest so he's finishing off the bits and pieces. I'll let him know you're here, but he may be quite some time yet.'

'He was supposed to give me a lift to the garage to pick up my car.'

'I think the garage will be closed by the time he's finished, but I'll tell him anyway.'

Rahim waited in the kitchen for Helen to return.

'I'm afraid he'll be another half an hour, but he says could you wait. Want a cup of tea?'

'If it's not too much trouble.'

Tea was brewed and Helen took the tray into the sister's office.

'Sit in here with us,' she told Rahim. 'We have to have our break on the ward in case Ethel tries to leave us again.'

Rahim sat in the small office with Helen and Mary, the other staff nurse. He was around six-foot-tall with a well-toned body and long slim legs. His shiny black hair was cut short at the back but left slightly longer on top and it lay in casual flicks above his eyes. He smiled as Helen handed him a cup of tea, revealing slightly crooked teeth that somehow made him all the more endearing. Mary left to check on Ethel, leaving Rahim and Helen alone, but it wasn't long before Aziz appeared at the door.

'See you two have met. Sorry about the car, but no can do just now I'm afraid,' he said.

'It's OK,' answered Rahim, 'I'll get it tomorrow. Shall I come back later and we can go for a drink?'

'No, wait here, I'll be about fifteen to twenty minutes. I'm sure Staff Nurse Singleton can take care of you till then. No alcohol though - I'm on-call.' Aziz vanished.

'We went to school together and he hasn't changed at all.' Rahim's voice was soft and he spoke English without a trace of an accent.

'Have you lived in England all of your life?' Helen asked.

'I was born in Kenya where there is a big Asian community. My parents are Indian, but we've lived in lots of different countries. They settled in Uganda but had to leave when Idi Amin started causing trouble.'

'How old were you?'

'Fourteen. I remember the soldiers coming in the early hours of the morning and telling us to go. We weren't allowed to take any belongings with us. My father arrived in England with a wife and four children to support and only fifty pounds in his pocket.'

At that moment, Aziz popped his head round the door.

'Oh no, not that old chat-up line again,' he said. 'Don't believe a word he says, Helen. He's just trying to get you to feel sorry for him and then he'll swoop in like a hawk.'

'You ready now?' asked Rahim, embarrassed.

Aziz winked at Helen and grinned. 'Ready as I'll ever be.'

Aziz called back as they left the ward: 'I'll be back later to see how she is. If you need me, I have my bleep.'

Helen watched them leave. She already knew Aziz had been brought up in Kenya in a place called Kisumu. He was not as tall as Rahim, probably around five-foot-nine and much stockier, but he had a mischievous twinkle in his eye, giving him a boyish appeal. She had worked with him for the past two months and, considering he was newly-qualified, he was an excellent doctor and she had become very fond of him. She cleared the cups away and went back to work. Before she knew it the shift was over, but not before Aziz came back to check on his patient.

'She's been great, in fact I think she's better now than before she arrested,' said Helen.

They went together to say goodnight to Ethel. Breathless but smiling, the old lady held on to both their hands.

'I can't thank you enough,' she said. 'I wouldn't be here now if it weren't for you two, and you know what?'

'What's that, Ethel?' asked Aziz.

'You'd make a lovely couple.'

'Don't get carried away now, Ethel. I wouldn't wish him on my worst enemy,' said Helen.

But, as they left the ward at the end of the shift, Aziz caught hold of Helen's arm and turned her to face him.

'Ethel's right; you were very calm and professional and she probably would be dead if you hadn't been there in that initial moment.'

'Anyone else would have done the same.'

'Yes, but probably not as well as you.'

She was embarrassed and it showed. 'I'm tired,' she said, 'let's go home.'

'There's a Halloween Party on at the doctors' res next week, do you fancy coming?'

'As I said to Ethel - don't get carried away.'

'I'm not. Bring a friend with you if you like, it'll be fun, but you have to dress up.'

'OK, I'm game for a laugh.'

Back at the flat Helen received a phone call. Her father wasn't well and needed to go into hospital to have some investigations carried out.

'Luckily I'm off for the next two days,' she told Jo. 'I'm going home tomorrow. Dad's going to have a brain scan. Apparently he's been having some kind of headaches and they appear to be getting worse.'

4 HELEN RUSHES HOME

It was a bright sunny autumn day; Helen pushed back the hood of her newly-repaired car and Duran Duran bellowed out from the radio: 'Please, please tell me now'. After that, she competed with Bill Withers and 'Lovely Day', trying to hold the note as long as he did. As she sped home along the motorway, she felt a pang of guilt. How could she feel so happy and so full of life when her father wasn't well?'

Once off the motorway, she drove down the bumpy uneven road and pulled up outside the white wooden gates that her father had so painstakingly put together. To him these were no ordinary gates; they were a symbol of health and happiness. Closing them at night, his whole family safe and sound behind them, was his way of shutting out the world. No harm would come once they were closed, so he believed.

She closed the gates behind her and thought back to when she was sixteen and it first became apparent that her father had a problem. She had seen how drained he looked and how, on occasions, he looked quite sad, but when she asked what was wrong, he would shrug it off, telling her how busy he'd been, that he was just a little tired. He was a self-taught craftsman and he could turn his hand to almost anything, but whatever he did he never felt it was good enough. He would spend hours sanding a piece of wood and filling in the tiny cracks before he was happy with his work. The perfectionist in him saw only the flaws and there were times when it drove him to distraction. Working long hours on the house, not sleeping much and running his business had all begun to take their toll. He was exhausted, but wouldn't stop and rest. Lack of money for renovations meant that he had to part with his beloved car, his 'Grand Old Lady'. It was a massive blow. When the car went he lost some of his energy and enthusiasm and began to suffer short bouts of anxiety and depression.

At the weekend, when all the girls were still at home, the whole family would join forces to help with work in the garden; everyone would rake leaves or lug branches pruned from the trees to a bonfire in the field. How Helen loved it. Mum would call them in for hot milky coffee and then they would be back out into the cold, working harder than ever. To earn pocket-money Helen and her sister Paula helped to clean the coaches. They had great fun collecting the money that had fallen out of trouser pockets and lay hidden beneath the seats and would compete to see who could collect the most. Standing one on each side at the front of the coach, Shelly would shout, 'One, two, three, go!' and Helen and Paula would race down towards the back pulling up seats as they went and gathering coins.

At that stage in their lives Elizabeth couldn't ever have imagined the consequences of her husband David's obsessive perfectionism. Night shifts at the local hospital, four children to care for, a house to run and helping with the business kept her busy. She and David stuck to their motto, 'work now, play later'. When the children were grown-up they would take holidays abroad and splash out on a few luxuries. For now, they were content to work, and the days spent out walking on the Yorkshire Moors or through the hills of Derbyshire became fewer and fewer.

Helen treasured her memories of those childhood jaunts: the big coach-loads of friends and family out for the day with packed lunches and waterproofs in rucksacks, walking for miles, singing as they went. But now it was different. For the last few years her father's low periods had become more frequent, and there had been times when, angry and frustrated, he would sit at the dinner table and cry. One weekend, Helen came home to find a gaping hole in the side of the sofa. When she asked what had happened, David continued to stare blindly at his newspaper without answering.

Elizabeth replied instead: 'I tripped whilst carrying a chair through and the leg accidentally rammed the side and tore the fabric.'

Later, when they were alone, Elizabeth told her the truth about the terrible week they'd had. David had not been able to sleep; he had spent hours crying for no particular reason and she had finally suggested that he see a doctor. He lost control and accused her of trying to make him think he was going mad. He threw an ornament at the wall and, as he stormed out of the room, he kicked the hole in the side of the sofa. It was so unlike him, so unlike Helen's dad who was always so strong and always very gentle. He would never normally lose his temper in this way.

Since then, David had found it difficult to cope with the business. During one of his more lucid periods he and Elizabeth talked about their plans for the future and decided to sell so that he could look for a job with less pressure. A friend suggested a local haulage company. David would be able to organise his own workload, be more or less his own boss and, with no long-haul deliveries, still get home in time for dinner. He was accepted, and for a while he seemed more at ease and life regained some normality, but the headaches were something new.

'Hi! I'm home!' shouted Helen.

The old black labrador waddled up to greet her, propelled by his furiously wagging tail.

'You smelly old thing, what've you been up to?' Helen scratched behind his ear. The dog rubbed his head against her knee and wagged his tail even harder.

Elizabeth came down the stairs. 'Hello love, how are you?'

Helen kissed her on the cheek and gave her a hug. 'How's Dad?'

'All right apart from the headaches. He's been better lately, just a bit down in the dumps now and again. He's having a lie down.'

'That's not like Dad. When did the headaches start?'

'Around two weeks ago, but he wouldn't do anything about them and just took painkillers. He only went to the doctor when he started experiencing a buzzing sensation in his ears, and then the pain started in his neck too.'

'So what did the doctor say?'

'He couldn't find anything wrong but suggested a brain scan - to exclude anything more sinister, presumably.'

'Dad agreed?'

'Yes. I think he's hoping that they find something, to be honest with you; he won't accept he might be suffering from anxiety or depression. I think he'd be delighted if they found a brain tumour.'

'Mum, don't say that.'

'I know, it sounds terrible, but for him it would be preferable to the humiliation of admitting that he's depressed.'

A couple of hours later, David stumbled down the stairs, bleary-eyed from sleep.

'What you doing home, Helen?'

'I'm allowed to visit, aren't I?' Helen smiled.

'I'm not so sure about that. I know my daughters, visits usually mean it's going to cost something.' David held out his hands. 'It's lovely to see you.'

Helen put her arms round his waist and hugged him tightly. Her head lay on his chest and she could hear the sound of his heart like the hooves of a horse. She felt safe and secure, tears stung her eyes. 'How can this lovely big man feel so lonely and insecure?' she thought. She loved him so much.

'I hear you've been having bad headaches,' she said. It was OK to mention them because this was a physical complaint.

'I don't know what's causing them. They're not too bad once I've had a sleep, but they creep up again a few hours later. Anyway, I don't want you worrying, I'm fine. I'll put the kettle on.'

Helen's two older sisters were married with children of their own, but Karen, her younger sister, still lived at home and that evening the four of them sat together for a family meal.

'Do you remember when you had a fight with Paula's friend?' asked Karen. 'She was twice your size, but you annoyed her so much that she caught hold of you by the hand and swung you from one bed to another, except that you landed on the floor.'

'Yes, I remember. I lay there not moving, pretending to be dead. She was so scared that she shouted my name and shook me to wake me, but then I started to laugh, and so she hit me really hard.'

'You were very pale though. I was scared myself,' laughed Karen.

David roared with laughter to discover the mischief the sisters got up to when they were young, unbeknown to their parents.

'Helen, you've always been one to play practical jokes on people,' said Elizabeth.

Helen looked at David. 'I wonder who I get that from?' she said. It was ten-thirty and he looked weary. 'Dad, you look tired. I think it's time we all went to bed.'

'You're right, love. I'm very tired and my appointment is at nine in the morning. I'll call it a day.' He kissed them all goodnight and went upstairs to bed.

§

The next morning, in true perfectionist style, David was ready to leave for his appointment with at least half an hour to spare.

'Good luck! We'll be thinking of you,' shouted Helen.

Karen waved. 'You'll be fine, don't worry. See you later.'

They watched as the car rattled up the path and out of sight.

'You think he will be OK?' asked Helen.

'I really don't know. Two months ago he told Mum that he didn't want to go on living. In a way, I wish they could find something on the scan today. At least that way it would be something he could talk about and do something about and not be such a big secret.'

'What do you mean?'

'A few weeks ago, Uncle Tony and Auntie Pam came to visit. Before they arrived Dad was very subdued and stayed in his workshop all morning. I know Dad doesn't have a close friend but I would say that if there was one it would be Uncle Tony. Anyway, when they arrived, Dad chatted away showing Tony the work he had done on the house, and everything was great. But as soon as they left, he slumped down behind the front door and broke down sobbing for over an hour. It was awful. Mum and I didn't know what to do. He'd made such an effort so that Uncle Tony wouldn't see that he wasn't well, that afterwards he was completely wiped out.'

'What happened after that?'

'He sat for quite a while and stared into space, not speaking. He looked like he was in pain - not physically but mentally. I felt useless. How can we understand what he feels inside?'

'What about Mum?' asked Helen.

'She sat next to him on the floor and cradled him, but she didn't want to try and move him in case he lashed out. She was scared; he's never been violent towards her, but he sometimes gets so angry that she doesn't know what he'll do next. He's like a stranger to her at times. When he eventually got up, he looked at her as though he'd never seen her in his life before then disappeared upstairs. The most peculiar thing though, is that in the morning he was fine - back to his normal self as though nothing had happened.'

'Oh God, let's just hope the doctors can sort him out.'

At one o'clock that afternoon the car doors slammed shut, the front door of the house swung open and feet stamped up the stairs. Elizabeth stormed into the kitchen and slammed her bag down onto the work surface.

'I can't take this anymore,' she said.

She explained that the scan and test results had shown a perfectly normal brain. The doctor said that, in his professional opinion, the headaches and the noise in David's ears were probably caused by stress and anxiety. He mentioned the word 'depression' and advised David to see his own doctor who would prescribe some anti-depressant medication.

'That was it,' said Elizabeth. 'As soon as Dad heard those words he was out of the room and heading for the car. God only knows how we got back in one piece.'

David did not emerge until the following morning. He had hardly closed his eyes all night and came downstairs unshaven.

'I need to speak to you both. Mum and I spent most of the night talking and I've agreed to try the medication. If the pills take away the headaches and this awful noise in my ears then it'll be worth it. And if they don't work, then at least I've tried, and it'll prove to you all, once and for all, that I'm not going mad.'

Karen hugged him: 'Whatever happens I hope you feel better. I don't care what the problem is so long as we don't have to see you like this.'

When Elizabeth went to pick up the tablets, she felt like waving them in the air and cheering. 'There is hope after all,' she thought.

Elizabeth had carried this burden for eight years. It seemed to have started when Shelly got married and left home. David had been heartbroken, although he kept his feelings hidden. When Paula married, he sank even lower. He was the same fun-loving person in public, but in private he started to talk about ending it all and how he would do it. His world seemed to him to be shrinking, he was losing control.

Elizabeth had told no-one about her husband's condition. If she betrayed him, he would never forgive her. As the youngest child, Karen had lived through most of it and Elizabeth worried about the effect it was having on her. Karen had heard the shouting; she had sobbed in her bedroom when she heard the stifled cries of her father. Forced to mature early and wise beyond her years, she had had to be the adult when Elizabeth needed comforting. But now, medication in hand, Elizabeth was sure that things were going to get better and they could begin to live the rest of their life without this dreaded curse.

'Bye Mum, bye Dad!'

Elizabeth and David stood on the doorstep, their arms entwined around each other and waved until Helen's tiny sports car disappeared from view. Helen drove back to her carefree life, relieved.

'At last something is being done' she thought. Her mind wandered to the forthcoming Halloween Party. 'What on earth am I going to wear?'

5 THE HALLOWEEN PARTY

'No way,' said Helen, 'I'm not going as Dracula's tart. You wear it.'

They were in the fancy-dress shop in town and it was the day before the party. Jo had picked out a little French-maid's outfit with plastic fangs and fake blood to drip down the side of the mouth.

'We've left it bit late to start being fussy now.'

'Doesn't mean I have to look like that. What about that one?' Helen pointed to a full-length, all-in-one, black leotard with the bones of a skeleton painted onto it in fluorescent white.

'You're on – let's both wear the same.'

They left the shop each swinging a carrier bag. Helen phoned home when they got back to the flat.

'Hi, Mum. How are you? What's happening with Dad? Is he taking the tablets?'

'Yes, believe it or not. And he seems much better. He's sleeping at night but he's usually a little drowsy during the day, around lunch-time.'

'He may get used to having a little snooze in the afternoon; it would do him a power of good.'

'They say people benefit from just a twenty-minute catnap.'

'Let's hope he does that. OK Mum, take care. Speak soon.'

The night of the Halloween Party arrived. Helen and Jo had a glass of wine in the social club first, to get them in the mood. Rahim was at the bar, talking to a friend. He excused himself and made a beeline for them.

'You two look drop-dead gorgeous.'

'Very funny, Mr Ismail. You'll have to do better than that if you wanna be in our gang,' said Helen.

Jo went over to talk with one of her colleagues.

'You going to the doctor's party?' Rahim asked Helen.

'Yes, and you?'

'I've got something else on.'

The DJ played Lionel Ritchie's 'All night long'.

'I love this,' said Helen.

'Want to dance?'

She was a little taken aback but followed him onto the floor where they danced a few feet apart. They chatted easily, he laughed when she told him about the Dracula's tart outfit.

'I think I might have preferred that one.'

She slapped him playfully on the arm. 'Cheeky!'

The song died and Jo returned from chatting to the other nurse.

'You ready, Helen?' she asked.

Helen looked at Rahim apologetically. 'Sorry, I have to go.'

'That's OK, me too. Have a good time.' He bent forward and gave her a peck on the cheek. 'Bye.'

'Bye.' Helen smiled as she walked away.

Helen and Jo approached the house which had been bought many years ago by the health authority to accommodate doctors. It was massive and old with a steep driveway but slightly rundown. The solid wooden door was sadly neglected and the lion's head that served as a knocker no longer shone brightly but hung tarnished and forlorn, its brass unpolished. A fantastic place for a Halloween Party though, thought Helen.

Two female skeletons leaned on the doorbell simultaneously

Someone dressed as Lurch answered.

'You rang?'

The entrance hall remained clothed in its original wooden panelling. The magnificent balustrade that ran up to the right of the stairs was well polished - but only through use. A bat followed them in, jumping out at the other guests and baring his fangs. Jo barred his way.

'Tom! Where did you come from? You're going to give someone a heart attack!'

Tom enveloped her in his long black cloak. She screamed, loving every minute of it. They were so good together. Jo was really in love and rightly so. He was handsome and funny and intelligent.

'Look who that is,' said Jo pointing across the entrance hall. 'You don't recognise him do you?'

'Yes I do,' said Helen. 'It's the doctor that treated me in casualty. He makes a great fallen angel.'

Helen, Tom and Jo pushed their way to the drinks table and, having placed their cheap plonk among the other bottles, they helped themselves to a glass of quality red.

'Cheeky, aren't we?' said Helen.

Tom shrugged: 'No-one will care what they're drinking later on.'

'And neither will we,' said Jo.

Just then the door opened and in came Dracula. He pulled up short as he wafted past Helen.

'Aha, my little beauty, I hoped I might find you here. Come to my castle and we can feast together on fresh black puddings - but no garlic, thank you!'

The voice was familiar.

'Oh no, Count Dracula Aziz von Shah, that would never do,' said Helen. 'What would Mother say?'

'How did you know it was me?'

'It could have been the breath. Did you cook tonight?'

'Rahim and some friends came over.'

'Where are they now?'

'Who?'

'Rahim and the friends.'

'They'll be here shortly. Shall we dance?'

An hour later they made their way back to Jo and Tom. 'I'm dying of thirst,' said Aziz.

Some late-comers arrived, the friends that Aziz had entertained earlier. He went to greet them, giving hugs and kisses to each of them including the men, who protested. He sniggered. 'You're no fun,' he said. Then, linking the women by the arm, he waltzed them off in the direction of the dance floor.

Helen was surprised to see Rahim. He stood to one side of the room with a dark-haired woman. She had seen her before; she was a doctor on the surgical side. He looked as though he didn't want to be seen and stood with his back turned slightly in. 'Strange,' thought Helen, 'he had said he wouldn't be coming'.

'Come on,' Aziz shouted. 'You skeletons have no back-bone. Come and dance!'

'Have you heard?' said Jo.

'What?' asked Helen.

'Lesley and Rahim split up the other day and now he's here with that doctor.'

'So what? He can do what he likes then, can't he?'

'You haven't heard the rest. Apparently, poor Lesley is upstairs crying and won't come down.'

'Oh no, poor thing.'

As the evening wore on and the drinks flowed, Helen began to feel the effects of the alcohol. She felt as though she was inhabiting someone else's body or looking out from behind a mask and that no-one could see the real her. Ghouls and monsters faded into the background and the music echoed inside her until she was unaware of anything else.

'You OK?' A hand touched her shoulder and steadied her as she stumbled towards the drinks table.

'Pardon?' She tried to focus.

It was Rahim. 'What would you like?'

'A glash of red wine, pleashe.' Her lips felt like elastic and they had a will of their own.

He handed her a glass.

'Thought you weren't coming,' said Helen speaking slowly and deliberately.

'I didn't think I was. Someone else was coming who I don't particularly want to see at the moment.'

'You mean Leshley?' The words slid out of her mouth followed by a hiccup. This meeting wasn't going well.

He looked horrified but not by the hiccup.

'How do you know?'

'Therrsh no sheecrets roun ere. Why'd cha come then?'

'Talked into it,' he motioned towards the group he had arrived with. His lady escort had vanished.

'Whersh your new woman gone?'

'She's just a friend.'

'They all shay that.' She raised her glass. 'Cheers!' and took a big mouthful, but the warm red solution wouldn't sink beyond her throat. For some reason it stayed there, like a stagnant pond, idling around her tonsils, refusing to budge.

'You sure you're OK?'

She managed to swallow at last.

'I think it might be time to go,' she said, and without warning - to herself as much as to him - she planted a slobbery kiss on his lips.

Aziz came up. He slapped Rahim on the back.

'Hey! What's going on here?'

'Helen's going home. We're saying goodbye.'

'I've ordered a taxi. If you want to share it, we could all go together,' offered Aziz.

Helen was oblivious to the arrangements they made to get her home safely. She didn't care. Her world consisted of muffled sounds, a feeling of apathy and the occasional ripple of nausea. Minutes later, a taxi pulled up on the drive and the three of them stepped out of the big old house. Rahim hung back so that Aziz could help Helen shuffle forwards. She slumped into the back seat and Aziz closed the door, but before he could walk around to the other side, the taxi suddenly took off, leaving him and Rahim on the steps. Helen turned and peered out of the back window, but was unable to muster the right words to stop the driver. Instead, she grinned at the two men like an imbecile and managed a sluggish wave goodbye.

§

The next morning, the soft cream curtains were still open and the autumn sun shot its golden rays directly onto the crumpled heap of Helen on the bed. She lay still, the skeleton outfit contorted, as was her body. She opened her eyes and squinted, then shut them again. With each pulsation of her heart, the pain inside her skull bore deeper, a churning in the pit of her stomach burned like the fires of hell and, lower down, her bladder, filled to capacity, screamed out to be emptied. She had to escape the clutches of her pillow, but right now it seemed preferable to stay where she was and pass away peacefully.

Jo crept into the room.

'There's a phone call for you,' she whispered. 'It's Aziz, he's asking how you are.'

'What time is it? Tell him I'm in the shower.' Helen's voice was a hazy croak.

'It's lunchtime. Speak to him.'

'I can't. Tell him I'll ring later.'

Helen slowly turned and managed to lift herself from the comfort of her bed. She staggered from the bedroom to the bathroom and tiptoed back to bed again.

'Never ever again,' she muttered, burrowing deeper beneath the bed covers.

'How many times have I heard that before?' asked Jo.

The day went by agonisingly slowly and the pain inside Helen's head began to ease. The flashbacks became more vivid and more frequent, until the whole evening's events illuminated themselves in multi-coloured splendour before her eyes.

'What am I going to do? What am I going to say? I'm never going to live this down.'

Jo laughed when she heard what had happened.

'It's not funny!'

'But it is, it's the funniest thing I've heard in a long time. I wish we hadn't left so early.'

Helen tried to be serious but couldn't and they rolled around on the floor in hysterics.

'Seriously, what shall I say? Shall I go and apologise?' Helen cringed at the thought. 'I wish I was a bloke, I could send flowers and that would make everything OK.'

'Ring Aziz.'

'OK, OK.' Helen reached for the phone.

'Hi,' she said, trying to sound casual.

'Hi,' said Aziz at the other end, 'how are you today? Got a sore head?'

'I'm so sorry. I didn't remember what happened until this afternoon when it suddenly dawned on me. Did you get home OK in the end?'

'You care?'

'Of course I do. I feel so embarrassed; I can't begin to explain how bad I feel. I'll think of a way to make it up to you.'

Aziz laughed. 'How about you cook us a meal sometime?'

'Us?'

'Rahim was left out in the cold too.'

'He was?'

'And don't worry, I won't mention it to anyone at work.'

She hadn't thought about that.

§

'Guess what?' Jo couldn't contain herself any longer. 'I'm finally going to meet Tom's parents. He asked if I'd like to go for dinner at their house on Friday.'

Jo and Tom had been seeing each other for four months now and Jo was convinced they were going to spend the rest of their lives together. Tom was in his final year of accountancy and he would soon be in a position to apply for a mortgage. They had begun saving a small amount already and had decided they would like to live in a little village about a mile away from the hospital. Jo could walk to work and, though Tom's job was a little further away, he would cycle so that they could save money.

Friday came round quickly and Jo was in a frenzy; half the contents of her wardrobe were on the floor.

'What shall I wear?' she shouted.

Helen didn't look up from her magazine. 'Something sensible, with a front and a back to it. Not your usual stuff.'

'Please! Help me, I beg you, I'll do anything.'

Helen dragged herself up from the sofa.

'For a start, no black. You need a high neckline, a low hemline and nothing too tight. Have you nothing of your mum's in there?'

Jo pulled out a brown skirt coupled with a cream blouse.

'I was joking, you'll look like a school teacher. They'll love you.' Helen rifled through the strewn clothes. 'Voila, just the thing.' She held up a simple blue dress 'Not too flash and not too frumpy. Now go and enjoy yourself.'

'Do I look all right? I'm so nervous my hands are shaking.' Jo tried unsuccessfully to button her coat.

Helen fastened it for her. 'Have a lovely time, don't worry, and I'll see you later.' She stood back and looked Jo up and down. 'You look gorgeous.'

6 RACIAL ATTACK ON JO

Once in the car, Jo was comforted by the warmth of the heater. On the radio, David Bowie sang 'Let's Dance'; Tom leaned over and kissed her full on the lips. He was wearing a casual blue shirt and smart black jeans; Jo loved his sense of style.

'Shall we go for a drink first? It might help you relax,' he suggested, as he could see that she was anxious. 'You'll be fine, they'll love you. You look lovely.'

'A drink sounds like a good idea.'

At seven-thirty they pulled up outside a large detached house. In the garden, an ancient oak tree peered down like a wise old man on guard duty and a weeping willow overshadowed the drive, its tentacles reaching out to passers-by. On the driveway two identical Mercedes stood side-by-side.

Tom took her hand.

'Ready?'

She thought she saw a frown cross his face, but it was quickly replaced by a smile.

Cream carpets covered the hallway, branching off into each room before meandering up the grand staircase. Sumptuous, deep red curtains hung against plain cream walls. Jo was dazzled by the sight of so many beautiful pieces of antique furniture. A television babbled in one of the rooms and Tom led her towards the sound. As he opened the door, somebody jumped up and switched it off. A woman turned to face them. Tom held Jo's hand so tightly that she had to wriggle her fingers to encourage the blood flow to the tips.

'Mum, Dad, this is Jo.'

A strange hush followed, as if his parents were transfixed, unable to move or speak. Tom ploughed on: 'Jo, th... this is my mum, Ann, and my d... dad, John.'

Still the couple stood and stared. Tom spoke a little louder: 'Mum, Dad!' he gestured towards Jo.

John broke the spell at last.

'Nice to meet you,' he said, stepping forward to deliver a limp handshake. He was a tall, jolly-looking man, with a full head of white hair, not particularly overweight, but with a slight paunch. Tom had inherited his blue eyes and warm friendly face. Ann, meanwhile, following her husband, held out a bony hand but only allowed her fingertips to hold Jo's, as though she were picking up a snotty handkerchief. She was tall and upright with square shoulders and Jo wondered if she had ever been in the army. Her hair, greying naturally, was backcombed and taken away from her face, fastened in a small bun at the nape of her neck. Twinset and pearls completed the picture. Jo imagined she was someone who held coffee mornings and was probably a member of the Women's Institute. There was nothing endearing about her.

'What about a drink for everyone?' said Tom.

'Not for me,' Ann's look was disdainful. 'I have things to do in the kitchen.'

Jo thought of offering her services, but decided to keep quiet.

'Where are you from Jo?' asked John.

'My family live just outside Manchester.'

'I mean, where are your parents from?'

Tom shot a sideways glance at his father.

'What I'm trying to say is that you have beautiful colouring and I wondered where you had inherited it.'

'My dad is from Pakistan and my mum is English.'

'John, could you carve the meat for me, please?' Ann shouted from the kitchen.

John excused himself. Tom looked agitated and Jo watched him closely.

'It's OK,' he said, 'they're always like this when we have visitors. Mum panics a bit, that's all.'

'What is it, Tom? What's bothering them? They looked shocked when I walked in.'

'It's nothing. They're fine. Let me get you a drink, a glass of wine maybe?'

'A glass of white if you have it please.'

He went through to the kitchen to get the wine and Jo sat alone in a chintz armchair by the door. She could hear animated voices. She heard Tom's voice, and he sounded angry. She strained her neck to hear. At first she could only detect the odd word, but the argument gathered momentum until, eventually, she could follow the gist of the conversation.

'Why didn't you warn us, Tom?' asked Ann.

'Because I wanted you to meet her first.'

'How could you do this to us?'

'Do what to you? She's the loveliest person you could ever meet.'

'You really should have been honest about it.'

'And then what? Then you would have refused to meet her. You still think only white people should be allowed to live in England, that's what it boils down to.'

'That's unfair.'

'You're scared because they are different and have their own customs. Why don't you get to know her first and then tell me how you feel?'

Jo crept closer, standing in the doorway just out of sight. She could see Tom with his back to her, facing his mother. His father carved the meat.

'Your mum's right, Tom. You've always known how we would feel if you brought a coloured girl home.'

'Coloured girl?' Tom spat. 'She's not a "coloured girl". She's of mixed-race or mixed-parentage, call it what you like, but none of that makes any difference. She is the only girl I've ever met that I want to spend my life with. I love her and want to marry her!'

Jo's heart hammered against her rib cage. Tears sprung to her eyes and her cheeks burned.

'You can't be serious!' said Ann.

'What are you going to do about it?' said Tom.

Jo stepped quietly forward into view and John's eyes opened wide in surprise. Jo placed a hand on Tom's arm.

'It's all right,' she said. 'I think it's best if I go.'

'Please don't,' pleaded Tom. 'We need to talk it through, that's all. Stay, please Jo, stay.'

'I need to get out of here.'

Ann stood motionless, aghast.

'But what about the food?' John blurted. He slapped his forehead with the heel of his hand, this was absurd.

Tears etched their way down Jo's cheeks. She ran towards the front door, reaching for the ornate handle. Tom grabbed her coat from its hook and ran after her. He turned and looked briefly at his parents when he reached the door. They stood in the hallway like two wounded soldiers, gripping each other for support. Meanwhile, Jo was running blindly down the road. Where she was heading she didn't know or care. All she knew was that she had to escape the humiliation.

'Jo, stop, please!' Tom caught up with her. 'Oh God, I'm so sorry. I never imagined they would react that way. I wouldn't have inflicted that upon you if I'd known.'

'But - you did know.'

She had stopped running but continued to walk quickly. He had led her into a situation for which she was totally unprepared. How could he have been so stupid and short-sighted?

'Please Tom, just take me back to the flat,' she said, shivering with cold. 'I don't want to talk about it right now. I need to get home.'

He flung the coat around her shoulders and pulled her close. He wanted to make it all better and protect her, but she shrank away in disgust.

'No.'

Her rejection tore his heart; the pain was almost physical, as if a bullet had bitten its way through his flesh.

'Stay here, Jo. I'll run back and get the car.'

Shortly after, she wilted into the soft leather car seat and stared ahead unblinking. Neither of them spoke until they pulled up outside the familiar red-brick building and Tom turned to her.

'I'm so sorry Jo. I really am.'

She looked at him, a tear on her cheek.

'So am I.'

The corners of her mouth turned upwards in a smile, but her eyes didn't reflect the sentiment. She got out of the car and, without looking back, slipped her key into the lock and opened the door.

Tom sat for a while then drove slowly away. He headed off into the darkness. The car spun along the country roads until he found himself in unfamiliar territory. After a mile or two, he swung into a lay-by sheltered by trees. Switching off the engine he punched the centre of the steering wheel.

'You're back early!' Helen turned to face Jo. 'What happened to you?'

'Oh, Helen, you won't believe it.'

Helen held Jo close and rocked her, smoothing the tousled hair until the sobs subsided. 'It's OK. It's OK,' she repeated. 'Tell me about it.'

Jo told her what had happened.

'Unbelievable,' said Helen. 'How can they say things like that, the small-minded bigots? They should be locked up. What are you going to do?'

'I'm too angry right now but tomorrow I'll go round there and let them know exactly what I think of them,' replied Jo.

'Is there any point?' Helen asked. 'It's not going to do any good is it?'

'I don't know; I'm too tired now to even think straight, I need to go to bed.' Jo hugged Helen and kissed her on the cheek.

'I'm so glad you were here. I'll see you in the morning. If Tom rings, tell him I'm asleep.'

'OK. You know where I am if you need me.'

Neither of them could sleep. After an hour of tossing and turning, Helen decided to get up and make a cup of tea. She found Jo in the kitchen, leaning on her elbows, a magazine open on the table in front of her, staring into space.

'You OK?'

'No - it won't sink in. I don't think they even begin to realise what they've done to Tom. How could anyone can be so blatantly racist?'

'Do you think, if they realise their mistake, they'll change their minds?'

'Don't know. They're not worth it. If they decide to accept me for Tom's sake, can I live like that? Knowing what they think about "coloured" people, as they put it?'

'And they couldn't have wished for a kinder, more caring, gentler, not to mention attractive, prospective daughter-in-law,' said Helen.

Jo laughed: 'Well at least I have one person who loves me.'

'Two actually - don't forget Tom.'

'Oh yeah - and him.'

'They'll be the ones that lose out. Did Tom go back home?'

'I don't know. I felt sorry for him, he looked distraught, poor thing, but I'm so angry with him too.'

Around midnight they crawled wearily back to bed and Jo drifted in and out of sleep until around six o'clock the next morning. Stumbling to the bathroom she looked in the mirror. Her reflection bore no resemblance to the bright, confident young woman who had stood there only a few hours before.

Tom stretched wearily. His eyes stung, his neck ached and he desperately needed to stretch his legs. He had spent a long night squeezed into the tiny cockpit of his car and couldn't bear the thought of going home to face his parents. He didn't even consider it his home any more. The previous evening had haunted his dreams. How could Jo forgive him? And how could his parents not see beyond their own stupidity? He needed to see Jo. A tremor ran through his body. Cold and tired, his stomach groaned, hungry for the dinner he had missed the night before. The digital clock on the dashboard said six-thirty and the sky was beginning to lift its heavy cloak of darkness. Tom switched the heater to full and coaxed the car into life.

He drove to the girls' flat and parked beside Helen's car. The light from Jo's bedside lamp was visible through the closed curtain. Tom felt a wave of nausea flow over him as his insides somersaulted. What if Jo refused to speak to him? Easing himself out of the car, he stood on the pavement. He ran his fingers through his unruly dark hair and rubbed his face to bring some colour to his cheeks. Standing at the window, the courage to tap lightly evaded him. He waited for a while and listened but there was no sound. Raising his hand to the cold glass he leaned his forehead against it and silently wept. He walked to his car and, before long was back at his parents' house. Creeping upstairs to his room, Tom cursed himself for being such a coward.

§

It was Saturday and Jo was working a late shift on the old Nightingale Ward where neatly-made beds lined the walls. She and another nurse were moving from patient to patient plumping-up pillows and making sure their ladies were comfortable. They shuffled the old linen trolley down one side of the ward and up the other. Jo was exhausted.

The other nurse gestured to someone standing in the main corridor outside the ward. 'He's been there for ages; do you think he's waiting for visiting time?'

It was Tom. Jo's legs turned to jelly. Clinging on to the trolley for support, she stared directly at him, waiting for the surge of adrenalin to run its course.

'Nurse?' A patient writhed to get comfortable and rubbed her chest. 'Could I have something for heartburn, please?'

'I'll be with you in a second.'

'Heartburn - that was one word for it,' she thought. Back in the sluice room she shunted the trolley up against the wall.

'I'll be back in a second!' she called to the other nurse and slipped out of the ward.

They stood a few feet apart. Jo felt as if she was seeing Tom for the first time.

'Jo, last night...,' he said, 'I can't tell you how sorry I am. I thought that once they met you they would see immediately that you were the one, but they didn't even give you a chance.'

'But you knew how they felt and yet you didn't warn me,' replied Jo. 'They were right, you should have been open and honest. You can't manipulate people like that. Have you any idea how I felt? It was beyond humiliating.' An angry tear rolled from the corner of Jo's eye.

'But then they wouldn't have agreed to meet you!'

'It's not a game, Tom. You should have told me how they felt. You should have been man enough to sit down and discuss it with them and with me.'

'Let me speak to them; I'll ask them to meet you again so they can get to know you.' He was almost incoherent. 'Please, Jo, I'm so sorry. I love you so much.'

'No, I can't go back there. Last night was the worst night of my life. How can I go and face them again after the things they said?'

'What are you trying to say?'

'I'm sorry... '

'Jo, we'll be fine, I promise.'

'No, I don't think we will. You ruined everything. I'll never let anyone put me in that situation again - not even you.'

She turned and walked away. It was so painful to see the injured expression on his face, especially when, deep down, her heart was breaking too.

Back on the ward, she locked herself in the staff changing room and gave full vent to the emotion she had been fighting to control. She loved Tom, but he was weak. He'd put his own feelings and, worse still, those of his parents before hers and she could never live with that.

Over the next few weeks, Tom tried hard to convince Jo that they could make a go of it. The phone rang often.

'It's for you,' said Helen, yet again.

'Is it Tom?'

'He sounds really upset.'

Tom phoned every day, sometimes twice a day. It hurt Jo to hear him plead. She loved him so much, but she had decided his parents had too much of a hold on him. He was looking to buy a house of his own, but nothing could change the fact that he hadn't trusted her nor prepared her for that fateful night. Out in the hallway she reluctantly picked up the receiver.

'Hello?'

'Jo, please, we need to talk.'

'Please don't phone. It's not helping; you're just making it more difficult. You know how I feel, and you know what your parents think, and nothing will ever change that. There's nothing more to say.'

She replaced the receiver, rubbed her tired eyes and went back to her room where she lay on the bed, staring into space.

The phone rang again.

'Jo?' said Helen, from the doorway.

'No, not again - I can't take this anymore.'

'It's not for you, it was for me.' Helen looked anxious.

'What is it? Is everything all right?'

It was eight o'clock in the evening and it had been dark for some time.

'Dad went out first thing this morning,' said Helen, 'and he hasn't come back. It was Karen on the phone; she said Mum's out of her mind with worry. I have to go home and see if there's anything I can do.'

'Where do you think he could be? Have they phoned the police?'

'Apparently the police don't want to know unless someone has been missing for over twenty-four hours. Mum told them that he wasn't well, but they still weren't interested.'

Jo was off the bed and standing in front of Helen.

'Go and pack a bag, I'll phone work and tell them you won't be in tomorrow.'

She hugged Helen. 'He'll be OK, don't worry.'

Helen went to her room. She pulled out a rucksack, gathered a few things together and stuffed them into the bag, but as she headed out into the hallway she bumped into Rahim.

'Where are you going?' he asked. 'Got a hot date, have you?'

'I'm off home, my dad's not well.'

'Sorry, hope he's not too bad. Take care how you drive and if there's anything I can do, give me a ring - OK?'

'Thanks I will, that's kind of you.'

Rahim kissed her on the cheek and gave her a hug and she was grateful for the comfort. Since the dreaded Halloween Party she had seen Rahim several times in passing and he always stopped to chat. She was becoming quite fond of him.

Helen chugged her way down the rugged path towards her parents' old house. A dim light shone from the kitchen; normally so welcoming, tonight it filled her with dread. Her stomach churned and she wanted to drive faster but the uneven road wouldn't allow it. The gates had been left open, which meant David wasn't back.

When she arrived Karen beckoned her into the kitchen.

'Shelly and Paula are in the lounge with Mum.'

'Any news?'

'Nothing. We phoned the police again; they said to contact them in the morning if he wasn't back.'

'He didn't say where he was going?'

'Just that he was going for a walk. He's been quite well recently so we didn't think anything of it. The only thing is - he stopped taking the tablets because he said he felt better and didn't want to become addicted to them.'

'Surely it was too soon to stop them. Did the doctor agree to it?'

'He didn't tell the doctor. Mum tried to get him to carry on, but he wouldn't listen.'

'Where could he be? Did he give any indication at all?'

'No. We only became concerned around five. That's when I phoned Shelly and Paula to see if he'd gone to see either of them. Of course he hadn't.'

'Poor Mum. I'd better say hello.'

They went through to the lounge. It was brightly lit and the television was on, the volume set low. Elizabeth was sitting in her usual chair by the fire looking pensive; Shelly and Paula were sitting on the sofa.

Helen put the lamp on and switched off the overhead light. 'Hi, Mum, how are you?' Helen didn't know what else to say. She gave Elizabeth and each of her sisters a hug and a kiss and joined them on the sofa.

'I'm sorry to drag you home, I feel so helpless,' said Elizabeth. 'I don't know what to do.'

'Why's he like this? I don't understand,' said Helen.

'I think he feels that everything he has worked for is being taken away from him. He no longer has his business or his car, the house still isn't finished and one-by-one his daughters are getting married or leaving home.'

'That happens in every family. We can't live at home forever – and if we did he'd soon get fed up with us.'

'He had such a terrible childhood. He craved this perfect life with his family around him forever. We've talked for hours. Our lives have to change as we get older, but he just can't come to terms with it. And now he refuses to take the tablets. I'm at my wits end. Put the light back on, Helen - I want him to see that we're here waiting for him. I don't want him to think we've gone to bed.'

Helen put the light back on and sat down next to Elizabeth.

'Have you looked outside - in the garage?' she asked.

'Yes, and in the attic.'

'We can't wait up all night. If he doesn't come back, we'll be in no fit state to do anything tomorrow.'

'Let's stay up till twelve. If he isn't back by then, I doubt he'll come back tonight,' said Shelly.

'Why don't we phone round to see if anyone has seen or heard from him?' said Paula.

'No! No-one knows about his illness. If I do that and he comes back tonight or tomorrow he'll be furious.'

Elizabeth began to cry. Her daughters looked at each other despairingly. Shelly went over and took hold of her hand. Meanwhile, Helen needed time to think; she left them and went to the front door, hoping to see a lone figure coming through the gates. It was a mild night, the sky was clear and the stars sparkled brightly, happily ignorant of the worry and fear beneath them. She hoped he had gone to stay with someone, but that was unlikely to be the case. He had few friends apart from Uncle Tony. He always said that you could count your true friends on one hand and there was no-one that he would confide in, not even Uncle Tony.

Helen closed the front door and went into the kitchen. Shelly stood by the sink, her nose buried in a tissue; she sniffed and wiped her eyes.

'What if he's finally managed to do something stupid?' she said.

'Shelly, he won't have,' said Helen. 'He probably needed some time on his own.'

'Mum says he talked of "ending it all" before he started on the medication. She went into the garage once and found a piece of hosepipe fitted onto the exhaust of the car.'

'What?'

'He often talks about going up over the moors at Saddleworth. Do you remember where we used to walk by the reservoir?'

'He's talked about that to me too, but only in the context of what he would do if he ever became disabled. He's petrified of having to rely on others. But then, if he was disabled, he wouldn't be able to get up there in the first place.'

They smiled at the irony.

Back in the lounge the television kept the silence at bay.

'Mum, Shelly just told me about Dad rigging the car up in the garage. Why didn't you tell the rest of us?'

'I didn't want to burden you.'

'But this is our problem too,' said Paula. 'We might have been able to help.'

'How could you? He wouldn't talk to anyone and he wouldn't listen to me. He wouldn't take the medication and now he has he thinks he's cured.'

'He may feel better if he knows that we're aware of how he feels.'

'I don't know how he'd react to you speaking to him Paula, and anyway, what if he doesn't come back?'

It was half past eleven and still no sign.

'Let's go to bed,' said Helen. 'We can leave the lights on just in case.'

Elizabeth wanted to stay awake in case David came home. It was midnight when she closed the door to her bedroom and sat fully-clothed on the bed touching the gold ring on the third finger of her left hand. Thirty-six years of marriage and some of its sheen had gone, but it remained a symbol of commitment to her husband and her girls. She turned it round and round and thought back over the years remembering the man she had married. Such a lovely man, tall and well-built, almost like a sergeant major, always immaculate and clean-shaven. His silver hair was dark brown back then and close-cut. The clothes he wore were inexpensive, but always beautifully laundered and pressed so that the creases in his trousers were razor-sharp. His black leather shoes shone like mirrors from hours of polishing.

She thought back to when she had met David, at a Christmas party, they had been the only people still sober at the end of the night. Sitting in the hallway on the bottom stair they had talked for hours, oblivious to the other partygoers. David had told her about his three brothers and how as children they had been beaten regularly with a leather belt, his sister the only one spared that humiliation. He told her his parents argued and fought most of the time.

Being the eldest, David had felt a responsibility towards his mother and siblings and had tried to protect them. He told Elizabeth about the day, when he was sixteen, and his dad turned on his mum yet again, landing a powerful smack across her face with the back of his hand. David had leapt over the sofa and grabbed hold of his father, pinning him against the wall. He was about to land a punch but wouldn't allow himself to be reduced to the same level. He had let go and gone to the room he shared with his brothers to pack a small suitcase. Within a week he found lodgings with a middle-aged couple and began working on a building site fifty miles away.

Elizabeth stretched out on the bed; the light was still on so that David would see that she was still awake if he did come back. She turned onto her side, the scent of him permeating her nostrils.

'Please let him be safe,' she prayed.

She had always believed in God, but then again, what sort of a God would do this to such a gentle, clean-living man? David didn't smoke or drink. He believed that if you treated others as you would like to be treated yourself, you deserved to go to heaven - if it exists.

Looking back, he had always been different. Obsessed with cleanliness and order, he didn't like soap to be placed on the side of the bathroom sink because of the slime that developed underneath; it had to be placed out of sight in the cupboard below. In the kitchen he insisted that all gadgets and equipment be hidden away in cupboards so the work surfaces remained bare and easy to clean, and around the house, ornaments were kept to a minimum. Obsessive yes, but he was also full of fun and jokes. Elizabeth could never have envisaged the fun-loving man she married becoming so pessimistic and so wretchedly desperate to die. There had been times recently when he had talked of nothing but the black hole that threatened to engulf him, and of how worthless he felt.

In the early hours she woke from a restless sleep. It was daylight. There was no sun, but no rain or wind either; it was a still, grey day. She went downstairs and opened the door to the kitchen, half hoping to see David in his usual chair at the table. She gave a gasp and stood rooted to the spot.

'It's all right, Mum, it's only us,' Shelly held out a hand. 'None of us could sleep either.'

'I didn't think I slept,' said Elizabeth, 'but I had the weirdest dream. It was about Dad and he was beckoning to me. There were two doors, one was to heaven and the other was to hell. God was calling both of us, but Dad was dragging me to the door of hell saying: "No, Bett, we're not good enough for there." Just as we entered hell, a bright orange light flashed and the heat was so intense it woke me up.'

'Oh Mum! Come and sit down,' said Paula.

'We must call the police; they have to do something, this is ridiculous,' said Karen.

'I'll do it,' said Shelly. She used the phone in the hallway. Muffled sounds filtered through to the kitchen.

'They'll be here in an hour or so,' she told the others when she was finished.

Shelly stood at the kitchen sink and looked out of the window. 'Why don't they come straightaway? Sorry Mum, I feel we're letting him down.'

'Let's see what the police have to say when they come.'

'Helen, why don't you and me go out now and look for him? We don't all have to be here when the police come,' said Karen.

'Why not, what's the harm?' said Helen.

'I'm scared,' said Elizabeth. 'I'm scared of what you might find; I'd prefer it if someone else found him.'

'Tell you what,' said Helen, 'if the police don't come in the next hour, we're going no matter what. All right, Karen?'

'I'll go and get dressed.'

Back at the flat, Jo drummed her fingers on the table before reaching for the phone. She dialled Helen's home and it was answered on the first ring.

'Hello.'

'Hi, it's only me,' she said.

'Hi Jo,' said Helen.

'Take it you haven't had any news?'

'Nothing, we're still waiting for the police. How are you?'

'I'm fine; it's you I'm worried about. I spoke to Sister Small; she sends her regards and says don't worry about work.'

'Thanks. Is it busy?'

'You can't go worrying about that. Is there anything I can do?'

'Not really.'

'Let me know as soon as you hear anything.'

'I will - thanks for ringing, Jo.'

Shelly was pacing back and forth to the window when her heart suddenly skipped a beat. Walking slowly, hands sunk deep into his pockets, was a man in an overcoat, strolling down the path towards the house. Was it him? It looked like him, but no, it was their neighbour.

'I can't stand this,' she said, 'it's driving me insane.'

'Let's go and sit in the lounge,' said Paula, 'I've got a massive headache and this isn't helping. When the police come we can make a plan; all this waiting is making matters worse.'

'Paula's right,' said Elizabeth, 'be patient, they won't be much longer now.'

Helen and Karen, dressed in thick coats and scarves, joined the others in the lounge. Helen studied her sisters, they were so different. She and Shelly had dark hair, like Elizabeth's side of the family. Karen and Paula, who sat with her head against the back of the chair to ease the tension headache that hammered at her skull, were like Dad with fair hair and blue eyes. Helen thought how there was nowhere she would rather be at this moment than with her sisters, and she said a quiet 'thank you' that she wasn't an only child.

By ten-thirty there was still no sign of the police.

'What are we going to do?' said Karen. 'I'm going to search for him. You coming, Helen?'

'Yes.'

Elizabeth wrung her hands and sighed. 'You two go and we'll wait here, but please don't be too long, I don't want to be worrying about you as well.'

'We won't stay out long,' said Helen.

Paula was prostrate on the chair but Shelly made her way back to the kitchen to keep watch. Suddenly a shriek from Shelly sent them all racing to the lounge.

'He's here! He's back! Quick, come and see!'

They dashed to the window from where they saw a forlorn-looking figure in a fawn-coloured duffle coat approaching the house. They scrambled over each other to reach the door and ran outside to open the gate. Elizabeth followed at a slower pace, fearful to be the first person to greet him, unsure how he would be. He smiled wearily as he stood by the gate, almost like a tramp or a ghost. Tears welled up in his eyes and he held out his arms as if to gather them all up at once. His eyes met Elizabeth's over his daughters' heads. Their gaze connected, Elizabeth put out a hand and lovingly smoothed his cheek. Neither of them spoke; the look of relief in her eyes was enough welcome for him. Unknown to her, he too was afraid of the reception he might receive.

The girls ushered him into the lounge. Shelly went to bring a blanket, Paula made him a warm milky drink, Helen brought his comfy slippers and Karen offered to run a warm bath. Elizabeth sat holding his hand, waiting for the right moment to gently coax out of him where he had been.

David couldn't believe the response his return had evoked. Seeing his family around him he felt deeply ashamed and asked himself how he could have been so stupid.

'Where did you go, Dad?' said Shelly at last, 'we've been out of our minds with worry.'

'I don't know where to start,' he said. 'I was back in that black hole again, only this time I couldn't escape and to be honest I didn't want to.' He searched the room as if trying to find his next words. 'I felt so lonely, which I know is ridiculous when I have all of you, but life didn't mean anything, I felt that you would be better off without me.'

'How can you say that?' said Shelly.

Paula broke in: 'So what did you do? Where did you sleep last night?'

'I didn't sleep, I didn't know what to do so I just walked for miles without following any particular direction.'

'David,' said Elizabeth, 'where are the sleeping tablets the doctor gave you? They were in the cupboard and now they've gone.' She had looked for them immediately she suspected that he might not come back. Normally, she either hid any tablets or threw them out - for fear he might take the lot. The sleeping tablets were from a recent prescription and she hadn't managed to get her hands on them. David pulled a small brown bottle from his coat pocket. She almost snatched it from him.

'Dad, we were worried sick. Were you intending to take the tablets?' said Paula.

David produced a small bottle of whisky out of his coat pocket. He held it up like an exhibit in a police investigation.

'But you don't drink!' said Helen.

'I know that alcohol increases the potency of the tablets and I thought the two of them together would do the trick.'

They couldn't believe what they were hearing. It was almost enough to evoke anger but his pain was tangible and the room fell silent.

'I got the bus to Rivington Pike,' he said, 'and then walked and walked, trying to sort out the chaos in my head. Eventually, I just sat on the ground with my back against an embankment. I felt dazed and so tired. I knew that I wanted to end it all, but I hated myself even more for not having the courage to do it. I don't know what time it was, but it started to go dark and somehow it seemed that the time was right. I took out the tablets and laid them in a line on my thigh following the crease of my trouser leg. I opened the bottle of whisky.'

He stopped there and stared straight ahead as if in some faraway place.

'What happened?' Karen's voice was barely audible.

A grin appeared on David's face: 'I couldn't drink the bloody whisky, it was like poison, and I couldn't take the damn tablets without a drink.'

Slowly, they all began to smile. Seconds later, they were laughing - laughing and crying, David included. They smothered him in kisses and hugs and, once again, Elizabeth and David looked at each other, their eyes communicating a million unspoken words.

'I can't believe this,' said Helen, 'if anyone saw us now - maybe we're all a bit mad!' She hugged him again. 'Thank goodness you're not an alcoholic, that's all I can say.'

A knock at the door surprised them. Karen opened it to reveal a young policeman.

'I've come about a missing person,' he said, looking puzzled. Karen didn't look like someone who had spent the whole night awake worrying.

'He's back!' she said.

'May I come in?'

'We're through here.' She led the policeman into the lounge where David sat like a Sheik enjoying his homecoming.

'Sir, I'm afraid I still have to take down particulars. It's for our records and also it is police policy to inform the psychiatric department, who will send a community nurse round to speak to you.'

David was too weary to argue: 'OK, do what you have to, but I can tell you one thing - there won't be any psychiatrists coming to this house.'

A psychiatric nurse arrived the following day. David responded cautiously, but slowly warmed to her. She seemed to understand him; he was able to talk to her without the fear of anyone else knowing his secret.

Two days later Helen decided it was time to return to work. David was in good spirits and, over dinner, he appeared much happier and had promised to take the medication again. He felt that he could now recognise when he was heading for a crisis and would be able to control his moods. She was reassured so she packed her bags and said her goodbyes.

Back at the flat, Jo ran and hugged her.

'How is he? Was he OK about you leaving?'

'He told me not to worry, that I had my own life and shouldn't be concerned about him.'

'You think he'll be all right?'

'Don't know, don't suppose we'll ever be sure. But for now, we have to believe him.'

'I hope so. I hate to think of him in such a state, Helen. By the way, Rahim has been asking about you. He wants you to let him know when you're back. He was very concerned.'

8 DISASTER STRIKES AT WORK

Helen wanted to get back to her old routine as soon as she could. The events of the previous week loomed vividly in her mind, but it was as though it had all been a dream. She was desperate to keep occupied so that she wouldn't think about what might be happening at home but, at the same time, it was difficult to stay focussed. Work was extremely busy. Extra beds had been erected to cope with the problems that winter brought. The elderly, as usual, were the ones to suffer, brought in with flu, bronchitis and hypothermia. Sickness among staff was rife too, placing a heavy burden on the remaining few. Helen took advantage of this and placed her name on the list of volunteers willing to cover the empty shifts.

Her first day back was dreadful. She was met in the office by Sister Small, the senior ward sister, a stocky woman who bustled efficiently. At her request Helen followed her through to the kitchen.

'I wanted to make sure that you're fit to be at work', said Sister Small, 'Jo told me about the problem. You can't usually take time off for something like that so I took the liberty of signing you off as sick. It's chaos here at the moment but if you feel you need more time then please say. I've not told anyone the nature of your father's illness so it's up to you if you would like to keep it private.' She placed a hand on Helen's arm. 'If you need anything, please ask.'

'Thank you.'

Helen was taken by surprise. Sister Small was no ogre, but she had never displayed this kind of warmth towards any of her staff before - or not that Helen had seen.

'Let's go and face this lot,' said Sister Small. 'The night staff had an awful shift and they'll be desperate to get off.' She led the way and Helen followed, a little awkwardly.

In the ward office, Helen was greeted with an array of looks, some curious, some concerned. Word had leaked from somewhere. She smiled and sat down quickly. Report started at seven-thirty and was over by eight and, when everyone had gone, she stood alone for a minute summoning the courage to go out onto the ward. Aziz came in, he was unshaven and unwashed. He had been on-call all weekend and had been awake for most of it, managing only a couple of hours sleep at a time. His eyes were bloodshot, his thick mop of hair greasy and un-brushed and he smelled a little too.

'Hi, what are you doing here? When did you get back?' he asked.

Helen smiled. He was so pleased to see her and welcomed her so freely and without awkwardness.

'I came back yesterday.'

'Rahim didn't say anything about you being back,' said Aziz.

'Why would he?'

'No reason. I thought you may have bumped into him at the flat, that's all. Anyway - how are you? How's your father?'

'He's fine thanks, but how do you know?'

'Oh er - Jo told me,' Aziz stuttered, he had been sworn to secrecy.

'I can't really talk about it here. I don't mean to be rude but I have loads to do.'

He smiled: 'Maybe catch up later?'

'OK, see you soon.'

Helen walked down the centre of the ward, heading for the sluice. When she reached it she realised that she had no recollection of the short journey. She hadn't noticed the two rows of beds with their green floral bedspreads, or the matching curtains that had been pulled back hurriedly and stuffed behind the lockers. Her mind had been elsewhere. She was trying to remember what she was meant to be doing when Sister Small's commanding voice reverberated.

'Helen?' she said, 'are you all right? I was calling your name.'

'I'm sorry, I didn't hear you. Is there something I can do for you?'

'I saw you talking to Aziz and you seemed flustered as you left the office. Has he upset you?'

'No, there was no problem. I just wasn't in the mood to talk to him right there and then.'

'If you don't feel you can cope, please say and we can call in another member of staff.'

'Please don't do that, I'll be fine. It's just that it all seems so surreal, it feels as though it didn't really happen.' Helen realised that she felt numb and detached, and she began to edge towards the door. 'I need to get on, if you don't mind.'

'If you're sure. Could you start by doing the medicine round? I have to speak to Mrs Andrews' son. He'll be here in five minutes.'

Sister Small held out a bunch of keys. Helen took them from her and headed for the clean utility room where the trolley stood chained to the wall. She made her way from bed to bed, checking the drugs against the prescription sheet and popping the multi-coloured pills into tiny pots. Her colleague, Julia, double-checked the labels, took the medication to the patients and checked their personal details on their wristbands before handing over the tablets.

Halfway down the ward, a frail, elderly lady asked for a bedpan.

'Can you wait a little while?' Julia replied, 'we're right in the middle of this.'

'Don't think I can,' the patient replied. 'I asked some time ago, but the nurses are so busy I think they forgot.'

'OK, I'll get one.' Julia completed the check on the tablets for the next patient and went off to the sluice.

To save time, Helen delivered the plastic pot. Julia returned to the medicine trolley and they moved on up the ward.

'Excuse me nurse, these are not mine,' said the patient holding out the pot.

'Yes they are,' said Helen. She was sure the tablets were correct. They had double-checked them.

'Mine are two white ones and a little blue one, but you've given me a little white one, and two big red and black capsules.'

Helen took the tablets and went back to the trolley. 'They're what the prescription sheet says,' she told Julia, with a sigh of relief.

'Yes, they're the right tablets - but you gave them to the wrong patient. Did you check the name band, Helen?'

Helen's mouth dried up instantly. She had given Digoxin, a heart tablet, to the wrong woman. She felt as though the life had been sucked out of her body leaving her totally incapacitated. Julia swiftly closed the lid of the trolley listening for the click of the lock and then brought a chair for Helen. Sister Small came out of her office.

'Sister, do you have a moment?' said Julia, 'it's Helen; I don't think she's too well.'

'What happened?'

'Can we take Helen to the treatment room?' said Julia. 'She needs to lie down for a while. I think she's feeling faint.'

When Helen recovered, Sister Small was sitting at the bottom of the couch, 'How are you feeling?'

'Better, but I feel awful about what happened. Did Julia tell you what I did?'

In an effort to protect her colleague, Julia had not mentioned the incident with the drugs and it was Helen's conscience that forced her to tell all.

'This is a disciplinary offence,' said Sister Small, 'the Digoxin could have caused heart failure if she'd taken it. You didn't follow the correct procedure and it could have had catastrophic consequences.'

'It was entirely my fault. I can't believe how stupid I was.'

'To be honest, Helen, I really don't feel that you should be here at all. You had a very traumatic time at home and it's not surprising that you made a mistake.'

'I'm fine. Please don't tell me to go off duty.'

'I'm sorry, but in view of what just happened, I have no option. Either you go now or I'll have to report this.'

Helen broke down and cried, something she hadn't done until now, and it brought great relief. A surge of emotion came over her like a warm blanket. The knot in her stomach and the ache in her throat were replaced by an over whelming need to sob.

Aziz tapped on the door and pushed gently until it was slightly ajar.

'I've handed over to Doctor Johnson and I'm now off duty,' he said, then he saw Helen.

'What's the matter?' he mouthed.

Sister Small tried to keep him at bay by standing close to the door and shaking her head as she spoke. 'That's fine, Doctor Shah, have a good sleep, you deserve it.'

'What's wrong with Helen?' he said.

'Please, Doctor Shah, she'll be fine.'

'It's all right Sister,' said Helen. 'Aziz is a friend,'

'Well, if you're sure.'

'Hey, come on,' he stroked her hair. 'Here, wipe your eyes.' He pulled a tissue from a nearby box and mopped her face.

'She's going to her flat,' said Sister Small. 'She needs a little time to herself.'

'I'll escort her,' said Aziz.

'OK, that would be a great help - if you don't mind.'

'Thank you, Sister,' Helen whispered. 'I'm sorry. I'll speak to you tomorrow.'

'Get some rest, you know where I am if you need anything.'

Aziz helped Helen off the couch and placed an arm discreetly on her waist to guide her.

'Come on, I'll take you home.'

She put her arm around him and leaned into him, taking comfort from his familiarity.

'I wouldn't get too close if I were you. After the weekend I've had I could do with being fumigated.'

'I don't give a damn right now.' She looked up at him and smiled: 'I'm glad you're here, Aziz.'

They walked slowly and she told him the whole saga, including why Sister Small had insisted that she left the ward. Back at the flat, he took the key from her and slipped it in the lock. He helped her to the sofa then went through to the kitchen and put the kettle on. She heard him opening drawers and cupboards looking for utensils but lacked the energy to get up and help and instead stretched out on the sofa, resting her head on a soft velvet cushion.

When Aziz returned with two cups of tea, she was snoring gently. He placed the cups on the coffee table, kissed her forehead lightly and let himself out. Still unshaven and unwashed, he went upstairs to see Rahim.

'Oh dear me, what a sight,' said Rahim.

'I could say the same about you. Aren't you working today?'

'Got a study day. There's a lecture in the education department later so I was trying to have a lie in, thank you very much. Since you're here, I suppose you'd better come in.'

Rahim's flat was a replica of Helen and Jo's, but without the womanly touch. The little knick-knacks were absent, the soft furnishings that brought warmth and comfort were nowhere to be seen and the kitchen sink still held yesterday's greasy pots.

'I've just left Helen, she's in a terrible state.'

'What do you mean?' asked Rahim. 'Is her father still unwell?'

Aziz described both episodes - her trip home, and the incident with the medicine trolley.

'Poor thing,' said Rahim, 'I'll leave a note asking her to give me a ring when she wakes up.'

'Don't think she'll phone you. She's not too keen to talk about it. Go down later, see if you can catch her that way.'

'OK, thanks.'

Aziz's head felt like it was stuffed with lead and his eyes burned in their sockets. He returned to his own flat, set the shower running and went through to the kitchen to make a hot chocolate. A minute later he switched off the shower, without stepping under it, placed the cup down on the bedside cabinet without taking a sip, and sank into the comfort of his duvet.

§

Meanwhile, Rahim showered and dressed quickly, selecting a pair of smart jeans teamed with a casual white shirt. He smoothed on a little of his favourite aftershave and gathered up his textbooks. He headed for the door, hoping that Helen would still be in her flat when he got back at lunch-time. His lecture seemed to go on forever. *'If anyone asks another stupid question,'* thought Rahim, *'I am going to walk out.'* By one forty-five and, with no end in sight, he was starving and convinced that he would have missed Helen by now. Then a miracle happened. The professor announced that if there were no further questions, they could leave the lecture theatre. Rahim rushed home as quickly as he could, slowing his pace for the last hundred yards so that he didn't arrive breathless and sweating. He reached for the bell of Helen's flat and pressed lightly. Helen opened the door. She looked neither surprised nor pleased, which was disconcerting. She seemed so indifferent to his presence that Rahim began to regret calling on her.

'Hope you don't mind me coming round. I wondered how you were,' he said. 'Would you rather I left you in peace?'

She opened the door wider.

'No, please come in. I've just woken up. I didn't realise the time.'

In the lounge, the cold tea made by Aziz stood untouched. Rahim thought how strange it was that this flat, though identical to his own, could have such a different feel.

'Hope you don't mind me being here. Aziz was worried; he thought it might be a good idea if I checked you were all right.'

'I suppose he told you what happened.'

'Would you have preferred him not to?'

'I don't mind.' A look of relief showed on her face. 'Actually, it saves me going over and over it. Can I get you a drink?'

'I'm starving. Do you fancy going for a bite to eat? We could have a walk along the seafront later if you feel like it.'

'Sounds great, I need some fresh air.' She went through to the bedroom to change out of her uniform. 'I won't be long. Put on some music if you like.' She chose her leggings and a thick woolly jumper. The sun was shining, but it was bitterly cold. When she came out of the bedroom, Rahim was listening to the latest Lionel Ritchie album. 'You big softy,' she laughed.

Rahim ran up to his flat to collect a warm coat and some gloves. They headed to the seafront, stopping to buy food from a little kiosk by the slipway. Eating burgers and sipping hot chocolate, they chatted easily as they'd done on the ward that day. Rahim was passionate about his work and, having trained as a dentist, was hoping to carve out a career in oral surgery although it would be a long haul.

Waves rippled back and forth on the sand. It was out of season and the beaches were deserted.

'It's beautiful here in the winter,' said Helen. 'I could come here every day and never tire of it.'

'Have you ever tried wind-surfing?'

'No - especially not in this weather.'

'When it's warmer, I could take you. You can hire a wetsuit to keep warm.'

'I'm game if you are. I bet you're an expert. I'll look a real idiot.'

'Don't worry, I'll teach you. It's great fun. Do I take it that's a yes?'

'It's a yes.'

He put an arm around her shoulders and gave her a hug. 'You won't regret it.'

'Promise?'

'Promise.'

They stayed out till way after dark, walking for miles, stopping to sit on benches, eating ice cream and doughnuts and even trying their hand in the amusement arcade. They were so relaxed in each other's company that, to the eyes of an outsider, they could have been an old married couple.

Back at the flat they stopped outside Helen's door and Rahim turned to her.

'Can I remind you that you never did cook that meal for Aziz and me. Why don't you come back to my flat so I can cook up a nice supper for you instead?'

'I don't know about you, Mr Ismail, but I couldn't eat another thing.'

'What about a hot toddy and a video, the perfect end to a perfect day.'

'Well,' Helen hesitated, 'now you're talking.'

'I knew you couldn't resist.'

'You conceited ...!' Helen thumped him hard on the arm. 'Can I ask one question?'

'Of course.'

'Why do both Jo and Aziz think that you should know my whereabouts all the time?'

With a glint in his eye Rahim replied: 'That could be because I told them that I was very attracted to you. Do you remember the day on the ward, when Aziz was going to take me to the garage to pick up my car? We arranged that so that he could introduce me to you properly.'

'You scheming ...!' she laughed, 'but you had a girlfriend already.'

'But then I met you. It wasn't serious anyway.'

'I suppose I should be flattered.'

'Damn right you should be.'

Helen cast her eyes around Rahim's flat.

'What you need is a woman's touch.'

'I thought you'd never offer.'

'Stop it! I meant your flat.'

'What's wrong with it? It's clean and tidy.' When Rahim had nipped in to pick up his coat he'd quickly hidden the pots that were in the sink and tidied up.

'It's a bachelor pad. Wait there, I'll be back in a second.' Helen disappeared and returned with a collection of large, soft cushions from her bedroom and a lamp, which she placed on the small table in the lounge.

'There now,' she said, as she switched on the lamp, 'a big difference, wouldn't you agree?'

'Now can we watch the film?' asked Rahim. Helen lay at one end of the sofa with her legs stretched out across his knees.

'Comfortable, I hope?' he said.

'Very!'

9 A ROMANTIC MEAL FOR... THREE

Helen crept in at midnight.

'Where have you been?' asked Jo.

Helen told her about her mistake with the medicine trolley and about Rahim.

'So – it's love?'

'Typical! It's just a friendship, but you wouldn't know what that meant, would you?'

'Oohh! I think I may have hit a nerve. When are you seeing him again?'

'He's invited me for a meal at the weekend,' said Helen.

'Look at your face! I haven't seen you with that expression in ages.'

'What expression?'

'You know what I mean.'

Jo waltzed out of the room and Helen followed her.

'Keep your nose out of my business, Jo. When there's something to tell, you'll be the first to know.'

'Seriously - be careful,' said Jo, 'you've enough on your plate. I'm worried you might get hurt. He's Indian. Don't get too involved. I know what I'm talking about. Look at my mum. She's had a lifetime of coming second-best to the Muslim faith and all that comes with it. Have some fun but leave it at that.'

They hugged each other.

'Sorry, Jo.'

'Don't you remember how Dad would send money to his family in Pakistan when Mum hardly had enough housekeeping money for food? And how he would make us all sit in front of him and recite the Koran. Do you remember him hitting my brothers for swearing? What a hypocrite! When he first came to England he used to smoke and drink and swore like a trooper.'

'I know you mean well, but don't worry. Rahim's good company, and that's it, nothing serious.' Helen tried to smile but it wasn't very convincing. 'Anyway, how are you?' she asked.

'I'm OK, but I've missed Tom so much this week. He's stopped phoning and I've been desperate to hear from him. That's so selfish of me. I heard that he's looking for a place of his own. What about you? Have you heard from home?'

'I don't phone every day but I know that Mum will be in touch if necessary. Now we all know about it she'll feel free to talk to us, which is a relief. I may go home for a few days in a week or so.'

'When are you going back to work?'

'I'll speak to Sister Small and see if she'll agree to me going back as soon as possible. They're so short-staffed I feel bad being off.'

Sister Small insisted that Helen saw her doctor to be signed off for another two days. When the two days were up, at the end of her first shift back, Helen was summoned to the kitchen for a quiet word. Not again, she thought. She was beginning to develop a kitchen phobia.

'Don't worry,' said Sister Small, 'this is not another of my pep talks. I have some news for you. Sister Turner is pregnant.'

'Wonderful - that's the best news I've had in ages.'

'The reason I'm telling you is because she's going to hand in her notice once her maternity leave comes up.'

'And..?'

'There'll be a sister's post up for grabs in a few months' time and I want you to apply for it.'

Helen's jaw dropped. Sister Small laughed: 'What's the matter? Don't look so shocked.'

'I am shocked, very shocked. How can you tell me this after what I did earlier this week? Plus, I haven't been qualified very long.'

'That was unfortunate and, yes, it could have been a lot worse, but I defy anybody in this hospital to look me in the eye and say they've never made a mistake. You'll have learned from it, and that can only be beneficial - and I know you're more than capable of doing the job of a junior sister. Now, are you going to apply or not?'

'Well - yes.'

'It will be advertised externally as well as internally, but you stand a good chance. Read up as much as you can on the latest developments and what's in fashion right now. Learn the latest buzzwords and you'll be fine. I'll help in any way I can.'

Sister Small turned on her heels and headed for the door. Helen stood reeling.

'Hi, you look like you saw a ghost.'

'Aziz! I swear to God you're a witch, a male one. You always turn up at the right moment.'

'What's the matter now?'

She told him about Sister Turner's pregnancy and that Sister Small wanted her to apply for the vacant post.

Aziz grabbed her by the shoulders, gave her a hug and kissed her on the lips.

'That's fantastic.'

'Hey! What d'you think you're doing?'

'Sorry, got carried away. Don't worry - I've also had some news.'

'Good news, I hope.'

'Depends how you look at it.'

'What is it?'

'After my on-call, I went home to see my parents and they've arranged a marriage for me.'

'What? Can they do that without telling you?'

'Well, we've talked about the possibility, but I didn't think it would be so soon.'

'What's she like? Do you want to marry her?'

'Don't know since I haven't met her yet. They want me to go home again for a few days to meet her and decide.'

'Unbelievable - surely they can't just do that.'

He pulled a photograph out of his pocket and held it out to Helen. 'This is her, she's a pharmacist.'

A very pretty girl gazed at Helen, her long hair was gathered up in a bun on top of her head with loose strands falling down at the sides. She was wearing a sari, but Helen got the impression that she was a modern girl rather than traditional.

'She's beautiful, Aziz, but how do you know whether you'll get on?'

'I don't. I've asked them to give me the chance to get to know her, which they have agreed to, but I know that they'll be upset and embarrassed if I don't accept her. It isn't very good for her family either to be told their daughter isn't suitable.'

'I suppose not. And I thought I had problems. When are you going?'

'Sometime in the next few weeks. I have some annual leave to take so I'll go home and spend the time getting to know her but I'm as nervous as hell.'

'Shall I come with you?' Helen joked.

'Oh yeah, that'll go down well.' He stuck out his chest to appear brave and courageous. 'No, this is a man's thing. I have to do it alone.'

'Why don't you come to Rahim's tonight? He's cooking a meal.'

'What, and be poisoned? No thanks.' With that, he was whisked away by his consultant to do the ward round.

Helen made a detour on the way home from work and called in at the corner shop to buy a bottle of wine. Unsure of Rahim's preference, she bought two, one white and one red.

§

'Get out of there right now!' Helen called to Jo.

Jo liked to spend hours in the bath with the latest bestseller, but tonight Helen had other ideas. She planned to spend at least two hours in there herself to concentrate on a whole-body home-beauty session, followed by manicure and pedicure. She was going for a natural clean and fresh look with minimal make-up.

'Won't be long, only another two chapters to go,' Jo shouted back.

'No - not another two chapters. I need to get in there now.' Helen headed for the bathroom to bang on the door, but Jo was already out of the bath and had slyly opened it. She was peering out to watch Helen's reaction.

'Oh, we are getting anxious - I thought he was just a friend.'

'You mean thing! He is just a friend - but I still need to get ready.'

'It's only five o'clock; you have another couple of hours yet. What's the rush?'

Helen's faced reddened. She gathered her things and pushed past Jo to commence her marathon cleansing, toning and scrubbing session.

At seven o'clock, wearing casual jeans and a sweatshirt, she had been ready and waiting for half an hour, but didn't want to arrive right on time. She hung around chatting to Jo, nervously twiddling the strands of hair that hung around her face – the habit of a lifetime and a sure sign that she was on edge. Ten minutes later she climbed the stairs to Rahim's flat. The door was slightly ajar and she was greeted by the aroma of exotic spices. A strange combination of hunger and excitement made her feel nauseous to the point where she didn't feel she would be able to eat a thing. Jo was right, she was in deeper than she realised.

'Hello!' she called.

No answer.

'Hi, it's me.'

She could hear music and the sound of pots and pans being shuttled around. Moving closer, Helen knocked on the kitchen door much louder than she had intended. Rahim spun round startled and let out an involuntary cry. This shocked Helen who let out a small scream and dropped both her bottles of wine on the floor. Splinters of glass scattered in all directions and the red and white wine merged into one as it made its escape.

'You OK?' said Rahim, 'I didn't hear you come in. You frightened the life out of me.'

'Oh God, I'm so sorry. Give me a dustpan and brush and I'll clean it up.'

'No, don't worry,' said Rahim. He began to look for a cloth but then a smell of burning rose from the cooker. 'Oh no, the curry!' He dashed over and dragged the pan off the electric ring. Clasping his head in his hands he muttered an expletive under his breath, then turning to Helen, he apologised: 'Sorry! Look, why don't you have a seat in the lounge while I get myself organised?'

'I wouldn't dream of it. Let me clean the floor and get some more wine while you carry on with the food.'

'All right, but there's no need to buy more wine. There's plenty of white in the fridge and red on the top if you prefer. I could do with a glass right now actually - you look divine, by the way.' He smiled, leaned forward and kissed her lightly on the cheek. She saw that he was wearing an apron with the body of a woman in a bra and suspenders on the front of it.

'Thanks - but would you like me to come back later when you're dressed?'

Rahim glanced down and burst out laughing: 'No, it'll be more fun dressed like this.'

An hour and two glasses of white wine later, both were much more relaxed. The kitchen floor was dry, the food had survived and they were about to sit down to eat when there was a knock on the door. Rahim groaned as in waltzed Aziz.

'Hi! Looks like I'm just in time. Thanks for inviting me, Helen. I decided to come after all. I've had a hell of a day.'

Rahim frowned and looked at Helen questioningly, mouthing to her: 'You invited him?'

Helen shrugged her shoulders awkwardly, turned to Aziz and smiled. 'Nice to see you,' she said.

Aziz sat down and started to help himself to food, unaware of the resigned look on Rahim's face. 'What a surprise! I never knew you could cook like this, you old dog. You kept that quiet.'

Helen cringed. When she'd asked him to come, she hadn't thought for one moment that he would turn up. After the meal was over, Aziz slept on the sofa while Helen and Rahim washed the dirty pots and tidied the kitchen.

'Sorry about Aziz. I felt sorry for him when he told me about the possibility of an arranged marriage.'

'He told you about that, did he? I know the family and she's a really nice girl,' said Rahim. 'Don't worry about him coming round. I'm used to him appearing when he's least wanted. He's a good bloke - but a pain in the backside sometimes.'

'He's brilliant at work. Whenever I need him to see a patient he's there like a shot. He teases the women no end, they love him.'

'Yeah, but he's still a pain,' replied Rahim. 'Actually, I have a really close friend who was with me at university in London. He's just moved up north, to work at Barrow Green Hospital. His name is Nadim. You'll like him, he's very funny. We could arrange to go over to see him and his girlfriend Amanda if you like.'

'I'd love to,' said Helen.

'Leave the pans, I'll do them later.'

'They won't take long; we might as well get them out of the way.'

'I have a better idea. Put the cloth down right now,' he said sternly.

'Yes, sir!'

Helen did as she was told and looked up at him, grinning. He turned to her. His dark eyes so full of warmth; they seemed to penetrate her mind, as though reading every thought, every expression of happiness and all the heartache she had ever felt, although in their depths she also saw a sadness that she couldn't place. He reached out and traced the outline of her jaw with his fingers. Helen's hands trembled, her heart fluttered and her legs went weak. Now she understood why the leading ladies swooned in old movies. She didn't dare take her eyes off his, for fear of losing this precious moment. He bent forward, his lips barely touched her face, yet he gently caressed and explored every detail. He pulled her closer and wrapped her in his arms. She responded eagerly, feeling the firmness of his body, and held on to him tightly, enjoying every second - and they kissed with a passion she had never experienced before.

Music played softly in the background. Aziz woke. He stretched and levered himself up off the sofa, but even tactless Aziz could not interrupt the two lovers in the kitchen. He let himself out of the flat, pulling the door to without a sound. He pulled the photograph out of his pocket and gazed at it for a few seconds before kissing the girl who smiled back at him.

10 JO'S NEW MAN

In the weeks that followed, Helen and Rahim spent most of their free time together. If Jo was working a late shift, they would spend their time in Rahim's flat, but if Jo was around then all three would have a meal in the girls' flat. Rahim kept his word and arranged a night out with Nadim and Amanda. He was right when he said that Nadim was funny and good company. He was much stockier than Rahim, with black curly hair. Born in Jordan and brought up in Kuwait, he was fluent in Arabic and spoke English with an accent that made him sound even funnier. Amanda was the same height as Nadim and slim; she too had black hair and dark eyes. She was scatty and that made Nadim laugh the whole time. They had been seeing each other for around six months, and Helen guessed that they were very much in love.

Helen had spotted a beautiful frosted glass vase in a florist's window in town and couldn't resist buying it as a present for Rahim along with some brightly-coloured gerbera to go in it. It was one of many items of soft furnishings and picture frames she had bought over the last few weeks to make Rahim's flat look more homely.

One day, Rahim had just arrived back from work and was settling down with a quiet cup of coffee when Helen burst through the door. He set his cup down on the small pine table in front of him – another of Helen's acquisitions – and held out his arms to greet her.

'Look what I got today.'

She handed him the beautifully wrapped vase and watched as he slowly opened the paper.

'Stop it! You're being slow deliberately, just rip it off!'

Rahim looked serious. 'You can't rush these things.' Eventually the vase was unveiled. 'Just what I needed,' he said sarcastically.

Helen slapped the gerbera in his lap and pretended to sulk. 'You need flowers sometimes. They cheer you up on a miserable day.'

'You think of everything, darling, but I can assure you it is not a miserable day and I don't feel miserable either.' He put the present on the table and kissed Helen. It was the beginning of December. 'What are you doing for Christmas?'

'I have Christmas off so I'll be going home, but I have to be back at work for New Year. Dad is really well at the moment and apparently all four of us will be home which rarely happens, so it will be good if we can all be together as a family. What about you?'

'Strangely enough, I was planning to do much the same. We don't celebrate in quite the same way, but it's an excuse to stuff our faces and have a good time.'

'Come and spend a day with us, my family would love to meet you.'

Rahim looked uncomfortable.

'It's probably better if you go alone in view of the situation with your dad. I don't want to be in the way.'

'You wouldn't be. Come on, it would be fun.'

'We'll see.' He changed the subject. 'Have you heard from Aziz since he came back from his holiday? I think he's in love.'

'You're joking.'

'I saw him at work today. He said that he had a great week at home and he really liked Serina. It looks as though it's all go.'

'What? You mean marriage? When?'

'He said it wouldn't be for some time yet. Serina is doing some sort of a course and they want to wait until she's finished her exams.'

'That's unbelievable, but at least they'll have time to get to know one another.'

'You seem to be under the impression that he doesn't want this, but don't forget, this is still very much a part of our culture - the same thing could happen to me.'

'Could it? But how would you feel about that? Is it what you want? When would they expect you to marry?' Helen asked the questions as though the concept was totally alien and she'd never heard of it before.

'Wow, slow down, one question at a time, please. Well, for starters, I wouldn't want to marry anyone without getting to know them first, but my parents have talked about the possibility of an arranged marriage. They have also offered to introduce me to suitable girls at functions like weddings and parties, rather than them choosing one in particular. That way I wouldn't be under pressure or in danger of insulting anyone's parents if I don't like her.'

'But you've lived in England for so long now and have become westernised. Surely this is so outdated.'

'Not to my parents it isn't. They still expect it of me, and it is so important to them because when I do get married they will live with me. My wife will care for them and become part of our family, leaving her own behind. For that reason, I will marry an Indian girl because an English one wouldn't even consider living with her in-laws.'

'What if you wanted to marry an English girl?'

'They would never accept it. I'm their only son so they're my responsibility. They know that I've been out with English girls before, but they've never met them. Helen, this is so hard for me to say, but it's important that you understand. There's no future for us as a couple. An English girl would be miserable living with my family, and neither they nor the Asian community would ever accept it.'

'So do they know about me?'

She wasn't sure she wanted to hear the answer. She knew it was early days in their relationship but she hoped that he had told them about her.

He raised his eyebrows and grinned mischievously, bringing light relief to the conversation. 'Not yet, but maybe when I'm home at Christmas I might mention your name.' Lifting her chin with his index finger he kissed her on the nose. 'They're always better if I talk to them face-to-face.'

Consoled by this thought, Helen gave him a hug.

Rahim looked down at her. 'I love you,' he whispered.

'I love you too,' she said, but his words stung so painfully that it made her wince. She felt confused. First he said they had no future together, but then, almost immediately afterwards, he had declared his love for her.

'Anyway, who said I wanted to marry you?' she said petulantly.

He smiled: 'I need to make sure you understand - I love you but I'm scared that you'll get hurt. Look at Nadim; he intends to marry an Arabic girl. He knows that his parents expect it of him and though they won't necessarily live with him, he just feels that it will be easier all round when it comes to socialising within his own circles.'

'Does Amanda know that?' asked Helen.

'Yes, she does. Nadim went to boarding school in England from a very young age and yet it is still ingrained in him that he should marry one of his own, which shows how strong the family ties are.'

'That's unbelievable,' remarked Helen. 'Well, don't you worry, I won't let it get too serious; I have no intention of ending up broken-hearted.' She needed to clear her head. 'Let's go to the social club. We can get a bite to eat somewhere afterwards.'

The social club was tucked in behind the nurses' accommodation within the hospital grounds. It was Thursday evening and there was only a handful of people there. One or two were propping up the bar and another group was huddled deep in discussion around a table in one corner. The coloured lights set up by the DJ cast subtle shades across the dance floor obscuring Helen's vision. She screwed up her face as she strained to see the couple sitting alone on the opposite side of the room. She was sure it was Jo talking to a tall fair-haired man. They were laughing and joking as though they knew each other well, but Helen had never seen him before.

'What would you like?' asked Rahim. He was more relaxed now that he had escaped the awkward questions from Helen.

'A dry white wine, please.'

Rahim turned to hand the glass of ice-cold wine to Helen, but she had disappeared. He saw her talking to Jo and her companion and went across to join them.

'Hi Rahim, how are you?' asked Jo. She stood and kissed him lightly on the cheek.

'I'm fine now,' he replied with a smirk on his face. Jo gave him an enquiring look, but before she could ask, the conversation moved on.

'Aren't you going to introduce us?' Helen asked.

'This is Sam. He's the new charge nurse on A and E. He started last week.'

They shook hands and everyone sat down.

'Nice to meet you, Sam,' said Helen. A sense of dread welled up inside her; she already knew what was in store.

Sam Garston was incredibly handsome. All six-foot-two of him was perfectly formed, not too fat, nor too thin; he obviously kept in good shape. Helen soon learned that he was football crazy and played at every opportunity. She could see that Jo was hooked; she was almost drooling, hanging on to his every word and laughing a little too enthusiastically at his football stories. Helen wished she could put everything into slow motion to protect Jo, but she knew it was too late.

'We're going out to eat,' announced Rahim. 'I don't suppose you two would like to tag along?' He glanced towards Helen.

'Yeah,' said Helen. 'Why don't you come? That would be great fun. We were thinking of a Chinese.'

'Were we?'

'Well, that's what I fancy.' Helen blushed.

'That's fine by me,' said Sam.

Jo gazed up at him admiringly and agreed.

'Oh no,' Helen whispered under her breath.

'What was that?' asked Jo.

Helen grabbed her handbag. 'I didn't say a word. Shall we go?'

As they headed for the door, Aziz was just entering accompanied by a young Indian girl who Helen recognised from the photo as Serina.

'Hi! Where are you lot off to?' asked Aziz, looking disappointed. He had hoped to show Serina off to his friends.

'We're going for a Chinese. Why don't you join us?' said Rahim.

'Well, if you don't mind.'

'Not at all,' said Jo. 'This is Sam. Sam, this is Aziz.'

'Hi!'

Aziz reached for Serina's hand: 'This is my fiancée, Serina, Serina, this is Helen and Jo.'

Both girls replied in unison: 'Hi! Pleased to meet you.'

'Pleased to meet you, too.' Serina shook hands all round except with Rahim, whom she kissed on the cheek. 'Good to see you again, Rahim.'

Helen looked at him incredulously. 'When did you two meet?'

'When I saw Aziz today in the canteen, Serina met him for lunch. I started to tell you earlier, but then we moved on to other things before I had the chance to finish.'

Helen thought back to their conversation of earlier that evening and realised that her shock about Rahim's family and the marriage issue had indeed turned the subject away from Aziz and Serina. 'You're right, sorry. Serina, you will come, won't you?'

'I'd love to.'

As they rounded the corner toward the taxi rank, Jo hung back a little to wait for Helen. She fought to keep her voice under control.

'Helen!' she squeaked. 'I just have to tell you - I'm in love.'

Helen closed her eyes in desperation. 'Oh please, spare me!'

11 A CHRISTMAS SURPRISE

Christmas was looming and Helen was exhausted, but she was excited at the thought of going home and being with her family. She also felt a sense of dread at being parted from Rahim for a week. She still hoped to be able to persuade him to visit them, but he was resisting, saying he didn't want to intrude.

For all Helen's good intentions not to become too involved with Rahim, it was very difficult. He was so different in every way. He would leave little notes hidden in her make-up bag or in her purse, saying how much he loved her, or he would place a heart-shaped chocolate in her lunch-box as a surprise. Rahim was impulsive and great fun to be with. He would often call round late in the evening when Helen was already in bed and take her for a midnight stroll along the promenade, or early in the morning take her for breakfast at some quaint café he had spotted. She would sit in the car on a freezing-cold day, watching whilst he windsurfed; she enjoyed every minute, though it wasn't difficult to resist the temptation to try it herself until temperatures had risen a little. Afterwards, they would find a snug little pub with a log fire where they could warm up again and eat. Her fascination with his culture was as strong as it had been with Jo's dad when she was a child. That Rahim was Indian made him all the more alluring.

Rahim had three sisters; the eldest, Zara, lived in Canada, and Sofia and Safina still lived at home. Helen loved to see the photos of his family. She imagined being with them and pictured herself learning their language and cooking their food. Drawn to the brightly-coloured saris, Helen longed to wear one herself. The intricate gold jewellery they wore, the metal much darker in colour than usual, added to the striking glamorous vision she created in her mind. She knew, though, that she must never let Rahim into her secret fantasy world. After all, he had been honest with her from the outset and told her not to get too involved. The question she often asked herself was why would he want to marry her when he had the choice of so many beautiful young Indian girls? She felt dowdy by comparison.

The next day was Christmas Eve and Helen would be heading for home the following morning. It would be their last day together for a while and Rahim had planned a special evening, although he refused to give Helen the details. He told her to wear something casual and to be at his flat for seven o'clock. When Helen went home to get ready, she found Jo in the bath already, beautifying herself in readiness for a date with Sam. Jo and Sam had been inseparable over the last couple of weeks but Helen still worried that he would hurt Jo just as other men had done previously.

'OK, I'll be there to pick up the pieces as usual,' said Helen.

'Don't worry, you won't have to this time, you'll see.'

'What do you think Rahim has planned?' Helen shouted through the bathroom door. 'I hoped we might go for a posh meal somewhere, but if I don't have to dress up then I haven't got a clue what it could be.'

Jo knew what was in store, but had been sworn to secrecy.

'Maybe it's ice-skating or a trip to the funfair; they have special deals at Christmas, free rides and complimentary sick bags, you know the sort of thing.'

'Very funny.' Helen was in no mood for joking. The idea of being separated from Rahim, combined with the thought of a disappointing last evening together, had quashed her Christmas spirit.

'He won't let you down,' said Jo. 'Stop worrying, have a glass of wine for goodness' sake.'

'But I wanted to do something memorable. I wanted to be wined and dined so I could savour the memories until I get back. I'm going to go up and ask if I can book a table somewhere.'

'No!' But before Jo could leap out of the bath to stop her, Helen had rushed upstairs to Rahim's flat. The unlocked door yielded to the weight of her body, and Helen stood in the hallway instantly regretting her decision. From where she stood she could see, hanging on the lounge door, the most elegant dress ever. It was beautiful. The fine material, in delicate shades of pink and cream, fell into gentle folds around the hemline.

Rahim stepped out from the kitchen. 'What are you doing here?'

Helen closed her eyes, she wanted to cry.

'I'm sorry, Rahim. Why do I have to be so stupid? Why didn't I trust you?'

'Hey, what's the matter? It's OK. So you got your surprise a little earlier than expected!' He held her close to him.

Helen hated herself for being so selfish: 'I'm so so sorry.'

'Let me show you.' He took the dress down and laid it across her arms. 'I hope it fits.'

'It's beautiful, thank you, I don't deserve it.'

'Yes you do. Go and put it on. I've booked a table at the Savoy Hotel.'

'Oh no, I really have ruined your surprise haven't I?'

'It's OK, stop worrying.'

'Well?' asked Jo, once Helen was back downstairs.

'I feel such an idiot!'

'He asked me to choose it with him last week. Try it on. Let's see if it fits.'

The dress fitted perfectly. It wasn't a sari, but Helen imagined that this must be how it felt to wear one. She donned her best jewellery and looked in the mirror.

'What do you think?'

'You look fabulous.' Jo hugged her. 'Go and have a great time. I'd love to see Rahim's face when he sees you.'

Moments later, Helen stood before Rahim. The adoration in his eyes made her want to burst with happiness.

'You look gorgeous. Let's go. We must make the most of our time together.'

'Can I just say that you look extraordinarily handsome tonight, Mr Ismail.'

'Well, thank you my dear, how very kind of you to say so.'

They laughed and hugged each other before heading for the door.

§

Christmas Eve was upon them and, as Helen made her journey home, her mind returned to the events of the previous evening. They had been greeted at the Savoy with ice-cold Champagne, before being escorted to a specially-chosen table that snuggled into a bay window overlooking manicured gardens. Outside, soft lighting brought bare trees to life in a way that would have been otherwise impossible in winter; inside, an open fire crackled and lighted candles lined the mantelpiece. Following a sumptuous banquet, they were escorted through to the grand ballroom where the band played softly and they had danced for most of the night. It was all over much too soon and, at the end of a wonderful evening, they had parted reluctantly, making a pact not to meet the next day as it would be too painful. What Rahim didn't see, was Helen hiding behind her curtain, watching as he loaded his car and left for home. One last glimpse was all she needed, and then she too set off on her journey.

§

The old wooden door swung open and David came out, waving. He marched across the yard to open the gate. It was heart-warming to see him looking so full of life and back to his normal self. Before Helen could reach for the handle, he had wrenched the car door open, helped her out and put his arms around her.

'It's so good to see you!'

'You too, Dad. You look great.'

'I feel great. I can't believe that everyone is going to be here. I hate it when the house is quiet. Poor Karen is the only one left and she has no-one to argue with now.'

'Dad, she's twenty years old for heaven's sake. We don't fight any more.'

'Well, I wish you did. All those years of telling you all to stop arguing and now the silence is almost unbearable.' Laughing, they entered the kitchen where the others had already assembled.

'Look, Bett, the last of our brood has arrived.'

'Welcome home,' said Elizabeth. 'It's lovely to see you, Helen. You look absolutely radiant. I don't suppose you have anything to tell us, do you? If I'm not mistaken I'd say someone was in love.'

'Mum! We'll talk about it later if that's OK.'

Helen embraced each of her sisters in turn and ignored further enquiries.

'Is it too soon to eat?' asked Elizabeth. 'If we wait too long, the dinner will be spoiled.'

Everyone was hungry and they began to bring the serving dishes from the oven to the table. Elizabeth had made enough to feed the entire neighbourhood - if they had had one. It took Helen back to when they were children.

'Mum, do you remember years ago, when I wanted a pony and you put a massive meal in front of Dad?'

'How could I forget? He asked if I thought he was a horse and you piped up, "oh I wish you were"!'

'That was the moment I realised I had no choice but to get one for you,' said David smiling.

'You always got what you wanted,' said Paula.

'Only because I was so determined; you used to give in far too easily.' They'd had this conversation before and Paula was obviously still upset about it; Helen was a very determined person and very stubborn when she wanted to be. Many times in the past she had got what she wanted through sheer doggedness. Despite the little spat the evening went well and they relived their youth, recalling events that their parents knew nothing about. Elizabeth and David loved it; it never ceased to amaze them to hear of the girls' escapades that they knew nothing of.

Helen spent Boxing Day at home. After dinner she was in the lounge reading when the door opened slowly. She was aware of someone next to her and peered up, expecting it to be her mother with a cup of coffee. It was Rahim accompanied by Nadim.

'What! Where did you come from? How long have you been here?' The words tumbled out.

'There you go again - so many questions.'

She leapt out of the chair and flung her arms around him. There was a peel of laughter from the rest of the family who had hidden out of sight to watch her reaction.

'What are you doing here, Rahim? Nadim, how are you?' She was overwhelmed.

'I hope you don't mind me tagging along,' said Nadim.

'Of course not, I'm in shock, I can't believe you're here.'

Rahim had phoned an hour earlier and spoken to Shelly and, instead of handing the phone to Helen, Shelly had arranged the surprise visit. David took Rahim and Nadim to see his workshop and Helen watched with pride as they chatted. Elizabeth served them a three-course meal and refused to let them leave till they were so full they could hardly walk.

'My mum has cooked for us as well,' Rahim protested.

Nadim rubbed his stomach. 'I knew this was going to be a good day,' he said.

After Rahim and Nadim had left, the girls sat and chatted in the lounge.

'How does Dad seem to you, Karen?' asked Helen.

'Apart from the occasional day when he's quiet, he seems a lot happier, but then we can all have off days. The psychiatric nurse got him back on medication and Mum makes sure he takes the tablets; she puts them out for him every morning and hides the rest away.'

'That's good, let's hope it continues.'

The following morning, Helen sauntered into the kitchen where her mother sat gazing out of the window.

'Morning, Mum, how are you? Did you sleep well?'

'Actually, yes. What about you?'

'Like a log. I think I slept too long. What did you think of Rahim? Nadim's a scream isn't he?'

'They both seemed very nice,' agreed Elizabeth. 'Is this a serious relationship - you look very happy?'

'I like him a lot, Mum. Well, actually, I love him and he says he loves me, but he also says that he has to marry an Indian girl so that his parents can live with him.'

'Oh dear, that won't be easy.'

'I know; he's so westernised I think he'll find it really difficult. But he's been totally honest from the outset and told me not to get too serious.'

'He's right, Helen, life is hard enough without looking for problems. Listen to him and be careful or you'll end up getting hurt.'

Helen put her arms round Elizabeth and gave her a kiss.

'I'll try,' she said.

§

Helen returned to work for the New Year, and night duty meant there was no time for celebrations. There was a month to go before the interviews for the sister's post and she was already preparing. The floor of her bedroom was .littered with professional journals, textbooks and articles and she waded through them laboriously. The latest developments, this year's buzzwords and emergency procedures, all waltzed around inside her head.

'It's Saturday! I'm off to the social club. Why don't you have a break and come with me?' asked Jo.

'You're right. I've had enough of textbooks, I'm coming.'

Once in the social club, Jo headed to the bar where Sam was waiting. Sam appeared to be genuine, he doted on Jo. He was always there to walk her home after she'd worked a late shift. He would phone her during the day to find out what she was doing. If they were both at work he found excuses to visit her ward, and they would always meet for lunch in the canteen. Helen said a little prayer in the hope that this time it would last.

The day of Helen's interview, Monday February 5 1984, came around. She was relieved that the time had come and she wanted to get it over with. There were six applicants, each looking equally nervous, they sat together in a small room where a connecting door led to the office of the Chief Nursing Officer. Helen was tense, but confident that she had the knowledge and experience to do the job. The door opened and a large severe-looking woman, stood surveying the candidates. Helen recognised the Chief Nursing Officer from the medical wards.

'Miss Singleton, please step this way.'

'How was it?' asked Jo later. 'You think you've been anxious. Look at my fingers, I've chewed all the skin from around them and I've been to the loo at least six times.'

'It wasn't as bad as I thought it was going to be - but it wasn't perfect either,' replied Helen. 'Well, I didn't come out in tears like one of the other girls.'

All Helen could do now was wait for the dreaded envelope to land on the doormat.

§

'One of my university friends is getting married,' said Rahim. 'Would you like to come to the wedding? It's in Wales - we could take the car and share with Amanda and Nadim.'

'That's great,' said Helen.

'It's this weekend,' he added.

'You're joking.'

'I accepted the invite some time ago, but until now I wasn't sure who to take with me,' he said mischievously, 'but if that's not enough notice for you then I could always ask someone else.'

'No way, I'll be ready and waiting. What time do we leave?'

'Eight in the morning on Saturday, coming back Sunday night.'

On Saturday morning Rahim and Helen set off to pick up Amanda and Nadim. Rahim's Golf GTI was his new toy and he couldn't turn up with it dirty, so they had to stop at a garage to wash the outside and vacuum the inside.

'We'll be late!' said Helen.

'It won't take long.'

The queue for the car wash took twenty minutes and by the time the car was clean they were forty-five minutes late picking up Amanda and Nadim.

'Where the hell have you been?' said Nadim.

'I had to clean my car.'

'What do you mean you had to clean your car, Rahim? It'll be filthy again by the end of the weekend. You do you realise it'll take a good four hours to get there?'

'We'll be fine, don't worry.'

'You Indians are all the same; you think you have all the time in the world. I've just spent two hours waiting for Amanda to decide what to put in her bag. You should see the stuff she's bringing.'

Amanda staggered through the door with an overnight bag, a vanity box full of cosmetics and two handbags. Helen turned away so as not to laugh as Nadim's sense of humour was running low. He slung the bags into the boot of the car and sat in the back without saying a word until they stopped at the first service station.

'I'm sorry,' he said, 'can we start again? How are you?' He kissed Helen on the cheek.

'I'm fine. Don't worry, we'll get there on time.'

The roads were clear all the way until they were ten miles from the church where the wedding was to take place and then they hit a four-mile traffic jam.

'We'll be fine,' said Rahim. 'We still have an hour to get there.'

'And how are we going to get changed?' asked Amanda.

'I hadn't thought of that.'

It was a boiling-hot day. The traffic moved slowly and tempers frayed.

'There's a service station here if anyone fancies a drink,' said Rahim.

'You serious?' said Nadim. 'I'm speechless. We're late because of you and now you want to stop for a drink.'

'Actually, it's not a bad idea,' said Amanda. 'We can get changed in the loos while we're there and the traffic might clear a little.'

The plan worked. They stopped for fifteen minutes and managed to arrive at the church just as the bride stepped out of her car. When she saw them running down the road, she paused to let them get there before her.

Nadim flopped into a pew gasping for breath.

'You and that bloody car of yours.'

It was an old, granite church. The bride looked up at her fiancé and smiled. Rahim looked down at Helen and tightened his grip on her hand, making her heart beat faster. At the reception there were the usual speeches, but they were followed by an open invitation to the guests to add their own anecdotes. The groom sat cringing, worried about what might be revealed from their wild days at university. Helen's sides ached from laughing.

The following day the bride and groom didn't go on honeymoon immediately; they stayed in the hotel overnight and spent Sunday on the beach with their wedding guests and a huge picnic.

'Rahim, I've had a fantastic weekend. Thank you so much,' said Helen, as they drove home, having dropped off Nadim and Amanda.

'Yeah, good, wasn't it? And even better because you were with me. I love you so much - too much in fact.'

She knew what he was trying to say.

'I know,' she said, 'I love you too, let's wait and see. Who knows what might happen.'

Rahim frowned: 'Please don't live in hope.'

'Look at Amanda and Nadim – they're perfect for each other.'

'Yes, but it will never happen. Nadim's parents want him to marry an Arabic girl, and it's also what he wants.'

'Then why go out with Amanda?'

'What's he supposed to do? Like me, he has to wait for the right time, but in the meantime does he stay single? It's very difficult.'

'But this weekend, when we were away and there was just the two of us, it was like no-one else existed and it felt so right.'

'Don't you think that I feel that way too?' Rahim sighed.

'I'm sorry, I shouldn't get carried away, but I don't understand how your parents can expect to live with you when you're living in England.'

'Look at Jo. I thought you would be more understanding having spent so much time with her family when you were young.'

'But that was then. Her dad came here when he was in his mid-twenties; you've been here much longer.'

'But my parents are of the same generation as him.'

They pulled up in front of the flat. Helen laid her head back against the car seat and groaned.

'Let's go and say hello to Jo,' she said.

§

A week later, Helen sat motionless on the hard wooden kitchen chair. A brown envelope lay on the table before her. Jo dragged herself sluggishly out of bed and into the kitchen for her usual cup of coffee and slice of toast.

'What's the matter?' Jo asked looking at the envelope. 'Don't tell me you didn't get it.'

Helen looked up but didn't speak.

'Oh, Helen.' Jo went over and hugged Helen tightly. 'Don't worry; you'll get another chance one day.'

'I haven't even opened it yet, you idiot, I'm too bloody scared.'

'What?' Jo snatched the letter and tore at it until the contents spilled out onto the table. They both stared for a moment.

'This is ridiculous,' said Jo, 'I'll read it to you.' She unfolded the piece of paper and took a deep breath: 'Dear Miss Singleton, We are very pleased...'

'I've got it!' Helen jumped up and grabbed Jo. 'I got the job!'

'Flipping fantastic - "Sister Singleton" has a nice ring to it, don't you think? How shall we celebrate?'

'We'll open a bottle right now.'

§

Rahim had been home for a couple of days to see his family, but Helen knew he was back because his car was parked in its usual spot. She hadn't seen him that day. She had phoned his flat and bleeped him at work, but had no reply. 'He must be busy', she thought to herself. She planned to cook a surprise meal at his flat before he came home from work, and then she would break the news about her sister's post. Following a trip to the supermarket, she came back laden with a variety of ingredients. She staggered up the stairs and plonked the bags on the landing whilst she found her key. It was a dreary day so she switched on the lounge lights before she went back out to the landing to collect her shopping, but the room seemed strange. Was she in the wrong flat? Everything had changed. The soft furnishings she had so carefully arranged had all but disappeared;

only one or two cushions remained. She couldn't see the beautifully-framed photograph of herself and Rahim on the beach or the one of them huddled on a bench on a freezing-cold day. In their place were photos of Rahim's family. She went into the kitchen. The garland she had painstakingly put together and hung above the door had gone and so had the vase and the candles from the window sill. She slowly made her way around the flat. In the bathroom, her toiletries had been taken from the shelf and her gown no longer hung behind the door; and in the bedroom her shoes and the few clothes she had left were nowhere to be seen.

Hearing a noise in the hallway, she turned to see Rahim and Aziz standing motionless at the door. Seeing the expression on their faces, a feeling of nausea took her by surprise and she held her hand up to her mouth as if to prevent the surge.

'What is it? What's going on? Aziz, tell me please.' Something had happened, but she couldn't think of a plausible explanation. What possible reason could Rahim give as to why all her belongings had been removed and the flat had reverted to the empty bachelor pad it had once been?

'Helen! What are you doing here? I thought you were working.'

'I tried to phone you. I bleeped you as well but you didn't answer. What's happening, Rahim?'

She felt the blood rush to her face and the nausea vanished and in its place anger brewed furiously.

'You'd better tell me what you're up to - right now!'

'I haven't told my parents about you yet - I put the photographs away so they wouldn't see them and jump to conclusions.'

'What about all the other things, the cushions and throws?' She could hardly contain her rage. 'Did you have to move those?'

'They would know. I didn't want them to start asking questions or think I had someone living with me.' He looked into her eyes, trying to gauge what damage had been done.

'You've moved all my stuff so that in theory I don't exist anymore, is that it? Well, if that's how you want it, then consider it done!'

'Helen!'

'If you have to pretend that you don't have a girlfriend then it's probably best that we make it a reality. And by the way - thank God I didn't move in!' She stormed out, leaving the shopping bags behind. Aziz ran after her.

'Let go of my arm and go back to your friend.'

She wanted to get as far away from Rahim and his family as she could. Not knowing where to go, she drove back into town and overcome by fatigue she found the nearest café and ordered coffee and cake. Sitting alone, Helen tried to picture Rahim and his family around the kitchen table. No doubt his mother had prepared her son's favourite curry dishes and they would now be sitting eating and laughing whilst she sipped the warm tasteless coffee, trying to make sense of it all. It was five-thirty and she'd been sitting there for at least an hour when suddenly it hit her, and she knew exactly what she had to do.

As she approached the parking bay, she saw that the lights were on in Rahim's flat. The curtains were open and she could see people moving around. Helen Singleton was going to go and introduce herself to Mr and Mrs Ismail, parents of Rahim Ismail, the coward! Once out of the car, her courage grew to enormous proportions. She raced into the foyer and up the stairs. Halfway up, she heard someone call her name.

'Helen!'

She stopped in her tracks. Jo was standing in the doorway.

'Jo, oh Jo, you won't believe what I have to tell you.'

12 HELEN MAKES A DRAMATIC DECISION

Jo knew why Helen was so upset. After Helen had left for her afternoon shopping trip, Rahim had arrived at the flat looking apprehensive. Jo had been getting ready for work when he appeared. He explained that his parents had decided to visit on the spur of the moment and he couldn't possibly let them find out about Helen this way. They would be totally unprepared and they would be opposed to any ideas about ever meeting her. He needed to sit them down properly to explain and let them get used to the thought of an English girl. Even then it would be difficult. For the whole of their lives they had dreamt of their son becoming a professional and with this in mind they had invested heavily in his education. He would then marry and become head of the family and at last they could relinquish all responsibility and enjoy retirement with a sense of fulfilment. How could he shatter their dreams by announcing that he wanted to marry an English girl? Even if they agreed to meet Helen it would have to be a gradual process that took place over a period of time. Rahim was also unsure as to whether it was what he really wanted or whether it would work.

He wanted to look after his parents and see them live in luxury without any worries. They'd had a hard life struggling to provide for him and his sisters, so the least he could do was show his appreciation. If he married Helen, would his parents still expect to live with him? What English girl could cope with such a situation? He realised that it was a lot to ask of any girl these days. Even Indian girls brought up in England were reluctant to accept the old tradition of living as part of an extended family. For now he'd had to remove any evidence of Helen's existence. He hadn't spoken to them about her as he'd intended on his last visit home, and now was not the time. The best thing to do was to talk to Helen in the hope that she would understand. Maybe he could introduce her to them towards the end of their visit if he could find the right moment to broach the subject.

Jo had listened intently to Rahim and managed to sympathise with him. She understood more than most because of her own upbringing. She could see that he really did love Helen, but was torn between his devotion and loyalty to his parents and his own needs and desires. She had agreed to help him move Helen's belongings and had promised to try to get hold of her. She had left a note asking Helen to phone her at work and had phoned the flat several times during the day, but Helen had gone straight from town to Rahim's flat. Now all Jo could do was to pick up the pieces and try to make Helen understand Rahim's motives.

'Come down Helen, please don't go up there. I need to speak to you.'

'No, I have to let them know what I think. I won't let him treat me like this!'

'Helen, you'll only prove to them that their image of English girls is right, and any chance you may have of meeting them in the future will be ruined. I've spoken to Rahim today and he's so upset.'

'How do you think I feel?'

'Listen, I can explain if you'll let me.'

Helen came down the stairs reluctantly and went into their flat. The warm familiarity was comforting. Jo reached for a bottle of white wine from the fridge. Ironically it was the one intended for Helen and Rahim's evening together. He'd asked Jo to take the shopping too, because alcohol is not permitted in the Muslim faith.

'You helped him do it! I can't believe it.'

'I'm sorry. Helen, I did warn you about this. It's another world and even I can't comprehend most of it. When Mum met Dad, he was very easy-going and was enjoying his freedom. They went out every Friday and Saturday night, dancing and having fun; they got married and had five children, but after he visited his home in Pakistan he arrived back in England a fully-fledged Muslim again. You wouldn't have recognised him as the same person. The trouble began when he wanted us to learn his language and his religion, but it was too late by then, we were aged between three and ten. We didn't know the man who came back; he had changed so much and it caused so many problems. You witnessed most of it. It's amazing that they're still together really. I suppose that's true love.'

'Yes, and that's how I feel. If it's meant to be then we'll find a way.'

Jo sighed. 'But why choose such a difficult life? Surely you don't want to live with his parents. Why not get out now while you still can?'

'Because I love him. He's so kind and considerate and he makes me laugh so much. And yes, I love the culture and background and the fact that he's different. I'd love to be part of it. I can't ignore the way I feel. Surely his parents will see that.'

'That's where you're wrong. They'll only see that you're scheming to take their son away from them. It's a completely different mentality. Believe me and spare yourself the heartache. What do I have to do to convince you?'

'But if they see how happy their son is.'

'You're not listening to me. It's not like that. They don't think like us. You won't be accepted by them. Look at it another way - what if you make Rahim miserable by chasing your dream? What if he's forced to make a choice between you and his family? That would kill him; he's been programmed all his life to take responsibility for his family. It would be a major disappointment to them and their community if he married an English girl. I know I'm being cruel - but they don't like English girls! Or at least, not as daughters-in-law. Could you live with that?'

'What has their community got to do with it?'

'A lot, believe me. They'll frown on Rahim's parents if he marries you. It's no different to the pressure that our family, friends and neighbours put on us for various reasons except that in the Asian community that pressure is far greater. Just leave Rahim alone, at least whilst his parents are here. Let them finish their visit then speak to him next week when they've gone - please.'

Helen reluctantly agreed to keep out of the way until Rahim's family left. Only once, when curiosity got the better of her, did she allow herself a quick glance from the window as they were getting into the car.

§

At last, Rahim dropped his parents at the train station, waved them off and headed straight to Helen's flat. Once at the door he took a deep breath and knocked gently. Helen opened it looking weary and dejected. After a tense few seconds she stepped forward and put her arms around his neck; Rahim breathed a sigh of relief and held her close. Then Jo interrupted to see who it was and they stepped back to look at each other.

'I'm going out for a while, Jo,' Helen shouted. 'I'll be back later!'

Jo smiled at Rahim and gave the thumbs-up before returning to her television programme.

'Where would you like to go?' Rahim asked nervously.

'Could we go up to your flat? I don't feel like being in a crowd. We've got a lot to talk about.'

His flat felt strange. The nest she had created had gone. She could have been anywhere and the fact that he had spent the last week here with his parents made her feel as though Rahim didn't belong to her any more.

He took hold of her hand.

'Helen, I'm sorry about the way things happened. I didn't know my parents were coming. They rang out of the blue to say they were coming later that day. How was I to know? I'd only just left them.'

'What difference would it have made if you had known? You'd still have asked me to move my things.'

'I could have spoken to you and explained. And I might have had the chance to speak to them about you before they arrived. I've tried many times to find the right moment to broach the subject, but when I'm with them they seem worlds apart from the one I share with you. When I'm here, I feel as though I was born here. We dress the same way, speak the same way, eat the same food and share the same humour; then I go home and I feel like I'm someone else. I go to mosque with my family, we have our own food, speak our own language and we wear different clothes.'

He looked haunted. 'Thing is, I don't know which of these worlds I belong to. I wasn't born here. I am different - and I love my own culture as much as I love the western way of life. I don't want to turn my back on my Asian background, I love it too much. Does that sound crazy?'

She reached out and gently caressed his cheek.

'No - and I wouldn't want you to turn your back on it. I never want to be responsible for that and I would never ask you to choose. You have to do what you feel is right. If that means marrying an Indian girl then that's what you should do.'

'And where does that leave us?'

'I think we both know the answer to that. At least you explained everything to me in the beginning. It was always a non-starter and we both knew it - but, I suppose, after a while you begin to believe that anything's possible.'

Rahim struggled to justify himself.

'I've explained before that I'm the only son and that has huge implications for me. I have three sisters, but the responsibility for my parents lies with me. I've been brought up to understand that I'll repay my parents for all that they've done for me by looking after them in return. This means that when I marry, my wife will live with me and my parents. Do you understand what I'm saying? And not only that, it's not just the fact that my parents will live with us, my mum would have more authority than you if you became my wife. In our tradition the daughter-in-law has to toe the line and do as she's told. How would you cope with that?'

'I don't know about that - but I think I could cope with them living with us if I had to.'

'And my two sisters? They would be at home with us too until they married or went to college.'

'Now you're just testing me!'

'No test, it's the truth. Do you see how difficult it would be?'

Helen fought to hold back the tears.

'I love you, Rahim, but I don't want us to be together at any price. Maybe we should never have let it go this far.'

'I love you too.' Rahim pulled her hands towards him and put them to his lips. 'I've always dreaded this. In the past I've tried not to get too involved with English girls for this very reason, but with you it was different from the start. I don't know what to say or do, to be honest with you. The two things in life that I want are incompatible. And the problem now is that I couldn't bear it if we split up, knowing that you are living just below me and I wasn't able to see you.'

'Why don't we see each other, but not quite so often? Maybe that will enable us to think more clearly and we might then be more rational about the whole thing.'

Rahim agreed, relieved to have a solution, temporary or otherwise. They talked for hours until eventually the sun rose lazily in the sky.

Rahim looked at his watch. 'I have to be at work in a couple of hours and I haven't slept a wink.'

'I take it you're kicking me out?'

'I don't want you to go, but I have no choice.' He said this mockingly, turning his mouth down at the corners.

'You poor thing,' said Helen. She pulled him to her and kissed him, but inside, her heart was heavy. 'We'll be fine, don't worry.'

She returned to her flat, fell into bed and slept soundly for several hours. When she woke she knew exactly what she must do. She had a plan and her mind was made up.

§

The two girls took a rare day off together. At lunch-time, they wrapped up warmly and sped into town. It was March and it was raining and blustery, so there was no chance of having the hood down on the car that day.

'This weather!' complained Jo, as they dodged in and out of shops to escape the showers.

'How would you like to live where the sun shines constantly all year round?' said Helen

'That would be lovely.' Jo closed her eyes to visualise it. 'And where might that be?'

'California?'

'California?' Jo saw the look in Helen's eyes. It was a look she'd seen before. 'You're serious aren't you?'

They stood face-to-face, rain dripping off their noses.

'Come on, spit it out!' shouted Jo above the noise of the downpour.

'Let's have a coffee and I'll tell you.'

Once in the coffee shop, Helen wrapped freezing fingers around her coffee mug. 'You know Dad's brother lives in Los Angeles? I thought I might write and ask if I could stay for a while. That way I can sort my head out and decide what to do.'

'But when and for how long? What about your sister's post?'

'I'll go as soon as I can sort out a visa. The sister's post doesn't seem important any more. I'll work my notice, sell my car, buy an open airline ticket and see how it goes. Who knows, I might never come back. I might meet a rich doctor and live happily ever after like they do in the movies. After all, my uncle does live near Hollywood, the land of dreams.'

'And you're asking me to come too?'

'Yes.' Helen's eyes danced with excitement. 'It would be fantastic.'

'But I can't do that. What about Sam? And what does Rahim have to say on the subject?'

'He doesn't know. We talked all night, and you're right, Jo, I can't ask him to change a lifetime's plan just for me. What if it all went wrong and we ended up divorced? That would be worse than if we go our separate ways now. There's no other solution. If we split up, I can't stay here and see him every day and if we stay together, I can't carry on knowing there's no future at the end of it. After hours of going around in circles, this solution sprang to mind. Sure you won't come too? What do you think?'

Tears mingling with raindrops clung to Jo's lashes.

'Oh Helen, I feel sad for you, but I think it's a good idea. I hate to watch you get hurt, although I'll really miss you badly. How do you think Rahim will react?'

'Don't know. He might be glad to be rid of me or he might kick and scream in protest, but I have to do it. I could organise a going-away party and invite some of his university pals. Then we'll have something positive to remember.'

'Send the first invite to us or you'll be in trouble!'

Surprise, shock, distress, and yes, relief too! These were just some of the emotions that Rahim was forced to endure when Helen told him about her plans.

'You don't have to go. What about your new job?'

'Some things aren't meant to be, I suppose.'

'That's rubbish! You'll make a fantastic sister.'

'But not a fantastic wife?'

'That's cruel.'

'I'm sorry,' said Helen. 'My mind's made up. It's too good an opportunity to miss.'

'Will you think about me?'

'Of course.' She pulled his head onto her chest and hugged him, gently running her fingers through his silky black hair.

'And will you miss me?'

'Course I will,' she repeated. She pinched his cheek, ' - like a broken leg.'

'Ouch!' He grabbed her and held her tightly so that she couldn't move. 'I'll miss you like crazy. Promise you'll write.'

'Only if you do.' She knew how bad he was when it came to paperwork. His correspondence and bills lay untouched for months before he did anything about them.

Weeks later, Helen was still waiting for her visa to arrive. She had arranged for it to be posted to her home address and she phoned periodically to check whether or not it had arrived. Today, she dialled the number and heard the click as the two phones connected. The persistent purr of the ring tone seemed to go on forever. No-one home, she thought, but just as she was about to replace the receiver, someone answered.

'Hi Dad, how are you?'

'I'm fine, but who is it?' The words were slurred.

'It's me - Helen.'

'Helen?'

 Silence.

'Dad - speak to me. You OK?'

'Sorry, I have to go.'

The line went dead. David's voice had sounded more than just sleepy - and he never stayed in bed late in the morning.

'Oh my God!' Helen said out loud, 'he's taken something.'

'What?' Jo was sitting in the lounge.

'It's Dad. He can hardly string two words together; he must have taken too many tablets.'

'You mean an overdose?'

'What shall I do?' Helen grabbed her car keys and ran towards the door, on second thoughts she shot back to the phone and picked up the receiver.

'You phoning your mum?'

'She'll be out on her rounds. I'll phone the college, see if I can get hold of Karen. She may be able to get home and find out what's happened.'

She managed to get a message to Karen who phoned back within ten minutes. Before racing home, she phoned the doctor's surgery where Elizabeth would be doing her clinic but was told that her mother had gone home for lunch. One of Karen's tutors offered to drive her home and when they arrived, Elizabeth's car was already standing outside the front door.

'Do you mind if I go in alone?'

The tutor left Karen and went back to work.

The house was silent. The door that led from the hallway to the kitchen was open but the kitchen was empty. Afraid of what she might encounter, Karen crept upstairs. Her parents' bedroom door was closed and her heart beat wildly as she reached out and pushed down on the door handle. The curtains were closed and her father lay prostrate on the bed in darkness. Elizabeth was rocking to and fro in the old high-backed armchair in the corner of the room. There were no tears and no smile, there was no expression on her face at all, just her eyes wide open.

'Mum, is Dad all right?'

Elizabeth didn't blink, and there was no emotion in her voice.

'I don't know, I think he's still breathing, but I'm not sure.'

'What do you mean, you're not sure? Call an ambulance!' Karen dashed to the phone, but Elizabeth leapt from her chair and smashed the receiver back down.

'You can't do that! It's not what he wants.'

'We have to call an ambulance right now.'

'He wants to die, Karen! If you do that, they'll take him to hospital and pump his stomach and if he survives who knows what might happen.'

'What do you mean? You can't just sit there. Do something!'

'I can't. He said that he would kill me if I ever found him like this and let anyone revive him.'

'You believe that?'

'Yes.' Elizabeth looked from her daughter to her husband on the bed. 'He'll be so mad that there's no telling what he might do. Karen, you can leave if you want to, but this is our promise to each other and I have to keep it. Your Dad is still that same loving person he always was and we love each other deeply, but he's not well. I can't bear to see him hurting this way.'

Karen left the room. Downstairs she phoned Shelly and Paula who both arrived within the hour, followed by Helen some time after. The four sisters sat in the kitchen staring at one another, not one of them able to offer any consolation as the hours crawled by agonisingly slowly. Occasionally one of them would take a cup of tea up to Elizabeth, but the previous one was always returned untouched. Finally, just after midnight, Elizabeth came down and said that David had begun to stir. She wasn't sure whether she should be thankful. The girls groaned with relief and hugged her. For the rest of that night and the whole of the following day David stayed in his room. At long last he surfaced; he apologised to them all and urged them to return to their lives, promising that he would know when the feeling was coming next time and that he would be able to deal with it.

'Dad, you don't realise how much we all love you and want to help,' said Helen.

'I know love and I'm sorry, but there are times when I don't have the energy to carry on. Some days I can hardly get out of bed and it feels like I'm being dragged down, like a bird trapped in an oil slick.'

'But you're on medication.'

'I was, but I can't take it forever.'

'Why not?'

'I don't want to become addicted.'

'That's absurd. Better addicted and alive than tormented - or worse still - dead.'

But for David, the stigma of mental illness was unbearable; he couldn't contemplate the idea of seeing a psychiatrist, and he had terminated his relationship with his community psychiatric nurse after she had broached the subject. There was nothing anyone could do to help him - and it was still a family secret.

§

Back at The Vic, unbeknown to Rahim, arrangements for the party were well underway.

Helen picked up the receiver and dialled Nadim's number.

'How are you Nadim?'

'I'm fine. What you up to? Have you packed your bags yet?'

'Not quite, it's a little early yet.'

'You're very brave. I hope Rahim appreciates what you're doing for him.'

'It's not going to be easy, but I can't see any other way. Anyway enough of that, the reason I'm phoning is because I'm arranging a surprise party for him. Would you mind contacting some of his old university pals to invite them? Once I have my visa, I'll give you a date.'

'No problem, he'll be over the moon,' said Nadim. 'You do realise that most of them are drunkards.'

'That's fine. Can we ask some of the ones that we met at the wedding, like Kieran and Mark - I don't mean that they are drunks by the way.'

'Consider it done.'

The party plan took on a life of its own. Jo and Sam offered to help with food, and Aziz and Serina were given the task of providing music.

At long last, Elizabeth phoned to say that the visa had arrived. By that time it was almost May and Helen had to work two months' notice. She decided that the beginning of August would be an ideal time to leave for America.

Once Helen had decided the date she phoned her uncle Richard in America: 'I don't intend to be a burden, I'll find some sort of work as soon as I can.'

Richard was excited about her coming to stay. His wife had died of cancer many years ago and he had lived alone ever since.

'You can be a burden for as long as you like,' he said. 'But if you want to work then I'll ask around and see what I can do.'

§

The day of the party was upon them. The food and drink that Helen had prepared downstairs had been transferred by Jo and Sam to Rahim's flat after he left for work that morning. Helen had invited the neighbours so that the party could go ahead without upsetting them. When Rahim finished at six o'clock he returned home to find a host of people already in party mode.

He looked at the sea of faces.

'Nadim! Dave!'

Nadim slapped him hard on the back: 'Surprised?'

'You can say that again.'

Amanda appeared, her arms full of baguettes laced with garlic butter and wrapped in foil, her lips pursed for a kiss from the host. Rahim recognised some of the guests from the hospital, others he hadn't seen in years.

Rahim and Helen didn't sit down for one minute during the whole evening. They mingled with friends, chatting and laughing, and danced till their feet were swollen and sore. Rahim loved the surprise, but it made him sad to think of the reason why it had been organised.

When the time came to depart for Californa, Helen left for the airport accompanied by her parents. She had said her goodbyes to Rahim, Jo, Sam and Aziz beforehand and stayed at home in the days leading up to the start of her new life. Not only would it be too painful to say goodbye to Rahim at the departure gates, but her father was well and she wanted to enjoy being with him and seeing her parents together, happy and smiling.

13 A NEW LIFE IN BEVERLY HILLS

Helen felt as though she had been slapped in the face with a hot, damp cloth. Above her, the blue sky, unblemished by a single cloud, offered no protection from the burning sun. She looked down at her crumpled cotton dress and tried to smooth out the creases. She hadn't seen her uncle for some time and today she looked like a vagrant as she dragged the heavy suitcase through the arrivals hall. She scanned the crowd in search of Richard's face (at his request, she had long since given up calling him uncle, 'It makes me feel ancient,' he protested). Now and then, when speaking on the phone, she would call him 'Old Uncle Richard', just to rib him and he would laugh and say: 'Wait till I get my hands on you, young lady!'

Out of nowhere Richard was suddenly before her. He was over six-foot-tall like her dad, and picked her up effortlessly, almost squeezing the life out of her. 'Hiya, darlin!' Although he had lived in Los Angeles for over twenty years, his accent had scarcely changed. Only occasionally would an American twang emerge although today it was the first thing Helen noticed.

Helen wriggled free enough to kiss him on the cheek.

'Am I pleased to see you,' she said.

They headed to his home outside Beverly Hills.

'I have some good news,' he said. 'I may have found a job for you. A friend of mine wants some help looking after his mother. She's ninety-four and a bit senile. What do you think? It might give you a start.'

'Sounds great; I'll see him as soon as I can.'

'Not too soon, I'd like to spend some time with you before you get into all that work shit.'

He always did have a way with words. There was no awkwardness between them; she felt comfortable in his company. She told him about everything that had happened at home, about Rahim and about her plans. She intended to take temporary work initially so that she could study and take the nursing exams that would enable her to work in one of the nearby hospitals. She knew she needed a green card in order to work legally and Richard offered to find a suitable lawyer who could sort this out once she had qualified. By the time they reached his house, her life was mapped out. It all seemed so simple. What could go wrong? She phoned her parents and Rahim to let them know she had arrived safely, and she tried to phone Jo, but there was no answer so she was probably out with Sam.

The new job was rather strange. Richard's friend Larry had two houses, one on each corner of the same street. He lived in one house with his wife of recent years and he also lived in the house opposite with his partly-demented mother. She had apparently arrived in New York many years ago as a young eighteen-year-old, and met and married a handsome young lawyer, Larry's father. Just after Larry's birth, his father had died from a brain haemorrhage leaving his mother to fend for herself. When, many years later, a new man came into her life and she wanted to remarry, young Larry had protested on the grounds that he would always be second-best. So she agreed not to marry and instead devoted her life to her son, and to her career as a successful saleswoman in a popular department store.

But the cruel twist in this strange fairytale was that just as her son had prevented her from remarrying, she then turned the tables, forbidding him to marry on the grounds that she had sacrificed her life for him. And this was why his girlfriend of over twenty years had only recently become his wife. When Alzheimer's had crept up gradually and got the better of the sad old mother, Larry decided he had nothing to lose and now he spent his time between the two houses trying to keep both women happy.

Larry's intention was that Helen would live with his mother as a companion and keep a watchful eye on her. They would make simple meals together as a form of therapy and Helen would help bath her a couple of times a week. The cleaner would spend two whole days at the house and provide relief whilst Helen had time off. It didn't sound too difficult and Helen agreed to a meeting, escorted by Richard of course.

When they pulled onto the drive in the smart Beverly Hills suburb, Helen felt a tingle of excitement. The detached white bungalow, mirrored on the other side of the road by the mother's home, was well maintained. A highly-polished Buick sat on the drive and as Richard parked his old pink Mercedes alongside, an elderly, but jolly man bounced out of the house. Helen was barely out of the car when he pounced on her, holding out a chubby hand.

'Hi, I'm Larry. You must be Helen.'

He took hold of her fingers and pulled her hand up towards his lips, but then lightly kissed the back of his own hand, chuckling as he did so.

'Pleased to meet you,' he said.

'And you too.'

Larry turned to Richard. 'And you, you old fart, how are you?'

'I'll have less of the old, thank you,' said Richard.

Larry led the way laughing. He guided Helen into the entrance hall. The house was immaculate with polished wooden floors and traditional furniture. Beautiful kilim rugs and rich tapestries, souvenirs of many visits to foreign countries, gave it a homely feel. Helen sat in the lounge and was introduced to the other two members of this strange love-triangle. She felt relaxed.

Larry's wife Sarah was pleasant and welcomed Helen as though she were a long-lost friend. Later, Helen came to understand that, to Sarah, she represented salvation. Sarah was quite tall and slim in comparison to her husband and, despite the odd grey hair and one or two crow's feet, she was obviously much younger.

Larry's mother sat hunched in a small armchair, a dear old lady, like anyone's favourite grandmother. Her name was Constantine and no-one was allowed to shorten it to Connie or use any other form of address. Her black dress was tailored to perfection around the shoulders and chest, and loosely fitted at the waist. A lacy grey cardigan complemented by a delicate string of pearls softened the look, but underneath that perfect exterior was a woman with an iron will. She had one thin leg and one fat leg. The fat one she called her milk leg and she explained to Helen that it had developed during pregnancy. Helen gathered that she must have had a deep vein thrombosis, which had probably been left untreated, and she was lucky to be alive. The meeting went well. Helen felt privileged to be offered her boss's old room in the house he had grown up in. She decided to take the job.

The following Monday, Richard dropped Helen at Larry's house.

'Let me know if you need anything, sweetie.'

'Thank you.'

Helen couldn't wait to start her new job, but she was in for a shock. Constantine's house couldn't have been more different to her son's. As Helen entered through a lobby at the back of the house she could hardly believe her eyes. Unlike Larry's house, this property hadn't been decorated or cleaned properly for years. In the kitchen the cream paint on the cupboard doors had peeled back to reveal the pale blue of a previous paint job; grease and grime that had obviously been there for some time nestled in the crevices; and the emulsion walls were coated in dust so thick that it formed balls of fluff that fluttered down onto the worn worktops below. On the floor, the faded linoleum curled in places and a broken light shade swung precariously above the kitchen table. It was like something from a Hitchcock horror movie. Surely her own room must be cleaner, she thought. Surely they had prepared it for her arrival?

Not so. A worse sight beheld her. It appeared that Larry must have various medical conditions because every surface in the room had become a pharmacy-shop counter, strewn with ointments, antibiotics, pain-killers, vitamins and a host of things that Helen had never previously come across, despite being a nurse. The bathroom reeked of embrocating balms, and its shelves carried yet more pills and potions.

A strange odour filled the house, a stale, heavy scent like bad breath. The windows, stuck down with paint, had not been opened in years and it was soon evident where the strange smell came from. Out of Constantine's bedroom trotted a large husky dog with thick matted fur. Helen noticed that the whole place was covered in a layer of white hairs.

Having accepted the job and moved in with her belongings, there was no way Helen would go running back to Richard to admit she'd made a mistake. She surveyed her room. 'What does the cleaner do when she comes in every week?' she asked herself. She began to fill brown-paper supermarket bags that she found in the kitchen with the medication that cluttered her room.

'What you doing?' asked Constantine.

'I'm clearing up.'

'You can't do that. That's my son's room, he'll be back soon and he'll need them.'

'Larry asked if I would tidy up a little.'

Constantine stepped towards Helen and raised her walking stick in the air, wobbling under the strain.

'I think you'd better leave. My son will come back and he'll be angry.'

'He's asked me to stay here to look after you.'

'No, he hasn't. I don't need looking after. If you don't leave, I'll call the police.'

Constantine lifted the receiver and dialled a number. 'Hello? I have a foreign girl here who says she's staying with me.'

Helen was very aware that she was working illegally and she didn't wait to hear the rest. She ran across the road to get Larry. By the time he reached the house Constantine had locked the door and was barricading herself in.

'Mother, let me in. Helen is here to help you. She's going to sort out my mess a little and spend some time with you.'

When Constantine had calmed down, Larry smuggled Helen back into the house. 'I'll take her out for a while so that you can settle in and unpack,' he said.

Helen sat on the bed and looked around the chaotic room. Her thoughts drifted to Rahim. She wondered what he was doing. Was he thinking of her too? Was he missing her as much as she missed him? She imagined Jo out walking with Sam, or Sam and Jo snuggled up on the sofa together. She pulled a double photo frame, hinged in the centre, out of her suitcase. On one side, surrounded by the tortoiseshell effect, were her parents, arms slung around each other's waists, smiling back at her. She imagined them joking: 'How will you get out of this one?' On the opposite side, Rahim sat at the kitchen table in the flat she had shared with Jo. He was knitting and laughing. It was a jumper that Helen was knitting for him and he had wanted to have a go. It made Helen want to cry. She closed the frame, bringing together the people she loved and made her resolve - that she would not be beaten by a senile old woman with a son so spineless that he'd wasted his whole life trying to appease her. She phoned Richard to invite him to the house - and burst out laughing when she saw the look on his face.

'Move back in with me,' Richard pleaded. 'I only ever visited him at the other place. I had no idea. You don't have to stay in this pig-sty.'

'I'll be fine. I'm going to clean up and transform it into a palace.'

'You've got a bloody good imagination. Come back with me right now, you won't have to speak to him. I can do that.'

'Let me give it a go. I'm not a baby. I can't come crying to you every time I have a problem.'

'But this is something else. Your mother would kill me if she knew I'd brought you to a dump like this.'

'It won't be a dump for long.'

'God, you're stubborn! Well - if you change your mind.'

Richard departed reluctantly and Helen rolled up her sleeves.

She had entered a bizarre world. Every other night, she was woken up when the old woman prodded her with her shiny wooden walking stick and asked her to leave. She would find herself in the street, in the middle of the night, knocking on Larry's door, whilst Constantine barricaded the doors with chairs and broom handles. Then it was up to Larry to find a way back in and settle Constantine back into bed before smuggling Helen back. After one such occasion, Helen found that her belongings had been rifled but the following morning she had to smile. Constantine joined her at the breakfast table and pinned to her nightdress was a badge that Rahim had given to Helen. On it was a picture of a big green monster with large white teeth and the caption: 'I've got a monster smile.'

Two weeks on, the house was gleaming and Helen gave Larry an ultimatum: his room must be painted or she would leave. Phil, Larry's decorator, arrived early on Monday morning and began to fill and sand the cracks.

'I can't believe you live here. The whole place needs decorating,' he said.

'Don't go on about it. Please, just do what you have to do.'

'Sorry, didn't mean to upset you.'

'Thing is, I've just arrived from England. I don't really want to live here, but I have no alternative apart from moving back in with my uncle, and I don't want to do that. I don't know anyone else here.'

Phil carried on sanding the woodwork.

'I won't say another word.'

'Sorry, I'm a little homesick as well.'

Phil smiled and continued with his work and Helen kept busy in the kitchen. At five o'clock it was time for him to leave.

'I'm off but I'll be back in the morning,' he said. 'Look, if you need company, there's about ten of us that meet up now and then for a drink or a bite to eat if you want to join us.'

She forced a smile. 'Thank you, I'll keep it in mind.'

Once he was gone, she dialled Jo's number.

'Hi, how's it going?' asked Jo.

'I've made the worst decision of my life, Jo. I have no-one here except Richard. I really miss you and Mum and Dad - and Rahim of course.'

'You'll be fine. Give it time, you'll see.'

'How's Rahim? Have you seen him?'

'He's finding it really hard. He misses you too but I keep telling him it's for the best. I'll give him a hint to write to you.'

Helen told Jo about Phil's invitation to join him and his friends for a drink.

'Go. You need to meet people. I'm sure Rahim won't be staying in.'

Six weeks went by and things slowly deteriorated. If Helen went out to hang washing on the line, Constantine would lock the door and refuse to let her back in; conversely, when it came to Helen's time off, Constantine would cry when Phil came to pick her up. The house had become a prison and Constantine, and Larry too, had become her jailers. Breaking-point came when Richard arrived unexpectedly to bring Helen's mail. Larry refused to let him in on the grounds that it would upset Constantine too much, and Richard left in a rage without Helen even knowing he had visited.

That evening, once he had calmed down, Richard phoned her.

'Helen, this is not what you came here for. You're locked up there like a criminal. You can get much better work - and, anyway, I'd love to have you here with me - come on.'

The following day Phil loaded his van with Helen's belongings and drove her back to Richard's house. Larry looked on helplessly as the vehicle trundled up the road. Helen felt bad but she couldn't stand it any longer.

Phil was one of a group of surfers; he was easy-going and good fun, and there was never any pressure on Helen to take things further with him. She made plans to go into nursing and arranged an appointment at St Joseph's Hospital in Santa Monica. Soon she was signed up to work one day a week as a 'candy striper', so-called because of the white uniform with the pale blue candy-stripe edging. The large basement of the private hospital housed everything from dressings to oxygen masks and tubing and a candy striper's job was to run back and forth to collect various items, which all had to be accounted for. In the meantime, Helen bought an enormous nursing book that she called her 'bible' and sat each night with her nose stuck between the pages trying to remember all the facts. To take the exams necessary to register as a nurse in America, she would need to study hard for the next few months.

Richard, like his brother David, was a perfectionist. Even when he had just finished work he still looked fresh, with his collar and tie tightly fastened and shoulders back in regimental fashion. Helen was slouched on the sofa with Phil watching television when Richard came in. He had a woman with him and Helen and Phil sat up at the sight of a stranger.

'Sorry, we were watching a film,' said Helen.

'Hi, sweetie! That's OK, this is Laura.'

'Hi Laura!'

'Laura and I have known each other for years. You've heard me talk about her. I called her this afternoon to see if she could find some sort of work for you and I may have struck lucky. Why don't we book a table somewhere and talk about it over dinner? Phil, you want to join us?'

Laura was twice-married with two daughters and, despite her expensive clothes, was struggling to make ends meet. A dedicated Buddhist, she was fascinated by karma, by cause and effect, horoscopes and precious gems. Helen was mesmerised by her conversation and dinner flew by in a rush of words. After Richard went to bed, Laura, Helen and Phil sat up till the early hours discussing a host of philosophies Helen hadn't even known existed.

'I feel like I know you already, Laura,' said Helen.

Laura's two daughters attended an expensive private school, paid for by their father, Laura's second husband.

'There's a school fete this weekend,' said Laura, 'join me. I can introduce you to some wealthy mothers who'll think it's very prestigious to acquire an English nanny. When they know that you're a qualified nurse, they'll be fighting over you.'

Within a day of the fete, Helen had a phone call from one of the mothers.

'I got the job!' she told Laura over the phone.

Richard poured two large glasses of wine to celebrate.

'I'll miss you,' he said, 'I was hoping we could spend some time together.'

'It's not that I don't want to live with you, it's just I need to be independent,' Helen explained.

'Don't forget where your old Uncle Richard lives. Meantime, you'd better let them know at home - and Rahim too, I suppose? Use the phone in my bedroom.'

Helen wrote to Rahim nearly every day, but didn't phone very often because of the extortionate cost, so this was a treat. Richard teased her about him and said he had never met anyone who was so much in love: 'I can tell from the way your eyes become big watery pools each time you mention his name.'

She spoke to her parents and Jo, then she phoned Rahim.

'Hi Rahim, how are you?'

'Helen!' The pleasure in his voice lifted her spirits further. She had worried of course that he would lose interest once she had gone, but he was evidently thrilled to hear her.

'What have you been up to? I've missed you, but your letters made me laugh so much especially when you described the old woman and her son.'

'I have a new job and a new home to go to.' She told him about Laura and the school fete.

'How are Aziz and Serina? Have your parents not found a wife for you yet?'

'Aziz and Serina are fine, and no, they haven't found a wife for me, but every time I go home I get dragged off to the mosque or to someone's house, who just by coincidence happens to have a pretty daughter.'

'You'd better be quick before the best ones are taken,' she said, but in truth she dreaded the day when he would say that he'd found the right girl.

'Stop torturing yourself. I'll tell you when that time comes - if it ever does. And what about Phil? You might find someone before I do.'

'Phil's nice, but you don't need to worry.'

When she put the receiver down, Helen sat for a few minutes to suppress her tears before returning to Richard.

'Mum and Dad send their love,' she said. The conversation came round to David's illness. Richard couldn't come to terms with the fact that his older brother suffered from depression; he had always looked up to him.'

'Let me speak to him, he said, 'I'm sure he would listen to me.'

'No, absolutely not! He doesn't want anyone to know about it and it's not something he can control, though he thinks he can. You can't just tell him to pull himself together. We tried that a long time ago. If only it were that simple. There's no way of reaching him when he's feeling low. He's alone in his own little world, and in that black hole he doesn't think about anyone else; it's a place where we don't exist.

That's how it is and, until he accepts treatment, the future is very bleak for him.' She bit her lip. 'You're going to hate me for saying this, but sometimes I wish he would do 'it'. It's awful to see him in such agony and know how useless he feels'

Richard thumped the table with his fist.

'We're all screwed up to some extent. I know it's easy to blame the parents, but in this case it's true. How can you grow up normally when, as a child, you were constantly belittled, called names and beaten by your own father?'

§

Helen packed her bags for the second time. The Stanton family couldn't have been more different from Larry's. Sean Stanton was a successful lawyer and he and his wife, Josie, had four children. The house stood on a steep incline in Benedict Canyon. It had umpteen rooms and a state-of-the-art swimming pool with wooden decking. They also had a beach house in Ventura an hour's drive away that they used as a weekend retreat where Sean could de-stress. Helen was given her own beautifully-decorated bedroom with en-suite bathroom. There was a car for her personal use and she got to drive the family station wagon when transporting the children around. All this plus two days off a week and twice the money she had earned looking after Constantine.

Over the coming weeks, Helen and Josie got to know each other. Josie was beautiful. She was slim with short blonde hair and, unlike many women in the neighbourhood, she was very natural and wore casual clothes and very little make-up. Sean was more distant - always polite, but always preoccupied with some big case. He promised Helen that he would introduce her to a friend of his who was an immigration lawyer so they could set the wheels in motion with a view to helping her obtain a green card. Within two weeks, she found herself sitting before Mr Braunstein. He could see no reason why Helen should not get a green card so long as she passed the nursing exams.

Helen ate with the family and sat with them in the evenings, although Sean spent most of his time in his office. The children were a delight. The two older ones teased her relentlessly, imitated her accent and played tricks.

One day, as Helen stood at the kitchen sink, the eldest boy slapped her on the backside as he passed, and said: 'Ooh! Jello!'

'Really!' said Josie.

'He's right,' said Helen. 'I've been eating too many burgers and pizzas since I came to America. I'll have to eat healthily and start some serious exercise before it's too late.'

Her working hours were from seven in the morning until seven at night and that meant she was too exhausted to go to the gym at the end of the day so, once the children were in bed, she would write a letter or two before plunging into a deep sleep.

'Surprise!' Josie skipped into the kitchen one morning waving two letters above her head.

'Guess who these are for?'

'Two?' asked Helen, lurching forward to grab the envelopes while Josie pretended to run off with them.

Helen recognised the handwriting. She decided to open Jo's letter first.

'Great news,' she said, 'my friends Jo and Sam are getting engaged. I'm so pleased for them. Would you mind if I took a ten-minute break?'

'And why might that be?' enquired Josie.

'This one's from Rahim,' said Helen holding the fuchsia-pink envelope close to her heart.

'Tell you what, I'll make a cup of coffee and we can sit and read it together. What say?' Josie smiled mischievously.

'I don't think so.'

'Go on then, but I don't want you back here all dreamy and starry-eyed, it'll make me jealous.'

Helen rushed upstairs to her room and propped herself up with soft pillows before carefully opening the long-awaited letter. Her hands trembled. Rahim had decided to visit his eldest sister and her husband in Toronto. Afterwards he intended to travel across the whole of Canada on a Greyhound bus. He still missed her and promised he would phone before he began his journey.

Helen returned to the kitchen and sat across the table from Josie.

'Would you think I was crazy if I went to see him?'

'When were you thinking of - and how long would you go for?'

'For a weekend? I would have to look on the map to see where we could meet, and the date will depend on his schedule.'

'My God, you're serious! Canada is huge and it's a long way to go. This is love like I've never seen it. What about Phil?'

'He's just a friend.'

'You sure?'

'What are you trying to say?'

'Helen, I've seen the way he looks at you and I think it's more than that.'

'We're just friends. We all hang out together.'

'Don't say I didn't warn you.'

The date was set. Helen and Rahim were to meet in Calgary on the twenty-ninth of November and spend a long weekend together. Helen would fly out on Thursday and return on Sunday. Over the next two weeks she couldn't concentrate on anything. What would she wear? What should she take? How was she going to greet him? What if, when they met, his feelings for her had changed? All these thoughts whirled around inside her head. She couldn't sleep. Tossing and turning, she imagined where they would eat, the sights they would see, and then - her departure.

Phil drove her to the airport.

'Got everything?'

'Think so.'

'Don't forget to come back.'

'Don't worry I'll be back.'

'I'll miss you,' he said.

She put her arms around him and they held each other closely for longer than friends ought to. She realised that Josie was right.

'I'll be back in a few days,' she said, prising herself away from him.

§

Her feet left the floor entirely as he scooped her up. With seemingly little effort Rahim swung her in a complete circle just as her father had done when she was a child and Richard had when she arrived in America. She clung tightly around his neck and buried her nose in the familiar warmth and smell of his flesh. He always wore Armani aftershave and she loved it so much.

His eyes, as usual, were searching and probing as though looking for clues.

'God, you feel so good,' he gasped. He put her down and stepped back, holding her hands out to the sides to get a good look.

'You're gorgeous,' he said and pulled her close again then stepped back for a second glance: 'A little plumper maybe - but still gorgeous!' Before the approaching slap could reach its target, he gave her a playful bear hug, rendering her helpless.

When he finally let her go, she adjusted the pale pink shirt that had ridden up under her chin. She wrapped her lamb's wool cardigan tightly around her body and sulked playfully.

'Thank you for the compliment; some things never change, do they?'

He kissed her on the nose and took her bag from her.

'You know I love you?'

With their arms intertwined they headed towards the airport exit.

'Come closer.'

'That close enough?' she squeezed her arm tighter around him.

'I want you much closer than that.'

'I can't get any closer.'

'Oh yes you can. I know a way!'

Canada was beautiful. Rahim's brother-in-law had arranged for them to stay at a friend's tenth-floor apartment situated close to some of the most stunning parks imaginable. The grass was a sumptuous green, bordered on all sides by trees, like an exquisite autumnal gold and bronze tapestry. In the early evening they sipped coffee and chatted to Fharad, their Arabian host. He was planning a trip to Peru and was feeling unwell after receiving his inoculations, at least that was the reason he gave for not accompanying them that evening or perhaps, knowing how little time they had together, it was an excuse to leave them alone.

Helen showered and tried on three outfits before deciding on dark brown trousers and a red roll-neck jumper. The strong colours suited her and it was quite chilly out and forecast to get colder. She felt like a schoolgirl on a first date. There was a rosy glow to her cheeks.

Meanwhile, Rahim sat in the lounge slurping a cold beer. He was debating problems in the Middle East with Fharad and didn't notice her. She stood for a few seconds wondering whether to interrupt then sidled up and touched his arm.

'Sorry, Helen, you were taking so long I thought you'd fallen asleep.'

'Cheeky.'

'Don't take any nonsense from him,' said Fharad.

Rahim placed his glass on the table.

'Come on, let's go and have some fun.'

'Rahim, you have the key. Go enjoy your evening. I'm off to bed.'

Once outside the apartment Helen turned to Rahim and kissed him.

'I've been dying to do that, you look so handsome. I'd forgotten how good-looking you are.'

The restaurant recommended by Fharad was perfect, small and cosy with soft lighting and candle-lit tables providing just the intimacy they needed. Helen and Rahim settled in, hardly aware of the existence of anyone else.

'I can't believe I'm sitting here with you,' said Helen. 'I really thought it was the end when we parted in England.'

'Who would have thought we would meet again, in Canada of all places, and so soon?' He took hold of her hand. 'Tell me everything you've done since you left me all cold and lonely.'

'You first.'

The hours raced by. Helen relayed the stories of Constantine and her big hairy dog and Rahim laughed until his sides hurt. He told Helen that Nadim was thinking of moving to Canada and Aziz and Serina were planning their engagement.

'Do you see yourself staying in America forever?' he asked.

'For the moment I must stick to my plan and see what opportunities come along. Now that I'm with Josie and Sean, I have a firm base.'

'I miss you so much. Do you miss me?'

'I miss you more than I ever thought I could, but I have to sort myself out. I can't keep thinking of what could have been.'

He longed to beg her to come home. She looked so small and vulnerable. He imagined her in Los Angeles, virtually alone because of him.

'I wish I could take you back with me.'

'Don't say that, Rahim, it'll only make it harder for us to say goodbye again.' Helen's chin began to quiver.

He reached for her hand.

'Let's go,' he whispered.

They held hands in the cold evening air and walked in silence, each in their own thoughts. Both had so much to say, and yet to voice those words would only make things more unbearable. The next two days were spent strolling in parks in the freezing cold, sometimes with temperatures as low as two or three degrees. When frostbite was imminent they would seek out a warm café and sip coffee until their frozen limbs had thawed. Helen was reminded of when they first met, and their walks along the seafront that they had loved so much. It was as though they had never been apart. So deeply engrossed in conversation they hardly noticed a red squirrel that scampered across their path. It disappeared up a nearby tree causing the leaves that formed a luxurious golden crown to rustle - but the sound fell on deaf ears.

Later, sitting in a bus shelter, they snuggled together for warmth.

'Tomorrow's my last day,' said Helen. 'It's over so quickly.'

'Let's pretend we have forever together.'

'You always were a big softy.' The cold air made her nose drip and she sniffed as she dug around in her pockets for a handkerchief. 'I knew you were a romantic from the beginning, when you put Lionel Ritchie on whilst I got ready for our first date. "All night long" will always remind me of you. Whatever happens, that will always be our song.'

'I'm dreading tomorrow. I don't want you to leave.'

'I feel the same; can't we run away together?'

'I wish we could.'

Cheek-to-cheek, staring out at the Canadian cold, they reminisced about their time at The Vic.

'If only we could turn back the clock for just a little while,' she said. 'I would give anything to re-live even a moment.'

It was time to leave. Helen packed her belongings and kissed Fharad goodbye. 'Thank you for having us to stay.'

'You only have one life, don't waste it,' he said as Rahim loaded her bag into the car. 'Whatever you decide, make sure it's the right decision for the two of you.'

The flight had been called three times and still they couldn't tear away from each other. They clung together like limpets to a rock, savouring every last second, hoping for a miracle. 'Have a safe journey,' said Rahim. His mouth was close to her ear, she could feel the words, and it gave her goose pimples that sent a shiver down her spine.

'Just remember,' said Helen, 'I love you more than anything in the world and some people never experience that. Whatever happens we will always have this love. No-one can take that away.'

'I'll always love you too. If nothing else, you have to believe that.' Cupping her face in his hands, he brushed back her hair so that he could memorise every detail. A tear welled and slowly forged its way down towards his lips, so that, as they kissed for one final time, Helen could taste it.

'Take care Rahim. Maybe it's better we don't stay in touch, this is agonising.' She slowly released her grip and walked backwards to the departure gate, where she waved, then turned and disappeared without looking back.

He stood for a long minute gazing at the image that had just left his line of vision. A woman bustled past him, knocking his arm, bringing him back to reality. He made his way back to the car. Caught between two different and incompatible worlds all his teenage and adult life, he had tried to avoid this situation and now here he was, stuck in the middle. Rahim was mad with himself. There in the airport car park, he made up his mind. He would stop being, in his own words, a 'pathetic creep' and start by telling his parents about Helen, but he wouldn't let her know - not yet anyway.

14 SOFIA AND SAFINA OFFER ADVICE

Rahim had something of a Pavlov's dog syndrome. As soon as he reached the front door of his parent's house, he began to salivate. Aromas wafted through the letter box and along his nasal passages causing his digestive juices to flow.

Hearing the lid of the car boot slam down, Fatima, his mother, rushed to greet him. It had been only a few weeks since he was last at home but still she missed him. He held his arms wide, kissed her on the cheek and embraced her for a few seconds.

'Smells good, Mum. Have you been cooking all night?'

They made their way through to the kitchen with his arm slung casually around her shoulders. The kitchen table was laden with food, from kebabs and samosas to biriani and daal. The drainer was stacked high with pots and pans all scrubbed clean and left to dry.

'I know why I love to come home,' said Rahim.

Jamal was a quiet man. He shook his son's hand: 'Good to see you, Rahim.'

'How are you, Dad? You look great.' Rahim wrapped his arms around him.

Jamal didn't like big shows of affection. He wasn't used to it and he was embarrassed, although because it was Rahim he secretly enjoyed it.

'I'm very well. You must be hungry, come let's eat.'

Rahim relaxed into his usual chair and loaded his plate with food. Fatima was a good cook and nothing in the world pleased her more than to watch as her son devoured her food. She had started early in the morning, preparing the samosa pastry, a long and arduous process, but that didn't matter. She peeled and chopped the onions and prepared the meat before making a luscious thick curry sauce. Her back ached, and her legs and feet swelled in the heat of the kitchen, but there she stayed for hours until at least four of her speciality dishes sat enticingly on the table. Rahim couldn't explain the effect that being home had on him. It brought a sense of belonging, as if to an elite society.

'Where are the girls?' he asked.

'Out with friends. We don't see much of them these days,' said Fatima.

Jamal frowned. 'It's not right. They shouldn't be out all the time with no-one to see what they're up to. They'll bring disgrace on the family, just you watch!'

'Dad, you can't keep them in day and night. Let them have some freedom. Once they marry, they'll have no choice but to do what's expected of them.'

'I want you to talk to them. I think they're smoking and drinking, it's a disgrace.'

'You're just guessing. You don't know for sure. They're probably at a friend's house watching a film.'

'Speak to them, Rahim. They'll listen to you because you know about these things.'

Jamal wasn't very old but, approaching retirement, he felt old and was weary with the demands that modern living made on him. He found it difficult to cope with two teenage daughters in a country that remained strange to him even after all these years. He couldn't understand the English mentality. It left him bewildered and confused.

'What if they are with boys - with English boys?'

Rahim burst out laughing; the expression on his father's face was comical. Rahim pictured his sisters walking in, with cigarettes dangling from the corner of their mouths, an English boyfriend on one arm and a can of lager in the other hand.

'Dad, you don't know your own daughters, they would never do that.'

Jamal slammed his glass down. 'Don't laugh, I'm serious, promise you'll talk to them while you're home!'

'OK, don't worry, I'll take them out and have a chat with them if that will make you happy.'

Rahim felt as though he was being manoeuvred into the role of head of the household and he wasn't sure that he liked it. Being made mentor to his sisters separated him from them in a way that he resented. He wanted to be their brother and friend, not a surrogate father who set down rules and told them what to do.

Rahim did nothing except eat and drink whilst at home; he was waited on hand and foot by his mother. Work at the hospital had been frantic recently. He had hardly slept a wink during his on-calls, had spent hours in casualty overnight or in theatre with his patients and then often had to work the following day. He was enjoying his time off. After dinner he slouched on the sofa glued to the soap operas, until his sisters came home. He then took them to the pub to read them the riot act.

'I'm not saying don't go out, but try to curb it a little so they don't worry quite so much. You know what they're like, they always imagine the worst.'

'Our friends go out all the time.'

'Your English ones maybe, but I doubt the Indian girls do. You have to respect their wishes, or I'll have to arrange weddings for you both to keep you in check.' It was a joke but a joke with an edge.

'Yeah, right!' Safina was the youngest. She put on an Asian accent and wagged her finger at him. 'Just you bloody well try it and see what happens,' she said, shaking her head comically from side-to-side as she spoke.

Rahim put on a thick Asian accent too. 'You will get a bloody slap in a minute if you carry on cheeking me. You should be in at night learning how to make chapati or no-one will want to marry you.'

Safina laughed and, continuing in an Asian accent, replied: 'I am making chapati for no bloody man; he must get his bloody mother to make chapati for him.'

Rahim reverted to his usual tone of voice. 'Then you'll be an old spinster and live at home forever.'

The three of them were in good spirits laughing at each other's jokes and funny stories. Rahim decided that now was a good time to broach the subject of Helen. He wanted to speak to his sisters to begin with to see how they would react. His parents would be a different matter, but if he could get Sofia and Safina on his side then at least he would have some support. If they were completely against the idea, then he didn't know what he would do, but he had to tell them how he felt about Helen. Maybe if he introduced her to them, they would like her and help him convince his parents.

'I've met a girl that I want to marry,' he said.

Their mouths fell open, they didn't say a word.

'Well? Say something!' Could they not ask him who, or congratulate him? If they reacted this way then how would his parents react?

'It's a bit sudden isn't it? Why haven't you mentioned her before?' asked Sofia. Then her eyes lit up. 'Has Dad arranged a marriage for you?'

'I met her at The Vic.'

'What's her name?' asked Safina, 'and what does she do?'

'Her name is Helen, and she's a nurse.'

'She's English!'

'That's the problem. Can you imagine what Mum and Dad will say?'

'You may as well forget the idea, Rahim. You wouldn't even dare to mention the word English and marriage in the same sentence,' said Safina.

Sofia's voice was almost a threat: 'If I were you, I would think carefully before deciding whether it's even worth talking about this.'

'I've thought about nothing else since I came back from Canada.'

'Why since then?'

'She flew over and stayed with me in Fharad's apartment. I asked Zara and she arranged it all for us.'

'Zara did? I can't believe that Zara would do something like that!' said Safina.

'She didn't know how close we were. I said she was a friend who just happened to be in Canada at the same time. When Zara was at university she had lots of friends, male and female, from all over the world, so she didn't think it was anything unusual.'

'She'll hit the roof when she finds out about this,' said Sofia. 'What are you planning to do? Are you going to move away? You'll break Mum and Dad's heart. Surely you're not expecting her to live with us?'

'When are you going to tell them?' asked Safina.

'I don't know, is the answer to all of your questions. Helen knows that Mum and Dad will come to live with me when I get married.'

'What did she say about it?' asked Safina.

'She thinks that she could cope with it, but I don't know about long-term. It would be very difficult.'

'Have you have asked her to marry you?' asked Sofia.

'I told her it wouldn't work so she's given up everything and gone to live in America with her uncle. But when she came to see me in Canada, it made me realise that I couldn't live without her.'

'Poor girl, that's really sad - and poor you,' said Safina. 'But I still can't see it happening. What about at mosque? What will they say?'

'I don't care what they say at mosque, for God's sake!'

'You should. They'll all be talking about it and if you end up divorcing they'll say, "I told you so". In the meantime, Mum and Dad's lives will be made unbearable because they'll have an English daughter-in-law.'

Rahim sighed and closed his eyes.

'I was hoping for your support, but I can see that it's asking too much.'

'It's not our support you need,' said Safina. 'It's Mum and Dad you need to worry about. We'll be gone in a year or so, but they're expecting to live with you for the rest of their lives.'

'I thought, if you spoke to them after I have, it might help persuade them.'
Sofia shook her head.

'You're wasting your time. They've lived their lives with this one dream and you'll shatter it for them the second you mention this.'

'You think I haven't thought about that? I have spent sleepless nights trying to find a solution. One minute I tell myself to forget about her and get married quickly so that I then have no choice in the matter; the next I'm trying to imagine how she would fit in and whether she would be accepted, not only by you and Mum and Dad, but by the other relatives and, as you say, the community. It's been going round and round in my head and the only definite thing that I've come up with is that I have to talk to them and ask them to meet her.'

Safina at least was intrigued. 'I would love to meet the girl who has stolen my brother's heart.'

'Don't joke about it. This is serious. I was counting on you both to help me as much as possible.'

'I would,' said Sofia, 'but I'm not sure I agree with what you're doing. Even if you managed to persuade them to let you marry her, it won't work out and you will end up divorced before long. Are you willing to risk everything, including alienating yourself from your family and everyone else? Even if you married her and lived apart from Mum and Dad, the strain could still split you up. You'll crumble under the pressure of knowing how much pain it would cause and you won't be able to bear the thought of Mum and Dad heartbroken and struggling to live alone.'

Rahim ran his fingers through his hair, his eyes focussed on the table in front of him.

'Please, meet her before you decide.'

'What good will it do?' asked Sofia. 'It will only build up her hopes and make matters worse.'

'I think we should meet her' said Safina, 'then we can decide whether she should be introduced to Mum and Dad. Let's fix a date.'

'Helen doesn't even know that I am intending to talk to them,' said Rahim, suddenly alarmed. 'I would have to get them to agree not only to meeting her, but also to getting to know her and giving her a chance. What if I asked her to come back and they don't accept her, or she decides that it won't work? It's a lot to ask and a huge gamble. She's already taken steps to qualify and work in a hospital out there. I can't wreck her chances when she could end up with nothing.'

'We can't decide just like that,' said Safina.

'My head is swimming,' said Sofia, 'I need time to think.'

Rahim raked his fingers through his hair again so that it stood on end momentarily before flopping back down onto his forehead. He was exhausted. What would he be like at the end of an ordeal like this with his parents? He wondered whether he should stop right now.

'It might help if you put yourselves in my position and looked at it from my point of view,' he said.

'One little problem with that,' said Safina. 'We're girls, so it's a hell of a lot different. You're a son - and an only son!'

Rahim had a sleepless night. He arranged to pick up his sisters from college at four-thirty the following day so that they could talk again. He arrived half an hour early in order to give himself time to think about the arguments they might raise and how he would respond. Parking his car in a side street outside the college, Rahim reclined his seat into a more comfortable position, slumped back and closed his eyes, tucking the gum he had been ferociously chewing underneath his tongue.

He drifted into a comforting slumber, the consequence of not having slept during the night. He dreamt that Helen was home. She appeared before him dressed in a wedding sari with full Indian make-up and adorned with jewellery. She looked beautiful. In her hand was an Indian sweet that she slowly broke in two. She placed a small portion into his mouth but he began to choke, he tried to cough but could neither inhale nor exhale. The wedding guests stood by and did nothing.

'He's not one of us,' he heard them saying. 'How can he marry an English girl? Leave him, let Allah deal with him.' And they all laughed. He felt a surge of panic as the life began to drain from him and, in a last ditch attempt managed to thrust himself forward onto the back of a chair. The pressure on his abdomen sent the crumbs hurtling from his windpipe across the room and he gasped for air.

Rahim was woken from his dream by a blow on the chest from the steering wheel as he lunged forward in his seat. Meanwhile, his head hit the windscreen and a large egg-shaped bruise formed in the centre of his forehead. In the blur, he saw the small piece of white chewing gum that had lodged in his windpipe come hurtling out. It came to rest in the air vent on the dashboard.

His sisters appeared. They rounded the corner chatting about something that had happened in class that day but stopped abruptly when they saw Rahim stumbling out of the car, clutching his head.

Safina stifled a giggle.

'What happened to you?'

'You've got an eggstra head,' said Sofia. She tried not to laugh and went to soothe his brow but, being over zealous, she delivered a painful prod instead.

'Sorry, you OK?'

Rahim told them about the dream and the chewing gum.

Sofia shook her head. 'See, it was a warning! You must take heed and listen to your conscience.'

'Oh, for God's sake, talk about the grim reaper. Let's go and get a drink somewhere. I need some anaesthetic.'

They headed for the nearest pub and made themselves comfy in a secluded corner. Rahim was so anxious that he forgot his change and had to go back to the bar.

While he was gone, Sofia shook her head.

'Poor thing, I've never seen him behave like this before. He's always so sure of himself - in fact, too bloody cocky for his own good.'

'Shall we make him sweat or make it easy for him?' asked Safina rubbing her hands together.

'You can see the state he's in. Tell him straightaway how we feel and what the plan is. OK?'

'OK!'

15 JO AND MAHMOOD CLASH

Jo's new flatmate was a nurse from the intensive care unit. Sandra was nothing like Helen. She was much more reserved, mouse-like even. She didn't follow fashion, food trends or football. She didn't follow anything at all, especially Jo's sense of humour.

'You could have more fun in a morgue,' Jo complained to Sam. 'Just as well most of her patients are on ventilators, the machine stops them dying of boredom. Rumour has it, one poor man tried to pull his tube out just to escape her.'

'That's not nice,' said Sam.

'Well, you don't have to live with her!'

'No - I mean being in hospital and having someone like that looking after you.'

'Oh you!' she said and thumped him on the arm.

Sam gathered her in his arms and smothered her in kisses.

'Don't worry, my little sweetheart, soon you'll be all mine.'

Ever since Sam had suggested that they name the day for their wedding, Jo had been consumed by the idea. Yet again, she called in at the corner shop on her way home from work to buy a bridal magazine. She couldn't wait to reach the flat and pore over its contents.

'Not another wedding magazine?' Sandra moaned. 'There are ten others here plus all the brochures you ordered.'

Jo mouthed the words back that Sandra had just spoken and she did it with a pout. Unfortunately, Sandra turned around in time to see her.

'Why are you always so rude?' she asked.

'Because you're no fun. Don't you want to look at them and imagine how you would look in, say, this big puffy one or this tight-fit one with the basque bodice?'

'Can't say that I'm interested. It's just a money-making exercise for the companies and most of the time it's a complete rip-off.'

Jo decided there and then that the wedding had to be soon. She couldn't live with Sandra a minute longer than she had to. That night she went round to see Sam, armed with a heavy bag.

'I brought one or two magazines for us to look at.' She lugged the bag through the door, but as she spoke the handles gave way and the entire collection spilled out onto Sam's foot.

'What the hell? I won't be able to play five-a-side on Saturday if you carry on like that.' Sam's eyes widened: 'We're only deciding on a date, not organising the whole damn caboodle!'

'Don't be a spoilsport, you're as miserable as her back at mine. I can't live with her any longer and I won't be held responsible for my actions, so we'd better get married soon.'

Sam launched himself at Jo and pinned her to the floor. 'Don't you dare compare me with her; we're not getting married just so you can escape a dreary flatmate.'

After much discussion, they decided that October the following year would be ideal. It would give them time to plan the wedding properly and save enough money to enable them to buy a house. In the meantime, Jo vowed to be nice to Sandra and even promised to try and lure her out for an evening once in a while. A year wasn't that long - was it?

§

The spotlessly-clean house, the audible silence and the sandals placed neatly outside the sitting room door indicated that it was prayer time. Inside the room, a lone figure knelt on a small mat facing Mecca. Head bowed and palms together, a low whisper issued forth as Mahmood prayed to Allah.

In the kitchen, Janice had cooked curry for her husband and was busy making rice and chapatis. Only the two youngest children remained at home.

'Hi, Mum!' Jo whispered.

Janice flinched. The sound of her daughter's voice amidst the deathly quiet had made her jump.

'What are you doing here?'

'Nice welcome!'

'Keep your voice down or he'll be complaining. You know what he's like when he's saying his prayers.'

'Sorry. Sam is with me.'

'What!'

'He's in the hallway, I'll tell him to come through.'

'No wait! What's going on, Jo? Why didn't you tell us you were coming?'

'I can't tell you yet. I need Dad here too.'

Janice knew this wasn't good. She sensed that Jo's news would not meet with her husband's approval. Having visited Jo in her flat on many occasions she knew Sam well and knew how much Jo loved him. She could see that they made a fabulous couple, but dreaded the news that she guessed Jo was about to announce. Their eldest son had recently divorced his English wife after he discovered that she had been having an affair with another man and this had reinforced Mahmood's belief that his son should have married a girl from Pakistan. He was now very determined to prevent this from happening again.

The sitting room door opened slowly and Mahmood reached for his sandals, unaware of the presence of visitors. He put them on carefully and brushed his hands together as if to clean them. Shaking the legs of his trousers down around his ankles, he looked up and his eyes filled with joy at the sight of Jo standing in front of him.

'Joanna, you didn't tell us you were coming!'

'I know, I didn't want Mum to go to any trouble.'

'Well, this is a very big surprise,' Mahmood saw Sam, 'and who is this?'

'This is Sam. I think Mum's already told you about him.'

'I don't think so,' Mahmood eyed Sam suspiciously. 'Nice to meet you,' he said, failing to hide his discomfort.

Janice listened. She had mentioned Sam to Mahmood many times, but he had chosen to forget. 'Amazing what the mind can do,' she thought. Mahmood had never visited Jo and Helen at the hospital. He believed that his daughter should have stayed at home until he could find a suitable husband for her. The thought of her living in the nurses' home, going out to parties and drinking alcohol troubled him to the point that, in the first few months after she left, he couldn't sleep at night. This wasn't what he had wanted for his daughter. Jo had refused to listen when he demanded that she stay at home.

'Shall I put the kettle on?' asked Jo.

'Good thinking,' said Mahmood.

They chatted uneasily, talking about anything that sprang to mind until the conversation ran dry and silence fell.

Jo shifted uncomfortably in her seat.

'Dad, Sam has something he would like to ask you.'

Mahmood pursed his lips, he knew what that question would be. He sat upright in his chair and uncrossed his legs, planting both feet squarely on the floor in front of him. Was he ready to pounce or make a run for it? Jo couldn't be sure.

Sam coughed.

'Mr Saheed, I want to ask your permission to marry Joanna.' He thought it a good idea to use her full name as her father did. 'I love her very much and we want to spend the rest of our lives together.' Sam knew it sounded corny but he had to keep talking to prevent another silence, and also because he anticipated an onslaught from Mahmood.

'So you think you can make her happy?' Mahmood looked Sam straight in the eye. 'And you intend to become Muslim? And you will bring up your children the same?' Mahmood raised his voice. 'What if I forbid it? Joanna should be marrying a Muslim boy with a good background.'

'Well, we weren't planning to change religion.'

Mahmood sprang forward coming face-to-face with Sam.

'What you mean, "we"? Joanna is already a Muslim.'

Jo intervened. 'I am not a Muslim, Dad.' she said.

'You're my daughter and that makes you a Muslim. You will not marry out of the faith, do you hear me?'

'We're going to get married, Dad, and we would like you to be happy for us.'

'No, I will not allow this. Think what you're doing. Think about the consequences.'

'How can you say that when your wife is English? That's so hypocritical.'

'You should learn from my experience. I should have made sure you were taught the ways of the Koran, and learned to speak my language. It is now very difficult for you if you want to go to the mosque or make friends.'

'But that's not what I want. You lived your life the way you wanted to and yet now I have to do as you say. Please, Dad.'

'Don't you dare speak to me that way. I'm your father and you should show more respect. I love your mother, don't you dare question it.'

'And Sam loves me. We love each other - and we are asking you to give us your blessing.'

'Yes, I'm married to an English woman,' said Mahmood, 'but I was very young when we met and I thought I was clever. Only when I returned to Pakistan did I realise that the Muslim faith is fundamental to the way we live. How can we live decent lives without it? I look around and I see youngsters drinking so much that they can't even stand up. I listen to people at work talking about who has been with someone else's wife and it disgusts me.'

'That has nothing to do with me,' replied Jo. 'It doesn't mean that I get drunk every weekend or that we won't be faithful to each other.'

'I have some very good books upstairs. I'll get them so you can read and learn from them.'

'Books on what?'

'They explain about Islam and how it can help us to live good lives.'

Jo sighed. 'Dad, we've been through this so many times before. You're not listening to me. I don't want the books. I haven't come to talk about religion.'

Mahmood looked from Jo to Sam, a strange, cold expression on his face. 'You will not marry an Englishman,' he murmured. 'Do you understand what I am saying? And if you do, I will not give you my blessing.' He turned and walked away, covering his face with his hands and shaking his head. 'I will not allow it, do you hear me?'

Jo fought the urge to cry. 'I'm sorry you feel this way - but we will get married, with or without your blessing.'

Sam moved forward to plead their case. Jo grabbed hold of his sleeve. 'Don't bother. It won't make any difference.'

'I'm so sorry, Janice,' said Sam.

'Don't worry, he'll be fine. He needs time to think about it.'

'It's probably best we go,' said Jo. Blinded by tears, Janice and Jo hugged each other.

Janice's heart was breaking. She knew there was no way Mahmood would change his mind but he was her husband so she had to stand by him; that was how it was.

§

The following week, when Jo had thought things through, she made a phone call.

'Hi, Elizabeth! How are you?'

'Jo. What a lovely surprise! I'm fine. How are you?'

'Fine. How's David?'

'Quite well, but you just don't know from one day to the next really. I play it by ear now, dealing with whatever mood he's in. On the whole though, he's doing all right.'

'Is it possible to speak to him?' asked Jo.

'Of course, I'll go and get him.' Elizabeth shouted to David, and then hovered in the background, curious to find out what Jo had to say.

When David replaced the receiver, he turned to face her.

'Bett, you won't believe this. Jo wants me to give her away when she gets married.'

'What about Mahmood?'

David explained about the problems that Jo and Sam had encountered with Mahmood.

'How do you think he'll react when he finds out you're taking his place?'

'I'll have to speak to him. I don't want him to read anything into it. Maybe he'll change his mind.'

'Probably best if you speak to Janice first. I wonder if he'll allow her to go to the wedding without him?'

'I'm not sure. It's a dodgy business. I'm honoured that Jo has asked me, but I'm concerned about our relationship with Mahmood and Janice.'

David decided to speak to Mahmood, but he was relieved when it was Janice who answered the phone.

'David, you don't have to worry. Mahmood is determined not to acknowledge the marriage in any shape or form. He has vowed that, even if the ceremony does take place, as far as he is concerned it will count for nothing.'

'What about you? Will you still go to the wedding or will he try and stop you?'

'I will be going. Nothing will stop me going to my own daughter's wedding. Take my advice, there is no point speaking to Mahmood because it won't make any difference.'

What she did not tell him was that Jo's approaching marriage had almost wrecked her own.

16 JAMAL'S DEVASTATION

Sunday lunchtime. The table groaned under the weight of another culinary masterpiece. Rahim cleared his throat nervously and massaged his temples with his fingers. His two sisters had slumped down in their chairs until they almost disappeared under the table. Sofia kept her head bowed and Safina had an overwhelming urge to giggle. The tension was intolerable.

'What's wrong with you three? What are you up to?' Jamal sensed that something wasn't right with his children.

Rahim had bitten into a samosa and almost choked.

'What are you talking about, Jamal? There's nothing wrong, you're always so suspicious.' Fatima had spent hours cooking and didn't want a full-scale battle at the table.

'They're up to something, Fatima, I can see by the look on their faces. Rahim, what have your sisters been doing?'

'Nothing, Dad - it's me.'

'What's the matter? Are you ill? Tell us.'

'Nothing's wrong, but I need to talk to you.' Rahim needed a sip of water but, as he reached out, the glass slipped from his fingers and went spiralling across the table. Cold water landed in his father's lap causing him to jump up from his seat.

'What you doing? What is the matter with you?'

'Sorry, Dad.'

Everyone calmed down and Rahim took a deep breath. This had to be the hardest thing he had done in his life. Throughout his training at dental school, nothing had made him feel so nervous.

'Mum, Dad, there's something I need to talk to you about - thing is, I've met someone that I would like to marry.'

Jamal was on his feet again in an instant.

'Why didn't you say something before? What wonderful news.' His face lit up. 'We must meet her and her family. Son, you have made your mother and me very happy.'

Sofia and Safina looked at each other in horror.

'Dad, please wait, I haven't finished yet.'

'We must celebrate; I can't tell you how happy I am.' Jamal was beaming and Rahim hadn't foreseen this. He'd imagined his father asking lots of questions before showing any kind of emotion; he had to stop him right now.

'Dad - listen to me - she's English!'

Jamal stopped in his tracks; Fatima took an audibly sharp intake of breath and held both hands up to her mouth, her eyes fixed on Jamal. Sofia and Safina tried to anticipate what would happen next; neither of them dared move.

Silence. Not one muscle moved in the room. Jamal looked from one to the other of his children.

'Did you know about this?' he asked Sofia and Safina

'Yes,' said Sofia, 'we did - but we've not met her and we've agreed not to do so without your permission.'

Rahim closed his eyes. All his hopes and dreams had vanished along with his appetite. The speech he had prepared now seemed feeble. He lifted his head.

'Don't blame the girls,' said Rahim, 'they've got nothing to do with it. I asked for their support, but I shouldn't have involved them.'

Jamal flopped down in his chair, exhausted and deflated, while Fatima sat bolt upright. She knew this was far from over. She took a chapati and tore it into tiny shreds, but not a crumb passed her lips.

'Let me explain and tell you how I feel,' said Rahim.

While Rahim spoke, Jamal and Fatima listened, deep frowns visible on their foreheads. They shook their heads, unable to comprehend what their son was saying. What did it matter if Helen was funny and intelligent? Why would they want a daughter-in-law who was a professional? They didn't particularly want her to work; she should be home looking after the family. Sofia and Safina urged Rahim on, supporting him with eye contact and the occasional nod of the head. Rahim told his parents that Helen had said she was prepared to live with them as a family and care for them.

'We can teach her our language and show her how to cook,' said Rahim.

'Isn't it easier to marry someone who can already do these things?' asked Fatima. She had dreamt of a daughter-in-law by her side in the kitchen and she couldn't bear the thought of it being an English girl. How strange it would be, she thought, like having a foreigner in their midst, a cog that didn't fit. She couldn't imagine how she could have a relationship with such a girl, or how they would be able to live harmoniously. Worst of all - how could she bear the shame of telling her friends? She imagined herself walking into the Friday night gathering at mosque, all eyes on her as she entered, the muffled whispers, everyone breathing a sigh of relief that it wasn't their son who had chosen a wife outside his culture.

Rahim stopped speaking and waited for a response. Jamal sat, deep in thought, a strange expression on his face. Then, to Rahim's total devastation, a tear welled in his father's eye until it could no longer be contained. It sprang out and rolled onto his cheek, coursing its way down until it came to the end of its pathway and plunged silently from his chin into his lap. Rahim had never before seen his father cry. Even through the darkest days when their belongings were taken from them and they were evicted from their home by soldiers, his father had been stoical and remained in control of his family and his emotions. Jamal stood and left the table. Rahim closed his eyes. Oh to turn back the clock and take away the pain he had inflicted a moment ago.

Jamal stayed in his room all day. That evening he asked Rahim to go and see him.

'Rahim, it will never work. You know that. We've seen it so many times before. You will ruin your own life as well as ours - and that of your lady friend.'

Jamal sat hunched on the edge of the bed, he looked tired and drawn.

'I can't agree to this and I'm asking you to think about what you're doing.'

'Dad, don't worry, I won't mention it again. I wanted to find out how you would react and whether there was even a remote chance of you considering the prospect of an English wife for me. Now that I know that it will cause too much hurt, I won't ask you again.'

Jamal laid a hand on his son's shoulder.

'It's for the best son. We will be happy if we stay together.'

Rahim looked his father in the eye. 'I will do my duty and marry an Indian girl, but it must be soon.'

He needed to seal his fate and didn't want to think about what could have been. If he couldn't marry Helen, then he had to take steps in the opposite direction and not prolong the agony of the inevitable. He left his father's room, dragging his heart and his tattered dreams behind him.

The rest of the day had passed by in a haze for Sofia and Safina. It had all had gone horribly wrong. Their plan had been to introduce the subject gradually by talking about a cousin of theirs living in Canada who was happily married to a Canadian girl, and then bring the subject around to what if one of them was to do a similar thing. They decided to continue to give Rahim their support and to try to convince their parents that it could work if everyone pulled together but only on one condition, which Helen must never know about. Rahim had to promise them that, if things did not work out, he would choose his parents over Helen.

§

A knock at the door brought Rahim back to life.

'Hi! You're back then? How's everyone at home?'

'Hi, Jo, come in. It's so good to see you. I came back a few days ago.'

'Oh dear, is it that bad? What's the matter? I haven't seen you like this before.'

The flat was never particularly tidy and today it was worse than usual. The sink was full of pots and there were textbooks, newspapers and magazines strewn over the floor and coffee table. A pile of clean washing dumped on a chair waiting to be ironed bore testament that Rahim had other things on his mind. Since the meeting with his parents, his mood had nosedived. He was unable to concentrate at work and asked if he could take some holiday. A bad decision; he spent the dismal days cooped up inside his flat, hardly eating, rarely showering and not speaking to anyone. The telephone was left unanswered for the most part.

Jo shook her head when she heard the story.

'I hate to say this, but your father's right. Don't do it, Rahim. We both know how difficult it would be. You'll ruin each other's lives, or others will ruin things for you. Leave Helen where she is, get on with your career and find yourself a nice Indian girl. Helen gave you the space to do that and now you're going to complicate everything by asking her to come back when it's all so uncertain.'

'I've promised Dad that I won't mention it again,' said Rahim, 'but I know I can't leave it at that. How can I think about meeting an Indian girl when I feel like this about Helen?'

Jo wanted to talk to him about her own marriage plans, but now wasn't the time, so she went to the kitchen and made them both a coffee.

'What if you asked Helen to come back and she refused?' she said. 'You can't presume she'll come running back to you the first chance she gets. What if she meets someone else?'

'She would tell me, surely?'

'Not necessarily. She might be worried about hurting you. What if she comes back and it all ends in disaster? What then? Are you going to put her on the next plane back and tell her it was all a big mistake?' Jo felt sorry for him, but she was scared for Helen also.

'It's a chance I have to take. I must at least ask her to consider coming home and then the choice is hers.'

'That's selfish, it's such a cop out. You can't do that to her. You know full well she'll want to give it a try. Just leave it.'

'I'm sorry, Jo, I know I promised my parents, but I have to try again. I have to get them to agree to meet her. Then I will ask her to come back home.'

His mind was racing; he imagined Helen walking hand-in-hand with another man, both of them laughing, and at that moment he knew he had to take the risk and try to convince his parents. But Jo, who with her own Muslim father knew about the problems that might follow, prayed that Rahim's parents would remain adamant and insist that he marry an Indian girl. She knew how much Rahim meant to Helen, and how strong-minded and obstinate she could be, and Jo prayed, without hope of success, that if Rahim did ask Helen to come home, Helen would refuse.

§

Three weeks had passed since Rahim had returned to The Vic following discussions with his parents. It was another gloomy day. Sofia replaced the telephone and turned to Safina.

'No change, he sounds depressed. You're right, we should speak to Mum and Dad. I'm worried about him.'

In fact, Safina had wanted to speak to them as soon as Rahim had left, but Sofia had convinced her that it was better to leave things as they were. They had always known that their parents would oppose any marriage other than an Asian one, although they had not expected such vehement opposition. Jamal had been withdrawn ever since Rahim broached the subject and so wrapped up in his private thoughts that he'd barely said a word. Fatima had tried to bring him out of his black mood, but all she could get out of him was a deep sigh and a motioning of his hand that he wished to be left alone.

Safina had argued with Sofia: 'If I had a son and he was feeling so miserable, I would want to put it right, and I'm sure that deep down they do too, don't you agree?'

'You've seen how Dad's behaving. He's bewildered that Rahim could even think of such a thing. Mum's putting on a brave face, but I spoke to her last night and she's devastated too. She's frightened at the prospect of having an English girl living under the same roof.'

'Frightened?' said Safina.

'Yes. Don't you listen to the conversations that take place? You know how difficult it is even for Indian girls these days to get married and leave their families to live with their in-laws. Are you going to go and live with your husband's family and look after them?'

'You've got to be joking!'

'And why?'

'I'm not having anyone tell me what to do.'

'Exactly! Mum knows that an English girl would feel the same as you do and it would tear the family apart.'

Fatima always did her chores on Saturday. She had just finished them and was reclining in the comfy old fireside chair, her feet resting on the small pouffe in front of her. She stared at the television in the corner of the room, but her mind was preoccupied by Rahim's request. She was in a muddle and had been so since he'd told them of his wishes. How could he think that it would work? How could she possibly live with such a girl? How could they converse on the same level? Her English was good, but she didn't possess the vocabulary of a native. The depth of feeling, the jokes, the intimacy, all this would be missing from any conversations they might have. She wanted to feel close to her daughter-in-law. She wanted them to share outings, go to mosque, cook for the family, so many things. None of this would be possible.

Rahim had always talked of them all living together and of how he would look after them.

'Fatima Ismail, you will never want for anything ever again,' he would tease. 'Your daughter-in-law will be the best, and you'll have your grandchildren around you and they'll keep you young.' He would pinch her cheeks and hug her. But she knew Rahim and she knew that, although he'd promised never to mention Helen again, he would not give up easily. What had made him change his mind? Was this girl so different? Was she going to take him away? How would they manage without him? One thing was certain: they would never be able to live together as a family. It was too much to ask of an English girl, and anyway Fatima didn't want it.

She turned to look at Jamal, who was sitting beside her hidden by the newspaper. Back in Africa he had worked hard for his family, only to have what he had earned snatched away from him by greedy, power-hungry good-for-nothings. It had broken him but he had refused to let the children see this. Only Fatima knew that the fire had been extinguished and that Jamal's zest for life and his drive to seek a better future had gone. Now he worked to survive and all his dreams, what was left of them, were pinned on his son. She saw the lounge door open and her two daughters crept in. Safina carried a tray laden with cups and snacks and placed it on the coffee table in the middle of the room.

Jamal looked out from behind his paper and frowned. The scenario wasn't new to him.

'What do you want?' he asked flatly.

'Nothing,' replied Safina.

'We want to talk to you,' said Sofia.

'How much is it going to cost me?'

'It's about Rahim.'

Jamal shuffled to get comfortable.

'What about him?'

'We think that you should go and see him,' said Safina.

'We're really worried about him,' said Sofia, 'he's been taking time off work for the last few weeks. He rarely answers the phone and when he does he sounds dreadful.'

'Who are you to tell me what to do? You have no say in such matters,' said Jamal sharply. He was cross with himself because for the first time in many years he felt out of his depth, he didn't know which direction to take. If he ignored the situation, how could he be sure that it would go away? If he went to see Rahim, did that mean he was considering the option of an English daughter-in-law?

'Dad,' pleaded Safina, 'listen to Sofia. We're not telling you what to do; we're telling you that we're worried.'

'You've said what you came to say, now leave.'

'Jamal, we should go,' Fatima whispered after the girls had left the room. She needed to see Rahim.

'Leave me alone.'

Fatima left the room and closed the door behind her. Jamal wearily reached for the phone and dialled Rahim's number. The ringing continued for some time before a subdued voice answered. 'Hello.'

'Rahim, we're coming to see you. We'll be there this evening.'

Fatima, who had been listening at the door, rushed down to the kitchen, took out her largest pan and placed it on the stove. Her heart sang as she prepared her son's favourite dish.

17 THE CONFRONTATION

Jo saw the silver car pull up outside. Hidden by a curtain, she watched as four members of Rahim's family got out and stretched after their tiresome journey. Their anxiety was plain to see as they approached the main door to the building, Jamal leading the way. She heard them climb the stairs and wished she could be a fly on the wall.

Rahim stood nervously with the door ajar, waiting to greet them.

'Hi, Dad, Mum.' He kissed his mother on the cheek and gave her a questioning look. Fatima closed her eyes and nodded to let him know that this was going to be a difficult visit for them all.

Sofia and Safina followed and hugged him freely, though without saying a word. It occurred to Rahim that they could be attending a funeral. He was sweating, having spent the last hour anxiously racing round the flat, shoving things in cupboards, under the bed, and behind doors. Compared to an hour ago, the place was immaculate. In the kitchen, the pots had been washed and put away, though a pile of ironing under the kitchen table would, unbeknown to Rahim, spill out and reveal itself later when they sat down to supper.

'It's good to see you, but why the sudden visit?' he said.

'Sit down,' said Jamal. 'Fatima, make some tea.'

Fatima disappeared to the kitchen, beckoning the girls to follow. Crockery chinked and cutlery clattered as it hit the table. In the corner, on the blue work surface, the white plastic kettle gathered steam. Soon everyone was sitting at the table.

'Rahim, are you really serious about this girl?' asked Jamal.

'Her name is Helen. You can say it if you want to.'

Jamal slapped his hand down hard on the table.

'Don't speak to me in that tone! I'm still the head of this family and you'll respect that, otherwise I'll leave now and this matter will not be discussed again, do you understand?'

'Sorry Dad. I was going to ask you to reconsider your decision, but I can see it's pointless. If you want me to marry an Indian girl, then I'll do it and I'll give you the grandchildren that you want so much - but she will be yours not mine because, having met Helen, I know I won't be happy.'

'Why did you get involved with her? We know of lots of relationships like this and they bring nothing but trouble and shame.'

'You think I don't know that? I'm surrounded by English girls, not Indian girls. You're asking me to go around wearing blinkers and not speak to anyone. Life's not that simple. I've avoided this up till now and even with Helen I tried my hardest to turn away, but the attraction was there and at the end of the day I am human.'

Jamal squirmed at the thought that this girl, Helen, could have such a hold on Rahim. In his mind's eye, he saw her, selfish and scheming, hatching a plan to lure Rahim away from them.

'She's done this on purpose,' he said. 'She just wants you for herself. She may say she'll live with us and look after us, but when the time comes, she won't.'

'You don't know her, she wouldn't do that. It may go wrong, but it wouldn't be because she planned it that way - it would be because it's difficult for us all to live together, for any family to live together for that matter.'

'What do you want me to say?'

Rahim leaned back in his chair.

'Just agree to meet her.'

Jamal sat stony-faced. If he agreed to meet Helen it would start a series of events that he might not be able to control, and the trauma of rejecting her could result in the breakdown of his family. Fatima would stand by him, but he risked losing his son and the support of his daughters. He thought of Zara. Living in Canada, maybe she was far enough removed that she could be more objective and make Rahim see things differently.

'I suggest we phone Zara and ask for her opinion,' said Jamal, 'she should know about this anyway.'

'All right - why not pour a little more petrol on the fire?' retorted Rahim.

Jamal wasn't a tall man, but he stood up quickly, sending his chair flying, and towered over his son, who remained seated.

'There you go again. We've come here to sort this matter out, but if you speak to me like that we can resolve nothing.'

'You've come here to try to talk me out of it, and, as we both know, Zara will back you and not me,' said Rahim angrily.

'Don't raise your voice to me. I won't have it!'

'You expect me to eventually become head of the family, and yet still you treat me like a child and expect me to have no say in the most important matter of my life. Is it fair that you ask everyone else for their opinion and yet you're not interested in mine? Who is the one that really matters? Go ahead all of you, decide my future for me and I'll accept your decision, but then I'll be your son in name only. I'll do everything you say if that makes you happy, but my heart will always be with Helen.'

Jamal walked over to the window and looked out. Fatima sat at the table clutching a sodden tissue to her nose. Sofia and Safina sat silently. Fatima shook her head; there was no escape.

Jamal turned round. He sighed.

'You're making this very difficult. You promised you would give up this idea.'

'I know, but I can't function knowing I may never see Helen again. I have to be sure there's no way around this. Phone Zara if you wish - she should be told anyway - but I won't speak to her.'

Both Jamal and Fatima talked with Zara for over an hour. Needless to say, Zara was opposed to the idea. Her arguments were along the same lines: an English girl wouldn't be able to adapt to their way of life, she wouldn't cope with living together with the family, and even if she made perfectly round chapatis, became a Muslim and dyed her skin brown, she still would never be fully accepted into their community.

Rahim submitted to their will.

'I suppose the decision is made. You have my promise. I won't mention Helen's name again - but you have to introduce me to some suitable Indian girls straightaway.'

Food was Fatima's remedy for any kind of upset and it seemed to work most of the time.

'Eat', she said. 'The food is getting spoilt.'

'I have an idea if you don't mind me telling you about it,' said Safina.

Rahim was too worn out for more discussions; he had hoped that they had come to an end.

'Go on,' said Jamal in a sarcastic tone, as though Safina couldn't possibly come up with anything constructive.

'Why don't we meet her first?' said Safina, as though the thought had never before occurred to her. 'If we don't think she'll fit in, then Mum and Dad are spared having to meet her, and of having to say no.'

Jamal's eyes narrowed,

'Who's "we"?' he asked.

Rahim shoved almost a whole chapati into his mouth, making it impossible for him to speak even if he wanted to.

'Sofia and me,' said Safina.

'But what if we say, "yes, she's the one" but then it all goes wrong anyway?' said Sofia, suddenly unsure.

'We can't make any guarantees, but we can at least meet her for Rahim's sake,' replied Safina.

Rahim suppressed a smile, wondering how his wayward little sister could suddenly come up trumps like this.

'I'll have to think about it,' said Jamal, darkly suspicious. 'Let's eat!'

The food was exquisite, and Rahim silently questioned whether an English girl would be able to produce food of the same quality, but he quickly dismissed that thought. He imagined Helen sitting at the table with them smiling. Of course she could learn to cook, didn't Indian girls have to be taught at some time in their lives? The conversation turned away from Helen and moved to the girls and their studies.

'No, Dad, I'm not becoming a bloody lawyer,' Safina said with her Asian accent and laughed.

'You'll do as you are told,' said Jamal, wagging his finger. 'What man is going to be interested in you if you have no prospects?'

'I can marry a lawyer; I don't have to be one myself. That's too much like hard work.' She knew just how to wind him up.

They all laughed. At nine o'clock Jamal decided it was time to go. He didn't drive and neither did Fatima, and he wasn't keen for Sofia to drive in the dark.

Fatima staggered to the door dragging a large black plastic bag behind her.

'Mum, what are you doing?' asked Rahim.

'It's your pile of ironing from under the table,' said Fatima. 'You can collect it next weekend when you come over.'

'But I'm not coming over next weekend.'

'Yes you are. You're far too thin; no son of mine goes without food.'

'Looks like we'll see you soon,' said Sofia.

Rahim carried the bag of washing and showed them to the car. He bunged it in the boot and hugged each one in turn, except Jamal whose hand he shook. He stood and waved until the car disappeared from view.

A hand came to rest on his shoulder.

'Heavy day?'

'Oh, Jo.'

'Thought you might need someone to talk to.'

'Somehow I don't think you'll approve.'

'Come to mine for a coffee, you can put me to the test.'

Jo was surprisingly understanding.

'I thought you'd be mad as hell. Why the change of heart?' asked Rahim.

Jo told him about her wedding plans and how her father had reacted.

'I've asked David, Helen's father, to give me away and he's agreed. You see, I would fight tooth and nail for Sam if I had to. Maybe I was being naïve before, or maybe I'm naïve now, it depends which way you want to look at it. Does love conquer all or is that just dangerous sentimentality? There's only one way to find out.'

'At the moment I'm waiting for Dad to agree to the girls meeting Helen.'

'Oh God, Rahim, I wouldn't want to be your shoes or Helen's for that matter, it's a lot to ask of her.'

'It's a risk I have to take.'

18 HELEN IS IN FOR A SURPRISE!

Josie was in the kitchen when the phone rang. She recognised the soft silky tones immediately.

'Hi Rahim, how are you?' She had never met him but she had become accustomed to his voice, his casual ease.

'Hi, Josie, I'm fine. What are you up to? Kids keeping you busy?'

'Tell me about it. It's non-stop from morning till night; don't know what I would do without Helen.'

'I can imagine.' Thankfully, she couldn't see his face when he grimaced at the thought that she might well have to do without Helen.

'Shall I get her for you?' asked Josie after chatting for a few minutes.

'If you don't mind.' The palms of his hands were moist, there were palpitations in his chest and his mouth dried up.

'Rahim!' said Helen. 'It seems like an age since we last spoke. I've missed you so much, it's been almost unbearable.'

'I've missed you too. Being without you has been ten times worse since I came back from Canada. I haven't been able to stop thinking about you.'

Earlier that day, Rahim had driven into town for a haircut. He'd chosen his outfit carefully; he wanted to reassure himself that he was worth taking a chance on. How could he speak to Helen whilst feeling worthless and empty? How could he expect her to love him when he didn't love himself?

'I wish I could reach down the phone to you,' said Helen. Since the Canadian trip she'd dreamt about him day and night, living out scenes in her head. She had imagined meeting his parents and family, had fantasised about being the perfect daughter-in-law, and had watched as they proudly presented her to their community.

'Listen, I've had some long discussions - first with my sisters and then with my parents - and they've said they would like to meet you.'

'What? How?' She could barely comprehend what he was saying. 'What did you say to your parents and how did they react? What about your sisters, what did they say?'

Rahim described his talks with his parents but played down the horror with which they had initially reacted. He omitted that the first talks had broken down within a few minutes, and that at one point he had given up all hope of the prospect of marriage between the two of them? He told her about his last weekend at home, the one immediately after his family had visited him at The Vic. His parents had been much calmer and had agreed to allow Sofia and Safina to meet Helen if she ever returned from America.

'Helen, this is only the first step. You need to think long and hard about this. What if you come home and things don't work out? I have to be brutal and ask what you'll do if they still say no after meeting you. How will you cope with prejudice from other members of the family or community if they say yes, or what if it's the other way around and I'm not accepted by your family?'

'You've met my family and you know they like you.'

'But that was when it wasn't serious. I didn't pose any threat to them then. They might not be so open and friendly if they think it's for good.'

'That's not true. I know how they feel about Jo and her family. When they first met there were no other Asians apart from Jo's dad, and my parents accepted him without question.'

'But he wasn't directly affecting your family. This is different. How will they react when you tell them that we intend to have my parents and my sisters living with us? There are so many things to think about, Helen. What if we're lucky enough to have children? How do we address the problem of religion? My mum has probably already dreamt about taking them to mosque with her.'

'Stop!' shouted Helen. 'Please don't say any more.'

'I just want you to put a lot of thought into all of these things before you decide whether or not to come home. You have to know exactly what you're getting into and what you're taking on - it's a mammoth task we're setting ourselves. At least acknowledge that.'

Helen agreed, although deep down she held an unshakable belief that she could make this work. She was determined to do everything she could to be accepted, not only into their family, but also into their society. She loved Rahim so much that she would do anything to be able to spend the rest of her life with him. She phoned Jo to tell her about her plans.

'Are you sure about this?' asked Jo.

'I'm so excited! I know you're worried and I do understand why, but I love him so much. I'll regret it for the rest of my life if I don't give it a try.'

'I don't know what to say. I'm pleased for you, but I'm petrified as well. I'm scared that it'll all end in tears.'

'It won't.'

'Nothing I say will change your mind?'

'Nothing.'

'In that case - when do you think you'll be back? I can't wait to see you.'

'I'll let you know as soon as I've booked the flights. See you soon!'

§

Phil stared out of the window.

'Do you have to go?'

'I'm sorry Phil, really I am. I didn't mean to hurt you. I honestly thought I would be staying here for a long time, if not for good.'

'It's not your fault; I know how you feel about him. I just hoped if I didn't rush things, you'd eventually get over him.'

Helen took hold of his hand. His eyes glistened with moisture, making them look so dark and sad. 'I'm so sorry.'

He lifted her hand and held it to his face, turned his head and kissed her palm tenderly. Moving closer he pulled her to him and held her, gently rocking to and fro, and she responded warmly. It was only now that she understood her true feelings for him, but even so it was still Rahim she yearned for.

§

Jamal prayed to Allah to give him guidance. He spent hours in his room in solitary confinement. He needed to be alone to weigh up the pros and cons of what Rahim was asking of them as a family and to consider in detail this meeting between the girls and Helen.

Fatima also prayed - and cooked. Cooking kept her busy and it dulled the pain and made her feel useful. She prepared all of her husband's favourite dishes in the hope of providing comfort and strength of mind for him so that he would come to the right decision. She also sought comfort at the mosque, feeling the need to listen and assess the mood of the community, and yet this was peculiar too.

She needed to hear the latest gossip in the hope that, should their story be leaked, some other event might draw attention away from them; not a word did she utter about her own predicament. She wouldn't have been able to bear to hear the exclamations, or for them to look down on her as she knew they would. She felt like a fugitive harbouring a dark secret, scared that someone could read her thoughts or see from her face that something was amiss.

Rahim arrived home and greeted his father cautiously.

'How are you?'

'I'm very well, Rahim. Tonight your mother and I are going to the mosque and I would like you to join us.'

In the past, Rahim had been excused from going to mosque on the grounds that he was studying. But he knew that, in the years to come, when he was considered head of the family, his presence would be compulsory. He dressed for the occasion in a dark blue suit, complete with a bright yellow tie, to assert himself and show that he could play a part in his community and yet still be integrated into the Western world. He wanted to be seen as a modern Muslim, different from the others.

The men gathered in the big hall in two groups. The elders sat huddled together by the wall to discuss the successes of their children while the younger ones congregated in the middle of the room to discuss business.

A large, bald-headed man gestured with his hands for attention then relaxed back into his chair with a smug grin on his face, interlocking his fingers across his chest like a Buddha.

'My son is now a top lawyer working in London,' he told them. 'The other lawyers have a great deal of respect for him. He owns a flat in Hampstead and he is doing very well.'

'You must be very pleased,' congratulated an equally large man next to him. 'My eldest son is an accountant; he is earning so much money that he goes on holiday four or five times a year. He has a Mercedes and a BMW. He will be getting married soon and then we shall live with him.'

A small wiry man with greased-back hair stuck out his chest: 'My daughter has just qualified as a doctor. Her fiancé is a very accomplished surgeon. We're so proud of her.'

Jamal kept quiet. He imagined what would happen if he came forward and announced: 'My son is going to marry an English girl, and she's going to live with us, and we're so happy.' He could hear it now, the sharp intake of breath, followed by stunned silence. The men would be angry with him initially for being spineless and allowing it to happen, but ultimately they would pity him and this was what he couldn't bear. He hated the thought of them gossiping and saying: 'Poor Jamal, he has an English daughter-in-law, how awful that must be for him.' For now though, he could relax, because hopefully the situation would be resolved, and he would never have to say those words or face the humiliation.

The younger men stood, hands in pockets, nodding in agreement or shaking their heads. One or two led the conversation.

'Luckily, we bought our property before interest rates went up,' said Mo, a handsome young man of around thirty. He wore an expensive Armani suit and a Rolex watch. 'Lots of people have ended up with negative equity and I blame the government for encouraging people to try and get on the property ladder. It's all very well them buying council houses, but then at the first sign of trouble, what happens? They don't have the money to pay the mortgage and the house is repossessed.'

'You can't blame the government for everything that goes wrong,' said a young man called Yousef. 'People are greedy; they shouldn't take on too big a mortgage if they can't handle an increase in the interest rate. It's a sorry state of affairs if you ask me.'

'How can you say that? You can't blame anyone for wanting to own their own home. If they're given a chance, then of course they're going to take it. Wouldn't you?'

Rahim kept out of the discussion. He wanted to be seen, but he didn't want to appear arrogant or opinionated. If he kept an air of dignity, it would be more difficult for them to ridicule him if and when the news finally got out.

Suddenly, from nowhere, a voice rang out.

'Rahim, how the hell are you? I haven't seen you for ages!'

It was Aziz, his old friend and ally - but Aziz mustn't be allowed to put his foot in it, in his usual style.

'Hi!' Rahim stepped in front of Aziz and pulled him to one side.

'What are you doing?'

'Sorry, Aziz. Whatever you do, please don't say a word about Helen. I'll tell you all about it later. How long are you home for?'

'Just a couple of days.'

'We could meet at yours afterwards and I'll explain.'

'OK.' Aziz straightened his jacket.

'Is Serina with you?' Rahim asked.

'She's talking to the other girls. I think you may be in luck, they keep glancing in your direction.'

Rahim was already aware of the attention he was getting. Serina stood among a group of around five or six girls, a stunning vision, which, absurdly, almost brought a tear to his eye. He had been to the mosque several times lately and enjoyed being among his friends and relatives. Tonight, seeing the girls dressed in their elegant saris with full jewellery and make-up made him feel good. He was home and it felt safe and comfortable. One girl in particular stood out. She was petite and very pretty. Her jet-black hair hung to her waist and its lustrous shine made him want to touch it. What caught his attention was her apparent shyness. She wasn't like the others. He could see she was listening intently to the conversation, adding a comment every so often, but on the whole she was restrained and appeared out of place. The others looked in his direction occasionally and giggled, but this girl paid no attention at all.

Serina was in deep discussion with a friend and hadn't noticed Rahim so he made his excuses to Aziz and seized the chance to escape, making a beeline for his mother, who, along with her friends, was giving out orders to the young girls as they laid out the food. It was noisy and chaotic and he wondered how Helen would cope with the mayhem.

Rahim saw his aunt, who was Fatima's sister-in-law, and called out to her. 'Mami!'

'Rahim!' she exclaimed. She planted a kiss on one cheek and grabbed hold of the other one too hard. 'How are you? Look at you; you've lost so much weight. Don't you eat when you're away?'

'Mami, you're exaggerating again,' he said as he rubbed his sore cheek. She went to take hold of the other one but he dodged backwards like a featherweight boxer. 'Oh no, you don't! I'm fine, honestly. What about you - are you well? Working hard? It's about time that husband of yours got a housekeeper for you.'

'I live in hope,' she laughed. 'Come, sit down and eat this.' She handed him a plate piled high with food.

Rahim shovelled up a big forkful and Fatima looked on dotingly as he ate. She was so proud of him and his achievements, but if he went through with the ridiculous notion that he could marry an English girl, then everything would change. A dark cloud settled on the horizon. She couldn't imagine how this girl would fit into their lives and she knew that they would never be able to bring her to this type of gathering. Deep ridges formed on Fatima's brow and she shuddered.

'You all right, Fatima?' asked Mami. 'You look very worried.'

Fatima forced a smile and Rahim looked at her questioningly.

'I'm fine. I felt a shiver but it's nothing.' But Rahim knew what she was thinking and felt a gnawing in the pit of his stomach.

Later that evening he met up with Aziz at his house.

'Auntie, no more food,' he protested, when Aziz's mother tried to entice him to eat. He slid down in his seat and stretched out fully to get comfortable. 'You have no idea how much I've eaten today.'

'You seem on edge,' said Aziz, once they were alone.

'I've asked my parents to meet Helen with a view to us marrying and her living with us.'

'You must be crazy. She'll be eaten alive.'

'I'm not at all sure to be honest, but I can't bear the thought of being without her. The idea is that Helen will come home and meet Sofia and Safina first.'

'God, Rahim, stop now. Don't take this any further. This is my fault. When I introduced you two I didn't think it would lead to this. It was only meant to be a bit of fun.'

'It's not your fault.'

'What if it doesn't work out? Where does that leave you, or more importantly - where does it leave Helen?'

'I think you know that my parents will always come first.'

'Poor Helen.' Aziz sat tight-lipped and frowning.

'I know, but my parents have nothing. They're relying on me to safeguard their future. What am I supposed to do?'

'Marry an Indian girl; there are lots to choose from and it'll be much simpler.'

'I thought you liked Helen.'

'I love Helen but sometimes you have to be cruel to be kind.'

'I don't know which way to turn.'

'Didn't you see all the young girls there tonight, some gorgeous ones too?' His voice had raised an octave or two in frustration. 'They were all trying to get your attention.'

The pretty girl sprang to mind. Of all the girls, she was the one Rahim would have liked to get to know even though she hadn't shown any interest.

'Don't tell me you didn't notice them,' said Aziz.

'I have to see what happens with Helen. I have to give it a chance.'

'Life is difficult enough without looking for trouble.' Aziz gave a deep sigh.

§

Rahim parked his car on the drive and let himself into the house. Music blared loudly from one of the girl's bedrooms. He hadn't been home for a while and was exhausted after another busy week at The Vic, followed by a long drive home for the weekend. He made a cup of tea and trudged upstairs to the lounge.

'Hey, Safina, turn it down a bit!' he shouted. He dropped down onto the sofa, switched on the television and took a big slurp of his tea.

Within a few minutes he was sleeping soundly.

'Rahim, you're going to scald yourself!' Safina took the cup that perched precariously on the arm of the sofa, and placed it on the coffee table.

'What?' He was still half asleep.

'I want you to meet my friend Mina. We met at college and then realised that her parents knew Mum and Dad from mosque.'

Rahim struggled into an upright position and tried to focus on Safina's face. In the background he was aware of someone else who looked familiar. Rubbing his eyes he realised it was the girl he had seen at mosque.

Mina smiled. 'Hi.'

'Hi,' said Rahim. 'Sorry, I must have dozed off.'

'Wanna come out for a drink with us?' asked Safina. 'You can pay.'

Mina was quite a few years younger than Rahim. She was studying fashion design and still lived with her parents. She wasn't as shy as he'd imagined and the three of them chatted easily about college and who they knew at the mosque, but what Rahim enjoyed most of all was the fact that they were speaking in their own language. It transpired that her family were also from Kenya and had lived in a village only a mile or so away from them.

Despite being worn out, he agreed to go to a nightclub with them. When they arrived, the place was heaving with people, all squashed together. It was very hot and the music was loud, so Rahim and the girls bought some drinks and found a less crowded place to stand. Safina and Mina spent most of their time on the dance floor, only coming back for a slurp of their drinks. Rahim yawned occasionally and watched as the people came and went.

Towards the end of the evening, Mina took him by the hand to a space on the dance floor just big enough for the two of them to sway together to the music. He tried to speak but it was too noisy and, as Mina leaned in closer to hear what he was saying, a drunken man slammed into them, forcing her into Rahim's arms where they held onto each other until she was steady again. Rahim pulled back a little to look at her and check she was all right. He could feel the warmth of her body next to his, and her hair, soft and silky, was entwined around his fingers. She looked up at him and smiled. Her eyes sparkled in the dim light, and Rahim placed his lips on hers. He wrapped his arms around her so that their bodies were pressed together and he could feel the soft mounds of her breasts against him. Mina responded and when they eventually parted, he was left breathless and tingling. He thought back to the first time he saw her at mosque and remembered why she had attracted him in the first place. As they made their way back to his sister, he bowed his head so that he didn't have to meet Safina's gaze.

The following day, he woke just before lunch and crawled downstairs. Safina was in the kitchen nursing a sore head.

'A little too much to drink?'

'You can say that again. I've already had an earful off Dad.'

'I've told you not to let him see you like this. He worries himself silly about you and Sofia. Was Mina drunk too?'

'She's much more sensible, but she can't be that sensible, she's got a bit of a crush.'

'On who?'

'Who do you think?'

'Don't be daft.' Rahim started to laugh.

'You seemed to think she was all right last night.'

'Yeah well, I'd had a few to drink, hadn't I?'

'I can't believe you just said that. That's so typical of a man to blame it on the booze.'

'I didn't mean it. You're right she's nice, but I...'

'Why don't you ask her out?' asked Safina, before he could finish his sentence.

'What? What about Helen?'

'Mina's really good fun as well as being pretty, and Mum and Dad would approve.'

'I know all that, but you know how I feel about Helen. I thought you were keen to meet her.'

'I am, but you've got to admit, Mina would be ideal, and a much easier option. Don't you like her?'

'Yeah...but...'

'Just take her out once and see what happens.'

'I suppose I could, but Helen's making plans to come home.'

'It's still not too late.'

Rahim agreed to ask Mina out, but two weeks down the line he still couldn't bring himself to do it. He tried to convince himself that it wouldn't do any harm, and might give him a chance to prove that Helen was the only one for him. But, no matter how hard he tried, he wasn't able to pluck up the courage and eventually Mina lost interest.

Six months had passed since Helen had arrived back from America. It had been heart-wrenching to leaving Josie and the family. The children had come to mean so much to her. Martin was only a baby. His toothless grin was so comical, and she would miss Darcy with her big blue eyes and golden curls that bobbed about as she ran and skipped. Kristen was the eldest and was so mature and ladylike at eleven years old, and then there was Stephen, the master of practical jokes, who never missed an opportunity to catch Helen out. Josie had become much more than an employer; she was a friend and confidante. They went shopping together and sometimes to the cinema, or, in the evening when Sean was busy, they would sit and talk over a glass of wine.

Despite all this, and the fact that she and Richard had both cried when they parted at the airport, Helen was still willing to give up everything to meet Rahim's family. She had spent hours daydreaming about meeting them. She could see herself chatting with his sisters, helping out in the kitchen and eating with the whole family. She had wanted to learn about their culture as she had with Jo's father, and now it was to become a reality.

When Rahim had phoned to say that he was moving back home and that his parents were happy to meet her (although 'happy' probably wasn't the most truthful way to put it), she had immediately begun planning. She needed a job; it would be a long time before she got another chance of being a ward sister so she decided to do something different. She would follow in her mother's footsteps and train to be a midwife. She applied to the maternity unit where her mother worked and was accepted without much difficulty. Everyone loved Elizabeth; Helen just hoped she could live up to her reputation. Two long months elapsed before Helen finally moved back in with her parents.

§

Helen sat at her dressing-table mirror. Turning her head from side-to-side, she examined the effects of the darker colour on her cheeks. Using a thick pad of cotton wool, she wiped off the foundation she had applied only a few minutes earlier. She would never normally wear full face make-up, but today she was worried that she would look pale and pasty alongside Rahim's sisters. She had seen photographs and knew that they were very pretty. How could she compete? How could she prove to them that she was worth the risk? Resting her elbows on the table, she cupped her face in her hands and sighed. What if they didn't like her? So much was at stake, her whole future rested on this meeting.

They had arranged to meet at two o'clock in a café just down the road from where Helen lived. She had been getting ready for hours, but still felt hopelessly inadequate. She wasn't glamorous or beautiful, she had no real sense of style or fashion, and this was suddenly something she wished she had paid more attention to. Elizabeth and Karen were out and she had no-one to consult.

'If only Jo were here,' she thought, 'she would have helped me find something to wear and would have done my make-up.' But Jo was busy planning her wedding and had other things to think about.

Suddenly it was 1.45 and, whether she looked good or not, it was time to go. She put on her smart navy-blue shift dress, simple but sophisticated, slipped her feet into shiny black court shoes, ran down to the car and drove to the café.

Rahim's silver Golf was visible on the side of the road. She parked round the corner afraid they would watch as she tottered from the car and crossed the road. She made it to the café door and reached for the handle but it opened immediately and Rahim was before her, smiling.

'You look great.'

'Thank you.' Her voice quivered.

Sofia and Safina stood up to greet her. Helen grasped each one tentatively by the hand and said 'hello' with a slight nod of her head and a smile.

'I'm Safina. It's great to meet you.' Safina smiled warmly.

'And you too.'

'I'm Sofia.' Sofia was a little more reserved.

'Hi Sofia.'

'Would you like a drink?' asked Rahim.

'Yes please, could I have a coke?'

Helen wished she hadn't got so dressed-up for the occasion. Sofia and Safina wore casual jeans, topped with baggy T-shirts, and still they somehow managed to outshine her. For some absurd reason Helen had thought they would be wearing traditional dress.

Once the drinks arrived and they were sitting comfortably, Safina could no longer contain her excitement.

'So you want to marry my brother?'

'Safina!' said Sofia.

'It's OK,' Helen laughed. 'In answer to your question, I think we have a long way to go yet. Apparently I have to get you to like me, and I realise that's a lot to ask.'

Safina rubbed her hands together. She liked Helen's sense of humour. 'I think it's fantastic,' she said and Sofia kicked her under the table; too much too soon, no conversation as yet, and they were already onto the subject of marriage.

'You were in the States weren't you? What's it like being back?' asked Sofia in an effort to start right at the beginning.

Helen told them about her stay in Los Angeles. They couldn't believe the story about Constantine wearing the badge on her nightdress. As she spoke, Helen appraised the two sisters. They couldn't have been more different. Sofia had short hair and wore tiny round glasses and looked studious, and she asked all the questions. Safina was the bubbly one. She talked openly and giggled at recollections of when they were young.

'Do you remember when we first came to England and it was Christmas? We wanted to celebrate like all the other kids. So Mum sent Zara out to buy a basted turkey – but when she returned she was so upset. She had asked for a bastard turkey and the butcher had laughed so much that someone else had to serve her.'

Time went by all too quickly. Helen felt at ease with the girls. They had talked about so many things, and she had laughed with genuine amusement at the funny stories Safina told. Inevitably the conversation turned to the possibility of a meeting with Fatima and Jamal.

'I have to be honest with you, Helen,' said Sofia. 'I really like you, but I think the chances of you being accepted by Mum and Dad are pretty slim. Their beliefs and culture are so ingrained that it will be difficult to make them see things differently.'

Helen tried to keep the smile on her face.

'I understand what you're saying, but do you think they would agree to just one meeting?'

'I really don't know.'

'What do you think?' asked Rahim, looking at Safina.

'I would love to take you to meet them right now Helen, but that would be just the beginning. And there are all the others that we need to worry about.'

'Helen,' Sofia frowned. 'You don't know what you're getting yourself into. We've seen it so many times. An English girl marries into an Indian family and it only lasts a few months, maybe a year if they're lucky.'

Helen looked across at Rahim hoping for support.

'We'll talk later,' he said to Sofia. 'It's difficult for you two to say what you really feel with Helen present.'

Shortly after, Helen said her goodbyes and left them to discuss her future.

§

The four doors snapped shut almost simultaneously as each passenger jumped into the car.

'Where are we off to?' asked Helen.

Rahim and Nadim glanced back at her then grinned at one another slyly.

'Don't tell them until we're on the motorway and there's no turning back,' said Rahim.

'You'll have to wait to find out,' said Nadim.

'Tell us,' begged Helen. 'Are we going into the country for the day?' This was a reasonable supposition. They would often drive out into the country and go for a walk before stopping at a local pub for lunch and that morning the boys had phoned her and Amanda to say that they would be taking them on a 'mystery tour'. The instructions were to dress casual, but not too scruffy, and be ready for pickup at around twelve o' clock.

'You get them to tell us.' Helen nudged Amanda.

'Come on boys, you can tell us now that we're on our way,' said Amanda.

'Shall we tell them?' Nadim asked Rahim.

The car sped on smoothly and effortlessly, past caravans and Sunday drivers. Rahim, barely took his eyes off the road but he gave his friend a sideways nod.

'Put them out of their misery.'

Turning in his seat to watch the full impact of his words, Nadim drew in a large breath and held it momentarily. He spoke slowly.

'We are going to ...'

'For God's sake, get on with it,' said Amanda.

Nadim's eyes were on Helen.

'We're going to Rahim's house to have lunch with his parents.'

Helen stared at him in disbelief.

Amanda grabbed her hand. 'Oh, Helen,' she said. She looked at Nadim, 'are you joking?'

Nadim's face softened, his eyebrows lowered to their normal position, he squeezed his lips together and shook his head slowly. There was a twinkle in his eyes.

'Honest injun,' he said.

Helen's head flopped back, reverberating against the headrest. She closed her eyes and let out a sigh. There was nothing she could do to stop this; it had all been arranged secretly beforehand.

'A little warning would have been nice. I could have prepared myself. I've been dreading this and now you spring it on me.'

'Exactly!' said Rahim. 'You would have been in a right old state if I'd told you a week ago, I wouldn't have had a minute's peace.'

'Oh, Helen, I'm so excited for you, I think I'm just as nervous!' Amanda squeezed her hand.

'I feel sick,' said Helen. 'What do I say to them? How do I greet them? Oh God, Rahim, I'll kill you for this.' She leant forward to stop herself vomiting. Her stomach churned and her head was spinning frantically.

'You'll be fine,' said Amanda, 'they'll love you.'

'Oh God, oh God,' was all Helen could say.

The car turned off the motorway and hurtled along a busy main road. They passed through the main shopping area of a village. Rahim took a right turn, proceeded slowly for a hundred yards or so and then pulled up onto the drive of a modern town house.

Nadim swivelled in his seat, he grinned at Helen and patted her knee reassuringly. 'Don't worry, they won't bite you.'

Helen got out of the car and Rahim and Nadim were already on the footpath.

Rahim saw the look of terror in Helen's eyes. She hung back only to be pushed forward by a prod from Amanda. He took her hand in his.

'You OK? I didn't want you worrying for days. Amanda's right though, you'll be fine. Come on, hold my hand.'

As Rahim reached out to put his key in the lock, the door swung open and they were greeted by Safina, along with a waft of Asian spices.

'Hi, how are you?' She embraced Nadim. 'I haven't seen you for ages!'

'I'm fine,' said Nadim.

Over his shoulder, Safina searched out Helen who looked like a child on her first day at school. Safina's heart went out to her. Releasing Nadim from her embrace, she gave Rahim a peck on the cheek.

'OK?' she asked.

'I'm fine, thanks. You remember Amanda?'

Safina greeted Amanda then bounded towards Helen like a puppy without any coordination and stood on Helen's toes as she went to kiss her.

'Sorry, sorry,' she babbled. It was so exciting; she couldn't believe that her brother had brought an English girl home. What next?

'That's OK, don't worry,' laughed Helen, 'it's nice to see you again.'

The accommodation was arranged on three floors. The lower floor was taken up by a small cloakroom and a large kitchen-diner; on the first floor was a huge lounge, a bedroom and the house bathroom; and on the top floor were three further bedrooms. Rahim led the way and Helen turned to look behind her for reassurance, but, to her dismay, Nadim was pretending to have a rope around his neck and proceeded to make a hanging gesture. Amanda stifled a giggle and Helen jabbed him in the ribs with her elbow.

'Ouch! That hurt. I was only trying to make you laugh.'

She felt her chest tighten, her hands shook and her head was whirling.

'Rahim, I can't do this!' she whispered.

She pulled Rahim to one side away from the door.

'I can't do it. I'm sorry, but I'm too scared,' she was barely able to speak. 'I need time to think and prepare for it.'

He put his arm around her waist, took her down the side of the house out of view of the others and held her closely for a few seconds.

'Trust me, Helen, they'll be fine. Mum has cooked a meal for us all. Why would she do that if you weren't welcome?' He stroked her hair gently, trying to calm her.

'I'm sorry, you're right. It probably wouldn't have made any difference if you'd told me beforehand. I'd still have been petrified.'

'Take your time and follow me.'

She breathed in a lung-full of air through her nose and blew it out forcefully through pursed lips, the nausea wouldn't go away. She rounded the corner and stepped reluctantly over the threshold, clinging tightly to Rahim's hand. Amanda and Nadim followed.

Rahim's parents met them at the kitchen door. To Helen's surprise they looked as nervous as she was. Rahim let go of Helen's hand as if it were a red hot cinder.

'Hi, Mum, Dad, how are you?'

He kissed his mum on the cheek and gave her an affectionate hug as usual, and then respectfully squeezed his father's arm and gave an appreciative nod. Then he put his arm around Helen, being careful not to actually touch her, stepped back a little and urged her forward.

'This is Helen,' he said. 'Helen this is my mum, Fatima, and my dad, Jamal.'

Uncertain whether to shake hands or give a kiss, Helen did neither for fear of offending them. She bowed her head slightly and smiled.

'It's lovely to meet you.'

Sofia was in the kitchen, preparing a salad. Wiping her wet hands on a towel she greeted Helen warmly.

'Sorry about the wet hands.'

Helen's first impressions weren't wrong. She had taken an instant liking to both the girls. They were warm and friendly and had offered to help Rahim smooth the way where his parents were concerned.

Nadim burst through. 'Auntie, how are you? Great to see you and you're looking so well!' He planted a kiss on Fatima's cheek and gave her a playful bear hug leaving her flustered but laughing. He turned towards Jamal.

'Uncle, it's been a long time! How are you?'

'I'm very well, thank you. Come in and sit down.' Jamal shuffled to one side. He couldn't look Helen in the eye and kept his head bowed, busy pulling out chairs and making them all comfortable.

For once, Helen was grateful to Nadim for dominating the conversation. He rambled on, laughing and joking and impressing Rahim's parents with his story-telling, and Helen allowed herself a surreptitious glance around the room. It was a modest house, homely and comfortable but in no way extravagant. She thought of how they had been thrown out of Uganda and lost all their belongings. Turning her attention back to the conversation, she focussed on Fatima and Jamal, who had obviously gone to great lengths to make them feel welcome. The table was carefully laid for eight people; in the centre were several small bowls, each containing different coloured accompaniments that intrigued her. On the cooker were four pans, each with its contents yet to be revealed. Apart from the curry that Janaice made, Helen had never had authentic Indian food before and her taste buds tingled impatiently.

'Do you like Indian food?' It was as though Fatima had read her mind.

'I do - very much. I love it actually.'

From the opposite side of the table Nadim winked and smiled and Helen smiled back and closed her eyes in order to relax. When she opened them again, Rahim was sitting beside her.

'OK?' he whispered.

She nodded, not wanting to attract attention.

The food was delicious; lamb bathed in a luscious red sauce, lentils steeped in spices, and aubergine cooked almost to a pulp. Was it really possible that she was sitting at a table surrounded by Rahim's family, eating food prepared by his mother and talking to his father? This was a scenario that only a few months ago would have seemed impossible.

By now, Amanda was totally relaxed and she too was fascinated by the food. She was an excellent cook and wanted to know how it had all been put together.

'Is this a piece of cinnamon?' she asked, pulling what looked like a twig out of her mouth.

Fatima couldn't hide her amusement and smiled. 'Yes, I should have warned you to look out for whole spices; there are some cardamom pods as well. If you chew one of those they have a really strong flavour.'

'I think I just did,' said Amanda screwing her face up. 'What else do you use?'

Fatima recited the ingredients and laughed when Amanda asked what curry powder she bought.

'I don't use curry powder, it's only the English who use that.' Realising what she had said, Fatima looked at Rahim. She didn't want him to think she was being rude.

Rahim laughed: 'You'll never find anything like that in Mum's cupboard. Everything is made from scratch, none of your ready-made stuff.'

Helen plucked up courage: 'Sofia, do you or Safina cook?'

'Sometimes, but cooking Indian food is very hard work.'

'I do a mean beans on toast,' said Safina. Even Jamal laughed.

The conversation flowed easily and Helen began to wonder why she had been so uptight. After the meal, the women helped clear away the plates whilst Rahim, his father and Nadim sat and talked. It was strange being in

Rahim's home. She glanced over to where he was sitting as he listened to his father and she knew he was aware of her gaze. As their eyes met, he smiled knowingly; this was going much better than either of them had dared hope.

A while later, Rahim stood up.

'Thanks, Mum, that was fantastic, but we'll have to go - it's a long drive back.'

Amanda politely rubbed her bulging abdomen.

'That was fabulous, thank you very much. I've eaten so much that I don't think I'll need to eat for a week.'

'You're very welcome,' said Jamal.

Helen sat mesmerised, and for a moment she still couldn't believe that she was part of this scene.

'Helen!' said Rahim and gave her a shove.

Helen came round to find everyone laughing at her.

'Sorry, I was miles away.'

'You're telling me,' said Rahim. 'I shouted to you at least three times. We're about to leave. Are you ready?'

She struggled to regain her composure.

'Thank you so much for having us. It's been lovely meeting you.'

'You're very welcome,' smiled Fatima.

Jamal bowed his head.

'Bye.'

Helen sat in the front seat this time while Rahim drove. She rested her head back and closed her eyes. Rahim turned to her, an expression of relief and amusement on his face. Without a word he fired up the engine and reversed the car off the drive. Amanda and Nadim snuggled together in the back, satisfied that all was well. But they now had to wait for the outcome.

After only a few minutes, Rahim swerved the car into the car park of the Barley Corn Inn.

'Don't know about you lot, but I need a drink!'

'Me too,' said Amanda.

'Make mine a double!' said Helen.

'And me!' said Nadim.

Two glasses of white wine and two beers sat triumphantly on the circular table.

'I would like to propose a toast!' announced Nadim. 'Here's to the future, whatever it may hold!'

'You're being a little premature if you don't mind my saying so.' Rahim had seen the look in his father's eyes when they left.

'That's always been my problem,' said Nadim. 'But we can enjoy and celebrate each step of the way, and I said "whatever it may hold". I think a small miracle occurred today, I never would have believed this could happen. So here's to love, life and happiness!'

Rahim leaned forward and kissed Helen.

'You were amazing. I'm sorry for putting you through such an ordeal, I promise never to pull a stunt like that again.' He hugged her. 'It's early days, but I think they liked you.'

'To Helen and Rahim!' said Amanda. 'Make sure you get some good recipes.'

'All you have to do now is meet the relatives,' said Nadim, 'and the whole Asian community at mosque, and learn the Koran from cover to cover and...'

Helen choked on her wine.

'One step at a time please. I have one question though - how did you manage to convince them?'

Rahim could not tell her that he had promised that they would always be his priority - and that if everything went wrong and he had to choose, he would choose them.

'I told them that, no matter what happens, I'll make sure they're well looked after.'

Meanwhile, Jamal sat at the kitchen table leaning on one elbow.

'This is going to be very bad for us Fatima, as I've said before, it will bring trouble and shame.'

Fatima gripped her prayer beads tighter.

'You don't know that, Jamal. She seems like a nice girl.'

'It's not right. We have to tell Rahim that it will never work.'

'Please, Jamal, give it some time, you might get to like her.'

'We shouldn't encourage this. They must see that it can never work.'

Fatima went to her room and prayed. She prayed that Helen would realise that she could never be one of them and that this was not what they wanted for their son.

20 THE PROSPECTIVE DAUGHTER-IN-LAW

Time went by quickly. Helen was well into her midwifery training and enjoying every minute of it. The wonder of a baby, emerging all shiny and wet, never ceased to amaze her. She had so many questions she wanted to ask: how the contractions knew when to stop, how the baby knew to take that all-important first breath, how did such a huge thing emerge out of such a tiny opening? She wondered how she herself would cope with pregnancy and childbirth.

'Go on, push! It's coming! Just one more push!' She found the whole process exciting and she would bear down along with the mother in an effort to expedite delivery.

'You're so lucky,' said Jo. 'I would love to see a baby being born. When you have yours, can I come and watch?'

'Jo, I think you are much closer to childbirth than I am. God knows if I'll ever have children at this rate. Can you come over soon? There's so much I want to tell you.'

'Same here, but it's difficult at the moment, we're so busy organising everything for the wedding, and you've no idea how much it costs. I'm working extra shifts to help pay for it all.'

Jo loved to hear about Helen's job and her visits to Rahim and his family but she was still worried and wished that Helen had stayed in America.

Helen enjoyed living at home again; in many respects it was as if she had gone back in time. There was only Karen left, but they sat around the table together in the evening and chatted like in the old days. The house was comforting. In winter, the wood-burning stove in the kitchen churned out a stream of heat that spiralled under the door and crept up the stairs leaving a charcoal smell that Helen adored. She was back in her old enormous bedroom too; the one that at one time had housed three of them. As each of them left home, the next in line would move to the smaller single bedroom. It seemed strange that here she was rattling around in the big bedroom by herself. Karen, who had moved into the smaller room because it was cosier, would come and sleep in one of the other beds, and they would chat till the early hours of the morning.

'Go to sleep now.'

'First one to talk smells,' said Karen. It was a game they had played as children, the three of them in one room, when it was difficult to get any sleep at all.

David was still working to get the house finished, rubbing down the wooden window frames, painting doors and decorating, but because the results were never quite perfect, he would start afresh and rub it all down again. It was painful to watch him. One day he was happy, whistling as he worked with nothing seemingly bothering him; other days he could barely get out of bed. He often wondered what it would be like to enter the black hole and never be seen again, but then he would get angry that he didn't have the courage to explore it. He told himself that his family would be better off without him.

Now that Helen was home again, David convinced himself that family life would return to how it had been back in the old days, but that could not happen of course. Helen was not the little girl who had left home a few years ago. Even Karen had her own life now, despite still being at home. They were both his daughters and he loved them dearly, but he found it hard to accept that they were no longer dependent on him. A battle raged inside him, threatening to turn him inside out and rip him apart.

'Mum! Dad! I'm off!' Helen shouted up the stairs. She was going to Manchester.

'Drive carefully,' David called from the landing. 'We'll be going to bed soon, see you in the morning.'

'That's good,' thought Helen, 'he's in a good mood again today.' It was lovely to see him back to his old self, laughing and joking and up to his old tricks. Last week, Helen had complained that the breakfast cereal in the cupboard was boring so she went out and bought her favourite one. David secretly took out the inside packet and replaced it with the boring one. He then sat quietly, trying not to laugh, when Helen poured her breakfast cereal into the bowl.

§

Since Helen's first meeting with Rahim's family, she had been back many times in an effort to get to know them. His sisters were fun and she loved them. Sometimes they would take her and Rahim to nightclubs in town. At one club that Safina regularly frequented, the queue was enormous and she pushed her way forward and asked the bouncers to let them in without having to wait.

'I've brought my brother,' she whispered.

'OK, no problem,' the bouncer replied but, when Rahim approached, the same bouncer put out an arm to stop him.

'Sorry, mate, we only let a certain type in here.'

'What?'

'This is my brother,' said Safina. 'He's not very trendy but he's OK.'

The bouncer waved him through.

'Sorry, mate, go ahead.'

'What was all that about?' asked Rahim.

'He probably thought you were the CID come to spy on them.'

Rahim enjoyed being with his sisters. It was strange, because he felt so protective towards them and yet, since he had moved back home, the roles had reversed and it was them looking after him. They also looked after Helen, and Rahim loved to see that.

'Helen, Mum asked me to tell you not to stir the rice, because it breaks it up.' Sofia was making chutney from fresh coriander and green chillies. She talked Helen through it as she prepared the ingredients. 'Just put it all in the blender together. Put plenty of lemon juice in with it and you'll love it.'

'What's this? It stinks.'

'It's Dad's favourite, I don't know what it's called, but it's a vegetable and it has a really strong sour taste and smell.'

Helen was learning so much but she was struck by Fatima's preoccupation with cooking. She was a good student, she was attentive and anticipated what was needed, chopping, stirring, frying and clearing-up when they'd finished, but it was hard work. At the weekends the two of them would spend the whole day in the kitchen, preparing and cooking the food and then the whole family would eat together.

'Why do you spend so much time cooking?' asked Helen.

'You have to make sure the men have good food. They work very hard and if we don't look after them, what will they do? They will complain and say that you are not a good wife.' Helen suppressed an urge to laugh but Fatima continued. 'On that day we first met, I could see you were a hard worker and Amanda wasn't.'

'Why was that?' asked Helen.

'I looked at your hands. Hers were very soft and smooth and yours weren't.'

Now Helen didn't know whether to laugh or cry.

'I've always worked hard,' she said, 'I enjoy it. I help out in the garden at home. When Dad prunes the trees I move the cuttings and put them in a pile or if he mows the lawn I help by emptying the grass box for him.' She turned away and smiled to herself and thought: 'Hand cream, that's what I need to buy.'

Helen and Fatima became friends. After dinner, they would sit in the kitchen and chat for an hour or so. This was a new world for Helen despite having grown up with Jo. In Jo's house only her father was Asian; in Rahim's house only Helen was English. Everything was new - smells, sights, the language, the people and the clothes and she loved it.

She wasn't doing so well with Jamal, however. He seldom looked at her and never joined in any conversation. He would often disappear to his room when Helen arrived and stay there praying. He could find no fault with her, but she wasn't what he wanted for his son or his family.

'How long have I been coming to your house?' Helen asked Rahim.

'About three months. Why?'

'Your dad doesn't speak to me. He does all he can to avoid being in the same room.'

'I noticed - I was hoping that he would come round in his own time. I'll talk to him.'

'Don't worry, I'll sort it out myself. I know what to do.'

Helen popped her head around the sitting room door where Jamal had settled comfortably into his favourite chair.

'Would you like a cup of tea?' she asked.

Jamal shifted uncomfortably.

'Yes please - if you don't mind.'

Jamal had asked Sofia to collect a prescription for him from the chemist.

'I'll go,' said Helen, 'it's no problem; I'm going into town anyway.'

When Fatima and Jamal were going to visit their friends, it was Helen who offered to take them.

'Don't worry. I'll drop you a few doors away so that it doesn't raise any questions for you.'

Jamal and Fatima still hadn't told anyone about Helen. Jamal prayed to Allah for guidance. He worried what would happen to his family if it didn't work out. It was one thing to have Helen coming round to the house, but another to have her with them permanently as a daughter-in-law. She was, and always would be, English.

Helen did as much as she could for Jamal, bringing cups of tea or newspapers, making phone calls to the doctor for him. He began to take notice and, before long, Helen was sitting with him to watch Indian films, chatting away happily. Sofia and Safina were incredulous. They could not believe the transformation in their father.

'Have you seen how Dad is with Helen?' Safina asked Rahim.

'It's unbelievable.'

'Mind you, she does a lot.'

'Do you think everything will work out eventually?'

'It's too early to say. We have a long way to go; we have yet to make it public knowledge. Introducing her to Mama and Mami won't be easy.' Rahim winced at the thought.

The name 'mama' referred to an uncle on the mother's side of the family and Mama was Fatima's brother, 'Mami' was the name given to a 'mama's wife. Mama was a formidable character, a businessman with firm ideas, who stuck to his culture and traditions. He would never tolerate one of his children marrying outside the religion.

'Maybe we should do it soon,' said Safina. 'And we also have to introduce Mum and Dad to Helen's parents.'

§

'What do you think about these for the tables?' asked Jo pointing to a picture of exquisitely packaged almonds in her magazine.

Sam wasn't paying much attention.

'Why do we have to have those?'

'They're called "favours". It's a way of thanking the wedding guests for attending.'

'We're spending a fortune feeding them. Shouldn't they be thanking us for inviting them?'

'Don't be so callous, it's a nice touch and they'll look lovely. Look at them.' She pushed the magazine under his nose.

'I'd rather look at your almonds instead,' said Sam and eyed up Jo's bosoms that were anything but almond-sized.

'You have a guest,' said Helen.

'Honestly, he's incorrigible.'

Sam grinned. 'What does that mean?'

'It means you're hopeless!' said Jo and laughed. She closed the magazine and jumped on top of him, playfully pummelling his chest with her fists. With help from Helen, she had planned every minute detail of the wedding. She wanted it to be a perfect day for everyone, not just themselves. Helen was to be a bridesmaid along with Jo's younger sister.

'I wonder if David's written his speech yet,' said Jo after Helen had left.

'If mine is anything to go by, the answer is no,' said Sam. 'Everything I put down on paper just sounds daft when I read it back. Can't you do one instead?'

'It's my job to look demure and blush appropriately. I'll ring him and ask.'

Elizabeth answered the phone.

'I wanted to find out how far David has got with his speech. Sam is having problems with his.'

'He hasn't been able to start it, Jo. We've had a terrible week,' said Elizabeth. 'Every day has been awful.'

'Oh dear.'

'He's been either really agitated, storming round the house grumbling about everything, or else completely subdued and won't even get out of bed.'

'Poor David. And what about you, how are you coping?'

'I stay out of his way most of the time. I'm in the background in case he decides to do anything stupid.'

Jo now knew what that meant; code for suicide, something that David talked about quite openly. He appeared to see it as an easy option, almost an everyday occurrence.

'Is there anything I can do?' asked Jo.

'I'm afraid not, but please don't worry about the speech. If worst comes to worst I'll write it for him. I'm sure he'll be all right on the day. He's been so well for such a long time that this has come as a bit of a shock.'

'I wish I could help.'

'He's a lovely man, but this ... thing ... gets hold of him and he becomes someone that I hardly know. Anyway, you don't want to listen to me rattling on. I'm sure he'll be there for you on the day. He is very proud that he'll be giving you away. How's your mum? Is she looking forward to it?'

'I think she'll be glad when it's all over to be honest. It's difficult for her; Dad won't even talk about it. Elizabeth, please tell David he doesn't have to do a speech if it's a problem. I'll be happy for him to just walk me up the aisle.'

'He'll be fine, I promise.'

But Elizabeth was out of her mind with worry. What if he wasn't well enough to give Jo away, or even if he was, what if he couldn't stand up and speak? In truth, David had fretted for hours on end and made hundreds of attempts to write a speech but couldn't seem to find the right words. He screwed up the bits of paper and threw them in the bin.

'I'm not going to bother writing it out,' he said.

'But what if you can't think of anything to say? That would be terrible, not to mention how disappointing it would be for Jo and Sam.'

'I don't have to drone on and on for hours. All I need to say is what an honour it is and all that sort of stuff.' He threw the pad of clean paper into the bin as well.

21 MR AND MRS S GARSTON

Saturday October 12th 1985; the doorbell rang for the tenth time.

'Karen! Can you get that?' shouted Helen.

'Suppose I'll have to,' Karen muttered. 'Get this, do that, go here, ring such a body.'

She opened the door and came face-to-face with Janice and Jo's sister, closely followed by the florist.

Karen hugged Janice.

'Morning, how are you two?'

'We're fine - and you?'

'A harmless drudge - I'm OK. Jo's upstairs in my room if you want to go up.'

'Morning, lovely day for a wedding,' said the florist. 'Where would you like the flowers?'

'Tempting', thought Karen, but she forced a smile: 'You can put them in the kitchen if you don't mind. Do you need a hand?'

Karen went out to the florist's car and helped bring in the freshly-made bouquets. Jo's was made up of cream freesias and tiny pink roses interlaced with variegated ivy. Each bridesmaid had a similar bouquet, but on a smaller scale and without the dangly bits. There were corsages by the dozen, sufficient for Karen to wonder if Jo had miscounted. The shrill of the telephone in the hallway startled her.

'Karen!' shouted Helen.

'Yes, I know - can I get the phone?' It was only ten-thirty, the wedding was not till two and already she'd had enough. The house was in chaos with dresses hung on every door: a wedding dress, a going-away dress, bridesmaids' dresses, mother's outfit and 'adopted' mother's outfit. Helen was in a total flap and Jo was even worse.

'Remind me not to get married,' Karen told Elizabeth as she reached for the receiver, 'or if I do I'll go to Gretna Green.'

'Hello,' she sighed.

'Dear me, you sound fed up.'

'Hi, Sam.' She tried to sound a little more upbeat. 'I'm fine - you know what it's like on these occasions, everything's a major trauma, and everyone's on the ceiling.'

'So, all normal then. How's David? Is he coping?'

'Know what? He's the only one who's being sensible and he seems happy enough. I think he's keeping out of the way till everyone's gone off to the church and there'll be just him and Jo left here. He's been so poorly, Sam, but he's going to be OK, he'll do her proud.' Karen couldn't finish, tears welled in her eyes and the words choked in her throat.

'It's OK. I know this is a big thing for all of you. I'll let you all get on and I'll see you later. Give everyone my love.'

Karen nodded, hoping that though Sam couldn't see her, he would understand. She hid herself away and cried openly for a few minutes. Her father giving Jo away was going to be an enormous challenge, and she knew that it would take all the courage and strength he could muster to hold it together for the day.

§

A cup of tea was placed carefully on the bedside table. David lay stretched out on the bed staring into space. He turned to Elizabeth and forced a smile. 'Thanks, love.'

'You all right?'

'Yes - but I need time to get my thoughts together.'

He didn't say that his heart was hammering at his chest wall and that his head was pounding. He knew that today was important, not just for Jo, but for him and his family too.

'Keep calm,' he told himself. 'Stop being a fool, you're behaving like a child.'

But beneath the surface, panic threatened to possess him and destroy all his efforts. 'They're all depending on you, you can't let them down,' the voice inside his head said. The voice persisted: 'Why are you bothering? They're better off without you! You'll look ridiculous and you'll be an embarrassment!' Beads of sweat formed on his upper lip and he suddenly sat bolt upright.

'David! What's the matter?' said Elizabeth.

He stood up and swiped his arm across his mouth absorbing the sweat into the sleeve of his dressing gown.

'I didn't realise the time,' he lied. 'I need to get ready.'

'The flowers have arrived. Shall I pin yours onto your jacket?'

He headed for the bathroom.

'Yes please. Is Jo all right? I'm sorry I can't go out there and join in, but there's too much happening. It's been like bedlam. Helen was almost hysterical because she couldn't get into the bathroom.'

'No-one's expecting you to do anything, just relax.'

'I'll have my bath now.'

'Do you want me to make some notes for your speech?' She was more concerned than ever that he would clam up and forget what he wanted to say. He still hadn't prepared anything. She had even prepared her own version in case he went to pieces but had not dared write it down in case he saw it.

'Stop going on about the damn speech, I've made a few notes, that's all I need!'

She backed off as she always did when he got annoyed. The past few weeks had been difficult. It wasn't that long ago that he had sat at the dinner table with the family and told them how well he felt, and now, here he was, again battling with the old demons.

It was a beautiful sunny day with the slightest hint of a breeze. The branches of the trees swayed and the blackbirds, robins and sparrows twittered happily providing a cheery descant as they went about their business. The house was peaceful now. Elizabeth, Janice and the bridesmaids had left, heading in convoy for the church. Only the soft purr of the Rolls-Royce waiting at the door interrupted David's thoughts. He drew in a long slow breath and filled his lungs to capacity, slowly releasing it in the hope of expelling all the tension that had built up. From the foot of the stairs he heard the rustle of silken layers and Jo's soft footsteps as she made her descent.

'I was coming to get you,' he said.

Jo emerged like a butterfly from a chrysalis and his heart melted. In that instant he knew that, even though he had played no part in her creation, nor been there at her birth, nothing in this world could bring them closer than they were at this moment.

Jo hovered in the big hallway, radiant as an angel. He swallowed hard.

'Jo, you look beautiful.'

He held her hands in his; they were so tiny, he thought he might accidentally crush them.

'I never thought that I'd have this privilege. You've always been like a daughter to us and to me, you've always been very special; so kind and gentle and funny. You spent so much time here with us and yet we hardly noticed because you just fitted in as though you were one of us.'

Jo managed a smile; she knew that she mustn't cry.

'I loved it here,' she said. 'I felt so happy and relaxed.'

A sudden pang of guilt struck her heart; 'Don't get me wrong, I love my family too, but being able to come here when things got tough at home was what got me through and kept me going.'

'We'd better go.' He offered her his arm.

As they sat in the car, David's worries trickled from him like tiny grains of sand through an egg-timer. Nothing could faze him now; not the walk down the aisle, nor the dreaded speech. He had already done it twice before and, after today, he still had two more occasions like this to look forward to. He was lucky; some men never had this pleasure.

The church doors opened majestically, the organ cranked up and the guests fidgeted in anticipation. Elizabeth and Janice stood side-by-side in the front pews. They glanced at each other and clasped each other's hands momentarily. Elizabeth closed her eyes and secretly prayed. Sam, meanwhile, couldn't resist a sneaky peak at Jo. She looked a vision and appeared to glide, arm-in-arm with David, towards him. The bridesmaids made him think of freshly-picked daisies, clean, petite and perfect. A boyish grin spread across his face and he turned back to the altar to await his bride. He closed his eyes and quietly thanked God for this special day.

Rahim admired the architecture of the old church. Ancient granite towered above him, softened only by the creaky timber beams and a kaleidoscope of colour that streamed through the glass. These were not windows in the usual sense, you couldn't see in or out through them, there were no openings to let in more air, and yet without them the old church would have no soul. One window in particular caught his attention; a scene depicting men and women going about their daily routines, a life long-forgotten, a child clinging to its mother, sheep roaming free. It took him back to Kenya and reminded him of the freedom they'd had there as children. The smell of furniture polish and old books combined with the scent of fresh flowers was also familiar and sent him back in time. He wondered what it would be like now, back home in Africa.

Helen sat upright in her pew. She felt humble and insignificant beneath the great expanse of the ceiling, and feared she was being watched or judged by some inconceivable force. The minister was about to begin the wedding service but Helen's mind wandered to Rahim and she stole a quick glance over her shoulder to where he sat. He looked handsome. His grey suit sat perfectly across his square shoulders and the crisp white shirt made a startling contrast against his dark hair and skin. The meticulously-knotted satin tie said it all; its intricate red and yellow pattern was daring and chic. Only Rahim could get away with it. He was smiling when their eyes met and when he winked without changing his expression, her heart began to race and her breath caught in her throat so that she had to turn back hurriedly to regain her composure and concentrate on the ceremony.

'Dearly beloved...' began the minister.

§

Outside in the bright sunshine, aunties, uncles, brothers, sisters and friends armed with fists-full of confetti milled around whilst the photographer snapped the happy couple on the church steps. An hour later, engines roared and the entire procession headed off to the hotel. The wedding party filed into the elegant dining room where circular tables were beautifully laid, adorned with flowers and delicate pink napkins. Janice stood by the doorway looking forlorn. Jo saw that her smile was there to hide the pain she felt inside.

'Mum, you OK?'

'I'm fine. Don't worry about me. You look beautiful. Are you enjoying your day?'

'I'm having a lovely time, but it would be even better if Dad were here. What did he say this morning? Did he ask where you were going?'

'He didn't say a word. I'm sorry, Jo. I'm sure he's hurting just as much as you are. He believes he's doing the right thing and he doesn't realise the pain it's causing.'

Jo shook her head.

'Mum, I'm sorry to put you through all this, but I'm glad you're here. I don't know what I would have done if you'd stayed at home with Dad.'

'Stop now. Let's enjoy the rest of the day and talk about this later.'

'I love you, Mum. Thank you.'

Once seated at the table, Jo relaxed a little.

'I still don't understand these things,' muttered Sam, fiddling with the silky ribbon that was used to tie the favours. Jo laughed, grateful for the distraction.

'You've a lot to learn about etiquette, my dear.'

'And you're going to teach me?'

'Yes.'

It was time for speeches. David rose to his feet and stood tall, looking around confidently. The room fell silent before him and, even though the silence was deafening, Elizabeth was sure her heartbeat could be heard above it. She sat hunched over, her head pounding and her eyesight blurred. David coughed and inhaled. Elizabeth clenched her fists so tight that her fingernails dug into the hot clammy flesh.

'Ladies and gentlemen,' he began, 'first of all I would like to thank you all for coming here today to witness the marriage of Joanna and Samuel - Mr and Mrs Garston!'

Elizabeth stole a glance at David. 'Could this be the same man?' she wondered. Now he was confident and she was petrified.

The guests clapped at the use of full Christian names and their new title and this made David smile.

'I have had two shocks today,' he continued. 'The first one was that I discovered that I'm not the real father.'

This brought a peel of laughter from the room and David laughed too. Elizabeth sat motionless staring at her husband. She couldn't believe her ears. She listened, hanging on to every word, careful not to distract him in any way.

'The second shock was being told that I had to make this speech and so I thought, well, I'll keep it short and to the point, but even so I had better make one or two notes.' He delved into his inside pocket and produced a six-foot-long computer printout which he held up at arm's length for everyone to see. The laughter grew louder.

Thirty minutes later he sat down.

'Why didn't you tell me you'd prepared a speech?' said Elizabeth. 'I was so worried and all for nothing.'

'I hadn't,' he whispered, 'I had one or two ideas - like the printout - but nothing in writing. I don't know where it came from.'

'You were fantastic!' She kissed him and squeezed his arm. 'I'm so proud.'

When the speeches and the meal were over, down went the lights to create a soft glow and on came the music, gentle and flowing.

The DJ made his announcement.

'Ladies and gentlemen, I would like to invite the bride and groom to take their places on the dance floor for the first waltz.'

Jo and Sam took up position and held each other closely, gazing into each other's eyes. It wasn't long before other guests joined them.

Rahim held out his hand to Helen. 'Care to join me?'

'I'd love to.'

They waltzed slowly round the dance floor and Helen felt as though she was floating.

'What a lovely day,' she said. 'I'm so happy for them. It's such a shame that Jo's dad wasn't here. Wouldn't it have been amazing if he'd turned up unexpectedly?'

'I didn't think for one minute that he would. The fact that he's refused to discuss the wedding at all in the last few months shows how strong his feelings are. It's a pity, they make a great couple. I'm sure they'll be really happy.'

'What about Dad? Wasn't he funny? I can't believe how well he did.'

'All that anxiety, and for what?' said Rahim. 'I haven't laughed so much in ages.'

'Hopefully, this will boost his confidence and make him feel better.'

She laid her head on Rahim's shoulder. It was so comfortable and familiar. All the bustle of the day was over, there was nothing else to think about or organise. He buried his face in her hair.

'I love you so much,' he whispered.

'I love you too. Can you believe that we're here together today? I'm so happy.'

He pulled her closer still.

'Do you think we should spend the rest of our lives together?'

She pushed away from him to see his face.

'What did you say?'

'You heard me.'

'Say it again.'

'I said, do you…?' He stopped and started again. 'What I meant to say was - will you marry me?'

'Do you mean it?'

'Will you marry me?'

'But your dad, what will your dad say? What about everyone else?'

'I've been trying to speak to Dad for some time and last Wednesday Mum and the girls went to the cinema to watch an Indian film, so I had the perfect opportunity. We sat and talked all evening. He's still worried, but he said he's lived his life and made his own decisions along the way and he realises that I should be able to do the same. After much thought he's decided that my happiness should come before anything else.'

'I don't know what to say.'

'You could start by answering my question.'

She hesitated, but only out of shock and only for an instant.

'Yes! Yes! Yes! Of course I will - I can't believe it - I'll make sure you never regret it, I promise.'

'Let's keep it quiet for a little while, I don't think now is the time to tell people.'

'You're right. Today it's Jo and Sam's day. We'll tell everyone tomorrow.'

He chuckled. He had meant a little longer than that, but he knew Helen wouldn't be able to contain herself.

'That's fine,' he said.

That evening, Helen and Rahim stayed at her parents' house and in the morning they went back to the hotel to see the Jo and Sam off on their honeymoon. They stood and waved until Sam's car disappeared. They had decided not to tell the newlyweds of their own plans for marriage until Jo and Sam returned.

Rahim squeezed Helen's hand.

'I'm starving. Let's go back inside and have a full English breakfast.'

When their breakfast was served, Rahim passed his bacon to Helen, a legacy from his upbringing. Having been brought up to believe that pigs were dirty, he could never bring himself to eat pork.

'There are a lot of things we need to talk about,' said Rahim. He was still nervous about the long-term prospects of marrying an English girl. He had woken up that morning with a stark realisation of the gravity of his proposal to Helen. Worried that he'd got carried away by the wedding atmosphere and high spirits, he now had a million concerns rushing through his head.

'We'll have to decide when and where and who we'll have as bridesmaids. Will you have Nadim as your best man or Aziz?'

'Please Helen...'

'I was teasing.'

'There are more pressing things - like you moving in with my family, and whether you will learn our language. Are you going to change your religion? If we have children, what religion will they assume?'

'I can't become a Muslim.'

'I just wanted to bring you back down to earth.' He took hold of her hand. 'We've got to think of all the problems and have the answers ready. Our families will ask and we have to show that we've given the problems some thought.'

'Let's make a list and see what comes up.'

They took their coffee through to the lounge area. First on their list was the prospect of Helen moving in permanently with Rahim and his family.

'I'll apply for a job in Manchester as soon as I qualify in October.'

'Do you think it'll be that easy to get one?'

'There's a shortage of midwives all over the country; there are a number of maternity units that I can apply to in Manchester.'

'So hopefully that won't be a problem - and by then Sofia will have started university so you may be able to use her room whilst she's away.' Rahim looked at their list. 'What type of wedding will we have? I'm sure both mums will have set ideas as to how it should be.'

'We could have a big Indian get-together and call it our engagement and your mum can invite whoever she wants and then we can have a registry-office wedding with a reception, like yesterday. That would be for my side of the family and our friends - but we could also invite a core of close friends and family to both events so everyone is happy.'

'I'm exhausted just trying to get my head around it all,' said Rahim.

'We knew it would be complicated.'

'OK, let's leave the marriage - what about children?'

'Four?'

'I didn't mean how many! I meant - what about their religion?'

'I've always wanted four blond little boys, but I think the blond part might have to be scrapped,' laughed Helen. 'As for religion, when we last talked about it, we said we wouldn't have them christened or registered as Muslim, so they could choose for themselves. Do you still agree?'

'And let them go to the mosque with Mum, or to church, as they want?'

'It would be good for them to experience both religions.'

'What's left on the list?' asked Rahim. Helen had an answer for everything.

'The dates, the places, the colour schemes. . . .'

'All right, you win - what date?'

'Next summer? By then, I'll have lived with your family long enough to know whether it'll work. That would be a lovely time for a wedding. You choose the date.'

'Let's have the Indian celebration around the beginning of June and the English one in July. How does that sound?'

'I can't believe we're even talking like this. It's so exciting!'

'All right, my little chapati, let's give it a try and see what happens.'

'You're so funny. Shall we break the news to my parents?'

§

They told Elizabeth and David their news but didn't get quite the reaction they had anticipated.

'You surprised?' asked Helen.

'That's a bit of an understatement,' said Elizabeth. 'Are you sure you know what you're doing?'

Rahim shifted uneasily from one foot to the other. He hadn't envisaged a hostile reaction from Helen's parents. He'd expected them to be thrilled but they were visibly shocked.

'We need to sit down and talk about this,' said David.

'I thought you'd be pleased, Mum' said Helen.

'Under normal circumstances I would be. Rahim - you know we're both very fond of you - but this is going to bring all sorts of problems. Look at Jo and her family – and the problems they encountered.'

'Every situation is different,' said Helen. 'There will be difficult times of course, but we might not have too many problems. Who knows unless we try?'

'What about your parents, Rahim?' said David. 'I thought they were going to live with you?'

'They are.'

Helen cut in: 'I'm going to Manchester to live with his family to see how we get along.'

'Well that's sensible,' said David. He looked at Elizabeth. 'What do you think?'

'It's their life. I don't suppose it'll make any difference if we say no in any case.'

'We've talked about it so much,' said Helen, 'and tried to go our separate ways, but we're still here - together.'

'Well, I think congratulations are in order. If there's anything we can do to help, let us know,' said David.

'Thank you so much,' said Rahim.

Helen hugged and kissed each of them. Rahim shook hands with David and hugged Elizabeth. In the car, they looked at each other.

'We thought that was going to be the easy part,' said Helen. 'I never imagined them reacting that way. We were so concerned about your parents that we didn't take their feelings into consideration. I'm worried, Rahim. What if your parents react in a similar way?'

'Dad is expecting us to make an announcement. Anyway, let's go and see them.'

When Rahim told his parents about the marriage plans they were obviously well-prepared. Jamal listened intently and Fatima pulled the prayer beads through her fingers, quietly praying for a life of peace.

'It won't be easy,' said Jamal, 'but inshallah, it will be all right.'

'Congratulations, all I ask is for you to be happy,' said Fatima.

Safina jumped up and flung her arms around her brother.

'Congratulations! I'm so happy for you both.'

'Congratulations,' said Sofia. 'Who would have thought we would ever see this day?'

'And from now on, Helen, you must call me Ma, and call Jamal, Bapa,' said Fatima.

'We must let Zara know,' said Jamal.

'I'll phone her,' said Rahim.

Zara was a little dubious.

'Well, if you're sure you know what you're doing.'

'It's not been an easy decision, but it's what we want more than anything - and we'll make sure that Mum and Dad are looked after,' said Rahim.

'I wish you all the best and I look forward to meeting Helen.'

'Thank you, that means a lot.'

'Can I be a bridesmaid?' asked Safina.

'There you go, that's one decision made,' said Helen.

22 THE HONEYMOON IS OVER

Sam would have turned over and gone back to sleep but, through a tiny slit between his eyelids he was aware of something wavering in the air above his head. He opened his eyes a little wider and saw the glimmer of a small shiny object. He squinted, trying to make sense of what was before him. When he lifted his head forward, everything came into focus. He watched for a second and grinned. Quietly laying his head back on the pillow, he watched without a murmur until he could no longer suppress his hilarity. It began with a small chuckle, but when Jo glanced his way and realised he was looking at her, he erupted into a quake of laughter, till the whole bed shook.

'You rotter!' she squealed, and belted him with a pillow.

He shielded himself as the blows rained down on him, but he was laughing so much that he didn't care.

'How long have you been watching me?'

'About half an hour.'

'No you haven't.'

'Look at me, Mrs Garston.' He held out his hand and admired his wedding band - just as Jo had been doing.

'You're horrible.'

She jumped up and grabbed the pillow again to beat him with it, but he was too strong and in his grasp she could only succumb. Blood surged like rapids around her body, the tingling began in her toes and rippled up till it was all-embracing and she responded to his caresses, which were now soft and sensual.

'I love you so much,' she whispered.

The phone rang. Sam groaned and stopped what he was doing.

'Shall I answer it?' he asked.

'If it's important they'll ring back later.'

The ringing stopped for a few moments, and then began again in earnest.

'Could be important,' sighed Jo

'Surely they realise that we've only been married for two weeks. We're only just back from honeymoon and we still have a lot of discovering to do.'

'Oh please leave us alone,' groaned Jo but she reached for the receiver. 'Hello?'

'Hi, Jo, how are you? How was the honeymoon?'

'Hi, Helen. The honeymoon was fabulous. How are you?'

Sam continued to massage and soothe every inch of bare flesh he could find, whilst Jo squirmed and tried to concentrate on Helen's conversation. Suddenly she stiffened: 'You're what?'

'Can you believe it?' asked Helen.

'You're engaged?'

Jo closed her eyes.

'Please don't,' she wanted to say. She covered the receiver and mimed to Sam: 'He's asked her to marry him.' She shook her head in disbelief and tried to think of a good response.

'He asked me on the night of your wedding, but I couldn't tell you then. You're very quiet - you don't approve, do you?'

'Of course I approve, there are no two people more suited - but I'm scared that other people will spoil it for you - you know that.'

'I can't pass up this opportunity. Otherwise I'll spend the rest of my life wondering what could have been.'

'Helen, I am pleased for you. I know this is what you want. I pray that it will work out and that you don't end up getting hurt.'

'I know what I'm doing and I know I can make it work. Rahim has been so supportive where his parents are concerned. Last week, his mum wanted to give me an Asian name, but Rahim sat with her and explained that it would be too complicated, and that my parents might not like the idea - and she was fine about it.'

'Well that's good.'

What Jo really wanted to say was that this was relatively minor compared to some of the things Helen would have to face, like people looking at her as though she were a piece of chewing gum stuck to the bottom of their shoe, or making snide comments and shaking their heads as she walked by, but she kept quiet.

'Have a word with Sam,' she said.

'Hi, Helen, I understand congratulations are in order.'

'You're not going to give me a lecture too?'

'Would I do that? I'm very pleased for you. When's the big day?'

Helen relaxed a little.

'Not for some time. I'm going to move in with Rahim and his family and see how it goes first.'

'You're very brave. Let us know if there's anything we can do to help.'

'That's really good of you. Once I can make a decent curry, you'll be the first to sample it.'

Sam made a slurping sound. 'I look forward to that. You get out there and show them what you're made of.'

Sam turned to Jo as he put down the phone.

'Now that it's official,' he said, 'we have to stop voicing our opinions and give them our full support no matter how we feel. Agreed?'

'You're right.' Jo lay back on the soft pillow and prayed out loud. 'Please, please let them be happy and don't let history repeat itself.'

'Please, please don't let the phone ring again,' said Sam. 'Now, where was I?'

23 EAST MEETS WEST

Elizabeth and David were keen to meet Rahim's parents if their daughter was to move in with them. They also agreed it was best to keep their views to themselves; it didn't concern them that Rahim was Asian, they weren't prejudiced. Hadn't Helen grown up with Jo? What did concern them was that Helen was intending to live with Rahim's family, possibly for the rest of her life. To live with English in-laws would be difficult enough, but it was hard to imagine how Helen would cope in such an alien culture on a long-term basis. They hoped that by meeting Rahim's family, their minds would be put at rest and some of their fears allayed.

Helen and Elizabeth sat in the kitchen.

'Why don't you invite Rahim's family over next weekend, I'll cook a Sunday roast,' said Elizabeth. 'Do you think they would like that?'

'I'm sure they would. What about Dad, do you think he'll be all right?'

'I think so. I'll talk to him about it tonight, you speak to Rahim and we'll confirm tomorrow.'

'Dad does seem to be much happier.'

'Fingers crossed, hey.'

Fatima and Jamal accepted. They were anxious about the meeting, but they knew they had to go for Rahim's sake.

'We'll be there too,' Sofia reassured them.

Rahim arrived with his family at two-thirty in the afternoon. Helen opened the gates and Elizabeth and David stood on the doorstep to welcome their guests. Jamal was in the front passenger seat; his arthritis was quite bad these days which made it difficult for him to manoeuvre. David went to his aid and helped him out of the low seat. The two gentlemen shook hands respectfully.

Rahim joined them. 'David, Elizabeth, this is my dad.'

Jamal bowed his head slightly. 'Please - call me Jamal.'

Rahim opened the rear door. 'Mum, do you need some help?'

Sofia and Safina emerged from the car relaxed and smiling. David liked them instantly because of their chirpy manner and they shook hands vigorously.

Helen hugged each of them, but not Jamal and Rahim. It would have been disrespectful to hug Jamal and it was forbidden for her to have any physical contact with Rahim in front of his parents. She bowed her head slightly in their direction and smiled before leading the way into the lounge where Fatima sat on the edge of her seat twisting the strap of her handbag around her fingers. Jamal looked around surreptitiously; he hadn't been in many English homes and he felt uncomfortable.

David was in a good mood. He wanted everyone to feel relaxed, especially Jamal, who was much older and half his size and looked ill at ease. David brought in a footstool.

'Here you are, young sir,' he said and lifted Jamal's feet to rest on top of it.

'Thank you, thank you, you're looking after me too well,' said Jamal, smiling.

'Let me know if there's anything else you need.'

'I'm very comfortable, thank you.'

'Look at Dad, he loves it,' said Sofia, and everyone laughed.

'If someone had told you,' Rahim whispered to Helen, 'that my dad would be sitting here in your lounge with his feet up and actually enjoying himself, would you have believed them?'

'Absolutely not, but on the other hand, if six months ago anyone had told me that any of this was possible, I wouldn't have believed that either.'

Elizabeth and Helen served the meal. Sofia and Safina chatted happily and kept the conversation flowing. Fatima dug around in her handbag and pulled out a small bottle of dark red powder. When her meal was placed in front of her she poured a tiny amount out into the palm of her hand and quietly sprinkled it around the plate.

'What you up to?' asked Safina loudly.

'I er...'

Safina laughed and apologised on her behalf: 'Mum always has to have her chilli powder; she can't eat food if it's not spicy hot.'

Fatima looked around the table to see who was listening; she wanted to kill Safina.

'Forgive my daughter, she's very rude,' she said.

'Sorry Mum, I didn't mean to embarrass you. I just think it's so funny,' said Safina.

'Don't you worry, put whatever you like on it,' said David.

'Any ketchup?' asked Safina with a smirk on her face, '- only joking.'

§

On the day that Helen moved in with Rahim's family David was distraught. He stood on the doorstep and sobbed uncontrollably as he watched Rahim's silver car bump up the road. He felt as though the life was being sucked out of him and tears cascaded down his cheeks. The big black hole was on the horizon once again. Elizabeth stood at his side, her arm around his waist. What could she say? This was a moment they had both been dreading, although for different reasons. David saw his family diminishing; Elizabeth recognised the fact that fledglings always flew the nest - but she knew how David would take it. It was a normal healthy process that any loving parent should welcome and enjoy, their job done properly, their children happy and independent. Today they should be happy and proud, but she knew that it wouldn't be the case. Elizabeth felt hopelessly inadequate. How could anyone understand David's level of despair? What could she do to ease his pain? Nothing, only David could expel his own demons.

It was twelve-thirty in the afternoon; an hour elapsed before David hauled himself away from the doorstep. He stomped heavily up the stairs and fell into bed, and apart from a couple of visits to the bathroom, he didn't appear until the following evening. When Elizabeth took him food, he simply turned over in bed to face the other direction.

'You need to eat something,' she coaxed. 'You've been in bed all day and all night and it's seven in the evening. Why don't you get up and have a wash, you'll feel better.'

He looked at her but saw nothing, his eyes were unfocussed, and red and inflamed through crying. Elizabeth almost felt that he blamed her. She knew this was ridiculous, but she was too frightened to ask what he thought. When he flew into a rage, she was petrified and she wondered if it were only a matter of time before he lashed out at her. He had always been a gentle man and she felt repulsed at the thought that he could be capable of physical violence. She reached out and stroked his forehead which felt clammy.

'Please, love, make an effort. I've made you a lovely roast dinner. It'll do you good.'

David's eyes slid shut. Out on the landing Elizabeth held her head in her hands to quell her overwhelming feeling of doom. She stood in the doorway of the girls' bedroom, now hollow and uninviting, and, for an instant, she understood a little of what he felt. She staggered over to Helen's bed and collapsed face-first into the pillows, giving in to her emotions, and sobbed until she fell asleep.

'Mum?' Karen touched her mother's shoulder. 'Mum?'

Elizabeth sat bolt upright. She screwed up her eyes and surveyed the room trying to get her bearings.

'Mum? You all right?'

Elizabeth jumped off the bed and made for the door.

'Mum? Where are you going?' asked Karen. She had just driven back from a weekend in Scotland with friends.

'What day is it?' asked Elizabeth. 'How long have I slept?'

'It's Sunday, and it's midnight.'

Elizabeth told her about David's behaviour over the last couple of days.

'I'm at my wits' end, I don't know what to do any more.'

'Why don't you arrange a weekend away, just the two of you, somewhere that Dad will appreciate? It might give him something else to think about.'

'Where?'

'Let's have a think over the next day or so and see what we can come up with, then, when he's in a better mood, we'll suggest it to him.'

'I'm sorry about this. You always get the brunt of it, Karen; you're always the one who picks up the pieces.'

Karen gave her a hug.

'Don't worry about me; I'm glad I'm here for you both. Let's get some sleep. You sleep in Helen's bed.'

At six o'clock the following morning David crawled out of bed. A mix of emotions tussled in his head. He yearned for Helen to be at home, but his conscience told him this was silly. He felt bad that he'd wasted so much time lying in bed when he had so much to do. He was cross with himself for causing Elizabeth so much anxiety - but cross with her too because she didn't share his pain. He dragged himself to the bathroom but the effort left him feeling weak, so he sat on the edge of the bath whilst he leaned over and placed the plug in its hole. He watched as water from the tap hit the white enamel. *'If only I was a droplet of water,'* he thought, *'fresh and clean, running down a river, free as a bird.'* He looked at his reflection in the mirror and was disgusted. He had worn the same clothes for three days; he could feel them sticking to his body and he could smell the sweat. He peeled them off and stuck them in the wicker laundry basket by the door and, holding the side of the bath tightly, lowered himself into the clear soothing water. Once in, he speculated about what would happen if he submerged himself completely and stayed under long enough so that he had no option but to take a breath and inhale the water into his lungs.

'Why not?' he asked himself. He slid down till he was totally immersed; it was like being in a warm silk purse, calm and peaceful, the way he imagined heaven would be - if there was one. He listened to the silence and allowed his mind to wander. The warmth of the water comforted him and he wished he could stay there forever. But, as the oxygen in his lungs diminished, a tight pressure started to build in his chest and his head felt as though it would explode. He could no longer hold the air in his lungs, but neither could he take that all-important killer breath. He emerged, blowing like a whale and gasping. Wiping the droplets from his eyes, he saw Elizabeth standing at the door.

'What are you doing?'

'Nothing, I'm fine.'

It sounded lame. Elizabeth knelt down by the bath. Her face was full of concern and confusion.

'Oh David, I've been so worried.'

'Sorry Bett, I'm useless.' He rubbed his eyes and stared straight ahead for a few seconds. 'Have you any idea how hard it is to kill yourself?'

It was as though he had stuck a knife in her chest, the pain was physical.

'Oh my God, it's my fault.' Surely if she could not make her husband happy, then she must be to blame in some way.

'It's not your fault Bett, it's me that's the problem but I don't know what to do.'

§

The following week Elizabeth called out to Karen from the lounge where she was watching television.

'Karen, look at this! It's a programme about the Orkneys. Dad's talked about going lots of times, but we never did anything about it. What if I suggest we go there?'

'You think he would?'

'Maybe if I wait until he's feeling a little better before I ask him. It looks so lovely. I'll get some brochures.' Elizabeth was full of excitement. 'It looks so wild and barren and they were saying it's like going back in time at least twenty years. He'd love that.'

Two weeks went by before she plucked up the courage to ask David about a trip away. He'd been too distant and preoccupied for her to contemplate mentioning it before. To ask him to make a decision risked overloading his mind, and that could be disastrous. As it was, each day saw a slight improvement. One day he offered her a cup of tea, another he sat with her on the garden bench for half an hour - small steps but in the right direction. She kept a close eye on him, never far from a window and within earshot so that, whenever he needed her, she was there.

'Bett?' David shouted from outside.

'I'm in the kitchen.'

'You fancy a walk?'

'It's a lovely sunny day for this time of year, I'd love to.'

She appeared enthusiastic but a feeling of dread shrouded her. When David invited her for a stroll it was usually for him to vent his feelings. Sometimes she was pleasantly surprised when he talked about things in general, but more often than not he talked of feeling hopeless and of how futile it was for him to carry on with life. It left her feeling sad and alone. She didn't know what to do; she didn't understand how a person could feel so desperately inadequate.

The first signs of autumn lay strewn along the path. Elizabeth kicked her way through the burnished leaves. She felt like a little girl again and part of her longed to go back in time. If only the two of them could be carefree and happy. She thought back to her childhood when she and her brothers and sisters would rake up the leaves and pile them high. They would count to three and then all dive in, shrieking with laughter and screaming as they picked on one person, pushing leaves up their sleeves and trouser legs. She smiled to herself; they'd played the same game so many times with their own girls and afterwards gone inside to a real fire and milky drinks to warm themselves up.

'What are you smiling about?' It was the first time in a while that David had appeared relaxed and comfortable.

'I love this time of year, don't you?' said Elizabeth. 'I was thinking of when the girls were young and how they played in the garden in the cold, but still managed to come in with warm rosy cheeks.'

He smiled at the thought.

'I'm so sorry for the way I've behaved over this last week,' he said, 'but that's the reason why - I find it unbearable to imagine life without them.'

'But you won't be without them. Shelly and Paula still come round, Helen will too, and we'll go and see them. Think of all the grandchildren we'll have. We can watch how they do things differently with their children - and the nice thing is that after they've visited, we can enjoy some quiet time and do the things we always wanted to do. Isn't that what we planned - "work now and play later"? Now it's our play time.'

They walked arm-in-arm.

'When you say it like that it sounds great, but last week I felt as if I was going to die. No, that's not true - I prayed that I would die. As each day passes, this feeling that I can't even begin to explain increases tenfold. I'm petrified of when Karen leaves; the thought makes me feel physically sick.'

Elizabeth placed her hand on his chest and massaged it gently as though to heal his heart.

'Try to see it differently. Look at their leaving as a positive thing that's healthy and normal.'

'I know I should be more rational - I can't explain it.'

'David, do you remember a while ago we talked about going to the Orkneys? I saw a television programme last week and it looks beautiful.

Let's go, it'll do us good. I think you'd love it, it's unspoilt and rugged. What do you think?'

David not only agreed but thought it was a great idea. Before he could change his mind, Elizabeth had booked a week away in a small guest house overlooking the sea.

24 HELEN MEETS MAMA AND MAMI!

Helen woke early so she could tidy the house ready for their guests before the cooking started. Today was her first real test and a day she had dreaded for a long time. Two relatives were visiting from Canada and they were staying with Mama and Mami. They were coming over for a meal along with a third aunt and uncle, and Helen would be meeting them all for the first time. Tongues would be wagging and this would be an interesting day for everyone. She knew they had been told about her and she imagined the conversation:

'Apparently she's been learning to cook.'

They would all laugh.

'Don't be ridiculous, an English girl can't cook our food the way we do.'

They would shake their heads in disbelief.

'Well that's what I've heard and I think she's even been to the mosque - and she wore a sari!'

They would gulp.

'You have to be joking! That can't be true. This is not right at all. Well, let's put her to the test if she thinks she can be one of us.'

It wasn't so much the family from abroad that scared Helen, but Mama himself. She'd heard so much about him. His sons and daughter still lived at home and would continue to do so after they were married. Everyone obeyed Mama without question, and there was no way he would ever consider the possibility of an English son or daughter-in-law. Today would be difficult, but then Helen had been told all along that none of it would be easy; she wasn't going to give in at the first hurdle and let them say: 'I told you so.'

She knew that, firstly, the house must be spotless; secondly, she must stay by her future mother-in-law's side the whole day and carry out every task to the best of her ability and as graciously as she could; and thirdly, she had to look her best no matter how tired she was by the end of it. The last thing she wanted was for Fatima and Jamal to be embarrassed or ashamed. She wanted them to be able to sing her praises and make the others wish that they had an English daughter-in-law too - even though, deep-down, she knew it was ridiculous to even think like that. They would probably rather lose a leg, she thought. Today would be difficult for Fatima and Jamal, because if things went really badly, Helen could walk away, but for them, the embarrassment would stay for a long time. The community would never let them forget and they would be reminded of their foolishness at every opportunity.

She had cleaned the kitchen and bathrooms and dusted and tidied as much as possible before the rest of the family came down for breakfast. Helen put all the ingredients for the day's cooking onto the work surface and pulled crockery and pans out of cupboards. She hadn't lived with them long but had already learned how to cook.

Each member of the family surfaced one at a time and staggered downstairs looking for a cup of tea. Safina ate breakfast and left for work.

'Morning,' said Fatima and smiled as she looked around. 'You've been busy. What time did you get up?'

'Six, I wanted to begin early so that we can make sure everything's just so.'

'You've done well.'

Helen grinned. 'I'll do the vacuuming before we start cooking.'

'Don't worry, I'll do that,' offered Sofia.

'Well if you don't mind.'

'But then I'm going out, so you'd better make use of me while I'm here. I'll see them all when I get back this evening.'

Helen hadn't reckoned on either Sofia or Safina not being at home. She needed their support. The phrase 'lamb to the slaughter' sprang to mind and she suppressed an urge to run. 'Stop it! You're a grown woman,' she told herself. 'You don't need help.' She pulled her shoulders back, smoothed down her clothes and continued with her preparations.

By two o'clock the food was ready. They hadn't stopped for one minute.

'All I need now is my fairy godmother to transform me,' Helen told Fatima.

'Have your shower and I'll come and put the sari on for you.'

'I'm so nervous.'

'We can only do our best,' said Fatima. 'These people are not with us all the time; they only visit and then they go. It's the family that's important. We'll look after them when they come and that's all we can do.'

'Thank you,' said Helen and hugged her tightly, knowing full well that Fatima too was probably petrified - while remaining gracious and dignified.

Rahim took Jamal to collect a newspaper and to buy some Indian sweets. Jamal was very anxious. He had not slept well and had worn a constant frown since crawling out of bed that morning. Rahim felt guilty about putting him through such an ordeal and wondered for the thousandth time if he was doing the right thing.

The doorbell rang.

'It'll be Rahim. I'll get it!' Helen called out. She wanted him to be the first to see her. The grey silk sari, adorned with silver embroidery, made her feel like a queen. Real silver dripped from her ears and an intricate necklace covered her chest, hiding any suggestion of a cleavage. Her hair was clasped loosely at the nape of her neck so that it fell in soft wisps onto her shoulder, and her make-up was barely visible. The intention was to create the impression of a gentle creature, timid and shy - it had been carefully and purposely orchestrated in the hope that the guests would like Helen immediately.

Rahim stood at the door - and behind him were his father and another six people. Rahim stood frozen to the spot; he had never seen Helen in a sari before. Fatima came to the rescue.

'Welcome,' she said in English, but then immediately switched to Kutchi, their own language.

Helen retreated into the doorway of the cloakroom to allow the visitors to pass. As they shuffled by, each one nodded courteously in her direction. She was trembling, her hands were clammy and beneath the fabric of the sari a trickle of sweat meandered down her bare midriff and burrowed into the tightly-fastened skirt.

Curiosity got the better of the women and they furtively looked her up and down but a very tall, stern-looking man paid no attention to her at all. Immaculate in his traditional cream-coloured salwar kameez, he marched past her looking straight ahead and took Fatima's hands into his. He bowed his head respectfully in greeting and Fatima smiled and returned the gesture, welcoming her brother into her home.

Once the guests were safely in the kitchen and out of sight, Rahim could no longer contain himself.

'You look amazing.'

Helen held out a quivering hand. 'But I'm so nervous - look, I'm shaking.'

'Oh, you poor thing.' He pushed her further into the cloakroom. 'Listen - they'll adore you. Just be yourself. Come on, my little chapati - we'll show them.' He quickly kissed and hugged her.

'It makes me laugh when you call me that.'

'Let's go.'

'Do we have to?'

'Afraid so.'

She checked her clothing and composed herself. When they put their heads round the kitchen door, Rahim and Helen could only smile. It was a sight to behold. The guests were hugging each other, laughing and talking loudly.

'Look at you, she's looking after you too well,' said one man, pointing at Jamal's protruding tummy.

Jamal chuckled and breathed in.

'Don't try to hide it; she's worked many hours to get you looking so good. Fatima, you're spoiling him.'

Everyone laughed and the banter continued. A few minutes later, the greetings were over, apart from the most important one. The moment Helen had been dreading had arrived.

As future head of the house, Rahim stepped forward; he shook hands with the men, welcomed the women, then turned to Helen, and said confidently.

'This is Helen, my girlfriend.'

Helen guessed that the tall man was Mama, she went to him first and gently cupped his outstretched hand in both of hers.

'Pleased to meet you,' she said.

To her surprise, he placed his other hand firmly on top of her head and replied: 'Pleased to meet you too.'

She continued around the room. The woman standing next to Mama was small and a little on the plump side. She wore a green sari with gold embroidery and lots of traditional jewellery, but there was no make-up or nail varnish.

'Hello,' said Helen.

'Call me Mami. I am Mama's wife and Rahim's aunt. Nice to meet you.'

'And you too, thank you,' replied Helen.

One couple were both quite elderly, probably in their eighties. The woman was tiny, with thinning grey hair scraped up into a small bun on top of her head. She had a kind face and wore an orange sari, which struck Helen as an odd colour for an old lady to wear, until she realised that it matched her spark and character.

'I'm a Mami as well,' she smiled, 'but you'll have to call me something else otherwise we won't know which one you're talking to. Call me Auntie!'

'OK, Auntie,' said Helen, as she gently squeezed her bony hands.

'This is my husband, he's also Mama to you - so you'd better call him Uncle.'

'Uncle, it's nice to meet you.'

The elderly gentleman beamed, revealing an almost toothless grin; what teeth were left were enormously long and stained brown from years of smoking. He held onto Helen's hands and bobbed his head continuously like a nodding dog in the back of a car.

Eventually, she broke free. So far so good, only one couple left to meet. Fozia and Bharrat were much younger and less traditional. Fozia, in salwar kameez rather than a sari, had cropped hair, which was unusual for an Asian woman. She looked very business-like with rolled-up sleeves and arms folded in front of her. Bharrat stood totally uninterested staring out of the window. Fozia dug him in the ribs, 'Bharat!'

He spun round and scowled: 'Hey!' he snarled, rubbing his side.

She gestured toward Helen: 'Helen is trying to say hello to you.'

'Sorry, I was looking at the garden - I've never seen it so tidy. Hi, I'm Bharat.' He said without shaking hands and turned back to look out of the window.

'Helen did the garden,' said Fatima. 'It is too much hard work for us now.'

Bharat glanced at Helen. 'You've done a good job,' he said, without much conviction.

Fatima was eager to get busy.

'Shall we eat? You must be hungry.'

All of the men, including Jamal and Rahim, sat down together, but none of the women joined them. The women rushed around babbling in their own language, bringing this and that to the table.

'Come on, Helen,' Fozia said, rather sternly, and ushered her over to the cooker where the food stood in large pans waiting to be served. 'Get the plates and put them on the table.'

Helen could hardly move in her sari. She rustled awkwardly between the wall and the chairs, trying to reach each person. Before she had finished giving out the plates Fozia said: 'Get the jug of water and pour them a drink.' There was no 'please', or 'thank you', or asking if she minded. Helen looked at Fatima for counsel.

'Don't worry,' Fatima silently mouthed and, gesticulating with her hand, urged her to carry on.

Meanwhile, Rahim kept his head down. Never once did he glance in Helen's direction. He listened to the male conversation and gave no inkling that he saw what was going on around him.

'Helen, please would you take the bowl of rice to the table,' asked Mami, but when Helen reached for the bowl Fozia butted in and gave her another job.

'Mami has asked me to put the rice on the table,' said Helen.

'It's no use putting rice out when the meat curry is still on the cooker. The men will want their rotti first, not rice.'

Perplexed and flustered, Helen scuttled back to the kitchen area and swapped over the two dishes. Her cheeks were beginning to burn and her mouth was dry. Keeping her eyes lowered, she went back to where the men were sitting and placed a dish of spinach and mince curry in the centre of the table. They prattled on regardless. Not one of them acknowledged her presence or the arrival of the food.

Back in the kitchen, Fatima gave Helen a dish of yogurt to take in.

'And this,' said Mami, handing her the salt pot.

'Where is the chutney?' asked Fozia, looking at Helen.

'It's in the fridge,' said Helen.

'Can you get it?'

'But ...'

Fatima stepped in quickly: 'I'll get the chutney, you take those please.' She gave Helen a reassuring smile.

Once the men had eaten, they went upstairs to the lounge for a smoke, whilst the women cleared away the dirty dishes and re-laid the table for themselves.

'Helen!'

It was Fozia again.

'Yes?'

'Make the men some tea and take it up to them.'

'Please!' Helen muttered to herself. She filled the kettle with water. A few minutes later, she struggled to climb the stairs in her sari whilst clutching the tray of tea. She placed it on the small wooden coffee table, lifted the first cup and shyly offered it to Mama.

'Would you like sugar?'

He looked a little surprised: 'No sugar or milk, thank you.'

Her heart sank, she had put milk in all of the cups and poured the tea. 'I'll just nip downstairs and make another one,' she said and rushed off to the kitchen.

Back in the lounge, and Mama in receipt of his black tea, she asked the old uncle if he wanted a cup of tea.'

'That is very kind of you, and could I have a glass of water?'

Her eyes began to prickle; she wiped her forehead with her hand and tried to smile, 'No problem.'

Again, she bustled down the stairs to the kitchen. When she arrived back with the water, Rahim had handed out the rest of the drinks.

'Thank you, Rahim,' she said. 'Would anyone like anything else?'

'We're fine now,' said Mama.

The men chattered on in Kutchi and Helen made her escape. She locked herself in the bathroom, leaned on the sink and sighed. The last couple of hours had taken its toll, what little mascara she wore, and the eye liner had roamed down onto her face and the blusher was far outstripped by the flush of natural colour brought about by stress.

A knock on the door startled her.

'Helen? Are you in there?'

'I won't be a minute.'

Fatima had come to find her.

'You all right? We're ready to eat.'

Helen opened the door.

'You've done really well,' said Fatima. 'We can relax a little now and enjoy our meal.'

'I'm fine,' Helen lied. 'I'll be down in a second.'

In the kitchen, the women were gathered round the table, talking loudly, laughing at each other's jokes, and shovelling food into their mouths. Helen ate without saying a word; she couldn't join in even if she wanted to because she didn't understand a thing they said. At six o'clock, just as they finished eating, in waltzed Safina. She greeted each one and then turned her attention to the food.

'I'm starving!' she said, 'what's for dinner?'

Fozia looked over to where Helen still sat.

'Helen! Get your sister-in-law some food.'

Shocked, Safina shook her head.

'It's OK, I can get my own food.'

'No, Helen will get it. You've been at work all day, you must be exhausted.'

Helen stood up and went to get the food.

'I'll do it, you sit down.' Safina repeated, but she could see from Helen's face that she couldn't push it any further or Helen would break down. The two girls spooned food onto the plate together and Safina sat down to eat. It was then the door opened and Mama told them it time to go home.

'Safina, how are you?' he asked.

'OK thanks,' she answered with a mouthful of rice.

'Thank you very much, Fatima, you must come to us next time.' He turned to Helen, 'Nice to meet you,' he said, but he sounded indifferent and Helen felt confused and deflated. She nodded and smiled feebly. After the goodbyes were done and the front door clicked shut, Rahim, Fatima and Safina joined Helen in the kitchen.

'You were brilliant,' beamed Rahim.

Helen kept quiet.

'What's wrong?'

She burst into tears.

'It was awful. I feel terrible,' she sobbed.

'I don't understand - you did so well.'

Fatima knew all too well what the problem was and went to Helen's side.

'Helen, even if you had been one of us, today it would have been exactly the same for you. A daughter-in-law automatically becomes the property of the mother-in-law and they have to do most of the work. Fozia wasn't being unkind; she was just making sure everything was done properly. Don't forget, we speak a different language and so sometimes we say things differently and it might not always sound very polite. You have to forget about your culture when you are with us and imagine you are one of us. Only then will you win.'

At that moment Sofia arrived home.

'What's happening?' she asked.

Helen wanted to curl up and die. Her first chance to prove that she had what it took, and she was crying like a baby. She felt she had failed miserably.

'Mum, you shouldn't have let them all tell her what to do,' said Sofia. 'You should have told them that you would instruct her.'

'I couldn't do that, Sofia, because then they would have said that we were spoiling her and that it would never work. I have to show them that Helen is strong and that she can be treated the same as any other daughter-in-law.'

'Mum's right,' said Rahim. He wanted to hold Helen, but he couldn't with Fatima present. 'If we're seen to be giving any concessions, they'll say that Helen is ruling the house.'

Helen blew her nose.

'But Rahim - you didn't support me at all. The only thing you did was pour the tea.'

'It's our tradition that the men don't do anything. It's the women who do all the domestic stuff and even though I don't agree with it, I have to fit in when I'm home. They would have been laughing if I'd helped you bring the food to the table or helped clear the things away. I'm sorry but these are the problems we're going to have to face.'

Safina gave Helen a fresh tissue. 'Helen, next time we'll be here to help you as much as we can.'

25 DAVID REACHES BREAKING POINT

Helen phoned home. Her father answered and after a brief conversation passed the receiver to Elizabeth.

'Hi, how are you?' Elizabeth sounded cheerful.

'Fine. What about you? Sounds like you had a good holiday.'

'It was just what we needed. Dad loved Orkney. It was like going back in time. Everyone was friendly, there was no graffiti, the phone booths had telephone directories, and even the toilets out in the middle of nowhere had toilet rolls and paper towels.'

'Doesn't take much to make you happy, does it?'

'Dad was back to his normal self. It was wonderful to see him chatting and laughing with people. There was only one day when he wanted to be alone, so I went out for a walk. I found a fabulous old church. The organist was teaching a student so I spent two hours there watching and listening and they even shared their packed lunch with me.'

'That was good of them.'

'I enjoyed myself so much and when I got back to the hotel, Dad had had a good snooze and was fine again. I just hope it lasts.'

'How has he been since you got home?'

'We've only been back a day, but he seems all right. Anyway, how about you? How's it going with Rahim's family?'

Helen told Elizabeth the whole visitor saga, but she made it into a joke and Elizabeth shrieked with laughter at the image of Helen up and down the stairs with drinks, falling over her sari as she went. Helen created an image of how she served Safina, bowing as she placed the food in front of her.

'I hope you know what you're getting yourself into,' said Elizabeth, not entirely fooled.

'Don't worry, you know me. I'll be fine.'

'You frighten me sometimes - you're so idealistic.'

'Why does that frighten you?'

'You see the world through rose-coloured spectacles. I worry you'll get hurt.'

'Mum, I won't. We have plenty of time to find out whether it's going to work, and if we don't think it will then we can call everything off.'

§

Helen and Rahim started to plan their wedding. They decided to call the Indian ceremony their 'engagement'. That way, Fatima could invite as many friends and family as she wanted to. She could organise the food and a band to play, but there wouldn't be an official ceremony as such.

The registry-office wedding was booked for the fourth of July, as Rahim had suggested.

'What do you think of peach for a colour scheme?' Helen asked.

'Yes, sounds good to me.'

'Who else shall we ask to be bridesmaids? We already have Safina, what about Sofia?'

'She's already declined; she doesn't want to look like a meringue.'

'I'll ask Jo if she'd like to be chief bridesmaid, and I'll ask Shelly and Paula if their daughters would like to take part.'

'God, how many more?'

'That's all - except that Karen might like to be one.'

'I'll ring Zara tonight so she can arrange her flights. It'll be her first visit home since she went to Canada five years ago.'

'Your mum will be in her element.'

'It'll be great to see Zara again,' said Rahim. 'The reception needs to be in a hotel, so that guests travelling from afar will have somewhere to stay for the weekend.'

'Are we going to have wedding cars?'

He nodded: 'I never realised how much planning went into these things. I suppose we'll have to - at least for you and the bridesmaids.'

'Will it be a horse and carriage, an open-top elite car, a motor-bike and side-car, or a three-wheeler?' She had him rattled and she knew it.

'I think a three-wheeler, don't you?'

'You sure you don't want me to get the bus?'

Finally, all was settled. Nadim was delighted when Rahim asked him to be his best man - but he was warned about the content of his speech.

§

November was almost at an end and it was unusually cold. The pavements were icy. Children clung to each other, shrieking with laughter as they made their way up the street, slipping and sliding. They jumped into the frozen puddles, ice and water scattering everywhere. Elizabeth and David were enjoying a leisurely breakfast.

'It's so cold,' said Elizabeth. 'Know what we should do?'

David wiped the grease from his plate with a piece of dry bread and stuffed it in his mouth; a slurp of tea helped him wash it down.

'What?'

'We should light the stove so the house is warm and cosy, and then go for a little stroll to blow away the cobwebs. On the way back we can call at the newsagent's and buy the Sunday paper and, when we get back, we can snuggle up for a quiet afternoon.'

'Sounds good to me. I have a couple of jobs to do first, but they won't take long. I'll give you a shout when I'm ready. That OK?'

'I'll do some ironing while I'm waiting.'

David had been in great spirits since the holiday in Orkney. He was working hard on the house with the hope of finishing it by the summer. He talked of the future and where they might go on holiday next year. Even the fact that Karen now had a long-term boyfriend didn't seem to bother him.

'I suppose she'll leave at some point,' he said.

It was noon when the pair of them set out in heavy winter coats, gloves and scarves. Frost lay on every surface like icing on a cake. They walked hand-in-hand, their conversation light-hearted. They laughed at the things that the children had said and done when they were young, and Elizabeth shared funny stories from work. Three children were running and sliding on the frost-covered road.

'Look at them, they're having a ball. Remember when you were that age, David?'

'I'm not sure I want to. It wasn't such a happy time for us. If ever I'd been out and really enjoyed myself like they are, I would come home to a beating from my father for something and nothing - as though I was being punished for being too happy.'

'David, I'm so sorry, I can't imagine how a parent could be so cruel to his children.' She wanted to change the subject quickly before his mood nosedived, but David continued.

'The beatings were nothing compared to the names he called us. The bruises would disappear within a week, but the real scars were the emotional ones that no-one could see, and they don't heal. He knew that the name-calling hurt more than anything else.'

'You don't need to rake all this up again.'

'I think you mean it's easier if we don't talk about it. That's the problem - it makes you feel uncomfortable, so it's easier to avoid the subject rather than "rake it up" as you say.'

'That's unfair, that's not what I meant at all.' She felt her throat tighten and she tried not to cry. 'I just thought that today would be special, and I didn't want you to get upset and for it to be spoilt.'

David walked on in silence, staring straight ahead. Elizabeth let go of his hand.

'Let's get the paper. I'll go in and get it,' she said.

She hurried towards the newsagent's but, with only a couple of yards to go, she forgot about conditions underfoot and slipped on a patch of ice. Her feet shot up in the air and down she thudded onto her right arm and shoulder. The pain was excruciating. She lay still for a moment, groaning, too afraid to move.

David ran to her aid.

'You hurt?'

'Not sure - I think I may have broken something. The pain is unbelievable.'

'Can you sit up?'

'I'm too scared. Leave me, I'll try in a minute.'

A young man who was passing offered to go in the newsagent's shop and call an ambulance.

'No, please don't, I'm sure I'll be OK. David, can you pull me up into a sitting position?'

David gently pushed a hand under her body.

'Where does it hurt most?' he asked.

She screamed out in pain.

'It's my arm! Leave me be.'

'We can't leave you here or you'll freeze.' He took off his coat and wrapped it around her.

Elizabeth tried to move but the pain was too intense. Tears streamed down her face.

'I'm sorry, but I think I'll have to go to hospital. Something is definitely not right.'

By now a small crowd had gathered. The same young man pushed forward.

'Can I give you a hand?' he said to David. 'If we go on either side and bring her up slowly, we could get her into a sitting position first.'

Between the two of them they managed to sit Elizabeth up, and then a second manoeuvre brought her to her feet. She stifled a scream, she'd never felt pain like this before.

'I'll go back home for the car. Let's get you into the shop where you'll be warm,' said David.

In the newsagent's, Elizabeth lowered herself onto a seat. Afraid of passing out with the pain, she laid her head back against the wall behind her and waited for David to return.

§

'What the hell is taking so much time?' David's face was dark. They had been staring at the walls in Accident and Emergency for three hours.

'They're very busy, there are always lots of accidents in this sort of weather,' said Elizabeth.

Just then a young man called out Elizabeth's name.

'Bloody hell, they've got twelve-year-olds working here now,' said David.

'David please, he'll hear you. He must be one of the junior doctors.'

'I don't care.'

The X-ray showed a hairline fracture to the upper right arm. One of the staff nurses, gently but firmly, arranged a sling around Elizabeth's shoulder and arm for support. The doctor wrote out a sick note and handed it to her along with a prescription for pain killers and, finally, they were free to leave.

'Why are you so angry?' Elizabeth asked, once they were back in the car.

'Because you always have to be in charge, and things always have to be done the way you want them to be done,' David replied.

'What are you talking about? What have I done wrong?'

'If you hadn't charged ahead to get the newspaper, this wouldn't have happened.'

'I was trying to help.'

'You always think you know best. Sometimes I feel that I'm not allowed to do things for myself, or have my own thoughts, without you interfering.'

'I don't understand.' She felt weak and her arm ached terribly.

'No you don't - that's the problem. You ask what I feel, but you don't really want to know - or maybe you're too thick to understand.'

She felt as though she had been physically struck and she couldn't contain her anger.

'That is so unfair,' she said. 'All I ever try to do is to spare you any unnecessary trouble or work.'

'You want to know what's unfair? You want to know how I really feel? I'm going to show you exactly how I feel!' David slammed his foot on the accelerator until the car was at full throttle.

'Please stop, you're frightening me.'

Deaf to her plea, his mind was crowded with a thousand voices, all shouting so that he could not decipher what they were saying. He drove faster and faster, but he could not escape the voices; they stayed locked inside his skull threatening to take over completely. He brought the car to an abrupt halt by the canal. In one movement he tightened the handbrake, took the keys from the ignition and jumped out of the car, demanding that she follow him.

'Where are we going?' said Elizabeth her voice filled with fear.

'Come with me.'

They walked until they reached a bridge where David made his way to the highest point. He looked over the rail into the murky water below, then, reaching out, he grabbed hold of Elizabeth and forced her to look too. She winced with the pain from her broken arm but David snorted like a wild bull, the steam of his breath streaming from his nostrils in the cold air.

'Now that I have you here I want you to see what I see.'

Elizabeth knew exactly what he was trying to demonstrate; she was face-to-face with the black hole.

'What are you going to do?' she asked.

'I'm going to throw you over. I want you to know what it's like to feel helpless like I do.'

She gripped the rail with her good hand.

'David you know I can't swim.'

'You think I've forgotten?' He pushed harder. 'That's why I chose this. I feel as though I can't swim either, like I'm drowning and I don't know what to do.'

'David, no,' she yelled. 'Don't do this; I'm begging you - please stop!'

Suddenly, he released his grip and began to sob. She stepped backwards to safety, placing herself out of harm's way.

'I'm so sorry, I'm so sorry,' she repeated.

He clasped his hands to his head.

'I'm weak,' he said.

She put her arm around him.

'You're not weak; you're strong. I wish you could see how much we all love and admire you.'

She began to walk, guiding him slowly back to the car. He didn't resist and plodded mindlessly beside her. Once in the car, he drove home at a slow even pace. He was exhausted, and not even sure he would make it. His mind had been purged of its tormentors and all he wanted to do now was to sleep. The atmosphere between them was strangely calm but Elizabeth was in agony. The pain killers had worn off and her arm throbbed - although this was nothing compared to the emotional anguish that he had inflicted on her.

26 HELEN'S BIG MOVE

Helen stood at the labour-ward desk, stomach churning and knees shaking. It was her first day in her new job at Withington Hospital in Manchester. She was a newly-qualified midwife. Everything was new; the maternity unit, the staff, the doctors, even the patients looked different. The labour ward seemed very busy. A woman shuffled to the toilet, huffing and puffing as she went; a midwife went bustling up the corridor carrying a piece of equipment; a weary-looking doctor ambled by waiting to be called upon for assistance. Helen knew how challenging a labour ward could be, but she loved looking after women in labour and hoped that, as time passed, so would the fear.

At home she and Rahim were enjoying living as one. No - as six actually. They spent much of their free time with family and friends and Helen loved all the new experiences. She had decided that, if she were to really fit in, she must learn the language, and she had bought herself a small notepad in which to write down key words.

'In your language, how do you ask, "what's your name"?' she asked one evening as they sat down to dinner.

'Tojonamcurui,' said Sofia.

'Pardon?'

Sofia and Safina burst out laughing. Helen wrote down in her book, 'Toe jo nam cur u I', and read it out loud, accentuating her northern accent. The whole family, even Jamal, laughed.

'What is a hair plait called?'

'A chotlee,' said Safina.

'Chotly! That's easy - what next?'

Every day she learned something new. Most evenings she cooked a different dish, experimenting with spices she had never heard of before. She was determined to perfect the art of making perfectly round chapatis, or 'rottis' as they were called.

§

Wednesday January 7th 1987 was a day Helen would never forget. She finished work at four-thirty and was walking home in the cold air. Her breath was like a puff of smoke in front of her face and it reminded her of a game she had played with her sisters when they put a pencil in their mouths and pretended to smoke cigarettes. She clasped her gloved hands together. Ice lay on the pavement and the windows of cars were opaque with frost. It had not been so cold in a long time. She reached Rahim's parents' house and let herself in. The girls were already home from college.

'It's so cold,' said Helen.

'I put the heating up higher, so it would be nice and toasty when everyone's home.'

'Thanks, Sofia, I'm frozen.'

She began cooking. She decided not to make curry and intead made an Irish stew, thinking that it would warm everyone up. At six o'clock the table was laid, the food ready to be served, and everyone was home apart from Rahim. Helen headed for the phone to check on Elizabeth who was still having some discomfort from her fracture and had been unable to return to work. Helen spoke to her mother regularly to keep her spirits up.

'Hello?' said Elizabeth.

'Hi, Mum, how are you?'

'Oh - it's you.'

'Who did you think it was?'

'I hoped it was Dad.'

'Why? Where is he?'

'I'm worried. He went out for a walk this afternoon and hasn't come back.'

'Did he say where he was going?'

'No. I was at the shops. He told Karen that he was going for a walk. She asked if he wanted her to go with him, but he said, no, he was fine by himself, and she didn't think anything of it.'

Elizabeth hadn't told the girls about the canal incident, partly because it was so horrendous and partly because, afterwards, David had picked up quickly so there didn't seem any point.

'Why didn't you phone me earlier?' asked Helen.

'I thought he would be back at any time.'

'What are you going to do?'

'Don't know; the police won't be interested, that much we do know - and it's dark now. He could be anywhere. I've phoned Shelly and Paula, they're on their way over.'

'What time did he leave the house?'

'Around one-thirty.'

'I'm coming over.'

'Thank you. I'm so sorry.'

'Don't say sorry. Let's hope he's all right, he's done this before after all.'

Helen put down the receiver, collected a few necessities and shoved them into a holdall. Shortly after, Rahim arrived home exhausted.

'Hi, how are you? Did you have a busy day?' he said.

'I have to go home, Dad's disappeared again.'

'Shall I come too?'

'No I'll be fine.'

'Don't worry,' said Jamal, 'he'll back soon, you'll see.'

Fatima pressed some prayer beads into her hand. 'Take these. Inshallah, he'll be all right.'

As Helen drove along the motorway her mind wandered. In her head, a vision appeared of her father hanging from a tree, his head to one side, eyes bulging, arms loosely by his side, his feet dangling. It was horrific.

She tried to imagine what she would do in those circumstances. Would she try to get him down? Would she scream or simply run for help? She shook her head to erase the revolting sight. 'Stop being dramatic,' she said out loud. 'There'll be an explanation.'

She concentrated on the road ahead, trying to blot out the image. She shuddered and opened the window a little, but she couldn't stay focussed.

'Where could he have got to? If I felt suicidal, what would I do? Where would I go?' She recalled that he had frequently talked about 'ending it all' at his favourite walking place on Saddleworth, but had never specified how he would do it. She imagined herself at the top of the reservoir where they had walked so many times; David slumped against a stone wall, his body cold as ice, an empty pill bottle by his side. 'Stop it!' she told herself, 'this is ridiculous. You know Dad will be home again soon. He could be there when you arrive.'

The silhouette of the familiar house stood ghost-like in the middle of its field. The trees were still, like ghouls, and tonight the house looked more like a mausoleum than a family home. An outside light was glowing and the gates were open. Elizabeth came out to meet her.

'Any news?'

'Nothing at all,' said Elizabeth. 'We've been sitting here for hours, watching and hoping, I don't know what to do, it's so dark. Shelly and I had a drive around to see if we could find him, and Paula and Karen searched on foot, but we can't do anything now.'

Helen threw her arms around Elizabeth's neck, to give comfort and also to receive it. 'Let's go inside. It's freezing out here.'

Heat belted out of the stove in the kitchen warming the whole house. Shelly, Paula and Karen hovered uncomfortably. Helen greeted each one in turn, then looked out of the window.

'We've been doing that all evening,' said Shelly. 'It's just like last time.'

'Mum said you were the last one to speak to him, Karen. How was he?' asked Helen.

'He seemed quite happy. I offered to walk with him but he said he didn't know when he would be back. Maybe that should have rung alarm bells, but I honestly wasn't worried at all. It's my fault. I should have insisted on going.'

'No it's not, Karen. He could have come back after an hour. You weren't to know.'

'Come on,' said Elizabeth putting her arm around Karen, 'let's go into the lounge and sit comfortably. We'll leave the lights on like last time so, if he does come back, he can see we're here.'

Paula sighed and plonked herself down into one of the armchairs while Shelly perched on the low window sill and continued to look out of the window.

'I can't see a thing except the street lights in the distance,' said Shelly

Elizabeth rubbed her eyes and yawned.

'You all right, Mum?' asked Shelly.

'I'm very tired.'

'Let's try to sleep so that we're fresh tomorrow. Assuming that he doesn't come back overnight - what's the plan?'

'Last time he went to Rivington Pike so it might be an idea to look there first,' said Elizabeth.

'Mum, I think you should stay here in case he does come home,' said Paula.

'I think so too,' agreed Helen. 'Let's wait up till twelve like last time then try to get some sleep.'

At midnight, they reluctantly headed for the stairs. Elizabeth lay on top of her bed fully-clothed. Every little sound sent her running to the window; she would drift off to sleep only to wake in panic, fearful of having missed an obvious sign or clue. All four sisters slept in the same room, Helen and Karen squashed into a single bed together; they weren't going to get any sleep anyway.

'It's absolutely freezing out,' said Shelly. 'Surely he has to be inside somewhere?'

'I hope so,' said Karen, 'there's no way he could survive outside overnight, it's below freezing and it's been so cold all day. Oh, why didn't I go with him?'

Helen stroked Karen's hair: 'Don't say that, it's not your fault.'

'Let's try and get some sleep,' Paula said, 'next one to talk smells.'

None of them slept for more than thirty minutes at a time. They listened out for their father's return. Weird dreams and peculiar noises woke them at regular intervals and when daylight arrived, it no longer seemed right to stay in bed. At six thirty, Helen turned to see Shelly in the bed next to theirs, her eyes wide open, staring at her.

'What a night,' said Helen, 'I feel like I haven't slept a wink.'

'Me neither.'

'You did, Shelly' said Paula. 'You were snoring.'

'I don't snore.'

'I'm sorry - but you do,' said Helen.

Karen lay with her eyes closed. The pit of her stomach lurched, nausea rising like a tidal wave; she climbed out from her tangle of bedclothes to make her way to the bathroom.

'She's still blaming herself,' said Helen.

Shelly got up and pulled on her dressing-gown.

'I bet Mum's downstairs already. You go down and I'll talk to Karen.'

Karen sidled back into the bedroom, and looked forlornly out of the window.

'Why did I let him go alone?'

'Karen, it really isn't your fault. How could you know what he was going to do?'

'Please let him come home safely. I just pray that he's all right.'

Shelly put a protective arm around Karen's shoulder. 'He will be, I'm sure of it. He probably needed some time alone to think and found somewhere to stay overnight.'

'I feel sick inside.'

'Let's go down and talk to the others, then we can decide what to do.'

Elizabeth had already set the kitchen table for breakfast. She'd been up since five and the stove was blazing making the kitchen as warm as toast. The old labrador lay stretched out on the hearth having his tummy scratched by Paula.

'Sit down, I'm making some tea,' said Elizabeth. 'There's cereal and eggs. Help yourself.'

Karen looked at the food and tried not to heave.

'I can't eat anything, Mum.'

'Eat or you'll be no use to anyone - especially Dad. It's better if we all sit down together. We need to plan what to do, so that we make the most of the daylight hours.'

They sat down round the table, all five of them.

'First we need to inform the police again,' said Elizabeth, 'although they won't do anything just yet. But at least, if we need them, we'll have the name of a contact. Secondly, we have to decide where to look for him, and thirdly - I know this goes against his wishes - we have to phone around and make sure he hasn't contacted or visited any one.'

They ate quickly as they made their plans and only Karen left the table with an empty stomach.

'I'll eat later,' she insisted when Elizabeth tried to force the issue. 'I'm not hungry right now.'

It was decided that Elizabeth would stay at home in case David returned. She would inform the police and make the phone calls. The girls would stick together and scour the area around Rivington Pike where David had gone last time. They would take with them a photograph of him to show to people in the hope that it might help jog a memory. They arranged to phone home on the hour, every hour, to check if there was any news and to keep Elizabeth up-to-date with their whereabouts.

27 THE SEARCH PARTY GOES OUT AGAIN

'Oh God, it's so cold,' muttered Paula wrapping her scarf tighter round her neck. 'My fingers are white; I can't feel the ends and we're not even out of the car yet.' She struggled to pull her knitted stripy gloves back on, having taken them off to examine her frozen fingers.

'You want these?' asked Shelly, holding out a pair of sheepskin mittens.

'I'm OK. let's get moving before we freeze completely.'

Helen emerged from the warmth of the car.

'This is weird,' she said wrapping her arms around her. 'What the hell are we doing?'

Karen closed the car door but held on to the handle. They were in the car park of a tourist area, surrounded by trees with not another person in sight. It was a beautiful place but an eerie silence hung in the air.

'Let's go in pairs,' said Paula. 'Helen, you come with me and Shelly and Karen can go that way. We'll go up from this side and meet at the top.'

Shelly agreed but Karen's face crumpled.

'I'm scared,' she sobbed. 'I'm scared of what we might find.'

'We all are, but we have to do it for Dad's sake,' said Shelly.

'I've never seen anyone dead before. What if we find him and he's done something awful.'

'Karen - look at me! Calm down. I promise if I see something first, you won't have to look - OK?'

'OK.'

'There's a phone box over there. Let's phone Mum and tell her we've arrived. She may have some news.'

There was no news and so their search began. Rivington Pike was as picturesque as Saddleworth Moor but on a much smaller scale. The climb to the top, where the remains of a stately home lay open to the elements, was only four or five miles up a gentle incline. The landscape was less rugged than the Yorkshire Moors, without sheer drops, but the girls left nothing to chance as they trudged up the narrow pathways. They moved slowly, checking under hedges, behind stone walls and down every gulley, looking up trees and searching more distantly as far as their eyes could see.

Near the top, Helen caught hold of Paula's hand.

'Paula!'

Two feet stuck out from behind a small wall. There was no movement or sound. The girls froze.

'Please - no,' whispered Paula. She closed her eyes and tried to pluck up the courage to take a step closer.

Helen looked at her and then, without a word, they stepped forward together and peered round the wall.

'Oh no!' said Helen.

Some poor man had sat down to shelter from the cold whilst he ate his sandwiches. He nearly choked with fright.

'What the..? You nearly frightened the life out of me.'

'Sorry,' said Paula.

He was a small stocky man, nothing at all like David. The khaki-coloured padded jacket he wore was tight around his middle making him look like Humpty Dumpty. It was difficult to tell his age. A knitted woollen scarf reached up to meet his flat cap and left no hint of how his hair might look, or if he had any.

'Sorry if I scared you too,' he said. 'I'm the ranger for the area. I was doing my usual rounds and there was a hawk hovering, waiting to go in for the kill, so I sat down to watch and have a bite to eat.'

'Seen anyone else around?' asked Helen.

'Yes, I saw two other girls wandering around on the other side.'

'Don't suppose you've seen a man by himself, have you?'

'Why?'

They told him the whole story and asked him to keep a look out. 'This is our home telephone number. Please let us know if you see or hear anything at all.'

'You poor things, of course I will. And this is my number if you need to contact me.'

Back at the car, all four sat dejected.

'He could be anywhere. We could be searching for weeks,' said Karen.

'We should look closer to home,' said Shelly, 'and I expect Mum could do with some company.'

§

Elizabeth was waiting by the gate. Shelly stopped the car and wound down the window.

'Nothing, we found nothing,' she said.

They dashed in out of the cold. In the warm kitchen Elizabeth had made their favourite dish; hotpot with a suet crust accompanied by pickled red cabbage.

'I've contacted the police,' said Elizabeth. 'They'll come round to take some details this evening - which means that nothing will happen till tomorrow.'

'What will they do? They're hardly going to send out a search party, are they?' said Karen.

'We still have to let them know.' Elizabeth moved closer to Karen and gently rubbed her shoulder. 'I don't know what anyone can do to help; it's like looking for a needle in a hay stack.'

They gathered round the table to eat, the delicious hot meat and potatoes slid down easily. After being out in the cold all day, each of them had rosy cheeks and a healthy glow that defied the circumstances. Even Karen asked for seconds.

'We should go over to Saddleworth tomorrow and take a look around there,' said Helen.

'You think he's all right?' Karen asked.

Elizabeth sighed: 'If only he realised what he was putting us through.'

'Why would he want to leave us? How can he do this?'

'He loves you all more than anything in the world,' said Elizabeth, 'but over the last ten years his mind has worked differently from yours or mine. He feels we'd be better off without him.'

'You think he's already dead, don't you, Mum?' Karen whispered. She placed her fork on her plate and wept.

'Karen, no-one's to blame, certainly not you. He's sick. I have no idea whether he's dead or alive - but the temperature is minus five degrees tonight. Unless he's found somewhere to stay, there's no way he can survive this cold.' Elizabeth looked drained and weary. 'I don't want to stay here tomorrow, but my arm is too painful for me to drive.'

'We have to stay positive,' said Paula, 'we have to believe he's alive. I'm not giving up until I know for sure. Tomorrow we should go to different places though, there's no point in all of us going to the same area'

'I'll phone Auntie Annie, to see if she wouldn't mind driving,' said Elizabeth.

'That's a good idea. Helen and Karen, you go to Saddleworth with Mum and Auntie Annie. Shelly and I will stay closer to home and ask around.'

At that moment, there was a knock on the door. A young policeman stood shivering on the doorstep.

'Mrs Singleton?' he asked.

Elizabeth made him welcome; it was such a comfort to have the police involved.

'I'm so glad you're here at last. I've phoned one or two friends and relatives,' Elizabeth told him once he was seated at the table with them, 'but my husband didn't have a lot of contact with people outside the family. The girls have been out searching for him but we don't know what else to do.'

'You say he's done this before?'

'He's very poorly, but we thought he was getting better so we weren't worried when he said he was going out.'

After making notes, the policeman put his book in his inside pocket and stood up. 'We'll do all we can but, in the meantime, let us know if you hear from him.'

'What exactly are you going to do?' asked Paula.

'We'll put out an alert so that our officers can look out for him and we'll keep his details on record at the station.'

'That it? What good is that going to do? We need you to help us look for him.'

'I'm afraid we don't have the resources to do that.'

'This is my dad you're talking about. He's very depressed and we need to find him.'

'No need to raise your voice, Paula,' said Elizabeth. 'Like the young man said, it's not possible to have a full-scale search. Thank you, officer.'

Just then the phone rang and Elizabeth answered.

'Oh, hello.'

They all sank back when they heard the disappointment in her voice. 'We're fine, Rahim. No, no sign of him.'

Helen took the phone: 'Hi, how are you?'

'I'm all right, what about you?'

'It's the not knowing and not being able to do anything that's so hard. I haven't been in touch with work. Could you tell them I don't know when I'll be back?'

'Don't worry about anything like that. I'll ring them. Is there any other way I can help?'

'I'll ring you when we have any news. Give my love to everyone and take care.'

The evening dragged. Elizabeth tried to watch the news on television but was annoyed that life carried on regardless while they were stuck in limbo not knowing what to do. She went up to her room to lie down. Karen and Helen sat together on the sofa, half their attention on the clock and half on the television. Eventually the girls followed Elizabeth to bed - but none of them slept.

28 SADDLEWORTH MOOR

Friday morning arrived cold and crisp, an ordinary day for most people, but another day of agony for Helen and her family. Elizabeth reached into the bread bin, pulled out a few slices of soft white loaf and began to make cheese sandwiches. Helen and Karen would be out all day. It was a tough walk up to the top of the Saddleworth reservoir and they would need to eat and drink. The girls put on lots of layers. It wasn't as cold as the night before, but on the hillside the temperature would be lower.

'We need hats - Karen, do you have a spare one?'

Karen was very subdued; she dug out a woolly hat for Helen.

'You ready?' she said quietly. 'It'll be dark by four-thirty which doesn't leave us much time.'

Elizabeth handed over two plastic boxes and two flasks of tea.

'I couldn't find the big flask so I've made two smaller ones. You'll need a hot drink in this weather. There are sandwiches in one box and snacks in the other.'

Annie, Elizabeth's sister, drove. She and Elizabeth planned to drop Helen and Karen at one side of the reservoir and then spend an hour or so with some close friends who lived nearby before driving round to the other side to pick up the girls again. Meanwhile, Shelly and Paula would stay at home for the morning in case David returned. If he didn't, they would go out searching in the afternoon.

The short journey along the motorway seemed to take forever. Helen felt as though she was in a bubble. Life continued around her and yet she was detached from it. They travelled in silence, both gazing out of the window. They left the motorway and narrow winding roads brought them closer to their destination. In years gone by, Helen would have been full of excitement and anticipation at this stage in the journey. She remembered competing with her cousins to get to the top of the reservoir first, singing songs and playing games as they went.

Along the path, piles of stones marked the way and every person left their mark by adding one more. Today, there was no excitement, no friends or relatives to laugh with, and no-one to greet them except the odd sheep that continued to graze, oblivious to their plight. Tears pouring down her face, Elizabeth hugged both girls. Clinging to each other, they said their goodbyes.

'I'm sorry you have to do this. Maybe I should go and you should stay here instead.'

'No, Mum, we'll be quicker, and if you hear from Shelly and Paula you may need to get home quickly. We'll find our own way home if we have to.'

Elizabeth blew her nose: 'I'm so angry with him. How could he do this?'

'Mum, he's not well,' said Helen.

'Karen, you're very quiet. I'm worried about you,' Elizabeth added.

'I'll feel better when we've found him and he's home safe and well.'

§

Elizabeth watched as her two youngest children went in search of their father. She felt numb inside and yet the worst-ever pain gnawed in her stomach. It was excruciating to watch them tramp the path toward the open moor. She wanted to find David to ask how he could torment his children this way. She watched as they became smaller and smaller. She had to walk a little way to get a better view; they were just pinpricks in the distance before they disappeared altogether. Still she stood, not sure what to do. It had been some time since she had been to church, but now she prayed: 'Please God, don't let them find him up there. Let him be somewhere else, safe and sound.'

Elizabeth walked slowly back to the car where Annie sat waiting. Only when she was back in the car did she realise just how bitterly cold it was outside. Her mind was on Helen and Karen.

'They must be freezing,' she said. 'What could he have been thinking?' She rubbed her face with her good hand, circling her eyes with her fingers, and let her head drop back onto the headrest. She was exhausted, but she had lots to do. They must tell Doris and Harry about what was happening. Doris and Harry lived in a small town near the moors. Although they had been friends for a long time, they didn't know about David's problems and the news would come as a shock to them.

Annie leaned forward and turned the key in the ignition, bringing the car to life. Elizabeth smiled. David always made sure their vehicles were running smoothly; if he detected any slight noise or bump he would vanish under the bonnet until the problem was sorted.

'She's running smooth as a bird, is what he would say,' said Elizabeth.

Annie laughed: 'You're right, that's exactly what he would say.'

They drove to Doris and Harry's home. It was eight-thirty in the morning and the drive took ages because the town centre was heaving with people on their way to work, but finally they pulled up outside a neat terraced house. The small wooden garden gate creaked as it swung open. A short path, flanked on either side by a tiny immaculate garden, lead to the front door, Elizabeth rang the doorbell. The ring echoed inside the house followed by the sound of feet shuffling over cold lino.

'Elizabeth!' said Harry. 'What a surprise. Come in out of the cold.'

'You remember my sister?'

'Of course I do. Annie, isn't it?'

He showed them into a cosy little lounge where an open fire was already ablaze and where Doris sat to keep warm.

'Oh my goodness, what a surprise,' said Doris. 'Why didn't you tell us you were coming? Is everything all right, Elizabeth, you look a bit worried?'

'That's why I've come to see you. It's David ...' Elizabeth's lips quivered.

'Oh no, he's not d... !'

'Doris!' said Harry, 'let Elizabeth speak.'

'You'd better sit down, both of you; I have a lot to tell you.'

She told Doris and Harry the story of the last ten years and of the past few days and that Helen and Karen were presently up on the moor searching for David.

'But he was always so happy and full of fun,' said Harry, in a daze.

'That was just a front; he was desperate that no-one should find out. He didn't want to believe he had a mental illness, let alone tell people about it.'

'I don't know what to say,' said Doris. 'Is there anything we can do?'

'It would help if you could stay home for the day. Annie and I are going to drive to the other side of the reservoir later to pick up the girls. I hope you don't mind, but they have your telephone number with them just in case.'

§

'How shall we do this?' asked Helen.

Karen thought for a minute.

'You look on the right and I'll look on the left. If we do it methodically we'll cover the area thoroughly. We mustn't leave the path though, it's too dangerous and we could easily lose each other.'

'I know I keep saying it, but this is so weird. It's the sort of thing that happens to other people or in films.'

The first few miles were quite easy. A well-worn path meandered through fields, over stiles and along the edge of a shallow stream. It was a clear day with no wind or rain but very cold. They tramped along the bottom of a rising valley. The hillsides on either side were beautiful, Helen had forgotten how beautiful. No wonder their father had fallen in love with this place. Karen remembered walking part of the way when she was small and, at such a young age, it had seemed vast. Today she was less impressed and, secretly, she despised it.

'My feet are freezing. Are we near the top yet?' she said.

'Don't think so. I think it suddenly flattens out when we get to the reservoir. The stream is formed from the overflow. You OK?'

'Keep going, it can't be far.'

They walked briskly so as to keep warm and to beat the daylight. They had to cover as much ground as possible, looking behind huge boulders, over stone walls and down ravines, whilst listening for unusual sounds - all to no avail. It was difficult to think of anything to talk about and, as the incline became steeper, their breathing grew heavier.

'I don't believe he could have come all the way up here,' said Karen. 'He would have had to get a train from home, then a bus and then walk for miles. At some point he would have changed his mind.'

'I don't know, it depends on how he was feeling. Let's hope he's somewhere warm and safe and we're wasting our time.'

On and on, the path wound its way to the top. Birds perched on fence poles, feathers puffed out to keep warm, and sheep wrapped in their woolly jumpers continued to chomp, oblivious to the bitter cold.

They rounded a bend and Helen shouted: 'Look!'

'What?'

'We've made it.' Helen pointed ahead.

'Thank goodness for that, but now what?'

'Let's have something to eat where it flattens out - and make a plan.'

The last half-mile was gruelling. The path became steeper and more dangerous underfoot, the temperature dropped and the cold bit into their cheeks. At last they had reached the top - they stopped in their tracks. By a stone wall that was part of the reservoir lay a familiar object.

'Oh God,' said Helen.

They held on to each other, unable to move.

'Oh, Helen!'

'He was here.'

'Helen - I'm scared.'

'Come on.'

A small rucksack stood abandoned like a toy soldier. Alongside it was David's old blue flask. It lay on its side capped by its gleaming white lid. Helen was suddenly icy calm.

'No wonder Mum couldn't find the flask this morning.'

Karen picked it up.

'Empty.' She looked in the rucksack, 'Nothing in here either.'

They looked around, there was no sign of David.

'I need to eat, Karen. Let's eat now, and then we'll split up and look around on either side of the reservoir.'

'What if we lose each other?'

'We won't go too far. If we eat quickly, we can spend an hour searching and meet up again here. It's all flat so it should be pretty safe. I'll meet you back here at two-thirty. Whether we find him or not, we'll have to think about getting back before it goes dark.'

They ate in silence, the sandwiches seemed tasteless but they satisfied their hunger and provided them with the energy to carry on. The hot tea brought comfort, sinking to the depths, warming as it went down. They split up.

'You sure you're OK with this?' asked Helen.

'Just hope we find him alive.'

'Me too.' Helen hugged her. 'See you in an hour. If you see anything, make your way back here and shout for me and I'll do the same - OK?'

Being out on the moors alone was not how Helen had envisaged it. She felt vulnerable and frightened away from the well-trodden path. Treading carefully, she scanned the ground. If he was dead, she wanted one of them to find him and not some stranger passing by on an afternoon out. She hoped, if they did find him dead, that he would somehow know that he was being looked after and treated with respect in his last few days on this earth.

'Come on, Dad, please be here somewhere,' she muttered. 'Please, please, please,'

Karen, meanwhile, walked slowly, trying to keep Helen within her sight. She did not want to be alone in this remote place. She found no peace and tranquillity in the wilderness. She called out in the hope that David might answer.

'Dad! Dad, can you hear me?'

Something strange occurred to her; when she shouted, her voice didn't carry, it stopped short on her lips as though stuck in a thick fog. She called again, but nothing. Even if he were alive, he wouldn't hear her calling out his name. Slowly, combing the area for clues, she looked near and far, in streams and down gulleys. She made her way back towards the meeting place and was relieved to find Helen already waiting for her.

'No sign?' asked Karen.

'Nothing - I take it you had no luck either?'

'It's beginning to get dark,' said Helen. 'I don't think we can make it down to the other side. Maybe we should go back the way we came.'

'What about Mum? She'll have gone round to the other side to meet us.'

'I know, but it's not far by car. When we get down, we can phone Doris and Harry and they can find her to tell her where we are.'

'If you're sure.'

They turned back in the direction they had come.

'At least we know he's been here. Tomorrow we can come back with the police and as many friends and relatives as possible and search a wider area.'

'We'll set out much earlier to give us more time,' said Karen.

Facing downhill gave the girls a different perspective on things. The whole place looked friendlier, perhaps also because they were homeward-bound. Helen was torn; she did not want to leave without her father but she wanted to be at home where it was warm and comfortable.

Meanwhile, down below, Elizabeth looked at the clock on Doris's sitting room wall. The hours had slipped by while the four of them sat discussing David's illness.

'We must get going,' she said.

It was freezing in the car.

'Annie, I'm scared. Do you think Helen and Karen are all right? I hope they haven't found him and are waiting safely for us on the other side.'

'If they haven't found him - what will you do?'

'Where do we look next? I can't imagine where he would go.'

'Let's wait until we see the girls,' said Annie pressing her foot on the accelerator.

At four o'clock Elizabeth's white Cortina, driven by Annie, pulled into the reservoir car park. The frost-covered tarmac bore no other tyre marks.

'No sign of them,' said Elizabeth, 'it's pitch black out there. What was I thinking letting them go up there alone?'

'They're probably making their way down slowly if it's slippery. Let's sit and wait a while,' said Annie.

'We should go up and look for them.' The thought of waiting was horrendous to Elizabeth. She had done too much of it. She cursed David: 'You stupid man,' she muttered.

'You don't mean that, Elizabeth.'

'Right now, I've never meant anything more in my life. Our children are up there. It's dark and it's the middle of winter. I can't believe he could do this.'

'Stop it!' said Annie. 'Calm down. Let's think about what to do.'

'I don't know what to do. Tell me, because I haven't a clue any more. I can't think sensibly.' Elizabeth stared hopelessly into the dark.

'We stay put. We need to be here when they arrive.' But Annie was out of her depth.

Having no children of her own, she couldn't imagine what might be going through Elizabeth's mind right now. Instead, she tried to put herself in the girls' shoes and imagine the difficulties they might have encountered and what she would do if it was her.

'I think we should drive back round to the other side. Maybe they had to go back down the way they came,' said Annie.

'But what if they come down here and we aren't here for them?'

'Tell you what, let's walk as far as that outcrop of boulders up there, but no further.' Annie pointed. 'If there's no sign of them, we'll drive right the way round.'

It didn't take long to reach the boulders and they couldn't see a thing. Elizabeth's fears began to grow. She shivered and pulled her scarf around her face for warmth. 'This hill, this massive lump of earth might already have swallowed up half of my family, and now it sits like a giant monster waiting for another chance.'

'Elizabeth, I think we should go back to the car.'

Elizabeth said nothing; she stood watching and listening, then turned and walked silently back to the waiting vehicle.

'Let's drive back round and if they're not there, we'll have to go to the police,' said Annie.

At that moment a car pulled up alongside them. Elizabeth let out a whimper like that of a wild animal caught in a trap. It was a police car.

'Not the girls, please,' she whispered.

§

'Karen!'

Having taken only a few steps, something caught Helen's eye, and she grabbed her sister by the arm.

'What is it?'

'Look down there.' Helen pointed towards the floor of the ravine where the water flowed black from the reservoir.

'What are you looking at?'

'Look, right in the bottom, it looks like a coat.'

They grasped hold of each other.

'Please no!' Karen cried.

They hurtled down the steep, frost-covered hillside towards the stream, leaping over boulders, and stumbling over rocks towards the object that lay at the bottom.

As they approached, Helen slowed her pace and held Karen back a little. She swallowed hard and closed her eyes hoping that the sight before her was an illusion.

'No Dad. No! No! No!' She turned to Karen, 'This can't be right.'

Karen stared, clinging onto Helen's hand. David lay face down in the freezing cold water; his fawn duffle coat covered in frost provided the perfect camouflage which was probably why they hadn't seen him as they made their way up. His arms were splayed out on each side of his body and the water danced over his hands and trickled through his fingers, teasing as it went. The black leather shoes he had spent so many hours polishing, now dull and sodden, remained firmly on his feet. One trouser leg had ridden up revealing a peculiarly mottled, yellow-looking calf.

The girls released their grip on each other and found the courage to go a little closer.

'Oh Dad, you poor thing,' sobbed Karen. She crouched down at the water's edge. There was no sign of life. They couldn't see the whole of his face, only one temple and a slither of his cheek which was also mottled; the rest of his face was obliterated by the water. Neither of them touched him, they sat on their haunches and looked, firstly at him and then at each other.

'I wonder what happened,' said Helen.

'Do you think he took any tablets?'

'Difficult to say.' Helen looked around for clues. 'We need to get back down and call the police and Doris and Harry, so that they can go and get Mum.'

'You go,' said Karen. 'I'll stay here with Dad till you get back.'

'No, it's too cold and dangerous.'

'I don't want to leave him alone again.'

'Come with me. It'll be awful for you up here once it's dark.'

Reluctantly, Karen agreed to go. She reached down to touch David's hand.

'Don't worry Dad, we'll be back as quickly as we can,' she said.

'We won't be long, Dad.' Helen caressed the side of his face. The skin she had kissed so many times was cold and solid but it was still him. She patted the back of his jacket affectionately as though to reassure him: 'We'll be back soon Dad.'

They set off at a rapid pace, a long trek ahead of them. The last three days had taken its toll and they were tired and frustrated. Helen suddenly let out a piercing scream; it was all she could think of to release her pent-up emotions. Daylight was now fading fast and a peculiar hush crept over the hillside. The birds had stopped twittering and the sheep stopped chewing momentarily as they passed by.

'What about Mum?' asked Karen. 'What shall we say to her?'

'Don't tell her he was face-down in the water, just say he was at the edge of the water, OK?'

The journey seemed never-ending. Concerned that they might take a wrong turning, they went slipping and sliding on loose cobbles as they tried to increase their speed down the hillside. Eventually, a towpath came into view and dim lights glowed in the window of a small stone cottage. An elderly man stood leaning against the white door frame. He drew in a long smoke-laden breath from his cigarette, the red tip glistened and a white cloud obliterated his face. As they trudged towards him, he seemed a little alarmed.

'It's all right,' said Helen. 'Please could we use your phone? We need to phone the police.'

The man's wife came scuttling to the door.

'What you doing, Fred? You'll catch your death!' she said, and then she saw the girls. 'Can I help you?' she asked.

Some while later, a police car pulled up quietly in front of the weather-worn gate. There were no blue flashing lights or loud sirens; it was too late for that. The passenger door swung open and a middle-aged policeman got out. He adjusted his jacket and plonked a hat on his head as Helen and Karen stood at the door to meet him. A second policeman jumped out of the driver's side.

'Good evening,' said the first officer, his breath curling in front of him in the cold of the evening. 'Is there anywhere we can talk?'

The woman came to the door.

'You're welcome to come in if you like,' she offered.

They gathered in the warm living room. Helen and Karen sat face-to-face with the two policemen in a stranger's house, in the middle of nowhere. Karen felt devoid of any emotion; she sat, wide-eyed, staring into the fire. Helen perched on the edge of the saggy old sofa and explained everything to the two officers. Sergeant Rothwell, the first policeman, asked all the questions. Judging by the crow's feet, Helen guessed that he was probably around the same age as her father. The other policeman pulled out his notebook and scribbled fast to keep up.

'I think that's all we need for now,' said Sergeant Rothwell, thirty minutes later. 'PC Hargreaves, can you radio for some extra help? We're going to need another car. Also, ring the undertakers and get them to come up.'

'Yes, Sarge.'

'This is what we're going to do,' said Sergeant Rothell. 'I'll arrange for Karen to be taken round to where your mother is waiting and have them escorted back to her friend's house, OK?' He turned his attention to Helen: 'Are you up to showing us where your father is?'

Helen swallowed hard. She hadn't imagined how they would bring her father down or whether a car could get up that far, but, thinking logically, she supposed the roads would have to be able take maintenance lorries to the reservoir.

'You sure you'll be all right?' asked Sergeant Rothell, seeing her expression. 'We could leave it till daylight if you don't feel able to return right now.'

Helen shuddered at the thought of her father spending another night alone, face-down in the water.

'No, that's fine. I'll show you where he is.'

'That's very brave of you. We'll get going as soon as the others arrive.'

It wasn't long before another police car, and a large black Transit van, came to a halt outside the cottage.

'Will you be all right, Karen?' asked Helen.

'But what about you? Do you want me to come with you?'

'No, you go and find Mum. She'll be out of her mind by now.'

They held on to each other before parting. Karen was ushered into one of the waiting police cars by PC Hargreaves. He gave the two officers inside it their instructions, and when Karen was safely inside, closed the rear door.

Helen got into the other police car. What if she couldn't find the exact spot? They should have taken note of an object or left something to remind them. Her head was fuzzy, her memory a blur and she couldn't think straight any more. Sitting behind the passenger seat, she leaned slightly to the right so she could watch the road ahead. She'd never imagined that she would ever make this journey by car. The headlights lit up a wide area. It was a clear night again and bitterly cold. A lone sheep looked up before turning quickly and scrambling up the bank out of harm's way.

'Let me know when you think we're getting close,' said Sergeant Rothwell.

'It was quite near the top.' Everything looked different and she was disorientated. The black van followed them, like a vulture waiting to pounce. She couldn't contemplate the thought of David's body being thrown in the back of it to make its final journey down from the place he loved.

When they drew nearer to the top, Helen knew where she was. She recognised a gnarled windswept tree to the right of the path.

'We're almost there now.' Her heart started to thud and she felt suddenly breathless. 'Can you stop here?'

The car gently halted and Sergeant Rothwell swivelled in his seat. He could see the fear in her eyes.

'We'll be right beside you.'

Helen was shaking. She made no effort to get out of the car and sat staring straight ahead, trying to gather courage.

'Helen?'

'I'm fine.' She reached for the door handle, climbed out and stood on the frosty grass verge, looking down into the gully. It was difficult to see clearly, despite the beam of light from PC Hargreaves' torch. Two men wearing thick black bomber jackets slid out of the black van. One was tall and slim with thick black hair. His colleague was exactly the opposite, a stocky, bald-headed man with a friendly smile.

'Maybe it was further up, it all looks the same.'

'Take your time,' said Sergeant Rothwell.

'There!' Helen caught sight of the familiar fawn duffle coat still glistening with frost. 'He's down there.'

They stumbled down towards the stream but the two undertakers hung back a little. One of them was carrying a black body bag. For a moment all were quiet, as each man paid his respects to the dead man on the moor.

'Carry on,' said Helen. 'Please do what you have to do.'

Sergeant Rothwell looked around at PC Hargreaves who continued to scribble notes.

'Have you got what you need?' he asked the two undertakers, then: 'Helen, I'll take you back to the car. We'll find out where your mother and sister are so that we can meet up with them.'

She followed as they made their way back up the slippery slope. Sergeant Rothwell hadn't even put the key into the ignition, when PC Hargreaves knocked on the window.

'Sorry, Sarge, but maybe we should get the body ID'd.'

Sergeant Rothwell grimaced and looked at Helen. He would never expect one of his daughters to experience such a thing.

'Surely that's not necessary right now?'

'If it's not done now, sir, someone will have to come to the mortuary tomorrow morning.'

'I don't mind,' said Helen. 'I'd rather it were me than Mum.'

Once again, the cold air hit her face. She pulled her coat around her tightly, and, totally unprepared for what she was about to see, made her way back down to where her father lay. He was now lying on his back at the side of the stream, his frozen body in exactly the same position, hands out like claws, legs splayed. What shocked her most were the bulging eyes, like two golf balls, his nose and the rest of his face were pushed to one side and contorted almost beyond recognition. She gasped and retreated only to stumble into Sergeant Rothwell.

'It's OK love, I've got you,' he said.

She shuddered and buried her face in his thick overcoat.

'Shall I take you back to the car?'

'No, not yet. He's still my Dad.' Slowly turning back she crouched down beside David and reached out to touch his hand, imagining that he could feel her fingers. 'You're safe now,' she said. 'They'll look after you.'

'Of course they will,' said Sergeant Rothwell. 'Let's get you back to the car. You've been through enough.'

She sat still in the darkness of the car and watched the road unfold in the headlights. She felt like an intruder, watching someone else's drama.

'Can I ask how old you are?' asked Sergeant Rothwell.

'Twenty-six; my sister is much younger and has never seen a dead body before. I'm glad Mum wasn't with us.'

§

The rear door of the police car opened and Karen appeared. Elizabeth fumbled with the door handle to get it to open more quickly, mother and daughter clung to each other.

'Thank goodness you're alive,' said Elizabeth then noticed that Helen wasn't there. 'Where's Helen?'

'She's fine - she ...'

'She's what?' Elizabeth's voice was high, she was almost in a frenzy.

'Mum - we found Dad. He was at the top of the reservoir.'

Annie, who had remained in the background until now, stepped forward to comfort her sister.

'Is he all right?' asked Elizabeth.

'No, Mum - he's not. Helen has gone back to show the police where he is.'

'Oh no, oh you poor things.' Sobbing, Elizabeth pulled Karen to her.

Helen arrived an hour later, escorted by PC Hargreaves and Sergeant Rothwell.

She scrambled out of the car. 'Mum, I'm so sorry!' She held out her arms to her mother.

'Helen, thank God you are all right. I need to see him,' cried Elizabeth.

'Not now Mum!' The sight of his face was still fresh; she didn't want anyone to see him like that, least of all her mum.

'Please, I have to!'

'No Mum, wait until tomorrow.' Helen hoped that by then his face might have returned to normal; she couldn't let any of them go through the nightmare that she just experienced.

'But I can't believe that he's dead. I have to see him.'

Annie coaxed her towards the car. 'Elizabeth, the girls are right, we'll go together in the morning, it's late now and getting colder again.'

Elizabeth agreed reluctantly. They drove to Doris and Harry's house in silence. Only a soft whimpering now and then could be heard from Elizabeth.

A post-mortem revealed that David had taken some sleeping tablets though not enough to kill him. The cause of death was a brain haemorrhage resulting from a fractured skull. At the inquest, Sergeant Rothwell read out a statement and Helen was asked to confirm that his statement was correct. The statement included the fact that David was found face down in the water. A combination of the effects of medication and hypothermia had probably rendered him confused and disorientated, and he had presumably stumbled and hit his head on a rock in the water causing the fracture and the haemorrhage. Taking into account the fact that David was inappropriately dressed for such drastic weather conditions, a verdict of accidental death was recorded. They did not take into account the history of depression or the previous suicide attempts.

'Why didn't you tell me he was in the water?' Elizabeth asked.

'We thought it would upset you too much,' said Helen.

'After all you and Karen went through and you're trying to protect me? I feel so ashamed of myself.' Elizabeth took hold of Helen's hand. 'I have only thought of my own sadness and not realised that you are also feeling the pain. I'll miss him so much but I'm glad he's at peace - but I still feel angry with him for doing this to all of you.'

A fine mist shrouded De Trafford House on the day of the funeral. Helen and her sisters had stayed there to give comfort to Elizabeth and to each other. The house seemed empty, David's absence creating a void that couldn't be filled. All five women stood on the doorstep and watched as he made his final journey to the home that was his castle. But this time, incarcerated in the beautiful oak casket, he didn't see the old dog sitting wagging his tail, or the tears being shed, or Elizabeth slowly making her way to his beloved gates, opening them for him to enter one last time.

The coffin lay before the altar beneath vibrant flowers. It seemed too small for such a big man. Friends and family occupied the cold wooden pews and stared in disbelief, trying to comprehend what had gone wrong. Helen, flanked by Rahim and Jo, stood and watched as Shelly comforted their mother. She was still unable to understand how her father could have ended his life in such a way.

§

'There are so many things to think about.'

'Like what?' asked Rahim.

'Like what Mum will do now? What about Karen? And if Karen leaves home, how will Mum cope with such a big house? And what about the wedding?'

'I wanted to ask you about the wedding. I probably shouldn't say this - but wouldn't you have thought he would have waited until afterwards?'

'If he was thinking logically there'd always be some reason to wait. How do we know he didn't wait to get Christmas out of the way?'

'I suppose. Have you thought about who could give you away at the wedding?'

'Yes, but as it's a registry-office wedding, I don't actually need anyone at all.'

'It would still be nice for you to have someone at your side. Who do you have in mind?' asked Rahim.

'What about Richard? After all, it will be the fourth of July, American Independence Day.'

'That's a fantastic idea. Would he come over?'

'I think so. What better way of paying tribute to his brother?' Helen smiled. 'Shall I ask him?'

Elizabeth went back to work as soon as she felt able. It kept her mind occupied. She'd always loved her job and now more than ever she was thankful she had her profession. It was the evenings she hated. She still expected David to walk into the room and sit in his favourite armchair and though she still had Karen at home for a while longer, she couldn't imagine what it would be like when she was totally alone. Sometimes, when the house was quiet, she would hear David call her name and she would look up expecting him to open the door, but there was nothing, only the emptiness that embraced the whole house.

Two months had passed since David's death. Elizabeth was in the kitchen washing the dirty pots from teatime. Tonight her heart lay heavy. Karen was out and she sighed as she stacked the cups - neatly, the way he would have liked it. Glancing out of the window into the darkness, she saw a car turn down the track and slowly make its way towards the house until it pulled up at the gates. She carried on David's tradition and kept them closed because she felt more secure that way. The car door opened and a passenger crossed in front of the headlights to reach for the latch on the gate. It was Helen, and Rahim was at the wheel. Elizabeth dried her hands and ran to the open door.

'What a lovely surprise! Why didn't you tell me you were coming?'

'Because, it's meant to be a surprise,' said Helen, 'and I didn't want you to go to any trouble.'

'If I'd known, I could have...'

'Exactly.'

Helen meant well, but Elizabeth was disappointed that she had been robbed of an opportunity to fuss over someone. The mothering side of her felt bereft, not having anyone other than Karen to care for.

'I'll put the kettle on.'

'I need the loo,' said Helen, dashing up the stairs. Reaching the top, she saw that her parents' bedroom door was open and peered inside. The room remained just as it always had. Helen went in and sat on her father's side of the bed. She stroked the pillow where his head used to lay. She spotted his wardrobe. Opening the door, she saw his clothes, still hanging limply from the hangers. Pulling them toward her she held them to her face. She could smell the familiar scent and, when she closed her eyes, she pictured him clearly in her mind and could feel his presence. For a moment, she forgot his torment and wished with all her heart that there could be a homecoming.

'Would you like something to eat?' shouted Elizabeth.

'Just a drink, Mum. We've eaten.'

Elizabeth pictured the whole of Rahim's family sitting around the dining table, eating and laughing together, just as her family had done not so long ago. She envied the Asian way of looking after their extended family. She would give anything right now to have a house full of people.

Back in the kitchen, Helen shifted in her seat.

'Mum, we've started thinking about the wedding again. It's not that far away so we need to sort out a few things. I wanted to ask you something - what do you think about asking Richard to come over to give me away?'

'That's a lovely idea. He'd love it - and I'm sure Dad would approve.'

'Well that's that settled,' said Rahim, with a sigh of relief. He hadn't been at all sure how Elizabeth would react.

'Shall we ring him?' said Elizabeth. 'He may already have other plans.' She reached for the phone book, found his number and dialled.

'Hello?' said a voice at the other end.

'It's Elizabeth. How are you?' She smiled at Helen and Rahim. 'I'm ringing to ask you to do something very special for me.'

'What is it you want?' asked the faraway voice.

'Would you like to give your niece away when she gets married on July 4th?'

'I'd love to!' shouted Richard. 'Is she there? Can I speak to her?'

Elizabeth held the phone out to Helen who clasped it to her ear only to recoil at the sound of Richard's booming voice.

'Hi there, sweetie, so he's making an honest women of you at long last. Of course, I would love to be there for you.'

'You don't mind?'

'Mind? I'm delighted you've asked me.'

'Thank you so much. Rahim would like a quick word,' she said handing over the phone.

'Hi, Richard, how are you?' said Rahim.

'I'm fine, but listen - you'd better look after her properly or you'll have me to answer to.'

'She's safe with me. Thank you for doing this - it means a lot.'

Once Richard had put down the phone, they sat back and smiled. Elizabeth felt good; she had something to look forward to and lots to keep her busy. Since David's death it was as though her life had come to a standstill, but now life would go on.

'We're having an engagement party,' said Helen.

'I thought you were engaged,' replied Elizabeth.

'We are, but we didn't make it official. At Asian weddings there are usually hundreds of guests, with an Indian band, Indian dancing and Indian food, but as we're having a traditional English reception there won't be the opportunity to do that. So we'll do it at the engagement party instead.'

'It'll be great fun,' said Rahim, 'and one or two of our English friends and Helen's immediate family are invited as well. Mum can do all the traditional wedding customs and rituals, which will please her. I think you'll enjoy it too.'

'Is there anything I can do to help?' asked Elizabeth.

'No. Come along on the night and just enjoy yourself.'

30 A NEW HOUSE

One Sunday morning in early March, Helen had been up for some time when Rahim came into the lounge carrying two cups of tea.

'Did you see the newspaper? They're building a small group of Georgian-style houses opposite the Marie Louise Gardens.'

'Where exactly are the Marie Louise Gardens?' asked Helen.

'A mile or so up the road. We should be thinking about buying a house; it's stupid to keep paying rent. Shall we go and see them?'

A few minutes later they pulled up in front of a building site. The houses were almost finished.

'Oh, Rahim, they look fantastic. Let's have a look through the windows.'

Helen glued her nose to the lounge window of one of the houses and Rahim was at the patio door when a voice called out.

'Can I help you?'

A well-dressed man came down the steps of a Portakabin.

'Would it be possible to see inside?' asked Helen.

'There are two left. The one that you're looking at now and the show house over there. You're welcome to have a look.'

The location was perfect; a quiet leafy road, away from the traffic and with a beautiful park opposite. Once inside, they were impressed; both houses were well-proportioned, each with four bedrooms and an integral garage.

'What do you think?' asked the man.

'It depends on the price,' said Rahim.

The man handed Rahim a brochure.

'All the prices are in here, along with the dimensions of the rooms and what's included.' He gave Helen a business card. 'If you're interested, give me a call.'

Back in the car, Rahim opened the brochure.

'Let me see,' said Helen.

He held the information up above his head, out of her reach.

'Wait till we get home.' He laughed, knowing how excited she was.

'Please, let me look.'

'Nope you have to wait.'

Instead of going home, they called at the local pub but Rahim kept the house details hidden away inside his jacket. He'd never seen Helen so impatient. Once they were seated with their drinks, he slowly opened his jacket and pulled out the brochure, placing it on the table in front of them. They read through eagerly until they arrived at the price - and horror struck.

'There's no way we can afford this,' said Rahim.

'It's ridiculous, what do they think it is - a palace?'

'The show house is even more expensive.'

Helen's mind raced, there had to be a way.

'Do your parents have any savings? What about your sisters? Will they be contributing?'

'The answer to both of those questions is no. Finish your drink, we'll go home and look at our finances and work out what the mortgage repayments would be.'

By the evening there were scraps of paper with scribbled calculations strewn all over the kitchen table.

'What if I do some extra shifts?' suggested Helen.

'I could work an extra hour a day,' said Rahim.

'I could sell my car and we could use the money for the deposit.'

'Let's go back to him,' said Rahim, 'see if he'll reduce the price a little.'

'You can't do that!'

'I'm Indian; Asians will haggle about anything.'

'I suppose it's worth a try.' She handed the man's business card to Rahim and he dialled the number.

'We've been looking at the figures,' he said, 'and wondered if there was any way you could reduce the price.' A long silence followed. Rahim nodded. 'Yes, I understand.' He looked at Helen, but she couldn't guess how the conversation was going. 'OK, I will do. Thank you for taking the time. Bye.'

Helen couldn't wait any longer. 'What did he say?' she asked impatiently.

'He says the prices are fixed and there's someone else interested who can pay the full price, so if we want it we need to act now.'

'Let's go to the bank and see what they say.'

'Don't worry, they always say that to make you panic.'

Monday morning dawned and Rahim was rushing to get to work.

'I'll phone the bank as soon as I get a chance,' he shouted to Helen. 'I have to go now, I'll ring you later.'

Helen dashed down the stairs.

'OK, I start at one o'clock today so I'll be at home all morning.'

'Don't get too excited,' said Rahim. 'A mortgage that size will stretch us to the limit financially.'

Helen kept herself busy, tidying and cleaning. Her stomach was doing cartwheels. The thought of living in such a beautiful brand-new house meant so much. At ten-thirty, hunger took the place of excitement. She popped a couple of slices of bread into the toaster and flicked the switch on the kettle. A minute later, she had just plonked herself down at the kitchen table for a well-earned break when the phone rang.

'Hi, Helen, guess what? The bank manager said yes! We can have the money.'

'When? How much can we have? We'll have to let the site agent know.'

'Slow down. Are you ever going to grow out of this twenty questions thing? Don't you think we should discuss it with the rest of the family first?'

'But what if it gets sold?'

'Helen, calm down. Don't forget this is about all of us as a family, not just the two of us. We can't jump in without consulting them.'

'They'll love it, I know they will.'

'Stop now,' said Rahim firmly. 'We'll take them to see it tonight and, if they're all in agreement, I'll ring in the morning to say we want to buy it.'

'OK, I'm sorry, I'm just so excited. I'll see you later then.' She swallowed down the toast quickly, pushed the plate to one side, took a slurp of the hot coffee, and reaching for the house details and read them over and over. Later that evening, when they sat down to eat, Rahim told his family about the house and showed them the brochure.

'We need to buy a property,' he said, 'rent is dead money.'

'When can we see it?' asked Sofia.

'Can we go now?' asked Safina.

'We could go now, but you'll only be able to look from the outside.'

'If we take a torch, we can look in through the downstairs windows,' said Safina.

'What about you, Dad, what do you think?' Rahim had always tried to encourage his father to buy a property, but Jamal was too cautious

Jamal looked apprehensive. The prospect of taking on a mortgage had been a major cause of concern to him ever since arriving in Britain.

'I'm too old to buy a house, I'll be retiring soon, but if it's what you want to do then I'm happy.'

'Mum, what about you?'

Fatima loved the idea; the thought of a new house was bliss.

'I'd like to see it.'

That same evening they set off in two cars.

'You'll love it,' Helen told Fatima. She couldn't get there fast enough. They turned the corner and Rahim began to drive very slowly.

'Why are you driving so slowly?' asked Helen.

'I'm prolonging the agony,' he teased.

'Oh no you don't, put your foot down.'

But as they neared the front door they couldn't believe what they saw. A large red 'Sold' sign sat in the bay window.

'It can't be! Rahim, do you think that the bank has contacted them to say we'll be buying it?'

'I doubt it. I told the bank manager where it was, but he didn't take an address or phone number for the agents. He just looked at the figures and gave me a verbal answer; we still have all the forms to fill in yet.'

'They can't have sold it without coming back to us first - we told him we wanted it.'

Rahim felt bad: 'I should have said yes to him and then sorted things with the bank; we could still have backed out if they refused to lend the money.'

'Don't blame yourself,' said Helen.

Fatima and Jamal said nothing. They could see how upset Helen and Rahim were at losing the house. Rahim got out of the car to speak to his sisters and Helen joined him.

'Don't worry, something else will turn up,' said Sofia. 'You haven't even looked at what else is on the market; you might find something even better.' But she could see that the house was perfect for them.

'Maybe you're right.' Helen wanted to believe Sofia, but it was hard. At that moment, she couldn't contemplate looking at other houses. Rahim drove home without saying a word and his parents sat in the back praying.

'Inshallah, we will find something,' said Fatima.

§

'Right, what else do we need to organise?' Helen asked Fatima.

'I've booked the band and we've hired some dandias.'

'What are they?'

'White sticks that we use in some of the dances. You click them together with your partner.

'You'll enjoy it, it's fun.'

Arrangements were well underway for the engagement party. Fatima had invited a hundred and fifty people, a conservative number apparently, and a few of Helen and Rahim's friends would also be there. There would be no alcohol, only coke and lemonade. The Indian band would play, they would burn incense and there would be lots of food.

'This is ridiculous,' complained Rahim.

'Stop complaining, it's for your mum. You said to let her do whatever she wants to do,' said Helen. She patted him on the head. 'After all, you're her only son.'

The party was being held at a nearby hotel and, on the day, the whole family, including Jamal, traipsed back and forth, transporting food and drink. Brightly-coloured decorations were suspended from the walls and ceilings to add an Asian feel and it all came together beautifully.

Fatima stood back to admire their work.

'It looks wonderful, I'm so pleased.'

'Thank goodness for that,' said Safina. 'I'm fit to drop. I don't know about partying, I could do with a sleep right now.'

Fatima shook her head.

'No time for that, it's four-thirty and we need to get back home so that we can get ready.'

'What a slave driver! Helen, do you realise this is your future mother-in-law?' said Safina.

'We'll be fine,' smiled Helen.

Fatima looked at Helen. 'Yes, we will - won't we?'

Back at the house, everyone was ready in no time.

'Bathroom empty!' called Sofia.

'Where's my sari?' shouted Safina.

'Dad, are you nearly ready?' asked Rahim.

Fatima was busy arranging Helen's sari in crisp folds before tucking it neatly into the purple cotton skirt. 'I'll put a large pin on the inside so that the pleats will stay in when you dance.'

Helen was nervous. Tonight she would face the whole community for the first time and all eyes would be on her.

'I won't be able to dance if they're all watching, I'll be too scared.'

'You must dance. Don't let them see that you're frightened,' said Fatima.

The whole family congregated in the kitchen.

'Everyone ready?' asked Rahim.

'Helen, you look lovely,' said Sofia.

'That colour really suits you,' agreed Safina.

Helen was wearing a purple silk sari with a silver border. Her hair was taken up at the sides, but left free-flowing at the back.

'You look amazing,' smiled Rahim. 'I can't wait to see their faces.' He was wearing a smartly-tailored black suit, with a white shirt and this time a bright blue and silver tie.

'All the young girls will be looking daggers at me when they see you,' said Helen.

Rahim knew that Mina would be there tonight with her family and he felt bad. He hoped that Helen wouldn't find out about the night out, and he hoped that Mina had got over her disappointment. Meanwhile, Jamal kept quiet, he shuffled nervously from one foot to another, quietly praying that it would all go well. He really did like Helen, but he still wasn't totally comfortable that she was about to become his daughter-in-law.

Fatima guided Helen out to the car protectively.

'Forget what anyone might say and make sure you enjoy yourself,' she said.

'What about you? Are you nervous too?'

'A little, but we'll be fine.'

Fatima knew that she wouldn't be the envy of any of the women there tonight.

§

Elizabeth arrived first along with Helen's sisters and soon the other guests started to arrive, laden with gifts and Indian sweets. Helen stuck firmly by Rahim's side with a fixed smile. She wasn't sure whether the thumping in her chest was vibration from the band or her heart racing madly.

'You look petrified,' said Rahim, 'try to relax a little and stop worrying.'

Helen stood as tall as she could with her head held high.

'Why is it,' she thought, *'that whenever I wear a sari, I feel like a princess at home and yet as soon as I'm among all the young Indian girls, I feel like a cheap imitation?'*

She wanted to sit down in a corner where no-one could see her.

Mami and Mama arrived with their family.

'How are you?' asked Mami.

Helen smiled, thankful for a friendly face. 'I'm fine, thank you.'

'Don't look so worried,' Mami whispered. 'You look good in a sari and that colour suits you.'

Fatima took Helen's hand.

'Let me introduce you to some of the people, you'll feel more comfortable then.'

Helen looked back towards Rahim. She beckoned him to accompany them, but he shrugged his shoulders and laughed. There were so many aunties and uncles and cousins that Helen couldn't possibly remember them all. She smiled and nodded, hoping not to appear totally dumb. Rahim, meanwhile, looked round for someone to talk to. He saw Sofia and Safina huddled among a group of their friends in a corner of the room and began to make his way over to them. Too late, he noticed that Mina was among them. He was about to head off in a different direction when she turned and saw him. She broke away from the other girls and approached him.

'Hi, Rahim, how are you?'

'I'm fine, thank you, and you?'

'I'm OK. Nice party. Your girlfriend looks lovely.'

Rahim felt that he ought to apologise for not calling her.

'Look, Mina, about...'

Mina's expression changed; she looked scared and shook her head slightly and, at that moment, Helen touched Rahim's sleeve. She smiled at Mina.

'Hi, I'm Mina. I hope you'll both be very happy.'

'Hi, thank you very much,' replied Helen.

Mina glanced at Rahim. 'Enjoy the rest of the evening, and good luck.'

'She seems nice,' said Helen.

Rahim watched as Mina went back to join the others. She glanced back and smiled wistfully. Rahim thought back to the night at the club and wondered what might have happened had he met Mina before Helen.

Nervous energy had used up all of Helen's reserves and she was now starving. The food was served early in the evening whilst Indian music played in the background, and, while the guests tucked in, she took time to look around the room. She longed to fit in and become part of the culture, but seeing the young girls so beautiful, dark and mysterious, she wondered how Rahim could possibly prefer her to one of them. At that moment, the doors opened and Jo and Sam along with half a dozen more of their English friends tumbled in. They bore gifts - vodka, Malibu and brandy to be exact, all neatly stashed in the inside pockets of their jackets.

Helen turned to Rahim: 'Now that the cavalry has arrived we can have some fun,' she said.

'Jo, Sam, everyone, help yourself to food, there's tons of it,' said Rahim.

One or two of them had already met Fatima and Jamal.

Helen gave Sam a knowing look: 'I wonder if you could get my future mother-in-law a drink, please,' she asked.

'No problem.' He took a large glass and filled it three-quarters full with coke, but before handing it to Fatima he sneakily threw in a large dollop of brandy and a couple of ice cubes.

'Lovely to see you again,' he said handing her the drink.

The food was cleared, the band started up and Mami pulled Helen and Rahim onto the dance floor. She demonstrated the moves so that they could follow her steps and beckoned Mama to join her. They were followed by one or two others until gradually the dance floor was full. Helen couldn't believe that here she was with all these people enjoying themselves at a party to celebrate her and Rahim being together.

Someone tapped Rahim on the shoulder.

'Surprise!'

They whirled around to find Aziz and Serina grinning in front of them. Helen screamed with delight and flung her arms around Serina. She was about to do the same to Aziz when he stepped back and raised his eyebrows. She corrected herself and retreated. Rahim beamed and shook hands with him. They hugged and patted each other on the back.

'You made it at last. What kept you?' Rahim asked.

'I've only just finished work,' shouted Aziz, above the music.

'I believe you.'

'It's true,' said Serina.

Jamal and Fatima stood near to the bar.

'Aziz, what time do you call this?' said Fatima.

'Not you as well. I've already been told off by your son.' Aziz shook hands with Jamal. 'Uncle, how are you?'

'I'm very well.' Jamal nodded his head to Serina. 'Please, help yourself to food and drink.'

'It's good to see you again after such a long time,' said Serina.

'Where's Nadim?' Jamal asked Fatima.

'He couldn't make it. His parents are over from Canada so he's gone to London to meet up with them.'

The music changed and the dandias were brought out.

Fatima took Elizabeth by the hand and led her onto the dance floor. Each person was given two sticks.

'It's a progressive dance,' said Fatima. 'Follow me. First you step to the right, then to the left, tap your sticks twice with the person opposite, dance around each other, tap your sticks again and then move on to the next person and do the same again.'

'I'll never remember all that,' said Elizabeth.

'Yes you will, just watch everyone else.'

Helen and Rahim, Safina and Sofia, and Jo and Sam joined in. It was a spectacular sight, saris in all colours spinning around, the sound of the sticks as they clicked together, and men and women, English and Indian, all partying together. Elizabeth soon got the hang of the dance steps, but when she came face-to-face with Sam she accidentally rapped him on the knuckles and then caused havoc when she stopped to apologise. It had been a long time since she had laughed without restraint, but tonight she did just that.

'Mum, you're supposed to have moved on to the next person.' Helen gave her a gentle push in the right direction.

'I don't know which way I'm meant to go.'

As Helen stepped to the left, she tripped on her sari, pulling the pleats out from her skirt.

'Oh no, look what's happened,' she shouted to Rahim.

'Go to Mami, she'll tuck it back in for you.'

'Are you enjoying yourself?' asked Mami as she rearranged the sari and secured it as firmly as she could.

'I love the music and the dancing. I hope everyone else is having a good time,' said Helen.

The evening was a phenomenal success. Helen's legs ached and her feet burned. She danced all evening, oblivious to any critical eyes.

After the guests had said their goodbyes and left, she turned to Rahim.

'I think everyone had a good time, don't you?'

'I think they did.'

'I told you it wouldn't be that difficult to win them over.'

'Yes, but the thing is...'

Before Rahim could finish what he was about to say he was dragged away by Sofia.

On the table was a huge stack of presents.

'I need some help to get all these out to the car,' said Sofia.

Only Elizabeth, Jo, Sam and a few stragglers remained. Helen was high on relief and excitement. She giggled and flung her arms around describing how she had almost fallen over when her sari had come loose yet again.

'How do you think it went?' Sam asked Jo.

'Difficult to tell really.'

'Helen is ecstatic'

'I know. It was a great night, but all that means is that everyone had a good time. I would bet my life that every one of them will wake up in the morning and think themselves lucky they're not in the same position as Rahim's parents.'

'You think so?'

'I know so.'

Helen came bounding over: 'Are you coming back to ours for a little while? I asked Serina and Aziz, but Aziz is working long hours at the moment and he was shattered.'

Jo reluctantly agreed.

'Only one drink though.'

They sat round the kitchen table.

'I'm so happy,' said Helen. 'I can't believe how well it all went. Mum, you were so funny; you caused chaos on the dance floor.'

'Yes, did you see?' said Rahim, 'she was apologising to people for hitting their knuckles, and then no-one knew who they were supposed to be dancing with.'

Jamal listened but made no comment.

'And did you see Sam? He and one or two others had bottles of alcohol hidden away in their jackets,' said Helen.

'They thought that I didn't know what they were up to,' said Fatima sternly.

'I don't remember you complaining about the drink he poured for you,' remarked Rahim.

Fatima smiled: 'I was cold and I needed it to warm me up.'

Helen put her arm round Fatima's shoulder.

'Leave her alone, she deserved it. Ma, what do you think they'll be saying now?'

'I don't know,' said Fatima. She looked at Rahim for a way out. 'I'm sure they enjoyed themselves very much.'

'Mum, you must be tired,' said Rahim.

'Me too,' said Elizabeth. 'I'd better get on my way.' Helen's sister's had left earlier and Elizabeth was driving home alone.

'We'll escort you,' said Sam. 'If we leave at the same time, we can follow behind until you take your exit off the motorway.'

So everyone left at the same time and the house fell into quietness after the day's hullabaloo. Helen and Rahim flopped onto the sofa and put their feet up on the coffee table. They were exhausted, but relieved that it was all over.

Rahim gave Helen a hug.

'How's my little chapati?'

'Past her sell-by date.' Helen yawned.

'You were brilliant. I didn't know you could dance like that.'

'Neither did I. It was fun though, wasn't it? Do you think they all had a good time?'

'I hope so.' He leaned his head back and looked at the ceiling so she couldn't see the pained expression on his face. But everyone enjoys a party no matter what the occasion, he thought to himself.

§

Helen pulled up at the side of the road and watched. As usual, no sign of life, she thought. She closed the car door quietly and walked across to the house that had been up for sale. Peering through the big bay window she saw that it was still empty of furniture, there were no carpets laid and no pretty curtains decorated the windows. She found it strange that every other house was now occupied except for 'theirs'. She could not let go of the idea that they were meant to own this house, just as she was sure that she and Rahim were meant for each other. Whenever she went out to the shops, she couldn't resist making a detour to drive past for one more look. She walked around the outside gazing through each window. She could see herself and Rahim at weekends doing the gardening and cleaning the cars, watching as Fatima and Jamal walked over to the park for a Sunday morning stroll. It was perfect. And it wasn't too far out of town for Sofia and Safina so they'd have no problem getting home after a night out. She returned to her car and sat at the wheel looking longingly at the front door - her front door - reluctant to drive away.

That evening they sat watching television.

'Rahim, you know I said to you that no-one had moved into the house?'

'Please, Helen, not again.'

'No, listen. I went past again today and it's still empty. I'm going to write a letter and put it through the door asking if they want to sell.'

'You can't do that.'

'Why not? I'm getting more Asian everyday?'

'I don't know, it just seems rude.'

'Well - nothing ventured, nothing gained.' Helen rummaged in the drawer for writing paper and a pen:

To whom it may concern.

We are very keen to buy a house in the area and, after speaking to neighbours, we have been informed that this property may be for sale. If so, please could you contact us at the above address.

Yours sincerely,

Mr R Ismail

'Will you sign it?'

Rahim looked surprised.

'Why me?'

'Because, sadly, this is still a man's world and they'll take more notice of you.'

She folded the letter neatly and put it in an envelope, placed it carefully on the passenger seat in the car, almost as though it was a sacred scroll, drove to the house, stood on the doorstep, kissed the small white package, said a prayer and pushed it through the letter box. Once back in the car she closed her eyes and prayed that a miracle might happen.

Two days later, a crisp white envelope dropped onto the mat in the hallway. It was addressed to Rahim. Helen rushed to pick it up and dashed upstairs to hand it over.

'Is it about the house?'

Rahim was enjoying a few extra moments beneath the covers after his alarm went off.

'Leave it there,' he said pointing to the chest of drawers. 'I'll open it later.'

'Oh please - open it now!'

Rahim grinned.

'OK.'

He opened the envelope and read the enclosed letter.

'Sorry, it's an invite to my cousin Nazim's wedding.'

'You're teasing me.' She snatched the paper out of his hand. The gold lettering indicated that this was nothing to do with the sale of the house and she handed it back. She knew she was behaving like a spoilt child, but she was desperate. The disappointment was almost unbearable.

Rahim saw how upset she was.

'Helen, I'm sorry. Come here.'

She sat on the edge of the bed and focussed on the cream duvet cover, avoiding his eye.

'No - I'm sorry,' she said. 'I shouldn't get so obsessed with things.'

'It's good to be like that. You're so determined, but sometimes you have to give in or you'll get hurt.'

She slumped forward and laid her cheek against his warm downy chest and he wrapped his arms around her.

'I'm stupid,' she said.

'You're just bloody stubborn, that's all.'

'I love you.'

'I love you too, my little chapati.'

The following day, Helen was on an early shift starting seven-thirty, so she left the house before Rahim. She was first to arrive home in the evening and was sitting in the lounge with a cup of coffee and the television on when Rahim popped his head around the door.

'Hi! Put your coat on, I'm taking you out.'

'What? Where to?'

'Just get your coat and come with me.'

'I'm tired, I just want to sit and relax.'

'Maybe this will get your attention.' He waved another crisp white envelope in front of her.

'It's a letter from the owners of the house. It arrived this morning after you left. They've invited us to go and see it; I phoned and arranged for us to go at five-thirty.'

'You're joking!'

'We have to be there in half an hour, but if you don't want to go then that's fine.'

Helen jumped up from her chair.

'I'll be ready in two minutes!'

'When we get there,' said Rahim once they were in the car, 'don't let them see how excited you are and don't tell them that we've seen it before. I don't want them to think we're desperate, otherwise they'll put the price up.'

'What are their names?'

'Mr and Mrs Simpson.'

'You do the talking.'

They pulled up outside the door to find the house lit up.

'Look, Rahim, even without curtains it looks homely and inviting.'

'It does. Fingers crossed, we might be homeowners before the night's out.'

They made their way to the front door and Rahim rang the bell. A middle-aged man greeted them warmly. He was tall and slim with slightly receding grey hair, dressed casually in an open-necked shirt and pullover. He stepped back to allow them over the threshold and Helen gazed around as though seeing it all for the first time. She noted the way the hallway opened out to provide a neat study area and how the ceilings were smartly finished with white coving. It was all perfect. The light and airy lounge-diner was large enough for a big family, and it was possible to step down into the garden from the patio doors. Pristine white, the kitchen was smaller than Helen had remembered, but still adequate. A small cloakroom completed the downstairs. Upstairs, two double bedrooms and one single were served by a fabulous house bathroom. Helen and Rahim walked into the master bedroom with its en-suite shower. The cream sanitary ware was the same throughout the house, and Rahim loved the fact that it was all brand-new.

'What do you think?' asked Mr Simpson.

'It's very, nice,' Rahim ventured, 'we might be interested.'

'Since we bought the house our circumstances have changed and I have to move to London for my work. We were going to put it back on the market, but if you're keen, we could come to an agreement without involving the estate agents, which would be of benefit to both of us.'

'What would you be looking at price-wise?'

Mr Simpson wanted five thousand pounds more than the original asking price and Rahim doubted they could afford the new price tag.

'We'll have to go home and discuss it,' he said. 'Can we get back to you tomorrow?'

Mr Simpson shook hands.

'I'll give you first refusal; I'll wait to hear from you.'

'Thank you, that's very kind,' said Rahim, trying not to let his disappointment show. Back in the car, he looked across at Helen.

'We can't afford it.'

'I know.'

Back at home the whole family sat together in the lounge.

'Why don't you offer to go halfway,' said Sofia. 'He might be prepared to do that.'

'I think even that's too much. We were already pushing it at the original price.'

Jamal and Fatima sat muttering prayers. Praying was all they could do to support their son.

'If you're sure there's absolutely nothing we can do, then we'll just have to accept it,' said Helen eventually.

'I'll phone tomorrow and see if we can negotiate, but I'm not hopeful.'

'If it's meant to be, then it will be, and if not we'll have to find another house. I'll see you in the morning. Night, night.' She wanted to kiss him goodnight, but she wasn't allowed to with his parents present. He was stretched out on the sofa and almost half asleep.

Saturday dawned. Helen woke early, went downstairs and made herself a large mug of coffee. Five minutes later she sneaked back upstairs, slipped into a pair of jeans and a top, and drove to see the house again. She loved it so much. Sitting in the car on the drive, it felt like home. She racked her brains for a solution, but she knew that ultimately it was Rahim's decision. She arrived back home to find Rahim up and in the kitchen having breakfast.

'Where have you been?'

'I'm sure you can guess,' she said guiltily.

'Don't build your hopes up, Helen.'

'I'm sorry, I just wanted another look.'

'We'll phone him later.'

That afternoon Rahim telephoned Mr Simpson. Helen and Jamal sat by his side at the kitchen table. Helen bit her lip as she listened.

'Yes,' said Rahim, looking at some figures he had jotted on a slip of paper. 'Yes,' he repeated. He looked at Helen, but gave no clues. 'OK,' he said and replaced the receiver. There was a long pause then he smiled at her.

'We can have it if we pay an extra two thousand pounds.'

She hardly dared speak. She waited a few seconds: 'What do you think?'

'It'll be tough.'

Jamal left the room and came back a minute later.

'Rahim, I want you to have this,' he said and held out a small leather purse.

Rahim opened the zipper.

'Dad - I can't - it must have taken you ages to save this.'

'There's three thousand pounds in there.' Jamal didn't earn much money and three thousand pounds was a fortune to him. 'Take it and buy the house. I can see how much you want it, and the money is there so why not use it?'

Rahim put his arms around Jamal and held him close as he had done when he was a small boy.

'Thanks, Dad.'

31 HELEN GETS A TASTE OF RACISM

There was only a week to go before Nazim's wedding. Safina and Helen were sitting together in the lounge. 'What are you going to wear next Saturday?' asked Safina.

Helen looked up from the bridal magazine she was engrossed in. 'I haven't a clue what to wear. To be honest, I haven't had a chance to think about it, what with trying to organise the move to the new house and finalising our own wedding plans.'

'We'll ask Mum, I'm sure she'll have something in mind.'

'At least I don't feel quite so nervous about big functions like this anymore,' remarked Helen.

'You've done really well. I never thought a time would come when Dad would ask you for advice instead of one of us,' said Safina.

'It wasn't without a struggle, it took a while to win him over, he can be very obstinate.' Helen put down her magazine. 'What are you going to wear?'

'Salwar kameez, but as an elder you'll have to wear a sari.'

'Well thank you very much!'

Since the engagement party, Helen's confidence had grown and she had no doubts about her future with Rahim and his family. Her relationship with his parents had continued to develop and she didn't see how anything could go wrong. She still hadn't met his sister in Canada, but even that didn't bother her as she had spoken to her on the phone on many occasions and they seemed to have a lot in common.

Later that day, Fatima returned from a shopping trip.

'Helen, come up to my room for a little while,' she said, 'I have some saris for you to choose from for Nazim's wedding.'

'You must be psychic; we were just talking about it.' Helen looked at Safina. 'Will you come too? I haven't a clue what's in fashion in the Asian world.'

Fatima laid out three different saris on the bed in her room, each one beautifully beaded and decorated with sequins. From her drawer she produced a box containing jewellery and hairpins encrusted with zirconium and pearls.

'Ma, these are beautiful,' said Helen. She looked at Safina for direction. 'Which one do you think I should wear, and what about the jewellery? They're all so gorgeous; I'll never be able to decide.'

'You look good in dark colours,' said Safina. She always knew exactly what suited. 'Why don't you try the maroon one and see what it looks like.'

The maroon sari was chiffon instead of silk. 'It feels light as a feather compared to the others that I've worn,' said Helen.

'It suits you and it might stay in place better than the purple one did at your engagement party,' said Fatima.

'Well, I was giving it some on the dance floor, wasn't I?'

'You can say that again,' laughed Safina.

'So - is this the one?' asked Helen.

Fatima held out an ornate silver necklace with matching earrings. 'I think so,' she said, 'and this jewellery set goes best with that sari.'

'That's you sorted then,' said Safina. 'Mum, what am I going to wear?'

'I can't tell you what to wear,' smiled Fatima. 'You wouldn't like it.'

'Too right I wouldn't! I think I have a nice little mini skirt tucked away in my wardrobe somewhere that would do nicely.'

'Safina you can't...!'

'Keep your hair on mother, I'm only joking.'

§

'We should be on our way by now. I'll wait in the car. Dad, what are you doing? Where's your tie?' Rahim called up the stairs to the girls. 'We're going to be late if you don't get a move on.'

'You'd think one of us was getting married,' said Sofia, 'can't you all just calm down.'

'Mum! Have you seen my gold earrings?' shouted Safina.

'Can you imagine what it'll be like when you do get married?' Sofia asked Rahim. 'I'll tell you what; I'll get ready at Mami's. I don't think I could cope with this.'

'But I'll need you here to organise everyone.'

'I'm not even thinking about it. Come on! We have to go right now!'

Helen had been ready for some time and was sitting in the lounge. The maroon sari was much more comfortable than the purple silk one and she felt confident that today would be another success. She made her way downstairs.

Rahim was waiting in the doorway.

'I'm getting used to seeing you in a sari.'

He kissed her on the cheek.

'Watch the make-up. It's taken ages.'

The car park at the wedding venue was heaving. Dozens of families, loaded down with gifts, shouted instructions to each other. Helen stood next to Rahim's car not understanding a word they said, and it struck her that they always seemed as though they were arguing. She felt calm although she noticed that one or two women and some of the young girls stared at her. But she felt good and she was ready to show them that she could be part of their social circle and fit in without feeling like an outcast. It helped that, over the last year, she had come to know many of Fatima's friends and they would be here today.

'You all right?' asked Fatima, as they headed for the entrance.

'I'm fine, Ma. Don't worry about me, you go and have a good time. I'll be OK.'

The usual pandemonium went on inside; women called out to one another and children ran round, while the men segregated themselves and sat huddled together discussing business and family matters. Helen stood by Rahim's side. She could see that she was the focus of attention from some of the guests. A group of young girls peered as she and Rahim passed by them, whilst three older women took sly glances and looked back at each other, eyebrows raised. None of this bothered Helen, her confidence was growing all the time and she knew that nothing any one could say or do would stop her marrying Rahim.

Sofia and Safina headed off to join the other young girls and Rahim was relieved that Mina wasn't among them. Meanwhile, Jamal sat quietly with his friends, unsure how they would react to him. He said very little in case attention was turned to him and he was forced to answer awkward questions. Fatima, acutely aware that she was being watched, smiled confidently and circulated, making conversation as she went. The last thing she wanted was for her friends to feel sorry for her.

'Helen, I'll have to join the men for a while,' said Rahim. 'You go over to Mum. You can stay with her and talk to her friends.'

'OK, I'll see you later.'

'How are you, Helen?' Mami was standing behind her.

'Fine thank you - and you? You must be exhausted after organising all this.'

'We've worked flat-out all week - to bed at two in the morning and up again at six.'

Helen had never known anyone who worked as hard as Mami, and yet she was always smiling and laughing.

'You've done really well. The decorations are lovely.'

'Have something to eat. There's so much food. Take as much as you like.'

Helen enjoyed watching the proceedings, especially the rituals surrounding the bride, who wore a bright red sari with an elaborate gold design. Her head was covered and she looked down at the floor the whole time, guided to her matrimonial seat by a woman who, Helen presumed, was her maid-of-honour. There seemed to be no order to the ceremony and the Mullah read out sermons and performed rituals in what, to an uninformed eye, appeared to be a haphazard manner. The couple placed morsels of food in each other's mouths and stepped on small pieces of pottery, crushing it underfoot, a practice which, apparently, brought them good luck. Helen understood very little but was captivated. After the marriage ceremony was over, she felt comfortable enough to mingle a little. She approached a group of Fatima's friends.

'Helen, I saw you a little earlier,' said Fatima's old friend, Gulli, 'but I couldn't get over to say hello. Let me introduce you to some of our friends.'

Helen had given Gulli a lift to the mosque many times and knew her quite well. The group of women were all friendly and made her welcome. Many of them asked about her wedding, where it would be and what she would wear. Fatima joined them and placed a hand in the small of Helen's back.

'Everything all right?' she asked.

'I'm having a great time.'

'I'll be with Mami if you need me.'

Helen excused herself from the group and made her way to the ladies' cloakroom. Back in the function room she couldn't find Rahim or any of his family, so unperturbed she found a quiet place out in the hallway and sat down on a sumptuous red sofa. She was joined by a pleasant-looking Indian lady.

'Hello, I'm Nazma, a friend of Fatima's. How are you?'

'Very well, thank you,' said Helen.

Nazma came across as a warm and friendly person, perhaps around fifty-years-old. She was keen to hear about the wedding plans and the new house. They joked about how she would cope with Fatima as a mother-in-law and Helen reassured her that they would get along well together. She explained that they had discussed the fact that it wouldn't be a traditional mother/daughter-in-law relationship. Nazma asked if Helen would become a Muslim, and go to mosque.

Rahim appeared and peered over Helen's shoulder.

'Where have you been?' he asked.

'Here - talking to Nazma.'

Rahim frowned 'I was worried; we looked all over for you.'

'You needn't have been. I've chatted to loads of people.'

'Dad's tired and wants to go home. You ready?'

Forty-five minutes later, they managed to leave the hotel, Sofia and Safina appearing from nowhere. They had spent the time catching up with friends and answering questions about their brother and his English girlfriend. Back at home the whole family plonked themselves down around the kitchen table to have a final cup of tea before bed.

Helen was buzzing; the day had been a huge success.

'Nazma was really nice,' she said. 'We chatted for ages.'

'What was she saying to you?' asked Fatima.

'She asked me how I had met Rahim and what sort of a wedding we would have and what religion our children would be. She asked lots of questions about you, and Bapa and how it would work between us.'

Fatima looked uncomfortable.

'Is something wrong?' asked Rahim.

'It's nothing.'

'Mum, something's bothering you. What is it?'

'I don't really want to say.' Fatima looked anxiously at Helen and then down at her hands.

She searched for the right words.

'After you had spoken to Nazma, Helen, she came to me and...' she fiddled with her prayer beads and took a deep breath, '...she asked what I was doing allowing my son to marry an English girl.'

Helen stared in disbelief. She shook her head.

'No, she can't have said that.'

Jamal took hold of the front of his jumper and pulled at the threads. This was exactly what he had feared, there would always be someone who would try to make things difficult for them and he didn't want to spend the rest of his life dreading every social occasion because he had an English daughter-in-law.

'That's ridiculous! How dare she say that to you?' said Sofia.

'Who the hell does she think she is?' said Safina.

'They're right, Mum.' Rahim leant towards Fatima and took hold of her hand. 'You mustn't put up with the likes of her saying that to you. Helen is a far better person than any of them will ever be.'

Fatima wiped a tear from her eye.

'I was so upset at the time that I didn't know what to say.'

'What did you say?' asked Safina.

'I told her that my son's happiness was more important to me than my own, and that, if he loves her, then who am I to spoil that for him - and that Helen is a lovely girl.'

'Well done, Mum,' said Sofia.

Jamal looked at Fatima and he knew she was right. If Rahim was unhappy, the rest of the family could never be happy, and he could see how happy Rahim was when Helen was around. She made him laugh, they did everything together and she made every effort to be part of the family.

'Your mum's right,' said Jamal, 'we've lived our lives the way we wanted to and now we have to let Rahim do the same. It won't be easy, but we have to ignore people like Nazma and think about what we want as a family.'

But Helen was still in shock, she couldn't speak. Rahim reached for her hand despite his parents being there.

'Helen?'

She didn't look up.

'I don't know how she could say that,' she said. 'She treated me as if I were her best friend. I trusted her; I feel so used, all she wanted was some gossip.'

'Don't get so upset. This is what I've tried to tell you all along. You'll always get people like her, but in time most of the ones that matter will accept you and love you as much as we do. Forget about her, she's not worth it.'

'Helen, I'm so sorry. I was so upset. I wasn't going to tell you.' said Fatima.

'I'm going to bed,' said Helen. 'I want to close my eyes and not wake up.'

32 HELEN CALLS THE WEDDING OFF

In the days that followed Helen tried to come to terms with what Nazma had said to Fatima. The words went round and round inside her head and they wouldn't leave her. How could Nazma be so two-faced? The episode raised other questions; what about Mami and the rest of the family, what about other so-called friends - were they laughing behind her back? Who could she trust? Had she been kidding herself the whole time? Had she not actually managed to do the impossible and fit in with such a different culture? Worst of all, she now had to tell Rahim that he had been right to have doubts all along. How could she go through with the wedding after this?

She lay on her bed.

'We need to talk,' said Rahim. 'I hate seeing you like this.'

She closed her eyes; the pain wouldn't go away no matter what she did.

'I've been so stupid. I should have listened to you and to Jo when you both tried to make me see the problems but I wouldn't. I bet they all see me as a silly, cheap English girl, who's not quite the full shilling. I bet they think it's hilarious to see me wearing a sari. I must be the laughing stock of the community.'

'No, you're not. Did you not hear what Mum and Dad said? They were so distraught, and what's incredible is they want to fight for you.' He took hold of her hand. 'You can't give up now, I won't let you. This has made me realise, for sure, that with their support we can make it work. What Nazma did was awful, and from time-to-time there will be people like her, but on the whole, the ones who really know you know how genuine and caring you are.'

'Last Saturday at the wedding I was convinced that nothing could get in our way, and now it's a sick joke.'

'We all love you - and we'll always be there for you.' He put his arm round her. 'Come here, my little chapati. I promise - we're going to be together forever.'

'I may be your little chapati, but they must be saying I'm not quite the full chapati!'

'See! You're so funny. Even in times like this you can still joke.' He laughed aloud. 'Promise me you'll put this Nazma thing to the back of your mind and forget about it.'

But Helen wasn't joking this time. She knew that no matter how she tried, she would never fit in completely. She smiled feebly.

'I'm not sure I can, to be honest.'

The move to the new house was imminent, and even though she now knew she would never live in it, Helen still wanted it to go ahead for Rahim. It would be a good investment for him and, although finances would be stretched, Sofia would contribute once she finished college and started work. Rahim and his family would be happy and settled there.

'Look what I've got.'

Rahim was dangling a set of keys from his index finger.

'When did you get them?'

'I just met Mr Simpson at the house and he handed over a whole bunch of them. We are now the proud owners of 92 Hampton Road.'

'That's good.' She loved the house even though her heart wasn't in it any more.

'We could go round after dinner tonight and at the weekend. Let's go into town and look around the big stores to get some ideas.'

She felt a small surge of energy. She had always dreamt of furnishing her own house and making it homely.

'I suppose that'll be fun.'

'It'll be more than fun. Come on - I want to see you back to your old self. I don't know what I'd do if I lost you now.' He caught hold of her and swung her round.

'You won't lose me,' she said, but a pang of guilt struck at her heart.

There was much to plan and do and the days slipped by. The carpets were ordered, and there was a new black leather sofa in a warehouse waiting to be delivered. The stylish dining suite was Rahim's choice; it consisted of a grey marble table and six black high-backed chairs and a matching marble coffee table.

Thoughts of Nazma were forced to the back of Helen's mind. She was too busy to dwell on her feelings. Rahim's parents had acquired so many belongings since they'd arrived in England that it was going to be a major task to sort them all out. The garage was packed with pots, pans and cooking utensils and a massive shelving system that housed at least fifty large, old-fashioned sweetie-shop bottles, filled with every spice imaginable. Deciding what to take and what to get rid of was impossible.

One day, while they were packing up boxes, Rahim said: 'You do realise the wedding date is only two months away?'

'Yes, I know.'

'Have you rung Richard to make sure he's booked his flights?'

'No, not yet, but I will do soon.' Her voice lacked enthusiasm.

'How do you feel about Richard giving you away?'

'I'm glad that I have him, but sad that it won't be Dad.'

'Jo will feel it too, won't she? Do you think she'll feel guilty?'

'Why should she feel guilty?'

'I suppose guilty isn't the right word - but if I were her, I would feel bad if your father had given me away and now wasn't here for his own daughter.'

'I'm so glad he gave Jo away,' said Helen. 'Life is full of twists and turns and that's one I'm pleased about.'

'What's the matter?'

She plonked herself down on a stool and faced him.

'I'm so sorry, I don't know how to say this - I don't think we're doing the right thing any more. It took someone like Nazma to make me realise. We'll be ridiculed for the rest of our lives and our children will be taunted and miserable.'

'What? You can't mean that! Nazma is a worthless nobody. We have family, friends and people we care about who are supporting us. Why let one person get to you like this? You've always been so strong and determined, please - don't say this.' He lifted her chin so she had no choice but to look at him. 'I love you and I know you love me.'

Rahim picked up the phone and handed it to her: 'Actually, I don't believe you. If you want to put a stop to the wedding, then ring Richard right now and tell him it's off!'

§

The move to the new house went smoothly. Helen had taken the week off work, and by Friday, with everyone else out, she'd managed to find a place for everything. Exhausted but satisfied, she looked at every room as though seeing it all for the first time. For now, she would sleep in the single bedroom, but once they were married she would move into the master bedroom with Rahim. She stood in the doorway admiring the fabric of the curtains and bed linen and realised she hadn't thought about Nazma once for five whole days. She hadn't been able to make the call to Richard to say that the wedding was off because she couldn't bear to see the pain in Rahim's eyes - but she still had her doubts.

Rahim walked in.

'Oh no, look at the time! Richard will be landing at any minute and we haven't even left the house yet,' said Helen.

'We'll still get there in time. He has to collect his baggage and get through customs. Stop panicking.' Rahim never rushed for anything.

'It's not very nice if there's no-one there to greet him.'

'OK, get in the car and I'll be with you in two minutes.'

They travelled at speed along the motorway and arrived at the airport just as Richard came striding purposefully into the arrivals lounge.

'Hi, sweetie,' he called out.

Helen ran to him as she had done as a child and flung her arms around his neck. 'It's so good to see you. How was your flight?'

'They don't make planes for people with legs; they're all for short arses like you.'

'You never change do you?' She laughed.

'It's so good to see you and you look amazing.' Richard stood back and looked at her: 'What's that?' he asked.

'What?'

'Oh I can see now - it's still that look of love. There's still time to call it all off you know.'

She looked at Rahim and smiled.

'No chance of that. Come on; let's get you home, Mum's dying to see you.'

The wedding was in six days and Helen had taken another week off. She had moved back home with Elizabeth in order to organise the final details. After dropping Rahim at the new house, Helen and Richard chatted all the way home and caught up on almost two years. Constantine had passed away peacefully after a short illness; Laura remained single and as crazy as ever; and Richard finally had a woman in his life. After the death of his wife, he had had many girlfriends, but none he had wanted to settle down with. But in Sarah Jane he had found something different and she was probably 'the one'.

'She has the most amazing blue eyes that twinkle when she smiles,' said Richard.

'Looks like I'm not the only one who's got it bad.'

'And you know what? It feels pretty good.' He took hold of Helen's hand. 'We're two very lucky people; you know that, don't you?'

'Yes.'

Helen filled him in on her news about Josie, with whom she was still in contact. 'She had another baby after I left and now she's pregnant again. Six children, imagine that.'

'No thanks - one would terrify me.'

'Think you'll have any?' she joked.

'It's a bit late for all that!'

As the car rounded the bend into their lane they could see Elizabeth waiting on the doorstep. The gates laid open their welcoming arms.

'Look, Mum's waving. I haven't seen her look so relaxed in a long time,' said Helen.

'She looks great.'

The car pulled up in the yard and Richard called out of the window: 'Get that bloody kettle on, I'm parched.' He was out of the car before it had come to a halt. He picked Elizabeth up and held her close.

'Hey, be careful, I'm not as young as I was.'

'You're as young as you feel. Let's get inside; we've a lot to talk about.'

It was well into the evening before the conversation dried up and even then it was mainly because Richard had downed one or two more whiskies than was good for him.

'Never in a million years did I think David was capable of doing what he did.' Richard stared at the carpet. 'I guess, one way or another, we're all pretty screwed up.' Then jet lag and the whisky took hold and he fell asleep. Elizabeth covered him up with a blanket and left him to it.

'You can't leave him there,' said Helen.

'He's a big boy. He'll go to bed when he's ready.' Elizabeth watched as Helen climbed the stairs. 'Sleep well,' she called.

Helen turned and smiled. 'And you.'

Next day, Helen and Rahim returned to the airport to pick up Zara, who had travelled from Canada for the wedding. Samir couldn't make it because of work commitments. Zara was smaller than Helen had expected with long curly hair and glasses. She dumped her suitcase at their feet and hurled herself at her brother.

'It's good to see you! How was the flight?' he said.

'I was so exhausted from work I slept virtually all the way. Now I feel fantastic.' Zara released Rahim and turned to Helen.

'It's so nice to meet you at last.'

'And you,' said Helen. 'Thank you for coming.'

'You're joking, aren't you? I wouldn't have missed it for the world.'

Zara was very direct, Helen liked that.

'Shame Samir couldn't make it.'

'Yeah, well - I'm starving. Can we get something to eat somewhere?'

'No way, Mum will kill us; she's been cooking all week.'

'Let's get home then before I collapse with hunger.'

Zara was different from her sisters and brother. Her high cheekbones and pouting lips made her look like a film star, and she had so much energy she left Helen feeling worn out. But she was good fun and the two of them got on well. After a huge meal at Rahim's house, Helen returned home to be with Richard.

When he was eighteen Richard had worked in a bakery and still boasted about his confectionary skills. Helen had been intending to make the wedding cake herself and had forgotten about Richard's skill until Elizabeth reminded her.

'Here it is!' said Helen.

'What?' asked Richard.

'The wedding cake.' She led him into David's workroom. 'You have a job to do.'

There were three cake tins on the table. Richard peered into the first of them.

'There's no bloody icing on it.'

'You're going to help me do it.'

'Do you know how long it is since I last did that job? It must be thirty-five years ago.'

'It's like riding a bike, you never forget.'

Day-by-day Helen and Richard added to the cake, first the alcohol and jam and then the marzipan. By the third day it was adorned with icing and roses and all that was left was to add a delicate row of tiny white icing-sugar dots around the edge. They beavered away in the kitchen and all was well until the gin and the whisky bottles came out.

'I'll teach you how to waltz.' Richard embraced Helen and took up the stance.

'You'll never manage it, I've got two left feet.'

He held her tightly around the waist and glided across the quarry-tiled floor with her in his arms - but her feet didn't once touch the tiles.

'You're good at this, not a step out of line so far.'

Her legs flew out to the sides and backwards and forwards like a rag doll. She laughed so much she was gasping for air. When he put her down, she could barely speak.

'We still have the cake to finish,' she spluttered, taking a large mouthful of gin. 'Let's put the finishing touches to it.'

Richard glugged the last of his whisky and refilled his glass.

'OK, pass that nozzle and I'll show you how it's done.'

She handed him the loaded piping bag. He started neatly with one tiny dot, then another. The next ones were slightly bigger and then one of them splattered onto the cake like a seagull dropping.

Helen burst out laughing.

'What do you call that? Give it here; I could do better with my eyes closed.'

She took over and piped a perfectly formed dot.

'Exactly the right size,' she said proudly.

'Yeah, but look where you've put it.'

The dot was perfect but completely out of line with the others

Elizabeth came in. 'What's so funny?' she asked.

'We're decorating the cake.'

'What the hell do you think you're doing? Look at the mess you're making.'

Richard put his index finger up to his lips like a schoolboy. 'Sorry,' he murmured.

Elizabeth was scarlet. 'Right you two, out of here now.'

Helen and Richard sloped off to the sitting room like two naughty children and Elizabeth, who had never decorated a wedding cake before, took up the icing bag and set about repairing the damage.

33 THE WEDDING DAY

Elizabeth sat in the lounge and sipped tea. She had hardly slept. If there were life after death, then David must be exhausted too because she had talked to him the whole night. If only she could satisfy herself that there was a good enough reason for what he did, or if she could understand what it was like to feel so low that you couldn't even stay around long enough for your daughter's wedding. And what about Karen? Had he thought about her? Did he think she no longer needed him? By five-thirty Elizabeth could stay in bed no longer. Careful not to wake anyone, she had crept across the landing to the bathroom and had a long soak in the bath. She was grateful to Richard for standing in, but it made her wonder whether David would have regrets if he could see them all now.

'Time to get up,' she whispered. She set a coffee cup down on the bedside table, sat on the edge of the bed and stroked Helen's hair. 'It's seven o'clock. How are you feeling?'

'Morning Mum, I'm fine. I wish Dad was here, but we can't change that.'

She had woken at six and stayed snuggled under the warm bedclothes thinking about her father. She eyed the cream ballerina-length dress that hung on the wardrobe and wondered whether he would have liked it. The flimsy veil draped limply over the back of chair would be brought to life in a few hours by a ring of fresh alstroemeria, roses and ivy. Would he have liked that too, she wondered.

There were tears in Elizabeth's eyes.

'If he were here, he would be so proud.'

'He must have been suffering so much to do what he did.'

'I still find it hard to understand,' said Elizabeth. 'I keep asking myself why - why did he want to leave all of you? Why couldn't he have waited?

We only had a few more years to work and then we could have done whatever we wanted to. I know he wasn't well, but I get so cross sometimes. I see other couples out walking hand-in-hand and I think that should have been us.'

'It's all right, Mum. It would be so lovely if he was here, but I wouldn't want him back if he was still so poorly and tormented. Richard's here and he'll make sure we laugh all day.'

'I suppose you're right. Come on, I've run a nice warm bath. I'll make some breakfast, but take your time.'

Saturday July 4th 1987 promised to be a very hot day. The sun was already glimmering in the sky and it was only ten-thirty. Unlike most households on a wedding day, the Singleton household was calm. Jo had stayed over the night before along with Karen and the two younger bridesmaids, and they were busy blow-drying hair and painting nails. Safina was getting ready at her home and would make her way over to Helen's to put on her bridesmaid's dress shortly. That left Richard who, in typical bachelor style, had ironed his shirt and pressed his trousers the night before. Helen found it peculiar to see so many of her father's traits in his brother. She had noticed this when she stayed with him in Los Angeles, but now she was even more aware of it. It made her sad to watch him polish his shoes.

The wedding was scheduled for twelve o'clock and Safina arrived at eleven.

'Oh my God,' she said, throwing her dress over the back of a chair. 'You wouldn't believe what it's like at home. Pandemonium! Everyone shouting at each other, the phone hasn't stopped ringing, and you won't believe what Nadim did.'

'What did he do?' asked Helen.

'Rahim had ordered his suit and picked it up for him, all Nadim had to do was buy a peach bow-tie to match the bridesmaids' dresses. This morning he couldn't fathom how his bow-tie attached so he asked Zara to give him a hand.' Safina was laughing so much she could hardly finish. 'Zara couldn't do it either, so he went to Rahim who had a look at the tie only to find that it wasn't a tie at all, but a Fergie bow.'

'What the hell is a Fergie bow?' asked Richard.

'It's a hair clip with a big bow on it like the ones that Sarah Ferguson wears - you know - Prince Andrew's wife.'

'Rahim was furious,' said Safina.

'That's so typical of Nadim.' Helen shook her head in amazement.

The shiny black vehicles arrived in quick succession. Elizabeth travelled with the bridesmaids, sitting up front with the driver in their vintage car. It wasn't an Austin Sheerline, like the one she and David once had, but the smell of the leather seats and the sound of the engine brought a flood of memories. 'David, how could you do this? You should be here with us today,' she told him.

Richard and Helen waited until the others were out of sight then ventured out to the old soft-top Rolls-Royce. Richard stood upright and proud, holding the car door open. He was immaculate in his grey flannel trousers and a navy-blue jacket that contrasted beautifully with his crisp white shirt.

'You look beautiful,' he said. 'Rahim is a very lucky bloke, I hope he knows that.'

'No, I'm the lucky one. I have Rahim - and, today, I also have you.'

He kissed her on the cheek. 'Let me take those while you get in,' he said and reached for the bouquet of fresh flowers. Helen dabbed her eyes carefully with Richard's handkerchief. They were tears of happiness mingled with tears of sadness for David.

'Head up,' said Richard, handing her the perfumed flowers, 'stop all that and smile. We're going to have a ball.'

'You're so bossy.'

'I don't want you crying, you look awful when you cry.'

She forgot how nervous she was and laughed. Richard winked and gave her a hug. 'That's better. It's hot, I need a drink. Let's get the job done then we can relax and enjoy the rest of the day.'

Rahim and Nadim stood on the pavement outside the registry office. The Rolls-Royce pulled up but the hordes of people milling around obscured Helen's view. She saw enough to see that Rahim and Nadim looked very handsome in their dark morning suits and 'white' ties, supplied by the couture shop. She held onto Richard's hand and spotted Rahim's parents looking lost and bewildered beside Zara. Seeing them was like a thunderbolt striking through her body. She swallowed hard. Now was the moment of truth for both families, a final opportunity for Helen or Rahim to change their minds. Mama and his family were among the guests, they looked relaxed but bemused at the spectacle.

Rahim ran to greet Helen.

'You look so beautiful,' he said stepping back to take in the vision.

'You look very handsome too, but where is your peach bow-tie?'

He shook his head: 'I could have strangled him, he's so annoying sometimes.'

She looked him in the eye.

'Haven't changed your mind then?'

'No way. You are about to officially become my little chapati - unless you change your mind.'

'I won't,' she said.

He kissed her on the lips.

'I was scared you might have second thoughts.'

34 THE NIGHTMARES BEGIN!

Helen's dress was sticking to her like a wet swimsuit and Rahim was desperate to take off his jacket, although he couldn't until after the photographer had done his job. It was a relief to get out in the open after the brief ceremony in the registry office. The room had been hot with too many people packed into a small space and no air.

Helen pointed to the car.

'Look, Rahim.'

Its hood had been pulled back and the Rolls looked like a grand old lady, her bonnet slung around her neck. They posed for the cameras and cowered beneath a torrent of rice and confetti.

'Time for a quick getaway,' said Rahim.

'See you at the hotel,' Helen shouted and the guests waved.

Richard stood like a centurion holding open the car door.

'The two of you make a lovely couple and I'm so glad you asked me to come over. It's made me so proud. I hope you'll be very happy together.'

'Thank you.' Rahim gave Richard a hug. 'You being here has meant a great deal to both of us.'

'See you at the hotel - though, I have to say, I'm not looking forward to this bloody speech malarkey.'

'You'll be fine,' said Helen. 'We'll see you shortly.'

'If you're lucky.' He headed towards Elizabeth, put his arm round her and escorted her to Shelly's car.

'Mum seems to be taking it all in her stride,' said Helen. 'Richard has been brilliant with her. He's stayed by her side the whole time apart from when he was with me.'

'I'm sure it's been difficult for her, but she wouldn't want to spoil your day by falling apart.'

'Our day, dear.'

'Sorry - our day,' Rahim corrected himself.

'Your mum and dad have been amazing too, considering it's all new to them.'

'Nadim kept them entertained. Don't think he'll ever change.'

They snuggled together in the back of the car and waved goodbye as it pulled away slowly.

The lavishly-decorated marquee was unbearably hot, even with the side doors open; the large ceiling fans were inadequate and the temperature soared. Nadim began his speech, reminiscing about old times, embellishing funny stories to make his listeners laugh and being a little risqué so that he could watch Rahim squirm. He spoke about Rahim's love affair with his car and told the story of a wedding weekend when Rahim had made them all late. 'There are two things in life that you should never lend to your best friend - one is your car, the other is your girlfriend,' he paused for a second or two, 'so far, I've borrowed his car...'

The guests loved it.

Now it was Rahim's turn. He thanked Nadim then proceeded to sweet-talk his newly acquired mother-in-law with tales of how wonderful life was going to be with his beautiful new wife.

'Before I finish, I must tell the story of a best man who was asked to buy bow-ties for himself and the groom...'

Finally, it was Richard's turn; the time he had dreaded had finally arrived and the sound of a silver spoon clinking on the side of a crystal glass rang through his head, leaving his nerves jangling. His name was announced and his mouth dried up.

Elizabeth nudged him.

'That's you.'

'I know.' He stood up and looked at the sea of faces. A hundred and ten expectant pairs of eyes gazed back. He cleared his throat: 'I would like to welcome...'

Elizabeth prodded him again: 'You should have your jacket on.'

'I'm being nagged to put my jacket on.' He did as he was told. 'It gives me great pleasure to come all the way from Los Angeles to...'

Nadim called out: 'Don't get carried away because it's Independence Day!'

The room erupted into laughter.

Richard tried to ease the tension round his neck by yanking at his tie. He took a breath, opened his mouth to speak - and nothing came out.

'Can't remember what I was going to say.'

He looked round for inspiration. Sweat dripped down his back and droplets formed on his brow, a muzzy feeling took possession of him, he felt dizzy and disorientated. He mopped his forehead with his napkin, gripping the edge of the table with the other hand.

'Don't keep looking at me,' he said, 'my mind has gone completely blank.'

People started to fidget in their seats, willing him to find the right words. He surrendered.

'I'm sorry, folks, I'll just have to ask you all to raise your glasses in a toast to Helen and Rahim. I hope they'll be very happy together for the rest of their lives. And I'm so sorry that my brother David isn't here today to witness this marriage.'

At his final words, and to his relief, everyone clapped and cheered. Then Elizabeth shocked everyone by standing up, asking to say a few words.

'I know it's not customary for the mother-of-the-bride to speak, but today is unusual in many respects. First of all David, Helen's father, sadly isn't here, but I know if he was he would have been very proud. He had already welcomed Rahim and his family into our home and given his blessing to the marriage. Secondly, I have no doubts that Helen and Rahim are meant to be together, but that circumstances may make their journey a little bumpy from time to time and, therefore, I hope that we will all provide support whenever it's needed.'

Elizabeth began to struggle and her bottom lip quivered, but she forced back the tears and continued. 'My dear brother-in-law Richard, I thank you from the bottom of my heart for coming over especially for Helen. Yes, it is July 4th, American Independence Day, which makes it even more poignant, so please all raise your glasses in a special toast to Helen and Rahim.'

'Mum, I had no idea you were planning to make a speech,' said Helen. 'Thank you, I don't know how you kept it together.'

'Sorry, Helen,' said Richard. 'I messed up.'

'No, you didn't, you did your best.' She reached out to him.

'And showed them all how bloody senile I am.'

'It's difficult when people are constantly butting in. Anyway, I don't care about a boring speech. I'm just glad you're here.'

'It wasn't going to be boring.'

'Oh yes it was.'

'Seriously, I feel like a complete idiot. I don't know what happened, all the things I had in mind went out the window - and when I looked around and saw everyone staring at me, I was completely freaked out.'

'Please Richard, Old Uncle Richard, it really doesn't matter. Dad will be looking down and laughing, grateful it wasn't him who had to make a speech.'

Richard pulled her close.

'Less of the old, I can still squeeze you to death.'

Helen released herself from his grip.

'I don't know what I would have done without you.' She pointed to the wedding cake. 'Look at that masterpiece - we decorated it! And just you wait till later when you see me waltzing around the dance floor; it was you that taught me how to waltz.'

She put an arm round him and lay her head on his shoulder.

Helen and Rahim took to the dance floor first and demonstrated that Helen hadn't learned a thing during her dance lessons at De Trafford House. They were soon joined by Richard and Elizabeth who glided effortlessly. Then Jo and Sam made their entrance. Jo shrieked as Sam picked her up.

'Put me down!'

'Can't, you're so small, it hurts my back to bend over like that.' They edged closer to Rahim and Helen. 'Look, Jo - it's Mr and Mrs Ismail.'

She struggled to break free. 'So I see. Put me down and we may be able to speak to them.'

The evening whirled by in a flurry of dancing. Nadim and Amanda, Aziz and Serina, family and friends from all over the country were joined together like old bosom buddies. Helen cried and laughed alternately; her heart ached for her father but at the same time she was elated. The dream that she and Rahim had dared to dream had come true and she wanted the evening to last forever. Suddenly, Nazma appeared before her. Nazma threw her head back and laughed.

'You stupid little English girl, it will never work,' she hissed.

Helen recoiled in horror.

'Why are you here? Who invited you?' She looked around the room but there was no sign of Rahim.

'Now, what are you going to do without your knight in shining armour?' said Nazma. 'Have you any idea what people are really saying? You think you're so clever, don't you?'

Nazma sneered at Fatima and Jamal.

'I told you not to let this happen,' she said to them. 'You'll be left on your own. You'll have no-one to look after you in your old age. She's got what she wanted and now she doesn't need you any more.'

'That's not true! Don't listen to her! I promised Rahim that I would look after you.'

Helen wanted to run away, but she couldn't. The whole room seemed to be folding in on her and there was no escape. Nazma came closer and Helen could feel her hot breath. She was about to scream out, when, from nowhere, a surge of energy grew inside her body, she gathered her strength and with one almighty shove, she pushed Nazma away from her.

'What do you think you're doing?'

Nazma flew through the air and landed on the floor with a thud. Someone took hold of Helen by the shoulders.

'I said what are you doing?'

Helen woke with a start. It was the morning after the wedding, she was in the bridal suite of the hotel and it was Rahim who had spoken.

'What?'

'What were you dreaming about? I was fast asleep and you gave me a right old thump in the chest.' He rubbed a reddened area of skin.

'Oh God, I dreamt about Nazma.'

Rahim laughed when she told him the contents of the dream.

'Come here,' he said, pulling her close, 'don't let her get to you. I thought that was all in the past.'

'We have done the right thing, haven't we?'

'Stop worrying! We're together now and no-one can harm us unless we let them.' He kissed her on the nose. 'You're my little chapati and that's the way it will always be. I love you so much.'

'I love you too,' she replied, 'more than anything.'